COILS OF THE SERPENT

JERRY AUTIERI

1

The ancient stone statue of a legionnaire still guarded the turn in the path Varro had walked in his youth. He examined this sentinel from his childhood, which now only rose to his chest. It had once seemed bigger than a real man. Time had worn the statue down to barely discernible, rounded features, and birds had splattered it white with droppings. The soldier's hand held empty space where he once gripped a wooden pilum. Varro had never seen the pilum, but his great-grandfather claimed the statue not only carried one but had even been painted in full color. Time had diminished it to gray rock, but the old guard had never faulted in his duty to ward off birds, even when birds had lost their fear of him generations ago.

"You've been on guard a long time, soldier," Varro said, then ran his thumb along the statue's shoulder. "Maybe it's time someone relieved you."

He rubbed gritty dust from his thumb, wondering if he was speaking to the statue or to himself.

Golden fields of barley stretched out in every direction. It was as if time had forgotten this place. Down the long rows between fields, the red tile roof of Old Man Pius's villa glowed with the midday sun. He expected the old man to step out his door and curse him for trampling his crops. Old Man Pius had no patience with children. Varro used to believe he spent his entire day standing at his front door, waiting for a child to pass whom he could then curse and chase away.

But unfamiliar slaves worked in the far fields and a dog barked in the distance, sensing Varro's presence. No one else had noticed a stranger traveling the old market path.

"A stranger." He spoke the words aloud as he turned from the stone legionnaire, leaving him to continue his watch until the end of time.

He was going home. Nearly eight years ago, he and his father along with Falco and his father, had climbed into Old Man Pius's wagon to travel to Rome. So much had changed, even if the fields and buildings remained the same. His feet trudged ahead, sandals scratching the dirt path. The knee-high barley nodded like old friends greeting him as he passed through the intersections of fields. The barking dog faded into the distance. He was seventeen years old once again and just as frightened to return home today as he used to be when Falco had blackened his eyes.

Though the reasons for his fear today were far different. He had no bruises for his mother to fuss over. Instead, he carried scars showing where he had almost lost his eye, or had been struck over the head, or white lines where enemies had carved their last act of life into his flesh. And those were the scars a normal eye could see. No one would know all his worst wounds were on the inside.

Today, he feared what awaited him at the end of this old market path.

He had ample time to wonder about it, lazing about a Scipio family villa for most of the summer. He had discussed visiting their old homes with Falco and Curio. Both wanted a break from the past.

Varro wanted to remember it and to discover what remained of it. He hoped to find the innocence he had left behind. Or had eight years of constant battle hacked away all of it forever?

The answer was plain to him, as it was to Falco who refused to join him. But Varro needed to confront that answer. He would not let an enemy linger behind him in battle. He would turn to fight him before advancing. So that was his plan today. Confront the past so he could move ahead in safety.

His childhood home was quaint compared to the new villa he had built for himself at Senator Flamininus's urging. It was smaller and more compact, sitting in whatever patch of field made sense to his great-grandfather when he built the farm with his war spoils. That thought brought a smile to Varro's face. He had just done the same.

At last, he saw the roof of his father's villa. The earthquakes that had been rocking all of Rome and the surrounding countryside had not damaged it. Some roof tiles were broken or missing, but it was natural wear. The walls surrounding the villa had been replastered and painted, though from the fading and cracking Varro knew the renovations were done a few years ago.

Past the villa, the same fields Varro had worked alongside his father were now occupied with different slaves and different workers. At a distance, if he squinted, any of the vague forms could've been men he remembered from his youth. He played the trick on himself, indulging in the fantasy.

The red door to the villa, a different color from Varro's recollections, hung open and light striking the atrium pool sparkled beyond. He could see that at least the floor mosaics remained the same. They would be too expensive to replace without good reason.

A shadowed figure appeared in the doorway. His throat closed as his sister Octavia stared out at him. He had expected none of his family to remain with the new owners. His vision swooned and his head felt feverishly hot. Such was the shock that he staggered back, putting his hand over his chest. Out of reflex, his right hand reached for a gladius that did not hang at his side. He wore only a plain brown tunic and sandals. This was not war, but he felt the same fear.

Yet now the figure of his sister vanished, her shouts echoing inside the villa.

He only carried his Servus Capax pugio, with the gold owl's head restored to him. Senator Flamininus had declared him worthy of it after his return from Iberia. While no one carried weapons legally in Rome, outside the city it was up to the individual to protect himself. Varro had opted for only his pugio, being as good as a gladius in any case. Yet now he feared it might still be too shocking for his sister to see him carrying such a weapon. When last they spoke, Varro had sworn to do no harm to any man. No wonder she had fled him. Between the weapon and all his scars, he must appear as a complete stranger.

Yet the person to reappear in the doorway was not Octavia.

Instead, he was a broad-shouldered man in a gray tunic pulled up high into the belt to reveal tanned legs in a soldier's style. Even with the ample cloth of his tunic covering the muscles, Varro knew his strength. His head was shaved clean, as was his face. Narrow, slanting blue eyes regarded him warily as he polished something in his hand using a brown rag.

The muscles of his forearm caused a red, lumpy scar and a blue tattoo to ripple as he polished the item in his other hand. Varro knew he hid a dagger there.

Behind him, another shape crowded the door, shadowed against the light of the atrium. A young boy by his size, Varro judged.

"What brings you here?" The man in the door's voice was like what Varro imagined the legionnaire statue would sound like if it could speak, hard and rough.

"Is Octavia inside?" Varro couldn't help but ask, his eyes searching past the door into the hall beyond. But the two figures blocked the view.

The man in the door raised his thin brow, and he continued to polish his hidden weapon. He also glanced at the pugio at Varro's left hip.

"No one by that name here. Are you lost, friend?"

Though the word did not sound like an acknowledgment of friendship, it eased Varro's worries. He felt the muscles of his torso release in response.

"I understand why you'd want to protect her from a stranger. But I am her brother. I think I frightened her just now."

The man stopped polishing the blade he kept hidden. Someone spoke behind him, the young man or maybe an older woman.

"I said no one is here by that name. Now, if you have no other business, you should leave. We'll be harvesting soon, and there's lots to prepare."

"I understand," Varro said, now looking out toward the fields. "I used to live here and helped harvest those same fields."

Varro had expected that revelation to generate a more genial reception. But the man in the doorway let his hands down, so that the cloth fell away and the shining bronze knife trembled in his white-knuckled grip.

"No one lived here when I brought this place. I've paid for this farm with my blood. I've done my service, and this is my reward. No one has a claim on it. I own it, and so will my sons after me."

The tattoo on his forearm was easier to see now.

"Second legion," Varro said, pointing to it. "I was also second legion. Tenth hastati. Macedonia and Iberia."

The man's narrow blue eyes blinked slowly, but the hard lines of his face remained set.

"Father, you were in Macedonia, too!"

Varro flinched at the suddenly bright voice to the right. A young boy with a mop of dark hair and the same narrow eyes as his father stood against the villa wall. It struck Varro that he knew just how the boy had turned up there. He had come around from a door on the far side, and followed the shrubs and trees that could hide a child like him. Varro had done it often enough to know.

"Get back," the father said. "What are you doing out here?"

Varro raised both hands. "I don't mean any threat to your family or property. Look, I'll throw my pugio on the ground, if it will ease your mind."

He reached for it, but the bald man shouted as he stepped forward.

"Don't touch it!"

The figure behind him slipped out, carrying a long spear used by the triarii. Varro knew from the boy's grip that he didn't know what he was doing. But he wore a look of firm determination. Varro couldn't help but smile in admiration.

His father's shaved head flashed in the midday sun as he did a double take. Varro could hear the unspoken question, "What are you doing with that?" But the son's grim stare did not waver.

"That's a long spear," Varro said. "I'm sure it put many Macedonians in their graves. Let's not tarnish its history with a good Roman's blood."

"All right," the father said. "Put that away before you stick me in the ass with it. Now, stranger, I'll let you put that weapon in the grass. I'll put mine away. I just get jumpy when someone reaches for a blade, even to peel fruit. We'll talk like fellow citizens, all right?"

"I completely understand. I do it, too." Varro let his pugio fall into the dirt and the man did the same with his knife. His young son walked with a lowered head back into the villa, where more figures swarmed him, delicate but chiding voices spilling out the door.

"My name is Marcus Varro. I'm sorry to come upon your home like this, unannounced and looking like a thief."

"I'm Gallio." The bald man at last smiled.

Varro hoped he did not cringe at hearing the name of a former friend turned traitor. But Gallio did not seem to notice.

"You met my son, Titus, and the lad over there is Tertius." He faced his young son and shooed him away. "Go back to work. Your father has company."

Young Tertius made to retreat, but Varro noted he stopped against the wall the moment his father turned away. He put his finger to his lips as if to extract a promise from Varro to not reveal his disobedience.

"So, I was certain the woman who came to the door was my sister." Varro allowed Tertius to remain just behind them, spying on his father.

"You're mistaken. That was my daughter, Soceillia. I'll call her out here if you don't believe me."

But Varro knew it was true and shook his head.

"No need. I was just so caught up in the past on my journey here. I imagined she was my sister. But she would not have stayed on. She should be married by now if Old Man Pius found her a husband before he died."

Gallio's narrow eyes widened. "That's who sold me the farm. At least his son did. He sold his farm too, after his father died. Became a rich man, too rich to work a farm himself."

Varro swallowed and it felt like he had a stone in his throat.

"What's done is done, friend. This is your home now. But it was mine once and should've remained mine. Pius was to mind our farms while we were gone. But his son did one better and made them his own. I'll never understand all the crooked dealings that went on here. I was too young. And now, I'm too old to care what happened then."

Gallio's face was an easy read for Varro, and now he had moved back to suspicion. So he held up his hand to forestall any argument.

"I'm far wealthier than I dress, Gallio. After this census, I find myself an equestrian now. I have a large farm and horses, fine clothes, slaves, and a villa that makes this old home seem a shack. I don't want or need it back."

"Then why are you here, friend?" Varro realized when Gallio called you a friend, it had the opposite meaning. His hands were flexing at his side, as if regretting the surrender of his weapon.

"Why does a man gone for eight years of war come home? Even when that home isn't his anymore."

Gallio sighed, and his eyes shifted as if suspecting his boy remained behind him.

"You're looking for your sister, for family. You want to know what happened while you were away bleeding for a city that only ever wants more of your blood. You want to know why your friends died and why you lived. You want to remember what you were thinking when you left here to become a man. Why were you so excited and happy? Maybe that feeling is still here, and you can dig it up in the old fields you played in as a boy. But I can assure you, none of that is here. Only an old farm that needed repairs and fields that had been left fallow. That's all that is here. Nothing else."

Varro inclined his head. "I assume you went looking for the same things, Gallio?"

"I did, though I had my family at home." He glanced across his shoulder and lowered his voice to mask it from young Tertius, hiding in the blue shadows of the villa wall. "Honestly, it was hard to come back to a family that had learned to live without me. Children that hardly remembered me. You're young still. You're better off restarting clean."

"I think—"

A sound like a thousand rocks plummeting down a mountainside cut off Varro. Something pushed against his feet and he stumbled backward, only barely catching himself.

Gallio did the same, though his shouted curses vanished into the loud crashing. He fell to the ground and landed hard on his side.

The earth felt like Varro was at sea in a storm, where the deck shifted and rocked underfoot. The sky was black with flocks of screaming birds.

Then he saw the tiles fly from the roof of his old home and the villa walls crack.

Varro sprang across the ground before he realized what he was doing. Tertius lay flat on his back, sprawled out by the sudden rocking. Shattered plaster had sprayed everywhere, and Varro knew the wall was going to fall.

He snagged Tertius by his tunic shoulder and dragged him away.

The villa wall slumped into a pile of plaster, stone, and wood framing. It just flopped into a heap, as if it had given up.

Varro lay with Tertius beside him, the boy clinging to his body and screaming. The ground shuddered for what felt like hours. It ended as suddenly as it had started. The volume of the crash lingered as a throb on Varro's eardrums.

"You're all right?"

Gallio appeared over them, snatching Tertius into his arms. The sniffling child buried his face into his father's shoulder and nodded.

A thousand birds circled aimlessly in the sky, their shrieks an echo of the confusion that sprawled out beneath them.

"An earthquake," Varro said as he got to his feet. But Gallio had already run into his house. Varro stood alone outside, the collapsed wall revealing the garden beyond where a table had flipped over. Cream-colored plaster lay in hand-sized flakes everywhere. Roof tiles had slid down into piles of shards.

Inside the villa, women screamed and cried. Varro looked around and retrieved his pugio and Gallio's knife. Both had been scattered far from where they had been set.

It was strange to enter his old home, particularly as an uninvited guest. But he found Gallio with his wife, two sons, and a daughter that had a passing resemblance to his sister. Two male slaves comforted each other in the corner.

The atrium pool had sloshed half its waters onto the familiar mosaic floors, which were now ruined with cracks and displaced tiles. Doors hung open, and he looked to his old bedroom, which revealed a mess beyond.

His father's old cubiculum was likewise a disaster, with toppled shelves and broken pottery. The niches along the walls where his family death masks had been displayed now held unfamiliar faces. Some had fallen out and shattered on the tiles.

Varro shuffled through the wreckage and presented Gallio with his knife. He took it without a word, his narrow eyes now pale.

His wife's face was streaked with tears, and she shook her head. "What have we done to offend the gods? We've always done our duty. We've always been pious. Yet they still destroyed our farm."

Gallio grunted. "It's not us the gods are angered with. It's Rome. Rome and the fucking Senate. They keep sending us to war, eating up a generation of men. If we keep having so many victories, there won't be anyone left to worship the gods. That's why they're angry."

The wife sniffed and rubbed her nose. "The Senate ordered everyone to pray for relief. I thought it was working."

Gallio pointed his knife at the sky, as if calling out the gods. "They won't stop until those rich senators have felt the pain themselves. To do that, they'll have to shake Rome right down to the foundations."

"Don't say it!" The wife looked to Varro as if to entreat him to agree. But he simply turned toward the open door leading to the garden. While Tertius clung to his father's leg, the older boy had gone outside. He now called back.

"Father! Come look at this!"

Everyone followed Gallio, even the slaves. In the garden, a wide crack had formed in the ground. It was as wide as Varro's stride and deep enough that he could sink up to his knees in it.

Varro stood outside of the circle of family. Tertius couched beside it and reached into it. "Where do you think it goes?"

His mother snatched him off the ground and carried him away. "Don't get near it."

"We'll have to fill that in," Gallio said. But his voice was hushed and fearful. The crack traveled to a collapsed wall section and beyond. "We're fortunate it isn't deep."

The older son leaned over it. "If it was deep, where would it go? What if a man fell in there?"

"If it was deep enough, it could mean the end of that man's life," Gallio said. "But it's not. So don't dwell on it."

His face was dark even as he looked at the sky where the birds continued to circle. Varro looked up with him.

"We're not safe until they land again," he said. "That's what my great-grandfather used to say."

Gallio nodded. "We should all stay outside for a while yet, and away from the walls."

Then he blinked as if a sudden realization overcame him.

"You saved my boy. One moment later, and he'd have been crushed. I owe you more than I can repay."

Varro shook his head. "Repay me by raising him to be a good, strong citizen."

Gallio's narrow eyes narrowed even more. "You really lived here, then? If so, I've got something you will want. If it survived this disaster."

While Gallio's family gathered away from the villa, he led Varro to the opposite side where a new wooden shed had been built against the wall. Despite the damage to everything else, the small structure remained untouched.

Inside was another matter, with crates toppled and their contents spilled. A broken jug released a liquid that smelled like sour wine into the dirt. Gallio patted the low roof.

"Me and my son built this. Seems like we were the better builders between our families. The walls are as firm as ever."

Varro tried to duck into the entrance, but there was not enough room inside for two grown men. Gallio cursed as he shifted through old things, opening two cloth bags until he found one that satisfied him. He then cinched it and both of them now stepped back into the sun.

"The house was empty when I bought it. But they left behind the family death masks from the previous owners. I was going to throw them out, but my wife is a pious woman. She thought to keep them in case the family ever came looking."

He extended the bag, and Varro took it carefully. He stared at it as if Gallio had handed him the actual corpses of his ancestors.

"Thank you for this," he said, his voice suddenly dry. "It means a lot."

Gallio gave a genuine smile this time.

"Some of them have been broken. Maybe from this earthquake, or maybe because I didn't treat them right. In either case, I'm sorry for it. But I'm glad to restore your family to you. It's what you came to find, after all."

Varro nodded. He didn't know what he came to find. He

wanted to confront the past, but discovered it was further behind him than he knew.

The two men stood in silence for a moment. Gallio at last cleared his throat.

"Look, if you've no place to stay tonight, you can stay here. But I'm not sure we'll sleep inside. After a shake like his, it can shake for days more."

"No, thank you. You've been kind enough. I have a ride arranged at the market to take me back home."

"The roads might be damaged, or the market flattened." Gallio put his hand to the back of his neck. "Earthquakes always seem to bring out bandits. You're welcome to stay until it's safer to travel."

The weight of the sack seemed to pull Varro down, as if begging him to leave.

"It's only noon yet. I hope to sort out something by evening."

Gallio shrugged, but his hand remained on the back of his head.

"You saved my son. I should reward for it. But everything is a mess now. So let me give you some advice, lacking anything else I can give a rich man.

"I've done what you've done, or something close to it. I've served Rome again and again, and never complained when called. I was in the triarii at Macedonia. We were sick of fighting by then. We had been fighting for what seemed our whole lives."

"I remember you triarii giving the consul a near-revolt."

Gallio smiled. "We didn't get all we deserved, but we got some of it. The longer you fight, the more you wonder when your brothers will dig your grave instead of the other way around. It just seems you can't go on surviving if they keep putting you in the line. But some of us still came home no matter how hard they tried to get us killed. It leaves a man with a lot of questions and a lot of bad dreams. There's no answer to those questions and the dreams are yours for life. The only way I know to live is to keep going forward. The legion never taught us to march backwards."

Varro nodded and gave a feeble smile. "Except for formation drills."

Gallio chuckled. "Respect your ancestors. Hang those masks in your new home. But always look forward and not behind. Take it from a sword brother who has walked that road already."

Varro thanked Gallio and offered to help clean up, but he declined. In the end, they all shared a small meal outside in nervous silence as the birds continued to circle. By early noon, he headed back along the path and left his old home for the last time.

Following the market path, he turned a corner and found the stone legionnaire on his side across the path between fields. The fall had broken off the pilum arm and head from the body, which itself had cracked open to reveal fresh stone.

Varro crouched over the toppled soldier and touched the rough crack that revealed glinting flecks in the rock. He squatted there in that familiar old path, watched over by tall and quiet fields of barley, and wept.

2

Varro squatted over the bag he set on the mosaic floor. Sprawling scenes of gods and battles covered the atrium floor, and subtle Greek motifs hid in its corners. Senator Flamininus had helped him find the workers and artisans to create what seemed a palace for Varro. It was no surprise that his fondness for Greece colored his choices.

"Besides," he had said. "Greece was where you became a man. You should memorialize that time, and how better than in tasteful flourishes like this?"

The reflecting pool behind him cast rippling lines of light along the wall where small alcoves were prepared. He had already set up the oldest of his ancestors' death masks. Shattered pieces of masks he could not remember filled the bottom of the bag he had carried to his new home. Despite how often his father made him honor these ancestors, he hadn't paid attention. Now he hoped he had the order and names correct.

He groaned as he slid out the next two masks.

His grandfather had meant little more to him than the mask

Varro now held in both hands. But he was his father's father, and apparently a hard man.

"And probably a criminal," Varro said aloud. "Just like his son after him."

He had not thought to capture a death mask of his father who had died on campaign. At the time, Varro had too much to deal with. Now, he found he only cared in so far as he would have to answer questions as to why he had nothing for his father.

Placing his grandfather's mask in its alcove, he then pulled out his great-grandfather's.

"Papa," he whispered as he traced the edges of that familiar face. He had worshiped the man as only a young grandson could. Papa had been his hero and would remain tall in his memory for the rest of his life.

"I couldn't do as you asked," he said, now standing and holding the mask to his eye level. "But accept some responsibility for that. You could've been clearer about what you meant."

He smiled, closed his eyes, then kissed the forehead of the mask.

"I forgive you for it, Papa. I swear I will still try."

Setting the masks in order, Varro stood back and admired his work. Now five of the eight alcoves were full. Presumably, his descendants would one day place his own mask at the end of this line. A grim smile came to his face.

"I'll leave a scowl that will scare those brats for generations."

As was customary, they created the masks after death, and so the expressions of his ancestors were mostly vacant. None of Papa's personality remained in his mask, nothing to express his giant spirit. Varro would have to do better when his day came.

After collecting the cloth sack and tossing in the mask fragments that had spilled to his beautiful mosaic floor, he started for the cubiculum. But a servant rushed in, a round Macedonian woman whose name Varro had not yet learned.

"Master! Thieves! They've hurt Siculus!"

Varro was already running across the atrium and out the front door. His villa was so new that he had not yet established a proper guard for it. He sprinted outside into the bright sunlight, rolling fields of gold and green crops, and three farm workers surrounding his slave, Siculus.

Down the path, three other men wrestled with a recalcitrant brown goat. They had squandered their lead for failing to properly truss the goat and now struggled to keep their prize.

Running at full pace, when Varro came within distance he shouted at the three thieves in his angered centurion voice.

"Halt where you are!"

They were young men, probably old enough to serve in the legions. But in one glance Varro knew these wretches wouldn't even pass for velites. They were thin and dirty, with stained gray tunics showing sweat stains at their armpits. Their faces were pinched and narrow. But they obeyed Varro's bellowed orders.

"What are you three doing with my goat? And what did you do to my slave? If he's hurt, you'll pay for it."

Even the goat froze from Varro's shouting. But soon it began pulling against the rope one thug held fast.

"Are you the rich bastard who built this place?" The tallest of the three spoke, now stepping forward with arms crossed.

"I'll be asking the questions, whelp. Arms at your sides when you address me, or I can pin them there forever, if you'd rather."

The two others looked at their leader, who seemed astonished. But then he blinked as his mouth twisted into a crooked smirk.

"Must be the owner. Only a rich fucker talks to others like that."

"Right," said another who was missing two front teeth. "They're all like that. He's why the gods punish us."

"Fucking piece of shit," said the third.

Varro put both hands on his hips.

"I'd be less concerned about the gods right now, boys. That's my goat, which I'll be having back. Then you're going to help tend to Siculus. And if he's seriously hurt, you'll be paying for that too."

The three roared in laughter, but then their leader drew his knife, as did his gap-toothed friend. The situation had become too complex for the third one holding the goat. He seemed unsure how to draw the knife at his belt and keep control of the goat.

"You don't count very good for a rich man," said the leader. "There's three of us here and you don't even have a weapon."

Varro sighed. He had left his pugio on the stand inside the villa entrance and hadn't thought to take it. Still, he widened his stance and shook out his arms.

"Ah, boys, you've brought me more knives than I need for this fight. Let's get the lesson underway."

Varro sucker punched the thug holding the goat, slamming under his chin and knocking him out. He plunged backward and released the goat, which sprang away into the grass fields with its poorly tied rope trailing.

The two others rushed at him, but Varro had visualized the entire fight. These weren't trained soldiers or even hardened criminals. They would fight with the same unimaginative tactics that every brawler tried in their first year of legion training. He'd fought this battle a hundred times before this day.

The lead thug slashed as Varro leaped aside, sweeping his foot in between his legs and sending him to the ground. The gap-toothed thug tried to readjust his strike, but found his friend now in the way.

Varro seized his knife hand, using superior strength to twist the arm around. But to his credit, the gap-toothed thug only moaned but refused to release his weapon.

With a decisive punch, Varro broke the thug's arm at the elbow. The bone cracked and the thug's moaning became shrieking to shake the world.

Using his free hand, Varro caught the dropping knife as he shoved his enemy away like discarding trash.

Next, the knocked-out thug propped up on his elbows while the leader scrambled to stand. Varro circled around and kicked the recovering thug in the head. His toes curled up and felt the shock of connecting with the skull. His head snapped to the side and he flattened out again. Varro grimaced. He feared he might have killed the thug with that kick.

With no more time to think, the leader rose, grunting and angry. But now Varro leveled a knife at him, and he stopped. His eyes went wide as he regarded the condition of his support.

"You should really give up. I think I hit your friend in the head too hard. He might be dead."

But the groan from the ground proved Varro wrong, and somehow emboldened the leader.

"Fuck you!"

He charged in. Varro stepped aside and used his momentum to throw him forward. The thug slammed face-first into the ground and somersaulted onto his back. He lay stunned, his knife lost, while the two others rolled around in the grass and groaned. Varro stood among them, examining the captured knife.

"This edge couldn't cut curdled milk. Gods, it's covered in filth, too."

Siculus arrived with two workers bearing him between them. Another worker ran after the fleeing goat, comically calling after it as both grew smaller in the distance.

"Did they hurt you badly?"

Blood dribbled from Siculus's side. He was a strong-framed, dark-skinned Macedonian with thick wavy hair and a thick beard, one of the thousands of slaves captured in their war with Rome. Varro had mused that they might have once faced each other across battle lines. But now Siculus was an honestly purchased slave, and a decent man despite his situation.

"It's not serious, sir," he said, looking at his blood-slicked hand. "But the bastard kicked me in the balls, twice."

Varro grimaced, looking down at the would-be thieves cowering in the grass.

"You let these dogs get the better of you? I thought you were a famous Macedonian warrior?"

"I had the rear pike, sir. If the enemy ever saw me, it was because we were broken. That only ever happened once."

Varro nodded placidly.

"What do we do with brigands here? In my father's time, if he caught them, he killed them."

"We're not brigands!" The leader, now weaponless and recovered from his tumble, sat up.

Varro tapped his finger against his nose as he regarded the thug.

"True. Brigands wouldn't waste time on a single goat. So what are you, then? Thieves? Come to see if the earthquakes have left an opening for you to steal from others?"

"There's a crack on the far wall," Siculus said. "From the shake we had yesterday. It wasn't much, but I think they used it for footing to climb over. Then they ran out the front gate with their spoils."

Varro shook his head.

"So my villa with its fine new walls is less safe than my marching camps in the wilds of Iberia. Good to know. I think two of our three thieves have a memory of today's lesson. But their loudmouth needs an education still."

Before the thug could slip away, Varro leaped atop him and pinned him. He drew the thug's own knife to set the point just below his eye and then grabbed his jaw. The trembling thug stopped resisting, wisely preventing an accident to his eye.

"You think the gods are angry because I came into some

wealth? Not because dishonorable, gutless scum like you exploit the misfortunes of others? I'd rethink that, boy."

He squeezed the thug's jaw as he jabbed the knifepoint into the flesh. Then he dragged it down, the dull blade cutting a jagged line from the base of his left eye and through his cheek. Blood bubbled up from the cut and ran backward into the well of his eye. He squirmed and growled, huffing against the pain.

"There's your lesson," Varro hissed. "One you can review every day. Lest it remind you of your good fortune. Because if you had done this yesterday when I was in a bad mood, you'd be searching for your right hand in the grass."

Varro stood up, wicked blood from the knife, then snapped it underfoot before tossing the handle into the field. The thug growled as he clambered up and held his face, blood flowing between his fingers. His accomplice with the broken elbow had already fled. The last one rolled on the ground, holding his head and groaning.

"Get off my property," Varro said cooly. "Or I'll practice my javelin throw with you two for my targets. Better be gone before I get them."

The groaning thug at last rolled over and vomited. His former leader, hand clamped to his bloodied face, ran past him. But he stopped when he was out of reach.

"You don't know what you've done. I'll find out who you are, rich man, and you'll pay for this."

Varro had started away with Siculus and his two bearers, but turned at the threat.

"Don't trouble me again, or I'll flog you before I sever your hand."

Despite his bravado, the thug followed his erstwhile companion vanishing into the midday sun. The last thug at last got to his feet and staggered after them, shouting for them to wait. Varro turned back, with Siculus now walking on his own.

"I'll have a look at that cut back at the villa," Varro said. He looked at his workers. "Anyone else hurt? If not, I'll send over good wine tonight for your thanks. Don't get too drunk on it. You won't have any relief from your duties for a hangover."

His workers bowed and thanked him. They were older men left over from the wars with Carthage. They hadn't had his good fortune and lost almost all they possessed. When Flamininus offered opinions for slaves and workers for the farm, Varro insisted on using as many veterans as possible. To his horror, he found Rome full of leftover soldiers whose wounds, both physical and mental, had denied their rewards. Flamininus thought slaves a more prudent choice, and Varro agreed. But he wanted to do something for the men who had sacrificed so much to save Rome from destruction.

After examining Siculus and his minor wound, he cleaned the long but shallow gash before dressing it.

"Their blades looked as if they had found them in an animal pen. I'd hate for you to die of infection after spending a small fortune on you."

Siculus smiled. "You're a kind master, better than the one who sold me."

"He said you were a drunk and stole from his casks." Varro sat on a stool in the doorway opened to his garden to use the light better as he worked. Siculus stood before him, a thin smile hidden in his heavy beard.

"I was a fine excuse for him. His wife believed I drank all the wine while he and his friends held their secret parties. Too bad for him. She got fed up and forced him to sell me."

"My gain," Varro said, now washing his hands in a wooden bowl his house slave brought to him. He then stood and regarded Siculus.

"All of this is new to me. I don't know what to do. Now I have a country farm and villa, horses, slaves, workers, more farmland than I know what to do with."

"The legion was good to you, sir." Siculus smiled. "I don't know many who have profited as much."

"I was good to the legion," Varro said. "It was no simple thing to earn this kind of reward. Most of that story is carved into my flesh. Maybe it was your pike that gave me this scar?"

Varro tapped the sharp white line over his eye where a pike had nearly skewered his head during the final battle of the Macedonia campaign. Siculus shrugged.

"If it was, I will not apologize for it, sir. When I was free, I had a duty to kill Romans. You were invading my homeland and killing my friends. Now I am your slave, and you may dispose of me as you will."

"You speak to me as if we are equals and as if used to being in command. You weren't always standing in the rear. I'm sure of that. I believe you're not honest about your former rank. Besides, you're too educated to have been a rear-rank pikeman. Your Latin is more than passable, and you can read it. I'll have your true story one day."

While Siculus said nothing, Varro noted that his back straightened and a distant look came over him as if he were reviewing a battle, perhaps the one that had ended his freedom.

Varro wiped his hands, and his house slave removed the chair and bowls. Varro walked Siculus into the garden. Everything was new, from the furniture to the bushes and colorful flowers. He and Siculus admired the tranquility until Varro at last sighed.

"I hate being here," he said. "I know it's a reward for all I've done. I can't just sit on my coins, but must invest them in something. With the census this year, I had to make a fast decision. Now all this has sprung up overnight. It's the worst ambush I've ever experienced, and I've had to deal with Macedonians, Numidians, and Iberians. Three peoples famous for their devious tricks."

"Thank you, sir." Siculus bowed. "Though I wouldn't mind suffering an ambush like this."

"It's the worst kind of trap." Varro folded his arms and looked around. "Look it all this responsibility. All these people who need my care, and all this land that has to produce or else I lose my investment. Give me a soldier to order about and a senior officer to tell me what to think. Give me a mission. Not four walls, four fields, and a stable of horses."

Siculus nodded thoughtfully, his dark eyes glinting with the sun.

"Do you think it's funny? Well, I'm glad someone can laugh about it. The worst isn't over yet. No, it won't be long before I have a wife and children to follow. Sure, I want descendants. But I don't want all the trouble in between."

"You can always adopt a son when you're older, sir." Siculus's smile now emerged from his thick beard. "You Romans will even adopt a full-grown man."

"I'm beginning to understand why." Varro watched his house slave from across the garden. She carried a clay jug on her shoulder and headed out of the villa toward the fields.

"Siculus, I'm not done with the legion yet. If I have my way, I will never be done with the legion. Gods, I just swore to my great-grandfather not more than an hour ago that I'd never embrace violence again. I've already broken it twice since."

The Macedonian slave again fell silent while Varro considered his situation. He recalled advice from the day before. Just move forward.

"I need someone to manage this farm and its defenses when I'm away. I don't even know the name of my house slave, or even the workers I'm paying to prepare my fields for winter barley. This is a disaster. But I know you and I know to trust my judgement about people. You've got it good here."

"I do, sir. You've not beaten anyone in the weeks we've been together, even though it was your right and you had cause."

"I will only beat them if they deserve it. I save flogging for soldiers. Anyway, you want to buy your freedom one day. Here's how you'll earn out that price. Take care of this place while I'm gone. I'll arrange for the funds you'll need. Right away, I want you to hire as many guards as we need to keep this farm and my people safe. Today, we got lucky with just troublemakers. If real brigands come, we need to be ready."

Siculus's brows sat high and his forehead wrinkled.

"Sir, you would entrust me to run your estate in your absence?"

"Who else can I entrust? Plenty of people have slaves to administer their estates. I think you gave more orders in Macedonia than you took. I need that kind of man here. Besides, you'll be watched. You'll remember Senator Flamininus is my patron. Help and revenge are both not far."

"Sir, I am flattered. But I'm inexperienced in managing an estate." Siculus's humor vanished and his face had paled.

"You'll learn as you go. I expect mistakes. As long as they don't cost lives or my fortune, l will be forgiving. At least you're experienced with taking blame. It'll save me face to blame you for all the same mistakes that I would make doing the same job. Give me time to become the rich countryside equestrian the census has marked me as. For now, I'd rather be on campaign with a clear enemy to fight and my sword-brothers at my side."

"Sir, I don't know what to say." The dark Macedonian was now a shaking white shade of his former confidence. It made Varro wonder if he had miscalculated. He had made horribly incorrect judgements of others in the past, especially thinking back to his time in Numidia. He liked to believe he had grown since then.

"You don't need to say anything, because I'm not allowing you a choice. Tomorrow we're going to arrange for a way to pay for things when I'm gone. I'm still learning what a bank is. Apparently, you just can't leave your money there or it risks disappearing. Makes me wonder why anyone uses it."

The rotund house slave once more rushed in on Varro. She no longer carried the jug and her face was red and sweaty, as if she had run far to speak to him.

"Master, you have a guest."

"That's right."

Falco emerged from the villa doorway behind the house slave. He dressed in a clean white tunic worn high to show his muscular legs.

"Looks like your place got a crack in the wall yesterday. Curio's home was fine, too. Seems like only I have the shit luck."

"Was it bad?" Varro locked forearms with Falco in greeting.

"Not as bad as what I'm here to tell you. Flamininus is calling us back to the Scipio estate. Looks like our days as country gentlemen are over. The Senate is sending us back to war."

3

Together with Falco and Curio, Varro sat in the gardens of the Scipio villa. Bees hummed and hovered over pink flowers washed in the amber light of dawn. They sat on marble benches amid a trellis of thick vines. Curio sat beside Varro, nervously flattening out wrinkles in his white tunic. He then licked his thumb and tried to rub off dirt from the hem.

Falco sat opposite both of them on another marble bench. Dappled sunlight fell over his head and broad shoulders. His heavy brows drew together and he nodded to Curio.

"No one would see it, anyway."

Curio paused and looked up. "I can see it. That's enough. This tunic cost too much to let it become dirtied."

Varro chuckled as Falco rolled his eyes.

The pleasant smells of cooking wafted into the gardens. It made Varro's mouth water, as none of them had eaten since the prior afternoon. They had rushed back to answer their summons to return to the villa they had lived in after returning from Iberia over a half year ago. Ostensibly, this villa was part of the Scipio family estate, though none of that august family ever seemed to make use of it. In Varro's estimation, it was the mark of true wealth. Who could afford a magnificent place such as this and not even care to use it? His new villa was meager compared to this place.

He set his hands on the smooth marble bench. The three of them waited in silence, except for the buzz of bees and the scratching of Curio's thumb as he fought the dirt his tunic had picked up on the road.

"You're going to rub a hole in it," Falco said. "That'll look worse."

Curio was unswayed. "Do you know what looks worse, Falco? I shouldn't have to tell you, since you see it every time you see your reflection."

"How I've missed your wit." Falco dusted his own tunic and squinted into the sunlight. "Remind me to shove you off your horse when we ride out next."

Their playful battle faded as Varro considered all that had happened since returning from Iberia. The events and visions of that time seemed to have happened to another person in another time. Now he was the guest of Rome's most powerful family and counted among the wealthy himself. As he sat and scanned the expansive garden, slaves dressed better than most citizens darted through the shaded areas on their errands. He was familiar with most of them from his short time here. Even that period seemed from a different time.

Falco and Curio fell to silence, and Falco once more produced the papyrus letter and scanned it.

"He said to be swift, and now we're sitting on our hands waiting for him to arrive. By Jupiter's beard, this is just like being in the army again."

Both Varro and Curio laughed. At last satisfied he had defeated the stain on his tunic, Curio sat back.

"I was hoping we'd have been allowed more time to settle our affairs. That villa cost me everything I had. I don't want it to fall to shit while I'm gone."

Both Varro and Falco nodded. It had happened to all of them. Senator Flamininus had been intent on getting them recorded appropriately in the census to reflect their new wealth. He had awarded them each a talent of silver for preventing the theft of the Macedonian war indemnity. A talent of silver might take average citizens several lifetimes to acquire. Now they had plowed most of it into property, which Flamininus assured them would make them even richer in time.

Falco stretched, then patted his stomach.

"We will not see our villas much, I'm sure. What I'd like to see now is some food. Where's the hospitality gone?"

Curio looked to Varro. "Do you think your slave could watch all our places? I'm paying a steward to look after mine, but I hardly know him."

"I hardly know Siculus," Varro said. "But I think he's a good choice. I'm not sure he can run all our places yet. Maybe after he has gained experience. Falco, what did you do?"

"Do?" He now craned his neck as if searching for the food he craved. "I came here like the letter said to do."

Varro's mouth gaped and he looked to Curio. Both of them couldn't find words, but Varro eventually slapped his forehead.

"Are you saying you didn't plan for someone to run the farm while you are away?"

Falco shrugged. "It'll be there when I get back."

"All right, you've just dumped a talent of silver into the Po River. That's what you've done. I told you I had people trying to steal from my farm. It'll be worse if the earthquakes continue. Bandits will be out looking for toppled walls and undefended wealth."

"You both worry too much," Falco said. "I will not worry about a fancy house while I've got enemy swords pointed at my face.

Look, I'm not completely stupid even if that's what I look like. I told the workers to keep things going while I'm away. I'll pay them a bonus for it. If anything is stolen or they take off, I warned them I'm good at finding people and killing them. In fact, that's how I got so rich. They seemed convinced. The details will work out, I'm sure."

Varro cocked his head as he considered it.

"I suppose it's not too different from what I did."

Falco waved his hand dismissively and returned to craning his neck in search of breakfast. Immediately his eyes widened and he sat up straighter, looking past Varro.

"I can't fucking believe what I'm seeing. What have we done to make the gods hate us so much?"

Now Varro twisted on his bench. He looked through the lattice and vines to see three people gathered at one entrance to the garden. A man stood taller than the others and wore a toga of searing bright white, and a grass crown rode his curled black hair. He was a young man, perhaps only three years older than Varro. As his regal head surveyed the garden, his eyes locked with Varro's through the gaps of the lattice.

"Marcellus Paullus!"

Curio twisted away and looked down, as if he couldn't bear the sight of him. "I thought we'd never see him again."

"Here he comes," Falco said, groaning. "I hope Flamininus saves us from Paullus's company."

With slaves and servants trailing him, Paullus crossed to the center where Varro and the others sat. He halted halfway and dismissed his attendants. Varro turned back to share a disgusted look with Falco and Curio.

Marcellus Paullus now appeared between them, stepping under the lattice and vines into the dappled light. The patches of it on his shoulders seemed to gleam. Only his smile was brighter.

"A joyous reunion of old friends!"

"Paullus," Varro said, nodding. He knew Paullus wouldn't leave them alone, but hoped his curt reply would discourage conversation. Both Falco and Curio repeated his name in greeting, but said nothing more.

"Really? You three are going to just sit there?" He scratched under his grass crown as if to point to it. The dried leaves rustled as he waited expectantly. The crown, of which Varro had two and Falco one, required even senators to stand and greet anyone who wore one. But this was generally saved for attendance at games or public ceremonies. Varro had never worn his own and enjoyed none of its benefits.

Yet Paullus cleared his throat. Varro reminded himself to respect traditions even if he did not respect the man. He dragged himself up.

"Paullus," he said again, hoping he sounded as dead dreary as he felt. Then he looked to Falco and Curio, who both stood as if fighting a great weight.

"Did you make that after weeding your father's garden?" Falco asked as he stood.

A subtle wince was all Paullus showed of his irritation.

"No, I won it for saving the life of a companion at great personal risk."

Falco nodded. "Ah, so you took turns nominating each other for a crown. Seems right for your kind."

Varro put his hand up for peace.

"All right, we're better than this. Paullus has done nothing to deserve hostility."

"If I knew it'd be a pissing contest," Falco said, returning to the bench, "I'd have worn my own crown. Say, does a crown holder have to stand for another crown holder? Varro has two of them, earned them too."

Paullus glared at Varro, but then it transitioned into light laughter.

"Congratulations. You have always been a hero, it seems. Rome depends upon heroes like us."

He crossed between them to sit on the marble bench beside Falco, who grudgingly stepped aside to make space. Paullus had acted swiftly, so that everyone would have to sit down after he had, which they did. Now Varro folded his arms and stared expectantly at him.

Paullus spread his hands.

"Why all the angry faces? This villa belongs to my family. If anything, I should be offended to find the three of you exploiting my family's hospitality."

Varro pressed his lips tighter. Years ago in Macedonia, Varro had led a team of soldiers to rescue Paullus from the Macedonians. Several of Varro's team died in the effort. Only they discovered he had become a plaything of King Philip's sister, Alamene, and refused to return to Rome. He had to be forced back, and rightly could be considered a traitor. Yet when Varro had last seen him, he was the decurion of his cavalry unit.

"We've been summoned," Falco said, brandishing the letter. "We're waiting on our orders and not lying about, unlike you."

Paullus leaned back as if the letter impressed him, though Varro knew he mocked them.

"Ah, yes, special orders. I understand you spent several months enjoying my family's hospitality. I am certain you must have done them a great favor to have been gifted such a privilege."

Varro cleared his throat. "It was certainly a privilege. Your family keeps a beautiful home."

"And the gods have not touched it with their violent earthquakes as they have others." Paullus looked around, smiling placidly. "It must be a sign of their favor."

The capriciousness of earthquake damage led many to believe they were in or out of favor with the gods. But Varro doubted the gods cared about anything other than themselves. He forced himself to be contrite in answering Paullus.

"I pray it will always be so."

"Of course," Paullus said. "My uncle is the greatest hero Rome has ever known, and that greatness runs in the entire family. The gods know their own, Varro. Have every confidence in that."

They fell silent a moment, but to Varro it seemed to stretch out forever. Paullus clearly enjoyed their discomfort, regarding them with hooded eyes and a sneer. But Varro would not play his game, and sat quietly while waiting for Flamininus to arrive.

At last, Paullus leaned forward and lowered his voice.

"This is no chance meeting of ours," he said, looking between them. "I received word you would be here soon, probably before you knew it yourselves. I came as fast as I could, and have made it in time."

Falco's heavy brows drew together and he folded his arms.

"It'd be a better thing if you leave as fast as you could."

Now Paullus's good humor cracked and he narrowed his eyes at Falco.

"You forget yourself. I am your better, in every way. You are a guest in my family's estate. You were always an oaf, but I would expect better behavior even from you."

Varro saw Falco's face redden and interjected before he could worsen matters.

"We are guests here, and should behave better. I apologize that none of us are especially glad to see you. We left off on difficult terms."

Falco let go a long breath. "Difficult terms? He was off running around with King Philip's sister, drunk on true love and all that bullshit. So drunk he could betray—"

"Enough of that," Paullus snapped. "I'll do you the favor of preventing an insult that would bring serious consequences."

Varro hated agreeing with Paullus, but it was indeed a heavy thing to accuse a patrician of treason. That opportunity had passed long ago, and like all the wealthy patricians of Rome, Paullus fell under a different standard of justice.

Now the four of them hung in desperate silence while Falco squirmed on the bench like a boy made to sit out his favorite game, which in his case was conflict and combat.

Paullus straightened the folds of his white toga.

"Better silence than false words." He nodded across the short distance between benches. "Learn from Varro and Curio. If you can't say anything of value, don't speak at all."

Falco glared at his feet while Curio kept his head down, as if hoping to be forgotten. Mention of his name made him shift on the bench.

"Here's the last thing you need to know about my time as a prisoner of war. When General Athenagoras realized my status, he had Alamene seduce me. Being a young man in a desperate situation, I was as weak as she was seductive. She then kept me drugged to be both pliable and tractable. Thanks to your brave efforts, I was spared from becoming a pawn in their games. Now, you have the official account, and I will hear no more about it."

The account was completely the opposite of what had happened. Paullus certainly had never been a prisoner of war. But Varro nodded and gave a smile that must be obviously false to anyone seeing it.

"Will you now explain why you rushed to meet us?"

Paullus clapped his hands together, using both to point at him.

"Do you see why he is your leader? He does not waste time in pointless battles he cannot win."

Falco folded his arms and opened his mouth as if to speak. Varro was sure it would be a jab at his abilities as a leader, but then Falco put a hand over his mouth. When no one responded, Paullus continued.

"I have learned all about your secret society."

Varro raised his brow and Curio sat back. Only Falco remained still, with his hand over his mouth.

"Don't look so surprised," Paullus said. "I know the significance of those pugiones you carry with the owl head. I have ways of learning things that you common people could not imagine."

Varro's hand unconsciously slipped to where his pugio should be, but he had surrendered all weapons upon arrival at the villa. Indeed, his whole kit of armor, greaves, shield, and helmet had all been left in the cart they had all used to travel here. Paullus noted Varro's reaction and smiled.

"Servus Capax. Really, whoever came up with that name must have no imagination whatsoever."

Now Falco unfolded his arms. "We're not supposed to discuss it with anyone. Direct orders from a higher-ranking man than you."

"He's right," Curio said, at last braving the conversation. "You know what you know. But that's all you know."

Paullus's brows drew together and he tilted his head. "What a profound thought. Apparently membership in this society doesn't make many demands on a person's intelligence."

Varro now sat up straighter. "We're not revealing anything to you. We'll not answer questions or confirm your guesses."

"That's fine," Paullus said, spreading his hands wide. "I'm heartened to hear it, actually. You need to protect the secrets you hold, especially where you've involved yourselves in the shadowed dealings of the Senate."

Now all three of them shared a glance while Paullus gloated. He flicked his eyebrows up and down.

"You didn't realize you had done so? Well, you can hardly be such dear clients of Senator Flamininus and not inherit his enemies at the least. And your oafish bumbling has probably brought a raft of enemies of your own."

"No," Falco said, waving his hands. "Anyone that makes an

enemy of us is dead in a few months. Just good policy not to let a snake hide under your sandals, you know."

"Don't I know it," Paullus said. His grass crown slid forward on his wavy hair, and he pushed it up as he leaned close. "And that analogy is very apt. Because you have a snake under your sandal in Senator Cato and his patron, Flaccus. Now there's a man you don't want to offend. He has the biggest mob in Rome behind him."

Shaking his head, Varro asked, "Is this why you rushed to meet us before speaking to Senator Flamininus? You just wanted to warn us that anyone aligned with Cato will want to do us harm? That's noble of you, but we already realized it."

Paullus sat back and also folded his arms, reflecting the stances of everyone around him. It seemed as if he were reevaluating why he had come. His dark eyes shifted around all of them until settling on Varro.

"I want to join your secret society. I want you to make me a member."

Falco chortled and Curio sat back then sighed. Varro, however, understood Paullus was serious and tilted his head.

"Do you know what you're asking? Do you really know the kinds of missions we are sent on?"

"He hasn't got a scar on him," Falco said. "Let's take him in and make him just like us—scars from toes to nose and nightmares that'll never fucking end. Sure, let him join."

"Scars aren't a measure of competence," Paullus said. "Any ranker can get himself a scar with enough bad luck."

Varro put his hand to the back of his head as he considered how to decline Paullus's request.

"Falco is telling you we are barely alive at the end of our missions. We are called Servus Capax because we're useful but expendable. Just like you might enjoy a nice pair of sandals until they become so beat up you throw them away. That's what you want to become? To go from a privileged life to that of a disposable servant?"

Paullus blinked, as if confused.

"You three have done exceedingly well for yourselves. You've got estates worth many times more than what your families could've earned in a dozen generations."

"You need more wealth?" Varro asked, chuckling.

And Paullus grew quiet. When that silence extended, everyone leaned forward for an answer.

"Maybe because the glory of my heritage is blinding, you do not see my real life. I have served my time in the legion and I should be a candidate for public office now. But yet my family does not advance me. I am tolerated, not embraced. I am patronized, not developed. My future will forever be to hide behind my brothers and cousins, and never become more."

"It's because of what you did in Macedonia." Falco slapped his knee. "Of course it is. Your family has too many enemies that would love to use your history against them."

Rather than become irate, Paullus adjusted his grass crown.

"I did earn this, you know. I can fight and be brave. I fought the same war as you three. I rode away from battles when my friends did not. I have the same questions that haunt me in the night. At least in this way, we are not much different."

"It is not for us to decide who joins," Varro said. "We were recruited, and we weren't asking for it. Senator Flamininus will be here shortly. You can speak to him about it. If your skills match what he needs, he may give you a pugio of your own."

"That's why I wanted to meet you first. I need your recommendation. Make an appeal to the senator for me. He has the same misunderstandings about me as the others. But if you were to recommend me, it would carry much more weight."

Varro saw Falco shaking his head while Paullus gazed at him.

"I can't do that," he said. "I won't deny your crown or your service. But I cannot see you fitting in with anything we've done thus far. You'd be a liability."

Paullus slumped and lowered his head.

"I thought you might say that. Make no mistake. I will become a member of your society. I can do anything you can do. More capable, in fact. But if you cannot see it, then let me give you an example of why you need me. I can keep the heat away from you when you beat up the relatives of powerful senators."

Falco snorted, and Curio laughed. But Varro felt a strange chill in Paullus's smile. He thought back to the three thugs.

"They were dressed like beggars," Varro said. "They carried knives that looked like they found them in a latrine."

"I had them dressed that way," Paullus said, smiling. "Instructed them on how to act like bitterly poor fools that are always complaining about inequalities. You know the kind. Varro, I sent them to you because I thought you'd go easier on them than Falco or Curio. But by the gods, you carved up one's face and broke the other's arm. That arm will never be right again and that scar is going to heal ugly. What kind of animal have you become?"

"What are you playing at?" Varro asked, teeth gritted. Both Falco and Curio had grown still, like they balanced on the precipice of a steep cliff.

"Just insurance that you help me get what I want. I deserve a spot in Servus Capax if I want one. And I do. I want to live the life of adventure that you three have. I'm never going to succeed in politics, at least not in public office. But I will always be a fine snake under the sandal, eh, Varro?"

Varro's eyes narrowed. "Whose relatives?"

Paullus shook his head. "You can't guess? I've already named him. Flaccus, of course! Won't he be enraged when he finds out you have struck the first blow in your mutual war, one certainly lopsided in his favor? But he doesn't know yet, and his little nephews don't know who you are. They're waiting for me to tell them. And I can tell them someone else's name. Just give me one. I can even do better and keep them quiet. I have many skills that will be a benefit to Servus Capax. But I need to get in first. So, will you help me? I think it would be in your interest to do so. It'll be a shame what Flaccus will have done to those fine estates you've just established. Fires, earthquakes, brigands, and who knows what else could plague them while you're gone? Plague them until nothing remains but rubble."

"You will never be one of us," Varro said.

Paullus smiled. "Think carefully about your decision. You've done some terrible things to powerful people, completely out of proportion to their offenses. You're going to need help anywhere you can find it. So you help me, and I help you. The choice is simple, Varro."

4

The pleasant garden now felt like a sweltering marsh to Varro. Sweat rolled down his back as he paced in circles around the trellis-covered marble benches. Once-bright flowers now appeared gray and the droning bees sounded angry, as if they were preparing to swarm him. Yet they simply floated from flower to flower, uncaring of Varro's relentless pace.

Falco and Curio remained in the shade of their benches, the white of their tunics shining through the vines and lattice. But both leaned forward, Falco with his fingers interlocked behind his head and Curio with arms folded tight across his chest.

Across the garden, Paullus turned a last time with his two servants trailing him. He waved at Varro before vanishing into the villa to "clean up from the road," as he said. He had tried to make it seem he had somehow traveled with no care for luxury. But Varro doubted he had done a single thing to prepare for his trip here.

Other than to arrange a trap.

Once Paullus vanished into the darkness of the villa, Varro

resumed his circular pacing. He punched his left palm, growling in frustration.

"You were going to devote yourself to peace again," Falco said. "And then you mangled three kids. What's with you?"

Rather than answer himself, Curio spoke up.

"You're always giving him shit for holding back, now you're complaining that he didn't. What's with you? That's the question."

"Hold on, Curio. This has got all of us in the shit. Now we've got more to lose than just our goods looks."

"And what would you have done?" Curio sat back and tilted his head.

Varro continued circling, trying to find peace in his confused thoughts. Both Falco and Curio continued with their disagreement.

"I'd have beaten them till they couldn't walk," Falco said. "But I wouldn't have cut off their noses."

"He didn't do that. You're exaggerating!"

"He came close enough. Cut up faces, broken arms, and broken heads. It's all the same result."

The argument vanished into indistinct chatter while Varro continued to circle. It wasn't so much that Paullus had forced his choices that angered him as it was his own mistake. Falco had been right to say they had more to lose now than ever. His actions could cost him everything he owned. Outside the legion, he was not a centurion, free to dole out whatever punishment he wanted. Indeed, he had failed to act like a civilized man. The thugs were no challenge to him. He could've reclaimed his goat, thumped the thieves for their trespasses, then sent them off. Instead, he had nearly killed one and marred the other two for life.

He had become the monster his great-grandfather warned him about. It both hurt and enraged him to realize it. Indeed, he might never be suited for civilian life again, and be better off living in an army camp.

He continued to pace as Falco and Curio's disagreement petered out. Varro, now shining with sweat, returned to sit beside Curio in the shade. Falco regarded him with a wrinkled brow.

"Did making yourself dizzy help?"

"No," Varro said, wiping perspiration from his brow. "But I couldn't scream and kick over flower vases, could I? I had to get it out somehow. Damn that snake! I'll have to ensure Flamininus approves him."

"And then what?" Falco asked. "How do you know he'll keep his word and not just hold it over you? Even if he honors his word, he'll just extort us another way."

"Once he's a member, he'll be subject to the same rules we are. He would work against Servus Capax if he works against us."

Curio cleared his throat. "I agree with Falco. He is rotten and nothing but trouble. We'll just end up doing whatever he wants."

Varro put his hands over his head, much as Falco had done a moment before.

"I don't know what to do. If we don't help him, think of the trouble he'll bring to all of us. And it will hurt more than us. All our slaves and workers will be endangered."

"You're a treat," Falco said. "You're worried about slaves after carving up three boys."

"They were not boys," Varro snapped. "They were—are—criminals that broke into my villa and stole my property. I could have cut off their hands for it. Instead, I gave one a gash on his face. Just stop talking about what cannot change. What we do next is more important."

They fell silent until Curio spoke up. "You still plan to support Paullus?"

"Yes," Varro said. "Anyway, if he does join, he'll soon find out there's little glory in our missions, and no acclaim for success. I suspect he thinks he can work his way into politics through Servus Capax. Somehow, he aims to influence from the shadows. He doesn't want to crawl through the mud with us, and certainly wouldn't survive the shit we've been through."

"There's a thought," Falco said. "Let him catch enemy javelins for us."

Curio's voice brightened. "After one mission, he'll be begging to be released. They'll make him a spy in a place far away. We'll rid ourselves of him for good."

Varro's chest released. "Maybe it's not as bad as I thought. I am just so mad at myself. My love of violence led us to this trouble. I have to do better."

Falco sniffed. "You were easy on those brats. You should've taught them a real lesson."

Curio leaped off the bench and pointed. "See? There you go again."

With his heavy brows stitched together, Falco leaned back.

"What are you excited about?"

Varro saw Senator Flamininus enter the garden through the main villa, his attendants and secretaries trailing. He dismissed them, as was his custom when dealing with anything related to Servus Capax. Varro stood up and waved away the arguments between his friends. Both turned and stood as well. Flamininus crossed the luxurious garden to meet them. He smiled, squinting in the sun. His hair had a dash of gray at the temples and the first signs of age reached into his face as lines between his soulful eyes. He dressed in a white tunic with a purple stripe to denote his senatorial status.

"I am sorry to keep you waiting after an urgent summons." He now stood between them, Varro and the others backing away to make room, and nodded to each one in greeting. "Varro, you look as if you've run a marathon with such sweat."

Falco laughed. "He loves his marching drills, sir. He can't wait to start again."

Flamininus gave a polite laugh then gestured for all to sit on the marble benches.

"There will be a lot of fast marching in the days ahead," he said. "But before speaking of that, how have you fared with your new investments? The gods have spared your homes from damage, I hope?"

They made small talk about the frequency of the earthquakes and how only Falco's villa had endured significant damage. The senator offered his thoughts on their arrangements for oversight while away. He did not react to Falco's choices as Varro had, and instead commented that brute force had its uses.

"The three of you will become proper citizens yet. You'll want wives and children, I suppose. But hold off on that for now. I can help find suitable matches when the time comes."

Varro swallowed hard. Once more, he would be indebted to Flamininus. They had a patron and client relationship, which is how all senators or anyone at all grew and maintained power in Rome. Flamininus had a deep interest in making his three young clients successful, as it would only enhance his own influence. Maybe because he had just stumbled into Paullus's trap, Varro wondered if Flamininus was binding them in chains disguised as garlands of flowers.

"Onto the business at hand." Flamininus's voice shifted subtly. Perhaps only men who served with him would notice. But Varro noted how the senator's voice gained the edge of a consul in the field. Battle plans and orders were about to be assigned, and the only words required from subordinates were "yes, sir."

"It's not enough that the gods torment us with earthquakes. These seem to have awakened the Ligurians in their mountain hideouts. The Senate has received a letter from the commander of Pisa, Marcus Cincius. The Ligurians have united their tribes and besieged the city. He is utterly surrounded and is begging for relief. He estimates forty thousand Ligurians besiege him. They first ravaged Luna before reaching Pisa."

Falco gasped. "We were just there! Well, a few years ago anyway."

Luna had been the staging point for Cato's campaign in Iberia, and where Varro, Falco, and Curio had rejoined the legions after time in Numidia.

Flamininus nodded gravely. "You wouldn't want to be there now. The Ligurian tribes have laid waste to everything. But that's not all. Another Ligurian army has sacked everything between their mountain homes and Placentia."

Varro grimaced. "This is a serious attack, sir."

"It always is with the Ligurians," Flamininus said. "Normally, they don't unite in such numbers. So someone or some group has organized them for this purpose."

He looked at all three of them with narrowed eyes.

"One day, we'll silence the Ligurians forever. It's no simple thing to dig them out of their mountain forts. But attacks like these show us why we must."

"They'll pay for it, sir." Falco shrugged. "We'll teach them they're a conquered people just like we did the Iberian barbarians."

Flamininus's eyes lit up. "Ah, this reminds me of other news. You three made quite an impact in Iberia. After you left, your actions had roused them to intense anger. An entire army of united Lusitani tribesmen descended on Far Iberia. The praetor was then justified to ask for more troops, which he received, and he used them to crush the Lusitani. He went deep into their territory and used your map in that invasion plan. A large part of that victory is thanks to the three of you."

"We're honored, sir," Varro said, blinking. "But we can't be credited with more than making a map and barely escaping with our lives."

"Nonsense," Flamininus said. "This is how Servus Capax works. We facilitate change. We goad the enemy into the battles we want to fight, then we crush them and advance Rome's power and influence. Now more of Iberia is under our control than ever before, and that's because of what you did and what you learned while there."

All three of them shared a bemused grin. Then Flamininus cleared his throat.

"But back to the mission. It's Ligurians this time. Much closer to home. Pisa can hold out only because the Ligurians are not wise in siege warfare. Eventually they will prevail, and we must meet them head-on before that happens."

Varro nodded. "Absolutely, sir. What is our part in this?"

Flamininus gave a sly smile.

"The consul assigned to Liguria this year would not have been my choice for this crisis. He's not a bad man, but an indecisive one. Too fretful and unimaginative. Not everyone selected to consulship is prepared for the challenge. But I am one man with one man's opinions."

Varro felt a tightness in his chest, and he looked to Falco and Curio. Both seemed as tense as he felt, and they probably expected an order to remove this consul by any means possible. Varro could not do something like that, no matter who ordered it.

"What's wrong? The three of you look like you're waiting for the scourge to hit your backs." Flamininus's soulful eyes narrowed. "The consul is Quintus Minucius Thermus. He's going to need as much help as he can get to bring a swift end to this uprising. This is where the three of you come in. Your experiences will be a great aid to him."

Varro slouched on the bench and laughed, as did the others. Flamininus frowned at the interruption.

"I'm sorry, sir," Varro said, regaining his composure. "We did not sleep well last night and are more foolish for it today."

Flamininus scanned them with hooded eyes before continuing.

"Consul Minucius has requested last year's reserves to assemble at Arretium, along with our allies. But the people are unwilling to serve. What have we come to when our citizens cannot be counted upon to defend their homes?"

Varro thought back to Gallio, who had bought his farm after a lifetime of service. He thought of the men working his own villa, who had done the same and lost everything for it. But he could not disagree with Flamininus.

"It is the duty of a citizen to defend the city from all threats. The Ligurians could sweep into Rome if left unchecked."

"Precisely," Flamininus said, shaking his head. "Yet they petition the Tribune of the People to be excused from duty. Or they claim illness or injury prevents them from service. I understand Rome has asked a lot of her people. But what shall we do when enemies attack?"

Falco sighed. "It's a sad state, sir. People have grown tired of fighting."

"And our allies as well," Flamininus said. "They won't answer their summons. Only the Numidians have been willing to aid us."

Varro smiled, remembering Baku and his fearsome raiders.

"King Masinissa and his people will always be Rome's allies, and we are doubly fortunate for it."

Flamininus nodded and rubbed his chin.

"The issue of who shall serve is still with the Senate. Pisa will have to hold out while we settle this. I will vote for action, of course. But I have met with other of my peers in private, and we see an opportunity for you three to shape the battle to come. You can take action while the Senate is delayed."

Varro shared a smile with Falco and Curio, then leaned forward on the marble bench.

"We're all eager to do what we can, sir."

With a genuine smile, Flamininus leaned forward as well.

"There are few men in this world who would rather be at war than idling in a fine garden such as this. How mighty would Rome be if every citizen were as loyal and brave?"

Falco cleared his throat. "No disrespect, sir, but I'd rather be campaigning. My new villa is nice and I think I'll learn how to enjoy it. But not now. Give me an actual enemy to fight, not profit and taxes to manage. By the gods, that's what I'm really afraid of."

"You keep fighting for Rome," Flamininus said, "and I will ensure your farms make a profit. No worries there. Now, I want the three of you to proceed ahead of Consul Minucius. Get to Pisa and assess the Ligurian strengths and weaknesses. Where are their supply lines? How unified are they? And most importantly, who has organized them? The Ligurians fight each other more than us. So who has taught them to march together? When you find that man, kill him if you can. Without a head, the army will become a mob."

Varro nodded throughout the instructions.

"Sir, with so many troops about it might be impossible to reach their king or whatever he is. At least impossible to kill him and live to tell about it."

"Just so," Flamininus said, now tugging at his chin as he considered. "Do what you can to reach him, but don't endanger yourselves. High-value prisoners for interrogation would be a suitable alternative. Consul Minucius would definitely benefit from what they know."

Curio raised his hand. "Sir, how many prisoners should we capture? There's only three of us. I don't know if we could handle more than one."

"Assess the situation and decide for yourselves." Flamininus again smiled and spread his hands. "I have learned that the fewer instructions I give you three, the better you perform. So you have my complete support in whatever you do to hamper, confuse, and damage our enemy. I've every confidence you'll do that and more."

"Thank you, sir," Varro said. "How long before we can expect Consul Minucius to reach Pisa?"

"I can't be sure. It could be a week or more after we settle the petitions in the Senate. Give it ten to fifteen days. If you've not seen the legions by that time, head to Arretium and await word there. When you locate Consul Minucius, he will expect your reports and after will assign you duties as he sees fit. He will probably place you in the infantry given your experience. Of course, you're qualified for the cavalry. But you might find their ranks closed to you, no matter what the latest census says about your class."

Varro waved off the concern. "I would be fine in any assignment, sir."

"Good. Now, one last objective. When you arrive at Pisa, you must get word to the commander that relief is on the way. I will write a reply to his letter, so he knows the veracity of your message. It is imperative that the people of Pisa do not abandon hope."

Flamininus now stood, and the others did as well. Varro saluted in acknowledgement.

"We will go as fast as possible, sir. You will know our work is done when Consul Minucius drives the Ligurians from the field and crushes them against their mountain homes."

Flamininus returned the salute. From his sheepish look, he seemed to realize he was no longer a consul.

Having been caught up imagining how he would handle his mission, Varro remembered Paullus, causing him to stumble over his words before the senator dismissed them.

"Sir, there is one more thing to discuss before we set out." He looked to Falco, who seemed disappointed he had remembered.

The senator frowned but inclined his head for Varro to continue.

"Sir, I want to recommend Marcellus Paullus for Servus Capax. I think he would honor Rome with his service."

Flamininus leaned back, his soulful eyes unfocused for a moment while he seemed to consider the request. "So that is why he has come? Well, do you honestly recommend him?"

Varro had not expected that response and looked to Falco and Curio. Both refused to meet his gaze and held blank expressions as they stared ahead.

"Yes, I do," Varro lied. "I'm certain he will do well."

The smile on Flamininus's mouth was hard to interpret. It seemed to report an impish delight at Varro's poor lying, but also hinted at something more sinister yet satisfying to him.

"Then I shall speak with him. I will find work for him to do, if he will accept the life this commitment demands. It is a dangerous duty, which could easily end in death."

"In fairness, sir," Varro said. "It is also true for service in the cavalry."

Again, Flamininus smiled. "I feel your work is far more deadly. In any case, I shall consider your recommendation carefully. If you think he should be accepted, then I will trust your judgement."

"Thank you, sir."

Varro felt queasy as the senator left them to prepare for their mission. He hoped he had not just invited a snake into their midst. Paullus would have duties befitting a member of the senatorial class, and not be sent to crawl in the mud behind enemy lines.

But he knew that was not how the gods played with mortals.

5

The journey from the Scipio family villa north to Rome took only a day of travel on foot. They now viewed Rome's hills as blue shapes in the distance as they followed a well-traveled road. Dust billowed up from the wheels of their wagon, drawn by the most forgiving mule Varro had ever known.

Even Falco had noticed the animal's uncommon demeanor. "How many times on campaign would I have given all my silver for a beast like this?"

Despite the mood of the group, Falco was in high spirits. Varro guessed that even with the addition of Paullus to their team, it still thrilled Falco to be going to war again.

For now, they marched without their newest member. Paullus remained behind to make arrangements, given the suddenness of the assignment. But since he would follow on horseback, he could catch up to them outside Rome where they would then set out for Pisa.

"You still act like footmen, marching everywhere you go. I'll have to teach you three how to become proper cavalry," Paullus had said. He brandished a new pugio with a Servus Capax owl head inlaid in silver on its pommel.

After they departed, Varro wondered why Flamininus had one ready for Paullus. Had he been aware of the impending request or just kept a spare handy? Whatever the reason, it didn't matter. Flamininus informed them Paullus was now part of their operation.

They marched with speed, but not up to the standard Varro would have set while active in the legion. He had maintained an exercise regimen these long months, but he had found it impossible to push himself when there was no urgency. Now, he paid for it with sore legs and feet.

Their cart rolled to a halt still a distance from the city walls. Weapons were not allowed in the city, never mind full war gear. So they would encamp with others not entering the city for various reasons. There was never a shortage of people camping outside of Rome. Indeed, it seemed a small community of its own that would form out of nothing then vanish again the next day.

They had left their scutum shields in Flamininus's care, as these would be too bulky for stealth work. Instead, they carried smaller shields used by the cavalry. This was the biggest part of their load, which was not much. They would still miss the use of their mule as they headed north. Their campsite fit among merchants and travelers, all collected together for mutual support. Curio had located a buyer for their mule and cart, which was no longer of any use past this point.

Pisa waited hundreds of miles north, and the fastest way to cover the distance would be to take a ship up the coast and land south of the invaded territory. From there, they would go on foot.

The next morning, they closed the mule and cart sale with a thin-faced merchant. Falco seemed sad to see the mule go. Now the three of them sat astride the road in armor and with their supplies in bulky packs. Their bronze helmets hung on their chests, feathers removed to cut down the profile for their stealth work.

They stood at every lone rider that approached over the crest in the road. But they sat back down in a cloud of brown dust as each time a stranger trotted by, giving them odd looks if noticing them at all.

"We'll give him to midday," Varro said. "Then we leave without him."

Falco waved his hands as if shooing away a fly. "He probably got cold feet and is riding back to Flamininus to hand in his pugio. We can leave now."

"He has a horse," Curio said. "Does he plan to take it? We'll never charter a ship in time if the captain has to take a horse aboard."

"Maybe he has a plan for it," Varro said. "Let's wait and see."

The morning passed with Varro becoming restless enough to pace. Falco dozed in the grass, using his pack for a pillow, and Curio wandered down to the stream that supported the roadside camps. Whenever Varro paced to his imaginary boundary, he turned to pace back. He repeated this for an hour until he at last turned to find what he hoped for.

Paullus trotted up the road, seated on his proud chestnut horse. The animal's coat shined in the midday sun. Another black horse and a rider followed behind. Paullus dressed in a cream tunic that turned amber in the sunlight.

Varro's gut immediately tightened and he balled his fists as he strode to meet Paullus.

"Any later and we'd have left you," he shouted before reaching the two riders. Varro saw the other rider was Paullus's servant, whose horse was piled with extra baggage.

"You could have," Paullus said jauntily. "I would've caught up before you reached our ship."

Now Varro stood beneath the horse, which cast its gaze down

on him with the same arrogance as his rider. The spirit of Centurion Drusus that informed all of Varro's leadership now stirred in his chest.

"You're not to catch up. You're to keep up and don't forget it. Forty thousand Ligurians besiege Pisa. They're not waiting on your convenience." He scowled at the servant seated on the packhorse. "And who the fuck is that?"

Paullus's eyebrows flew up in an expression of bewilderment.

"Never mind," Varro said. "It doesn't matter who he is. Send him back. And whatever mobile palace you've packed on that horse's back goes with him."

"Have a care how you address me. I am not some dirty recruit."

Varro's fists tightened until his fingers hurt.

"Then get off your horse and send him back with your servant. We go on foot to the port. It's not far. After that, we'll have no use for mounts. You don't infiltrate an enemy camp on horseback. You should know that much."

Staring down with head tilted as if he did not understand, Paullus remained atop his horse. Varro shook his head in disgust, then called out for Falco and Curio to rejoin him.

Falco flipped up from the grass as if a mule had stepped on his stomach. He seemed about to curse, but then looked at Paullus and his assistant.

"Who's the boy? What's he carrying on his horse?"

Circling around Paullus's mount, Varro addressed the servant who hid behind the neck of his black horse. Varro pulled the hem of his tunic and used his brashest centurion's voice.

"I don't know what your master has told you. But ride back to your home, take all this baggage with you, and speak nothing of what you've seen or heard. If you do, I'll have your tongue on a plate."

"Enough!"

Paullus vaulted down from his saddle with practiced ease, his face red and taut with rage. He grabbed Varro by his shoulder and turned him about.

"You do not order my servants around, and you do not treat me with such disrespect."

Varro did not wince from Paullus's stare. Instead, he glanced down at the hand gripping his shoulder.

"I'm in command of this operation. You are my subordinate. If any of my subordinates arrived late, carried unauthorized baggage, and broke the secrecy of our mission with his very first action, then I'd flog him. Since we're old friends, I'll just ask you to remove your hand and correct the situation. Can you do that, Paullus?"

The two glared at each other, but Paullus's dark eyes shifted aside. He gave a contemptuous sniff, then looked up at his servant.

"You heard the commander. Return home, and take my horse as well. Your life depends on keeping all you know a secret."

The servant did not seem especially frightened at the threat. Varro guessed Paullus routinely threatened his life. Yet he acknowledged his orders and dismounted with ease to attend to his master's horse.

Now Curio ran back up the slope, his face reddened, and joined Falco who had already shouldered his pack. Varro met them, leaving Paullus to coordinate his horse and excess baggage.

"Our fourth member has arrived with his house packed on his horse," he said as he met Curio and Falco. They stood amid a field of amber grass that stroked their knees as it waved from a gentle wind. Unfortunately, the wind delivered the less pleasant odors of Rome even at this distance.

"Fucking patrician brat," Falco said. "You wanted him, so he's all your problem. Still, that's a fine horse. Could be useful if we need to send a swift message."

Varro nodded. "If we need a horse, the enemy will provide one for us."

The three chuckled and watched Paullus order his servant.

"He's not even in armor," Curio said. "It's like he never served the in the legion before."

"I don't think he understands this is the legion," Varro said. He patted his pugio with the golden owl's head. "It is an exciting life of adventure. So let's get him straight before we reach enemy territory."

"Dreamy bastard," Falco said. "Remember how he went on about his true love, Alamene? You'd figure he'd grow up after that disaster."

Curio laughed and mimicked Paullus kissing his love. This made Falco roar with laughter and Paullus turn to scowl at them.

"Better not to mention that around him," Varro said, waving Curio down. "It'll just make him angry."

Falco rubbed at the corner of his eye as his laugher ebbed.

"His face makes me angry."

"Listen," Varro said. "Like it or not, he's one of us now. It will do no one any good to mistreat him. He just needs to adjust to the idea of not being in charge. We're forever going to be beneath his class. So there'll always be friction if he has to answer to any of us. But since Senator Flamininus has not given us any other direction, I'm considering him a junior member. Once he learns to play the game, I'm sure he'll be fine. He wants to get through this period so he can start waging shadow wars in the Senate, or so he probably thinks."

The three of them fell silent as Paullus approached. He now shouldered a heavy pack, larger than anything the others carried. Varro guessed it held his armor and as many luxury goods as he could bear to carry. Behind him, his chestnut horse followed the servant's black horse, tethered by a long rope. To Varro, who knew much about horses from his service in Numidia, this horse seemed happy to leave his master behind.

"What are the three of you laughing about?" he asked as he

joined their circle. "Was it a joke at my expense? You'll not be laughing long, not once you see me in action."

"We've seen that before," Falco said.

"All right, all of you," Varro said, cutting in front of Falco. "No more foolishness. The port is near. We'll have a rough time finding someone to sail toward trouble. So we need to be swift."

Curio sniffed. "There's always someone willing to go. Always someone wanting to profit from war, even in their homeland."

Varro knew the truth of it, but did not want to suffer any more delays. So they formed up their tiny column and marched along the road for the port of Ostia, with its bustling trade and travel traffic. He set a vigorous pace, expecting a complaint from Paullus. So it surprised him when Falco spoke up.

"To be clear, we're not running to Pisa? At this pace, we won't need a ship."

"That's the price for sitting on your ass all season," Varro said. He could see the sparkle of the ocean and smell the salt in the air. He picked up the pace.

"Show off," Falco muttered.

Paullus then inserted himself. "No chatter on the march. I thought you were veterans."

The tone rankled Varro, since it was doubtless an order. But he was correct in theory. Before Falco halted the march to argue, as Varro knew he would, he instead reissued the same order. He had never issued orders to Falco and Curio when it was just them. Paullus's presence changed all of that.

"Silence in column. And I'll give the orders, Paullus."

While he did not turn to see the effect of his order, he could feel eyes boring into his skull. He couldn't help a small smile as they marched on toward Ostia, chasing distant columns of traders and travelers headed to the same port.

Their arrival drew only cursory glances from the crowds. With the invasion of the Ligurians, it surprised no one to see armed men looking for travel. It took a few attempts to find a captain willing to deviate from his course and head toward the fighting. But using the denarii from the sale of wagon and mule and adding heavy-handed appeals to patriotism, they secured passage for the next day.

Varro tried to wrangle a swifter departure, but the captain insisted he had granted his crew leave and he would not disturb it. Conceding defeat, Varro prepared to find lodging for the night.

They stood beside the wide-bellied trading ship at the dock, its plank lowered. The captain, a wiry man of middle age and sun-shriveled skin, climbed back into his vessel. Varro and the others turned toward the port city again.

All except Paullus, who bounded up the plank to follow the captain.

"See here, Captain. We've offered a generous fee for the use of your ship. Our need is urgent."

Varro whirled around to see Paullus, who had donned his chain shirt like the others, grab the captain by his shoulder. A half-dozen crew sprang up from out of sight, and all reached for something to use as a weapon.

"What is he doing?" Varro asked.

The captain pulled out of his grip, his dark face now shaded darker.

"Keep your hands off me. No one comes aboard uninvited."

"Then I invite myself," Paullus said grandly. "Look at this."

Varro watched as more crew emerged from wherever they had been hidden from view. They carried clubs, spears, and a few held long knives. But none took any more action, as their captain was now examining Paullus's extended hand.

"That is genuine," he said. "The Paullus family signet ring. Now, in the name of my family, I will have you set sail immediately."

The captain stared at Paullus's hand, grabbed it then turned it side to side before being satisfied. He stepped back.

"You'd have some balls to show that if it were stolen." The captain looked down at Varro. "Is it true?"

But Paullus commanded the attention. "Marcellus Paullus, dear captain. That is who I am. Now, recall your men and I shall see them all compensated for their lost leave. We sail immediately."

The captain looked toward the sky. "You're fortunate the wind favors the journey tonight. All right, all of you come aboard while I fetch my crew."

Varro raised his brows at Curio, who shrugged, then led all of them up the plank that bounced underfoot.

Paullus stood at the center of the deck beneath the mainmast, his head tilted back in triumph. He looked down his nose at Varro.

"Do you see what I can do for us now?"

"Listen to me," Varro said, lowering his voice and leaning into Paullus. The crewmen nearby looked on as Falco and Curio flanked Varro.

"You do not act without first discussing your intentions with the team. You don't reveal your identity to anyone while we are on a mission." He filled his voice with as much threat as he could muster. "Do it again, and you'll sit out this mission and I'll report your failures to my commander."

The smug look on Paullus's face vanished. "Oh, yes, sir. Very good, sir. I'll be sure to ask the next time you roll over if you would like to be a man or remain a whipped dog. The mission is urgent, isn't it? Sir. I secured what we needed. You would've delayed us another day. Pisa is besieged, sir. The Ligurians are not waiting on your convenience."

"Let me break just one finger," Falco said. "He can still fight without his little fingers."

Putting up his hand for silence, Varro stepped back.

"Don't be coy with me. We operate as a team, with a single leader who directs a single purpose. I am the leader. You are a junior member. In my estimation, you are probationary. Now, you'll obey your orders like a good soldier, just like everyone else."

Paullus's expression flattened, and he pursed his lips. "I can always let Flaccus know who roughed up his nephews. You should think carefully about my probationary designation. We had an agreement, and if you won't keep it, then neither shall I."

"He doesn't know when to shut up," Falco said. "Let me break his jaw. He can still fight without having to speak."

"Threats?" Paullus slipped out of the semicircle, leaving himself an escape in case Falco was serious. "None of you would do a thing against me. You know who I am, and you know what would happen if you assaulted me. So don't bother with threats. Now, is there anything more, sir? Thanks to my initiative, we will soon be at sea."

Disgusted, Varro waved him away. He then left Curio and Falco to stare out at the harbor. Ships arrived in spaced out lines, but only a handful departed. The sun was low in the sky and shined orange on the rolling water.

True to his agreement, the captain had them underway faster than Varro hoped for. He paid the agreed price in advance, and the rowers chatted excitedly about Paullus's bonus for ending their shore leave.

No one approached Varro while he stewed over the problem he had invited into his life. He should've taken his chances with Flaccus. He might have sued him into destitution, but he wouldn't have cared. Now, with Paullus under his command, he might be killed. Not because of any direct threat from Paullus, but for him acting alone and believing himself more skilled than his true abilities.

He rubbed his brow as the ship rocked over the waves and headed north toward Pisa and the siege that awaited them.

6

The ship dropped anchor off the coast still miles south of Pisa. They had sailed all night, using the wind and then rowing when necessary. The water had been calm and to Varro it was one of the more peaceful sea voyages he remembered. Now that the dawn had arrived, the captain shouted orders to prepare the ship's boat to ferry passengers.

The crew yawned and stretched, either those who had awakened after their sleeping shift or those in desperate need of one. Curio and Paullus stood in awkward silence under the mast, their packs shouldered. Falco leaned over the rails and searched the distant shore. It was full of dark trees, which provided excellent cover for them to slip into hiding before approaching the Ligurian siege camp.

Varro hefted his pack, body stiff from a poor night's rest on the rocking deck. He joined Paullus and Curio, who both seemed as bleary-eyed as he felt.

"Not much for sleeping accommodations," Paullus said. "At least it will make it easier to sleep on the ground again."

Curio grunted in agreement.

Stretching, Varro looked once more toward the trees. "I hate forests. It seems I'm doomed to spend at least half of my life living in one."

While the crew untied the bindings for the small boat, the wiry captain joined them. He smiled to reveal yellow teeth.

"This is as far as we dare go. I've not heard good things from the north. The Ligurians sacked Luna, as far as I know. They're prickly traders to begin with. I can't imagine what they're like now."

"If we have our way," Varro said. "Rome will silence them forever."

The captain barked a laugh, then extended his palm toward Paullus.

"We've done our best service for the Paullus family. Now, that bonus for my men?"

Paullus smiled easily. "Of course. Varro, sir, pay the captain, please."

The captain's hand and smile swiveled to Varro.

His own hands went cold. He did not bring enough coin to pay the entire crew of thirty men. Worse yet, they were hostages to the captain with no weapons but pugiones. These were still formidable blades, but the captain had requested all their real weaponry and shields be stowed for the brief trip. It was a reasonable safety precaution and Varro knew he could reclaim them if needed to face a threat to the ship.

The pale, creased palm callused from a lifetime of hard work hovered before him.

"You don't have the bonus?" He looked hopefully at Paullus, who seemed genuinely surprised.

"Why would I carry around my family fortune? Flamininus must have granted you funds for the mission. Pay out of that. My family will reimburse you later."

The captain's left eye twitched, but he remained rigid with his palm extended to Varro.

"Can you give me a moment? I need to speak with the others."

The captain's palm lowered, and his smile didn't fade. "Of course, sir. We'll hold the boat and your other belongings until you're ready."

The captain stepped back and circled his hand in the air in a gesture that made no sense to Varro. But the crew stopped their work and stared down as if expecting trouble.

He called Falco over and then drew them into a huddle. He leaned into their shadows and spoke in a low voice.

"I have about ten denarii with me. Curio, Falco, put in what you've got."

Groaning, Falco scratched his nose. "Remember the wine merchant we met just before leaving for the Scipio villa?"

"Shit," Varro hissed. "Give what you have left."

"Sorry, it was good wine."

Curio spoke up. "I've got twenty denarii. I'll put all of it in."

"You'll have to," Varro said. "That's a denarius per man. It will not knock them over, but should suffice. Paullus, what have you got?"

He pulled back and frowned. "Well, you just said a denarius per man is enough. You don't need my coin."

Falco hissed through his teeth. "We're all broke because of your fucking generosity. At least pay us back."

"You spent all your coin on wine," Paullus said, narrowing his eyes. "And who was going to pay for you when you needed it?"

"Forget it," Varro said. "We've got to collect our gear and get off the ship. If the captain isn't happy with the bonus, then we'll leave him Paullus as a hostage for what we owe."

"We owe him nothing," Paullus sneered. "We paid him his fee. If his flea-bitten crew demands more, then it's his trouble. We never stated a price. I'm not a fool, Varro. The captain is. Surprised he has made it this long as a trader."

In the end, they scraped their coins together and made it clear to the crew that each was due a denarius from their captain.

While expressions soured, no one seemed overtly hostile. They had expected more from a wealthy patrician passenger. But to Paullus's point, no hard deal had been struck. So the captain thanked them before a crewman rowed them and their gear to shore.

"A shame," Falco said. He and the others rocked inside the crowded boat. "I'd have been glad to hand Paullus over as a hostage."

Curio laughed, gazing out toward the pale dawn on the horizon. "Now we're united in poverty again. We've got fancy houses and servants back home. But out here, we couldn't buy a pot of spoiled pig slop."

"Friends," Paullus said airily. "We are on this adventure together. What's mine is yours. We'll not be eating slop."

Falco raised his heavy brows at Varro, then pointed at Paullus. "A moment ago, what was yours was only yours."

Paullus waved him off. "I wouldn't waste my money on a ship of dirty, ignorant sailors if it wasn't necessary. You covered their bonus. It was my fast thinking that got us this ship."

The crewman rowing the boat coughed. Varro winced and offered an apologetic smile. He shrugged and put his back into rowing across the final distance.

They rolled into the shallows on gently curling waves. The crewman put up his oars and announced they could disembark. Varro was the first over the side, splashing into the cool, foamy water that rushed around his calves. He reached in to retrieve his pack and shield. The others stood and the boat rocked from the sudden motion. Curio and Falco both leaped off the boat rather than fall. Paullus stumbled back into it, cursing.

The crewman handed Falco his pack and Curio had already begun wading for the beach. Paullus now recovered and made it over the side into the flowing surf. He then turned to reach for his pack. Varro watched as the crewman helped retrieve it for him.

With a fake smile, he tossed it wide to Paullus so that he either had to dive to catch it or let it fall into the rolling waves.

The dive and catch failed, splashing Paullus into the water along with his pack. A wave immediately pushed him down, as if the sea had slapped him in the face. Varro put a hand over his mouth and turned aside. Or else he risked bursting out in laughter.

Falco had far less circumspection. He guffawed as Paullus blustered and cursed while fumbling in his chain shirt to escape the small waves. As he got to his knees, a wave shoved him over again.

"Sorry about that, sir! How ignorant of me." The crewman spoke in a tone that showed he was anything but sorry. In the distance, those aboard the trading ship cheered. Wisely, the offending sailor shoved off back into the waves as Paullus continued flopping around in the water.

"I'll have your head!" he shouted between mouthfuls of seawater rolling over him. "Fuck! I'm in armor. Help!"

Both Varro and Falco sloshed through the waves and then dragged him upright. Curio plodded back to fetch the pack that had sunk instantly below the waves.

Sodden and blowing water from his nose, Paullus shoved free of them and then staggered over to tear his pack from Curio. He snatched it aside with such force that items spilled into the water. Curio retrieved what he could, but shied back from the raging Paullus.

"It's all ruined." He held up the pack, water rushing out from the bottom. He turned back to the ship and pointed. "I'll have all of your heads for this! Laugh now. You'll not be laughing after I catch up with you!"

The crew waved back as if saying farewell to an old friend.

Varro steadied himself against the rolling waves and stifled his laugh. Falco didn't even try but shook his head.

"Don't forget the little man's revenge. They can be as evil as your senator friends. And there's more of them than you."

"Don't lecture me, you oaf!" Though Paullus was enraged, his soggy condition robbed him of any threat. "You think this is funny? My rations and supplies are all doused in seawater. Fuck! My armor will rust from all this."

"It was just a dunk," Falco said, turning to wade toward the shore. "If you've kept it oiled, it should be fine with some care."

Paullus gripped his pack to him like a child that had nearly drowned. His shield slipped down his shoulder. He seemed to tremble, his eyes boring into Falco's head.

"All right," Varro said, turning toward Falco. "Enough playing in the sea. We've got our mission ahead of us."

"What was his name?"

Varro paused and tilted his head as if he hadn't understood. He knew the captain's name was Herius. They had chatted after setting sail and before Varro found a spot to sleep on deck. He had a son close to Varro's age whose wife was expecting her first child soon. He was excited about becoming a grandfather.

"He said his name was Damianos. A Greek from the Achaean League. I believe he is headed there now."

Paullus nodded and sniffed. With all the wetness in his nose from the seawater, it sounded like sniveling. "I'll find him and his crew then drown each of them myself."

Varro considered a talk about how treating all people with decency would make for a more peaceful life. He knew such advice would be wasted on Paullus. Yet, if his rations were indeed ruined, then his actions had led to yet another setback. They would have to share with him, reducing the time they could devote to their actual mission.

So they at last all gathered up the slope of the beach and on the grass. A dark forest of mixed trees rose before them like a great green wall. Varro extracted from his pack a map of the general area. Scouts had carefully created it in ink on goat-skin vellum. Flamininus had handed it to him with a sly smile. "Flesh out the details for Tribune Minucius, would you? Maybe your map will again become a key piece of the battle plan."

They all leaned in to see the details stretched out between Varro's hands. He was careful to keep any water from staining the ink. Fortunately, Paullus's interest rebounded off the map the moment he realized what it was. Instead, he went toward the trees and then sorted out his wet gear.

"This is already well drawn," Varro said. He ran his finger along marked paths, streams, and potential forage locations. "Scouts have already done their work. We'll need to get details around Pisa."

"How far are we yet?" Falco asked. Varro ran his finger along a stretch of forest and hills stated in spidery ink lines.

"About a day out, I would estimate. We'll need to assess their camp and find a base of operations. Our first mission is to get the senator's message into Pisa. After that, let's see what mischief we can make for our uninvited Ligurian friends."

"He's talking to himself," Curio said.

At first, Varro didn't understand but then followed Curio's gaze around to see Paullus setting out all his gear in order as if taking an inventory. He could hear him muttering as he squatted over his pack.

Falco groaned. "We're really stuck with him? Who is the Flaccus character, anyway? Maybe it's better to risk him than to let Paullus get us killed."

"I really thought he'd be better than this," Varro said. "He was cavalry and served admirably. I can't figure out why he's acting like this."

"I know why," Curio said, raising his chin to look down his nose. "He was always treated better than the others, even as a recruit. I might've been a velite then, but I got around. I heard the gossip that a relative of Scipio Africanus was in the cavalry. There's no way they treated him like any other recruit."

"I bet his tribune rubbed his feet," Falco said.

"There's nothing we can do." Varro looked toward the horizon to see the trading ship turned south again. "He's with us until the end now. Let's form up and head out. A forty-thousand-man army has the reach to scout as far as we are. We can't linger on an open beach for long."

Varro had to cajole Paullus into a column with the others. His rations were mostly ruined. Falco offered unhelpful comments about just having added a bit more salt for taste. In the end, though, Paullus repacked his gear and marched out in sullen silence.

The forest was thick and cool. Varro hated forests, believing them to become mazes for the spirits of those who had died within their confusing and gloomy confines. He had never directly seen a forest spirit, but he knew their presence from all the misfortunes he suffered when under the trees. As they picked their way toward the paths indicated on Varro's map, he prayed to Fortuna to keep him safe.

By the afternoon, they had gone deeper and climbed higher into low hills that created a ridge for them to follow. Curio took point, as was his usual role when on such marches. Varro kept checking on Paullus, but he had remained in line and at the rear. His unusual silence worried Varro, but perhaps he was at last convinced to follow the lead. The mission was now underway, and what he called a grand adventure might now feel more like a potentially deadly trek through enemy territory.

Varro expected to reach the Pisa area by nightfall. They would rest a short while, then scout the encirclement for a way through to the city walls. From there, they would have to gain the attention of a wall guard without first becoming casualties.

With Curio in the lead, Varro followed the ridge, looping through trees and bushes and struggling for balance across exposed rock. Branches grabbed at his brown tunic, which he had reserved for stealthy missions like this. Falco and even Paullus had changed into the same. He had been shocked Paullus had the foresight to dress practically. Maybe he didn't need to be so worried about him.

Their short chain shirts were dull metal over their tunics, and being padded made no noise. It was only when their hobnails struck exposed stone did they offer nearby enemies a chance to hear them. The hobnails inevitably slipped on stone surfaces, which is why Varro hated wearing them into cities or other paved areas.

The march was tedious, but Varro did not pause for a rest, consulting the map as he went. He couldn't use it for a precise location, but he knew approximately where they were. The late day sun dappled the vellum page as if highlighting sections for his review. He rolled it up and tucked it into his pack.

Curio now led them across a prominent ridge where trees were sparse, but large stones assembled in lichen-covered groups. Patches of sunlight glided across his shoulders and bounced golden flashes off his helmet. It reminded Varro they needed to dull their metal before reaching Pisa.

Two shapes flickered up the slope at Curio's rear. They were gray and black smudges, but circular shields and swords were clear enough.

"Ambush!" Varro roared. "Scatter!"

He wheeled left as he raised his round cavalry shield. It

obscured the ambusher springing for him, but Varro heard his feet scratch across the rock.

The attacker rammed into the shield. Where a scutum would've deflected the attacker as if he had run into a wall, this shield shuddered and bent Varro's arm.

"Too many!" Falco shouted.

Varro shoved down at the enemy behind his shield. They had set a worthy ambush, but on the wrong ground. Varro used his height advantage to push the enemy back while he drew his gladius. The man tumbled onto his back with a curse and skidded down the way he had come.

Varro whirled to the sound of feet behind him, striking out with the shield. It was still a firm, round, wooden shield with bronze rims. The rim connected with the skull of the rearward attacker, and he flipped away and dropped his sword.

Another came right behind him. He was a tall man with thick black hair drawn together at the back of his neck. His face was red as he roared a war cry.

The sword slashed in and Varro skipped aside to feel its edge glide harmlessly across his mail shirt. He had this single instant to assess the field. Curio and whoever attacked him had all vanished. Falco struggled with two men, and being at the rear, Paullus was too far to see. Varro had three men on him. They had likely assessed him as the leader.

The original attacker who had stumbled down the slope now staggered back up. The enemy on the ground held his head where Varro had cracked him with his shield edge.

That glance cost him initiative, as the thick-haired attacker slashed at him again, shouting, "Roman!"

This time the blade connected with Varro's helmet, knocking it sideways so the chin strap bit into his throat. It seemed he was finished.

But he had a plan. He feigned a worse blow than he received, staggering back behind his shield, yet guiding his attacker toward the stunned man on the ground.

The enemy followed on, hoping to deliver a telling blow. But Varro slipped behind the fallen man just as his attacker drove for him.

The black-haired enemy's foot caught against his companion struggling to stand up. Both now collapsed in front of Varro.

With his own shout of triumph, Varro slammed his shield rim into the back of the attacker's head. He flattened out atop his companion. Both would've died at Varro's hands, but the original attacker had now regained the ridge.

He wore long, brown hair in a braid, and his teeth appeared sharpened into fangs. It was a ghoulish smile that made Varro's skin crawl.

"Look like a dog," Varro shouted, rushing forward with shield up to engage the enemy. "Die like a dog!"

He dropped to his knees and held his shield overhead as he reached the enemy. Now under the shield, the enemy's belly was exposed as he crashed into Varro. His knee came up, clipping Varro under the chin and driving his teeth into his tongue. But it did not prevent him from ramming his gladius into his foe's gut.

As the enemy flipped over, he wrenched free of Varro's sword, tearing out his own guts in the process.

Varro twisted aside, his mouth now flooding with salty, metallic blood from biting his tongue. The enemy crashed on his head as pale violet guts unspooled from the opening carved into his abdomen. He was dead before he landed.

The air filled with the reek of the disembowelment. Varro staggered up. His two enemies were still piled on the ground, the one on the bottom trying to shove out from the semiconscious man atop him. But down the opposite slope, Varro saw more men coming. Two specifically, and one whose enormous size and muscularity were obvious even at a glimpse. He carried a sword in one hand and a chain manacle in the other.

The others had scattered. Shouting came from all around. He was confident he heard Falco's voice among them.

So he bolted down the slope, away from the oncoming enemy, and sought the concealing confusion of the trees and boulders below.

7

Rushing down the slope, hurdling rocks and woodland debris, Varro fled the ambush. The number of Ligurian scouts—they had to be Ligurians this close to Pisa—remained unclear. He had counted at least nine, and a patrol might have even more if they were expecting conflict. Yet his headlong rush had drawn no pursuit, and as his feet slapped against the hard earth, he realized he could halt.

For a moment, he allowed himself to lean against a tree and catch his breath. Sweat ran from his brow and his saliva was thick with salty blood. His tongue throbbed where he had bitten it, but it was the least of his concerns. As he hung against the rough bark, he realized blood mixed with his sweat running down his forearm. For an instant his stomach tightened, then he realized it was enemy blood and not his own.

When his panting slowed, he turned back toward the slope. He heard thin shouting and curses through the trees. But no sounds of combat. The fight was over, but someone still resisted.

"A captive," he muttered and started jogging toward the commotion.

As he remounted the slope, he now crouched down and removed his helmet to let it hang from its strap. He remembered the flash from Curio's helmet just before the ambush. Now he moved from bush to tree as he neared the top. He spotted Falco crouched behind a rock. Fresh blood ran down the shield he set beside himself.

Varro gave a soft whistle, and Falco turned. In three bounds, Varro reached him and looked from behind the rock alongside Falco.

Curio wrestled between seven men. Of these, one was the huge brute Varro had noted, only now he was attempting to place the manacles on Curio. Two held him by each arm, yet he kicked and struggled against them still.

"Do we rush them?" Falco asked.

"Not only are the odds bad, but they'd probably kill Curio or hold him against us."

"Fuck. Where's Paullus?"

Varro shook his head, then reached for the map in his pack.

"That slippery bastard," Falco said. "He's probably hiding in a ditch and crying for his mother."

"He has a lot of terrible qualities," Varro said, unrolling the map. "But cowardice isn't one. This commotion should draw his attention, just as it did ours. I'm sure Curio is making this fuss to lead us here."

"Where did these scum come from? Brigands?"

"Ligurians," Varro answered. But he wasn't listening too closely. Instead, he pinpointed where he believed they were on his map.

"What are you doing?" Falco now pulled back and hooked his finger over the vellum. "What's this got to do with saving Curio?"

"Everything," Varro said. He angled the map to let Falco see it. "They're going to take Curio prisoner. They will want to take him back to camp for interrogation. It's getting dark. So the instant they subdue him, they'll head out. We now have the advantage."

"My balls have just crawled into my stomach, Varro. That doesn't feel like an advantage to me."

"The Ligurians now have something to lose, whereas before they did not. Curio represents intelligence. These barbarians might not know how to bring down city walls, but they're at least smart enough to know Rome is coming. They don't know more than that, but Curio could enlighten them."

"I get it," Falco said. "So they will do anything to make sure he reaches their leaders."

"Right," Varro said. "And they won't accept any delays. What if we're just ahead of a major force? They don't know we aren't. They've no time to waste. So, we must get ahead of them."

Falco leaned into the map and pointed at the range of hills inked on the page. "Is this where we are?"

Varro shifted the map under Falco's finger.

"About here, actually. They will head along this ridge before dipping down to this path here. But you'll also see that our scouts have marked something near here, too."

Again, he shifted the map so that Falco's finger now pointed to a mark on the map and a note aside it. "Danger. Potential ambush site."

Falco took back his finger and looked around the rock again.

"You lead them there, and I'll see what sort of trap I can arrange."

"Exactly," Varro said. "And because they have Curio, they will split their force to pursue me. Two captives are better than one, and unless these barbarians have more sense than I give them credit for, they'll chase. Your ambush will take care of the majority and I'll try to stop the two escorting Curio back."

"Looks like they've subdued him," Falco said, his face hugging the rock. He pulled back. "You better hope they're as dumb as you believe."

"Just do your part," Varro said. "And I'll work with whatever comes of it. Curio will aid his own escape. Don't forget it."

"What about Paullus? He'll become lost without us."

"He's got enough sense to stay put if he's lost. We'll come back for him. Curio is in immediate danger."

Without further discussion, they shadowed the Ligurians escorting Curio back. Two held Curio between them. Three casualties, two seriously wounded and one dead, burdened three others. The giant warrior held the dead man over his shoulder. That left only two free, and those would likely chase after Falco.

As expected, the Ligurians followed the trails Varro identified on the map. He was glad for his knowledge of the terrain. Too often, he had been confounded by natives who knew every root and rut in their territory. Whether he could parlay this into victory was another matter.

He and Falco paused nearby the way toward a potential ambush. Falco took the vellum and oriented himself. "Right, I'll hold on to this. You won't have time to read a map, anyway."

So they parted, Falco running deeper into the trees and Varro racing to keep pace with the Ligurians. Curio aided them by dragging his feet, wrestling against his captors, and screaming for help. Eventually, the Ligurians gagged him and this delay allowed Varro to race ahead.

The path wended through trees, being little more than a game trail that had evolved into something wider from frequent use. The Ligurians sought the fastest route through the trees, making their movement predictable.

Every waving branch or bush Varro left in his wake made him fear discovery. But Curio was doing his best to burden his captors. They had not been prepared to take a prisoner, even though they carried manacles. Otherwise, Curio wouldn't have been able to cause so much delay.

Seizing on their delay, Varro raced ahead of them to find a blind spot along the path where he could spring his trap. He barely had time to slow his breathing before their shapes flickered through the dappled orange light of late day. Their shadowed faces were grim and focused as they struggled to increase their pace under all their burdens.

Varro hefted a palm-sized rock, aiming for the brute. His long hair was greasy and flat to his wide head. Fortunately, he shouldered his fallen companion on the opposite side. As the Ligurian's neared, Varro weighed the right moment to strike. Wearing a chain shirt and carrying a shield, he was not as nimble as he would have liked. So he had to ensure a lead on the lighter armored enemies.

The stone hurled out of the trees and bashed the brute on his head. The distance had robbed the cast of its force, but it still thudded on flesh and the Ligurian staggered to the side, the corpse on his shoulder causing him to lose balance.

"Curio!" Varro shouted. "We are near!"

He then bolted into the trees, deliberately taking no care to hide his flight.

Just as a hound cannot resist chasing a fleeing rabbit, the Ligurians leaped to follow. Their shouted curses rang out through the trees.

Varro held forward his shield to slam a reckless path toward the ambush point Falco set. He couldn't pause to see who had taken up the chase. It would not be all, but enough that the Ligurians were divided. Their cries sounded arrogant to Varro, as if he could not escape them.

But he had fled through harder terrain than this sparse woodlands, and was confident of success. He lumbered up a slope, then turned to see three followed. They were just gray snatches of men in tunics with swords raised. He could see no more, turning again and scrabbling up the slope.

The thicker woods of the ambush site lay down a sharp, rocky slope. Now he could see why it had been marked as dangerous. Another game trail vanished into the trees, but behind these a steep hill rose into view. It would be a prime spot for slingers or other ranged attackers to lie in wait for those passing below. Falco could easily hurl stones on anyone closing on his position.

Varro's arms wheeled as he struggled to balance with a shield on his back and running downhill. His stride became like that of a titan, every bound gaining him incredible ground. But with each stride risked a catastrophic fall.

The Ligurians came whooping over the ridge. Varro paused at the game trail to glimpse them a last time. They slowed, leaning back and not risking the flight down the slope Varro had taken.

He smiled, then bellowed Falco's name to alert him.

Now he vanished into the forest.

From here, he applied all he had learned of misdirection and stealth. He flattened to the cold ground and prepared to hide beneath a fallen log. When the Ligurians entered the trail, he tossed a heavy rock away from himself so that the bush shook as if he had passed that way.

To his relief, Falco shouted in the distance.

Varro removed his shield and forced it under the log. Then, sucking in his gut, he slipped under the log as well.

The Ligurians shouted and cursed, having lost him. But Falco's indistinct shouting drew them away. Varro waited only long enough to be certain they had left him behind.

Once more, he was dashing back the way he had come. When he remounted the ridge, he knew to follow it this time. The other Ligurians would've continued on toward their camp, eager to deliver Curio to their leaders. Varro knew the ridge had a few trees and circled around to intersect the path. If he was swift, he could cut them off. Now that Curio was alerted, he would struggle, forcing them to subdue him and causing more delays.

He followed the ridge, racing to the limits of his strength. The curve soon appeared, and Varro experienced a surge knowing he was in the final stretch. The weight of his chain shirt pressed on his shoulders. As the ridge swept down into the trees, Varro spotted a shape flickering through them.

His gladius sprang to hand and his shield came up to defend himself as he charged down toward a figure that raced toward him.

"Wait!"

Curio's voice came directly ahead. But Varro was already crashing down with the momentum created from the slope. He drove his heels into the ground to slow down, but it only caused him to trip and crash atop his shield.

His vision spun in a circle as he rode the shield like a sled down the slope. Then he struck something that upended the shield and sent him sprawling into a trunk. His back struck square between his shoulders and drove the air out of his lungs, turning his vision white.

When the fog cleared, Curio kneeled before him. His face was cut and bruised, slick with sweat, but also creased with concern.

"Are you all right? Sorry to throw you off, but you'd have gutted me."

Varro shook his head, then stared hard at Curio. He seemed unhurried and calm.

"Just out for a stroll in the woods? No one chasing you?"

Curio looked back. "No one was a moment ago. Still looks clear now."

Varro licked his lips. He pressed into the tree so that it forced his helmet over his eyes and yanked the chinstrap into his throat.

"And no manacles, I see."

Standing up, Curio raised one leg to display a reddened and scraped ankle.

"They must have made the manacles for elephants. I couldn't believe it when they thought me captured. I slipped the manacles easily enough."

"Good work." Varro remained breathless and resting in Curio's shadow.

"Thank you!"

"Curio, is there an explanation you'd like to share? You were in a bit of trouble last I saw you."

"Those bastards caught me off guard back there. They were hiding along the ridge we followed."

"Yes, so I guessed." Varro groaned and then extended his hand. "Help me up before the blood flow to my head is cut off."

Groaning as he pulled Varro upright, Curio continued.

"If I'd have seen them, no way they could've caught me. They were too big for their own good. But they caught me and you all ran."

"Sorry about that," Varro said. He dusted himself off, then retrieved his shield that had shot into a tangle of dead bushes.

"I figured you'd come back. So I just gave them all sorts of trouble until they gagged me. The big one had the manacles you saw. When they pinned it on me, I knew I could work out of them. They were barely tight enough to stay on my feet."

"Sorry for interrupting," Varro said. "But I need to know if the Ligurians are nearby. You didn't kill all four of them alone?"

"Oh no," Curio said, looking back toward the trail hidden behind gray tree trunks. "Paullus helped. As soon as you drew off the others, he came running out of hiding. I only had one man guarding me then, and the others were all carrying their dead and wounded. After I got the better of the Ligurian on me, I found Paullus had taken out the other three. They were all fumbled up with their burdens and easy targets."

Curio mimicked falling about with a heavy weight on his shoulder.

"Including the big one?" Varro shook his head, thinking how he might've coordinated a better plan if Paullus had acted with them.

"Of course, or I wouldn't be out here looking for you."

Varro sighed. "We better hope Falco prevailed against the three I sent his way. Where is Paullus, then?"

"He's searching their bodies for intelligence."

Varro rolled his eyes. "What does he imagine he'll find on regular soldiers? I doubt they're carrying strength reports and battle plans. I doubt the Ligurians even have a plan."

Curio shrugged and rubbed his cheek.

"I did take a few good hits to the face."

"The swelling is an improvement." Craning his neck and enjoying a satisfying pop, Varro then removed his helmet again. "Take me back. We'll fetch Paullus and follow this ridge to link up with Falco again. I'm sure he got the better of them, but we shouldn't delay."

Curio ran to alert Paullus while Varro dusted off. He looked back across the ridge as if he could see Falco through it. While he held the advantage of surprise and a superior position, Falco was still in danger. Three to one were not good odds no matter how often he had been victorious in worse situations.

He heard Curio shouting for him, and it wasn't the calm of before.

Springing through the trees, Varro reached the path to where Curio stood in the middle. His gladius was in hand now. Around him were four Ligurian corpses. They spread out on the trail. The muscular one stared up into the light, a black and wet stain spreading across his abdomen through his brown tunic. Others lay on their faces or sides, congealing blood beneath them drawing flies and insects out of the woods.

"He's not here."

Varro blinked, then looked around. "He's not off taking a piss behind a tree?"

"He's not here," Curio repeated, scratching his head.

Joining him amid the carnage, Varro looked over the bodies sprawled out on the obscure path. Black flies danced on their ashen faces. From the branches above, a crow called out as if warning Varro to not interfere with its planned meal.

"He's not here," he said in a hushed voice.

Curio pointed to the ground with his gladius. "He helped me get out of the other manacle."

Both looked down at the large manacles, one pinned closed and the other opened. The long chain lay discarded under bushes.

"All right, explain exactly what happened." Varro retrieved the manacles, running his thumb along the wide edges. There was a story to them he would never learn.

"After the fight, Paullus caught his breath." Curio leaned on his knees as if he were also catching his breath. Then he straightened and turned aside as if facing a memory of himself. "Then he asked if I was all right. I told him it was a good plan you had to divide the enemy. He laughed and said something under his breath."

As Curio described the scene, Varro walked among the dead.

"I told him we had to find you, and he said you and Falco had a plan and would be fine. That's when he helped me out of the manacles. We both rested over there." Curio pointed to a rock large and flat enough for two men. "Then I said you'd probably follow that ridge you showed us on the map because it was mostly clear ground. Paullus said I should go check the area to find your trail and that he wanted to search the bodies for intelligence. That's it."

At the end of the path, Varro pressed his hands to his temples. "By the gods, Paullus. You're supposed to be helping us."

"He saved me," Curio said. "But his reaction was strange, like he didn't know why he did it or even if he was glad he did it. I'd say he seemed confused."

"I'm sure selflessness must be a confusing feeling for him," Varro said, kicking at a loose stone. "But there is something wrong here. There is no sign of a fight where Paullus might've been captured. We'd have heard it in any case."

"Unless they stabbed him in the back," Curio said, imitating a dagger thrust with one hand and clamping a hand over his imaginary victim's mouth.

"Maybe not killed," Varro said. "Otherwise, his body would've been here. Maybe knocked out in a single blow and carried off."

Curio toed the manacles now dropped into the track. "So another Ligurian patrol got to him? Why didn't they collect their dead and not even try to capture me?"

Varro shrugged. "I don't know what happened. Something still bothers me. Right now, we're divided in enemy territory, which is not good. We at least know Falco's general location. Let's find him and then figure out what happened to Paullus."

They left the slaughter behind and took the ridge path to where Varro hoped he'd find Falco waiting with three dead Ligurians.

But he knew when a plan was slipping out of his control.

8

The dead Ligurians were obvious. Varro and Curio came upon their crushed bodies at the base of the steep hill where Falco had set his trap. A stone as large as a man had rolled down on them and had crushed one of them. The enormous stone pinned his shattered body and the surrounding ground was sticky with blood. Farther up, two more lay dead amid the sparse vegetation at the foot of the steep incline. One stared up with blood dribbling from his mouth and his head shaded blue. His neck was also bent to show it had clearly snapped. The other lay a short distance from this one, and he had two broken legs and a stab wound on his neck.

"Here's the other stone," Curio said, indicating a round, knee-high stone that had smashed into a tree and gashed out a hunk of wood. "Looks like it clipped his legs, then Falco finished him."

Varro nodded in agreement, looking up to the perch where Falco must have looked down on his prey. "So where is he?"

"Vanished like Paullus?" Curio examined the Ligurian with the broken neck. He found a heavy stone nearby with blood on it and held it up for Varro.

"He should've stayed put," Varro said, nodding at the evidence of Falco's successful ambush. "Why is it so hard for anyone to remain in place?"

"Maybe he had to move," Curio said, then pitched the stone into the shadow of the trees behind them. "We should search for other tracks. Maybe more patrols?"

"That's the only thing that makes sense. But how did Falco and Paullus see enemy patrols that neither of us did?"

Curio shrugged. "Should we collect some of the Ligurian gear? We might need it for disguises."

"Good thought. Their tunics are of no use and our mail might give us away. But the shields are a peculiar design. Let's trade ours for theirs, at least."

The Ligurian shields had scattered near their bearers. One was crushed beyond use, but the other two were sturdy wood, shaped in an oblong with flat tops. Both were faded red, almost brown. Varro hefted one and found it more like the scutum than the cavalry shield he carried.

"This one was wearing some sort of over shirt." Curio crouched beside the man under the rock and yanked out a striped cloth. "Maybe he was a leader?"

They did not linger, but climbed to find where Falco had been. They found fresh earth where the stone he used had been, along with sturdy branches for levers used to dislodge them. His caligae had left some tracks, but none that showed where he might have gone. The ground was too rocky and hard.

They backtracked to where he and Falco had first parted ways, and then even farther back to where they had been ambushed. But they found no sign of either Falco or Paullus.

Varro put his hands on his hips and peered up at the darkening sky. "Now, if only the Ligurians would all disappear like this. Think of how peaceful our world would be."

After debating different plans, they both decided to camp here for the night and resume searching in the morning. Varro cursed himself for his hasty plan. He had not discussed a rally point with Falco and instead had become caught up in his own cleverness.

Their camp was little more than a lean-to against a large rock, camouflaged with dead branches and debris. Varro was more afraid of wolves or bears sniffing out their location than of any enemy. But with the Ligurian patrol's elimination, the enemy might dispatch another patrol to seek their missing companions. So he and Curio decided to each take a watch.

He had an uneasy rest for the first half, and then Curio awakened him for his shift. The forest was pitch black, cold, and filled with strange noises. Branches cracked, owls hooted, and breezes rustled through the forest. To Varro, it seemed night would last forever as he pressed into the rock behind him. But even in his alert state, he found his head drooping. He would rock back every time he did, and was satisfied he had fought off his weariness.

Then it was dawn and he realized he had slept through the last part of his watch.

Falco sat on a small log he had dragged close to the tent. He was sharpening his pugio when he realized Varro had awakened.

"Too bad I didn't bring a scourge," he said with a smile. "I'd love to flog you for sleeping on duty."

Varro yawned and stretched. "I'd deserve it. Then I'd borrow it to flog you for leaving your post. Where did you go?"

Falco stuffed the whetstone back into the pack he set between his legs then sheathed his pugio.

"I figured I was to follow the ridge to you. The Ligurians you sent me were easy to put down. They came running and yelling, blind to everything around them. There were plenty of big rocks that have been loosened up from all these earthquakes. So I set these up to crush them. But the first stone rolled too slow and only caught the bastard at the rear. I'm sure you saw what happened to him. I nailed another with a rock I threw and by that time the last one advanced to where I had another huge stone ready. Rolled it right over him. It only broke his legs and so I had to go down to finish him. Shit, Varro, I was good. Too bad no one was there to see it."

"Too bad you didn't remain there to show it to me." Varro slapped Curio's hip, and he awakened with a start. It took a moment for him to realize Falco had rejoined them.

"Where did you go?" He sat up, bumping the flimsy lean-to he slept beneath.

"I went to where Varro said he was going." Falco gave a sheepish smile. "But then I realized I wasn't following the right ridge. You know, there's more than one. Anyway, I found my way back to the ambush site, and then I followed the path back here. It was scary business traveling at night, even following a path."

Varro shuddered and now stood to stretch. Falco stood with him.

"But it wasn't all a waste of time," he said. "I found another camp."

"More Ligurians?" Varro paused in the middle of his stretch. "What are they doing this far from the siege?"

"Watching for Romans," Curio said. "What else?"

Falco agreed. "At least thirty men there. They've got a perimeter atop a short hill and what seemed like excellent paths leading out in a few directions. They could patrol from that camp and spot any force coming this way. A fast runner could warn the main Ligurian army of approaching danger."

"Consul Minucius will come from that direction," Varro said. "Crossing overland from Arretium. We'll have to mark that camp on the map for the consul. Good work, Falco."

"It was my plan all along."

They then caught up Falco on all that had happened. He snorted at Paullus's disappearance. "It's Macedonia all over again.

He probably fell in love with a Ligurian camp follower and is now joining her tribe."

They all chuckled, but Varro shook his head.

"He rescued Curio and helped him escape the last of his bonds. He was searching for intelligence. Maybe his search took him farther away than he realized and he became lost."

It was Curio's turn to shake his head. "Then he'd be the stupidest man I've ever met. He couldn't have wandered far before we returned to him. He'd have heard us, or vice versa."

Deciding they couldn't guess why Paullus had vanished, they broke camp and then marched up the trail the Ligurians had taken. Their corpses lay where they had fallen, but now had their eyes and most of their faces eaten away by scavengers during the night. It was ghoulish to behold, but Varro had long ago inured himself to such gory scenes. He stood amid the dead, hands on his hips.

"Take a Ligurian shield," he said to Falco. "It might help us pass unchallenged if we're spotted at a distance. And you'll probably like the size of it better."

They poked around the scene, all of them putting a finger under their noses against the odor of death. Falco had gathered a shield, gingerly plucking it from the dead as if he feared the corpse might fight him for it. But in the end, none of them turned up anything to show what had happened to Paullus.

"Spirits took him," Falco said. "Simple as that. They knew him for the bastard he is. Serves him right."

"Don't say that." Curio looked around him. "Maybe the spirits like Ligurians better."

Falco and Curio argued over what merits forest spirits would find in Romans or Ligurians. But Varro stared hard at the seven bodies sprawled out. They had moved little, other than from animals pulling at their flesh. At last, he realized what bothered him.

"Curio, you said he wanted to search the bodies for intelligence?"

"That's what he said."

"He never did it," Varro said. "Look at their packs. None have been opened. Also, none of the bodies have been moved. He didn't turn over anyone who fell atop their packs or move anyone to see if they carried anything of use. From what I see, no one has touched these corpses since their killing blows. At least not touched by a man."

Falco and Curio stepped back as if the dead might rise against them. Falco prodded one body with his drawn gladius. "You think he was taken before he could search the bodies?"

"Not taken," Varro said. "I think he left by his own will."

Falco's mouth froze with a half-formed word on his lips. Curio, however, snapped his fingers.

"He sent me away and then fled. That snake!"

"We're searching the wrong ground," Varro said. "We need to cast a wider net and we'll find signs of his flight."

"Why?" Falco finally got the words out. His heavy brows drew together. "That's desertion."

"It wouldn't be his first desertion," Varro said, frowning. "I don't know why he struck out on his own, but I'm sure he believes it's to his advantage. He wanted to order us like we were his soldiers. Instead, he had to obey me. I think that bothered him more than we know."

"Then let him go," Falco said. "I never wanted him in the first place."

"We should at least search for more signs." Varro stepped into the bushes, trying to think about what Paullus was after. "Just to be sure he's not lying injured somewhere."

Falco groaned, but Curio chimed in.

"He came to my rescue. So he's not all that bad. Let's at least be sure he's not like Varro said."

They searched the area around the ambush site, finding some signs of passage, but nothing that identified Paullus. After widening their search and spending an hour combing through brush and branch, they declared Paullus officially lost.

"He ran off," Falco proclaimed. "And so we can brand him a deserter and kill him on the spot when we find him."

"That's a bit bloodthirsty," Varro said. "I think we can use his actions to get Senator Flamininus to eject him from Servus Capax, at least. Then if that means death, so be it."

"No," Falco said. "Got to kill him before he can do anything else. Otherwise, he's going to carp on about this Flaccus character and threaten you with all sorts of violence if you don't keep his secret."

Varro waved off the concern. Paullus might still be in danger, and if so, he would do his best to save him. In fact, Paullus had showed trust by going out on a mission. Since once they were away from Rome, any or all of them could have wrapped Paullus in chains and threw him into the sea. Indeed, it might have been the prudent thing to do. But such a vile thought never passed Varro's thoughts until this moment. He understood it made him naïve. But better to be that than a ruthless murderer.

"We've wasted enough time," he said after his moment of reflection. "Pisa suffers and we are walking in circles here. Time to refocus on the mission. The senator's letter must reach the commander of the city, Marcus Cincius. Paullus will either show up or else be counted among the missing. Every battle yields scores of those names from every class."

Falco gave a firm nod. "True, and I bet Paullus's family won't be sad if his did. They might even reward us for getting rid of him."

He spoke in jest, and both he and Curio chuckled at it. But Varro's hackles rose at the thought. Something had seemed wrong in the way Flamininus so readily accepted Paullus and that he made no special precautions for such an illustrious person to go on a dangerous mission. It made Varro stop in his tracks. Falco, who joked with Curio, ran into him.

"Whoa, stopping for a rest already?"

"Could that be why he vanished?" He looked between his friends, who both tilted their heads. So he explained his thoughts to them. "Do you think he realized it and fled?"

"Who the fuck knows what that arrogant prick thinks?" Falco spit into a bush. "No one said to kill him."

"And no one said to keep him safe or else the Paullus and Scipio families will have our skins." Varro rubbed his jaw. "But would he really believe we'd put a dagger in his back? Why even join us if he suspected we might kill him?"

"If he did, then he wouldn't have saved me," Curio said. "He'd have killed me instead and blamed the Ligurians."

"Of course you're right," Varro said. "I'm overthinking things again. Bad habit. Let's just put this from our minds. Like I said, refocus!"

They resumed a faster march through the rough trees, now eschewing known paths for fear of running into another patrol. Paullus continued to nag at Varro's thoughts, but soon faded when they came to the camp Falco had discovered.

They spread out and watched the Ligurian camp. It was atop a hill and not well hidden. A half-dozen tents scattered around the top, mixed between trees and stones too large to move. After long moments of careful study, Varro saw lookouts stir. They wore gray and brown tunics they pulled overhead, helping them to blend in with the surroundings. Once satisfied, Varro drew the other two together in hiding behind a cluster of stones. They had to sit to remain hidden from view.

"About thirty men," Varro said. "Good job estimating that in the dark, Falco."

"I've had enough practice. There's six tents big enough for five men. Easy to figure."

"They're not concealed, but they've taken care not to set fires and to camouflage themselves. Definitely a watch post. We'll detail the map and give it to the consul. He'll send a force to cut them off from the main Ligurian camp. But I suspect the patrol we destroyed came from here. They'll send word back that Rome is getting nearer."

Falco shrugged. "It's an easy guess. I say we can bypass this place and let the consul deal with it."

They allowed Varro time to use his stylus and ink to rough in the basic surroundings and notes about the camp and approaches. He worked on a flat rock, and Curio held the bronze ink pot rather than risk spilling it. If they had more time, he could capture more details about the enemy themselves. But this was an aside to their primary mission to warn Pisa and then sabotage the Ligurian siege lines.

Just as he sat back and wiped the ink from his stylus, a sharp shout came from the top of the distant hill. Falco, who kept watch, now ducked back.

"They're fighting with someone up there."

Varro stuffed his map and supplies into his pack, then scrabbled to Falco's side. He looked up into the morning light, where three Ligurians struggled with a man in a brown tunic and sack over his head. He wrestled against their grip, blindly seeking a way free. But he was outmatched and shortly pulled back so that the scuffle was no longer in their sight.

"Paullus," Varro said, his voice flat. "He either stumbled on the Ligurians or they caught him."

"Fuck." Falco put his head to the rock. "You're going to rescue him."

But Varro did not answer immediately. Instead, he looked across to where he knew Pisa hid behind the hills and trees.

Curio remained staring ahead. "They put a sack over his head and stripped him to his tunic. That means they're going to take him back to their camp."

"Of course," Falco said. "Even for Ligurians, they're not stupid enough to kill a valuable source of intelligence. They bagged his head to keep him disoriented."

"Well, that's the answer," Varro said. "Just like Curio before. They'll want to waste no time to get him back for questioning. We will intercept them, just as we did the others. I expect they won't send more than a few men to escort Paullus back. They should be easier to handle this time."

Curio slipped back behind the rock, his face bright with a smile. "Mine was like a practice drill for this one."

With a chuckle, Varro peeked out from behind the rock again.

"That it was. Except now...."

A rider exited the camp, mounted on a sleek and groomed black horse. He wore a bronze helmet and had an oblong Ligurian shield and spear set on his mount.

Tied across the back of the horse, Paullus hung with hands and feet bound and a sack cinched over his head.

The rider trotted down the slope, and once reaching the path through the trees could easily outstrip anyone pursuing on foot.

"We've no time to waste," Varro said. "We've got to follow that rider or Paullus is done for."

9

The horseman reached the hill's bottom as Varro and the others weaved between trees to avoid being seen. If lookouts on the hill spotted them, they would end the pursuit before it could even begin.

"We can't catch a mounted man on foot," Falco whispered from behind.

Varro pushed through loose bushes and ducked under low branches as he shadowed the path. Ahead, he could see Paullus bobbling across the rump of the horse. The rider followed a narrow path, but it was not clear enough for him to gallop. That gave Varro hope of catching up.

"We could let him die," Falco said, keeping close behind. Being taller than anyone else, he groaned as he struggled with more branches.

"They'll torture him," Varro said, keeping his sight on the vanishing rider trotting away from them.

"And?"

"Falco, he may be arrogant, but he does not deserve torture and death."

"He came to my aid," Curio said. His voice was muffled, coming from farther back. "I owe him."

"We saved your life," Falco snapped. "He couldn't have done it without us, be we could've without him."

Varro turned with a finger over his lips, hushing them.

The path narrowed and twisted through the woods. Varro and the others had some advantage in being able to push a direct line through the trees, whereas the rider curved with the trail. The black horse was well trained and navigated the woods without difficulty. But the rider had to slow as trees and bushes clogged the path forward.

"Here's our chance," Varro said. "He's slowing down. We'll bluff him. Try to hide behind our Ligurian shields until we're close enough. Curio, you focus on getting Paullus down. Falco and I will dismount the rider."

They raised their shields. Varro appreciated its coverage, but it was not as heavy as he would've liked. However, it was an improvement from a cavalry shield. He led the others into the path, then jogged up the remaining distance until he could see the black horse's swishing tail.

His hand slipped to his gladius. "Here we go. I hope we're still obscured enough for him to mistake us for his friends."

He called out, unsure of how the Ligurians greeted each other. The rider wasn't expecting to be hailed. He drew his horse to a stop and turned in his saddle. Varro noted the saddle looked much like the Roman four-pointed saddle.

The rider called back, and Varro raised his hand as if in greeting. But he dropped it back to his gladius as he and the others approached the horse.

The rider called back something to him, and Varro just smiled and shook his head. Whatever the words, they were incomprehensible to him. He just needed him to remain unaware a few strides longer.

With less patience, the rider snapped what sounded like a repeat of his question. When Varro didn't answer, rather than twist around on the saddle, the rider turned his graceful black horse.

"Now!" Varro shouted then drew his gladius.

Behind him, he heard the ring of bronze blades escaping their sheaths.

To his credit, the rider seemed unsurprised by the sudden charge. He pulled back on the horse, and it reared up with its hooves flailing to the front.

Varro ducked behind his shield, fearing a strike from the horse. He had seen plenty of battle-mad horses break heads like eggs. The delay was all the rider needed to draw a long spear and retrieve his shield. When the horse thumped back to the ground, he was ready to fight.

Without any longer weapon, Varro and Falco both were disadvantaged. Their only chance was in flanking to either side, forcing the rider to choose an opponent and leaving his back exposed.

Falco broke left and Varro went right. He crashed along the edge of the trail, snapping branches and bushes with his shield as he charged. The rider had decided Falco was more dangerous. Being the tallest of them, he had the better reach. Meanwhile, Curio ducked into the trees to loop around the back of the horse.

A glimpse was all Varro could spare. He heard Paullus's muffled screams as he rolled around the horse's rump. When it had reared, his bonds appeared to have loosened as now he hung dangerously close to falling off.

But then the horse snorted and side-stepped toward Varro. The rider deftly covered against his attack with his shield to Varro, while using his spear to keep Falco at bay.

Varro thrust up, getting under the shield but only succeeding in scoring the rider's saddle. The horse turned and slammed Varro back into the trees.

Curio emerged, gladius in one hand and shield on his back. He crouched as if ready to spring away as he sought to grab Paullus.

But Varro slipped in the bush and collapsed to his back. The horse screamed and both Falco and the rider cursed each other. When he fought back to his feet, Varro found the rider had again turned his horse, this time to face Falco. Curio slapped his hand onto the rope securing Paullus, but the horse shifted again and threw him off.

Cursing, Varro leaped back into the fight. He could see the rider wanted to angle his horse toward his intended path. Despite the rougher terrain, he would bolt away and escape for good. Varro couldn't risk it.

He plunged his gladius into the side of the horse. The blade sank down into the muscle and slid between ribs. He tore the blade out as quick as a striking snake, spilling bright red blood over the black coat.

The horse reared up, surprising the rider and sending Paullus toppling to the ground. No matter how well trained, a wounded horse could not be convinced to remain in battle. The rider understood this and leaped off his mount and into the cushion of the bushes. But Falco followed on.

Curio, however, had sheathed his sword and now lifted Paullus to his feet. The sack on his head had twisted around and was brown with the dirt of the path. Hands and feet were still bound, Curio had just managed to get him upright.

The rest unfolded to Varro's sight like some viscous fluid oozing down a rough wall.

The injured black horse screamed and reared, its blood flowing from the hole in its side as if watering the vegetation around the path. Its eyes were white and rolling, its teeth flashing yellow. It slammed down on its front hooves, then bucked backward.

The hooves came up so slowly Varro felt as if he could have

walked over to reposition both Curio and Paullus out of the way and still have time to saunter aside. He was also snared within the gelid pace of time, unable to react to what unfolded before him. He could barely open his mouth and shout a warning before the hooves connected.

One stuck Paullus directly in his chest. Varro could see all of it caving in, a disgusting and horrifying bowl forming where his heart and lungs should be. The ripples of the impact blew through his brown tunic, puffing it with air. The force of the kick sent his bound hands flailing forward while his body launched backward and into the air.

However, Curio had an edge in seeing the danger, unlike Paullus. Even after sitting idle for most of a year, and suffering the injuries from a lifetime of battle, Curio still displayed amazing speed. Varro had always been aware of Curio's lightning-fast reactions. It was what made him so formidable in battle despite his height. But even now, trapped in a world where time oozed away, his speed stunned Varro.

He snapped aside, releasing Paullus to his fate. The hoof that also should have struck him high in the chest instead clipped his shoulder. Even so, Varro saw the painful rippling of flesh and cloth. His chain shirt sleeve would not relieve him of the damage. His shoulder slipped up, popping out of joint and raising a bulge under the mail. His face squeezed tight in an expression of agony and his hair flew back as if in a strong wind. He too launched into the air and fell out of Varro's sight.

Then time resumed.

Varro's heart raced. The horse spun around and bucked, forcing him to back away and shelter under his shield. He heard Falco shouting, but whether in rage or victory he couldn't be certain. The massive black shape of the horse cut between them as it danced wildly, spraying blood everywhere.

Now out of danger from the horse, he ducked though the trees to seek Curio. The beast continued to scream and stamp, and ran a dozen feet before collapsing into the bushes aside the path.

As Varro reached Curio, he heard Falco's shout of victory behind him.

"My shoulder!" Curio rolled atop his stolen Ligurian shield, his good arm holding the dislocated one to his side.

"I'm here," Varro said, crouching beside his agonized friend. He put a hand to his chest to ease him and felt Curio's wildly throbbing heart. "You're all right. Just a bump on the shoulder."

"That's no bump!" Curio lifted his head and attempted to see the dislocation. His reddened face shined with sweat. The effort made him groan and then he set his head back in surrender. "What about Paullus?"

"Dead," Varro said. No one could have survived such a blow, particularly when Varro saw Paullus's chest collapse in vivid detail. "Stay put. I've got to help Falco."

Dashing back across the path, pools of steaming horse blood caught his reflection as he leaped past. The horse was still crying and trembling in the bushes ahead. Nearer still, more bushes trembled.

Varro pushed them aside with his shield and cocked his gladius.

"It's me!" Falco tried to bring up his shield, but the dead rider had pinned it flat. He stared down the white edge of Varro's blade, then their eyes met.

They both relaxed, and Varro lowered his sword.

The rider's spear seemed as if it had been carefully set against a tree, though Varro knew it had been an accident of combat. The rider was facedown in dead leaves and forest debris, his sword arm bent out of shape where Falco had broken it.

"These fucking vines," Falco muttered as he extended a hand to Varro. "Did your map makers point out these vines? They grab your feet. If that rider had a friend, I'd be dead by now."

"Well, you're not." Varro hauled him upright, and Falco picked twigs and dead leaves off his tunic. "But Paullus is."

He snapped his head up, his expression caught somewhere between terror and joy. As they both rushed back, Varro summarized what had happened.

Curio remained prone, rocking side to side and sucking his breath. Falco kneeled beside him while Varro went to find Paullus.

He sprawled out half on the path and the track. His legs bent at the knees, but were still bound at the ankles. His hands remained tied at his wrists and the sack remained tied overhead. His posture confirmed he was dead. He was draped over a thick bush and his head hung backward.

His chest was flattened. Though Varro saw no blood, he could see the ribs had been staved in and likely driven through his lungs and heart. He did not breathe or move, but just hung like a rolled-up carpet discarded aside a forest path.

There would be a price to pay for allowing Paullus's death. Even if Falco had been right in thinking his family wouldn't mourn his passing, they would still assign blame. Would it be Flamininus? He had allowed him on this adventure, after all. But he was too high in the social order. So it would fall on Varro and his friends to bear responsibility. In fact, he could imagine the outcome with perfect clarity.

The Paullus family would come after his wealth. They would demand recompense for the death of a beloved son. No reasoning or point of law would sway them. Even if Flamininus defended them, the Paullus family could not resist claiming three rich estates for themselves. Those of the patrician class are never satisfied with their own wealth. Even the idea of one obol in the possession of another agonizes them to distraction. So they would snatch a coin from the palm of a beggar without hesitation.

Varro knew he was doomed to lose all he owned. It remained to be seen if they would allow him his life at least.

He shook his head at the bleak thought. The citizens of Pisa were in dire peril and Consul Minucius depended on his intelligence gathering. He had a mission to complete and recalled Falco's earlier comments. He could worry about his fancy estate later, but not while he faced enemy swords.

Returning to Curio's side, he and Falco looked over the injury.

"Dislocated," Falco said, nodding to the lump in Curio's shoulder. "He's out of action for weeks at least."

Curio's eyes opened and his groaning stopped.

"It'll be fine in a few days. I've had it happen before."

Varro touched the shoulder and felt warmth there. Curio instinctively flinched away.

"It was the same kick that flattened Paullus's chest. You've probably got a broken arm in the bargain."

"At least put my shoulder back in place." Curio bit his lips for a moment, then continued. "Let's figure out what happens after."

Varro looked up at Falco, and they shared a knowing look. The pain of resetting Curio's shoulder would be short but intense. He needed a distraction from the sudden push back into the socket. While Curio squeezed his eyes shut, Varro mouthed that instruction to Falco, who nodded in acknowledgement.

When he got into position to push, he looked at Falco and then patted Curio's shoulder.

"All right, I'm going to do this on the count of three."

"No! I know how this works! You'll go on one!"

Then Falco seized Curio by the sides of his head, violently twisting to face him. His eyes flicked open and looked up at Falco, whose heavy brows were knitted in earnest.

"Curio, I love you."

Varro shoved down on the shoulder.

"Wha—" Then Curio screamed in shock and pain. But it was after the moment Varro felt the bone shift and the shoulder pop into place. He had missed the instant of intense pain due to Falco's distraction.

He blinked as if he had been hit on the head. Varro leaned back to admire his work.

"Better now?" Falco asked. He withdrew his hands and clapped them as if dusting off dirt. He raised his brow at Varro. "What? You said to distract him."

"Distract. Not shock him to death."

"My shoulder does feel better," Curio said. "Falco, is it true?"

"Not a fucking word of it."

"Well, it distracted him. That's all we needed," Varro said. He looked about for something to serve as a splint, then realized the rider's spear shaft would work. "You'll need to brace that arm for several weeks. You're without a sword arm."

They all knew what that meant, and all fell silent. Curio struggled to sit up, and Falco helped raise him.

"It'll heal in a few days," Curio said, clutching his arm tight to his side. "Don't worry about me."

Varro put his finger to Curio's arm just beneath the shoulder and gave a gentle press. But Curio howled so loudly that Falco drew back as if he feared his aid had injured him.

"That's not your shoulder," Varro said. "That's the bruising and swelling where the hoof struck you. And I'll wager everything that the bone is cracked as well. You deflected a good amount of the force, but not all. We better get you out of that chain shirt before your arm swells too much."

"All right," Curio said, lowering his head. "But it's not a mission about fighting only. We're gathering intelligence. I don't need an arm for that."

Falco rubbed his chin and studied Curio's arm.

"He should find the nearest town and see a real doctor."

"No." Curio used his good arm to push against Falco. "There's no sending me to rear. There is no rear yet. I'm on this mission and can still help. I can fight with my other hand if I have to, or at least carry a shield."

In the end, Varro knew he couldn't dissuade Curio from remaining with them. While it made sense to get him medical treatment, Varro was not sure a doctor could do more than splint the arm and order him to rest. Besides, it was too dangerous traveling alone and on foot to wherever was the nearest town.

"I'll use the spear shaft to splint the arm," he said. "Don't take unnecessary risks and make it worse."

"Of course not. I'm no fool." Curio smiled and sat up straighter, but the motion made him wince and paw at his wounded arm. "At least I wasn't killed."

"Which reminds me," Varro said, returning with the enemy spear. "We've also got to bury Paullus."

"Do we really need to do that?" Falco remained kneeling beside Curio and slapped both his knees. "It'll take half a day to dig a proper hole with just our entrenching tools. It's just me and you doing the work, too."

"When did you become such a heartless bastard?" Varro worked the pin on the enemy spearhead, using his pugio to pry it up. "He gave us trouble before and made some threats recently. But he doesn't deserve to rot under the trees. Besides, do you want his shade to come for you in the night, tormenting you for not putting him to rest?"

Falco shared Varro's fear of the restless dead, and his eyes immediately widened.

"All right, calm down. I was just thinking of the mission. By now Pisa could be a pile of rocks."

"If it is, then there was nothing we could do for it yesterday that we can't do tomorrow. But I'm sure the Ligurians have confounded themselves trying to figure out how to enter Pisa. There is still time to save them."

First, they settled Curio, who did his best not to show any pain while getting out of his mail and then setting the splint over his arm. They left him breathless and dripping with sweat from his ordeal.

"We'll fold your mail shirt later," Varro said. "Right now we've got a hole to dig."

He waved them off without reply, then drank deep from his canteen. Falco, however, groaned as he dug out his entrenching tool, the dolabra. Its main use was for creating a staked trench surrounding a marching camp. They had all carried one since their days as recruits. The iron head had a spade on one side and a pick on the other. They stored it disassembled from the handle, which was a long and heavy shaft of wood worn smooth and dark from long use and sweat. They pushed and pinned the sections together, then found a clearing with soft earth beside the path.

As Falco had predicted, the dolabra did not excel at digging deep holes. It served their purposes, though consumed more time and effort. Eventually, both were in a hole up to their waists and their picks constantly struck stones too large to pry out.

"It's deep enough," Falco declared, wiping sweat from his brow. "Shit, I'm out of shape. Imagine what Centurion Drusus would think of us now?"

"He wouldn't think anything," Varro said. "His cane would just reflexively smack across our backs and he'd make us dig until we passed out."

They both laughed. Their helmets rested aside the grave like two heads watching them. Varro didn't like the omen and turned his around while they finished up. At last, the stones defeated them.

"All right, it will have to do. Hopefully, it's deep enough to keep wolves away from his body."

"If his shade drops by to complain, I'll lend him a shovel." Falco pulled himself out of the hole. "See if he could do better.'

They both rested for a moment, admiring their work. The

scent of the earth piled beside the hole filled Varro's nose. They went to retrieve Paullus's body, which had not moved. The legs hanging off the bush had turned the color of a week-old bruise. The blood had stopped flowing and now pooled in his feet.

"Oh, he's dead all right," Falco said. "What a way to go. Kicked by a horse. When I was a boy, we had that happen to a slave once. His head looked like someone had stepped on a tomato."

"Paullus's chest was crushed," Varro said and led Falco to the body. "If Curio had taken the same blow, we'd have two holes to dig."

They stood over the corpse draped across the thick bush. A dark stain had formed on the sack tied about Paullus's neck, showing where blood had run down the interior.

"Help me get him up."

But Falco barred him with his arm.

"Varro, how's your eyesight?"

"What? It's fine."

"Then why can't you see that's not Paullus?"

Varro stared down, his chest suddenly tight. He was going to protest but realized immediately that the legs hanging off the bush did not match Paullus's musculature and the skin was darker.

Falco growled. "Don't tell me I dug that hole for nothing and that Curio broke his shoulder for a stranger."

He then wrestled the sack off the head. Tossing it aside, he was about to curse.

But he paused in shock.

Varro did as well.

They did not look down on Paullus.

They looked down on his servant.

10

The corpse of Paullus's servant slipped through the branches of the heavy bush that had held it and rolled out at Varro's and Falco's feet. His blue face stared up in an expression of horror and confusion. He died without knowing or expecting the blow that ended him. His hands and feet remained bound, the flesh around the bindings raw and bloodied from his struggles.

"I don't understand," Falco said. "What is Paullus's servant doing here? I saw him ride off."

"On the horse I just killed," Varro said, completing Falco's sentence. He turned back and saw the rear legs of the dead horse extended into the path. "I should've known that black horse was too good for Ligurian barbarians."

Curio now rested against a tree with his arm braced and in a sling of brown cloth cut from the dead Ligurian's tunic. He called out to ask for an explanation. But neither Varro nor Falco could do more than stare at the dead man at their feet.

"It makes no fucking sense," Falco said. "How did he get ahead of us?"

"Why did he get ahead of us?" Varro rubbed his temples in thought. "And how did he know where to find us?"

"Was he looking for us or Paullus?" Falco toed the corpse's side. "Do you think he's got anything on him to explain what he was doing out here?"

"Probably not on him, but the Ligurian might."

Now Curio, groaning from the effort, staggered up to them and then stopped at the corpse.

"Who's this? Where's Paullus?"

Falco hissed at the name. "After I find him, he'll be in Hades getting a hot iron rod jammed up his backside for all eternity. This reeks of Paullus's treachery. Somehow, he's going to lead us to ruin."

"But for what?" Varro put his hand to his forehead, struggling to imagine what Paullus intended by having his servant follow. "I don't see how he benefits from abandoning us and bringing his servant here."

Curio crouched over the dead body, struggling for balance with just one arm free. "So Paullus's servant got captured, but Paullus did not. If he had been, then both would be prisoners headed to Pisa."

Varro was uncertain where Paullus was or what his plans were. He turned his back on the confusion and searched the dead Ligurian, but found nothing other than trinkets of no value to anyone but the bearer. After thumbing a rectangular wooden charm depicting an unknown god, he flung it into the trees out of frustration. He rejoined Falco and Curio, still staring at the corpse as if expecting it to provide an explanation.

"Nothing," Varro announced, raising his hands in frustration. "And you know what? I don't care anymore. We've wasted too much time chasing him around. Senator Flamininus sent us to warn Pisa and gather intelligence. But all we're doing is thinking about Paullus."

"I'm sure he'd love that," Falco said, kicking the corpse once more. "Well, we dug the hole. Let's drop this one in there and cover him up."

Varro nodded. "It'll be a better burial than what Paullus would've given him."

"Right. And we won't have to waste time thinking up something nice to say over his grave."

Even a perfunctory burial consumed more time than Varro hoped. Curio could not help, and so watched the surroundings for them in case the Ligurians sent more patrols from their camp. When it was finished, Falco blew out a long breath.

"We're not done with this yet. Paullus is using us somehow. We're going to pay for it. Curio already paid for it with a broken arm. There was no point in suffering that injury."

"That's not true," Curio said. "We couldn't let Paullus's slave reach the Ligurian lines either. It's just too bad I couldn't have saved him for questioning."

"That's the positive spirit we need," Varro said. "Now, there's plenty of daylight left. We must reach Pisa early enough to establish a post to operate from while we get our message through."

Despite the urgency, they ate from their rations. It made Varro think of Paullus and his ruined supplies, and once more his thoughts spiraled down into confusion. Falco was right. Paullus had his own agenda that at the least would not help them on their mission. He had not carried on about leaving snakes underfoot as a metaphor. They would become snakes to the truth of whatever misdeeds Paullus planned, and he would not leave them underfoot.

They set out at the fastest pace they could manage along the path. The map showed the trail petered out into thin woods, but before that it narrowed and became harder to follow. Curio kept pace even after such a staggering wound. He carried his Ligurian shield more as a disguise than anything else. Varro would not allow him into combat. He would be more of a liability than an aid.

They smelled Pisa before they saw it. At least they smelled the hordes of Ligurians surrounding it. Odors of smoke, animals, and filth swept through the trees on gusts of wind. Varro did not even need to ask the others to be wary. No one could miss that a massive army encamped nearby. The trees parted and the most raucous sounds of camp life now echoed as distant shouts and thuds.

It is one thing to hear that forty thousand enemies have come to do battle, and yet another thing to see them arrayed against you. Varro and the rest emerged onto a prominent ridge with few trees. He silenced a gasp as he glimpsed the highest walls of Pisa and the myriad campfires surrounding it.

"Normally I'd ask Curio to get up a tree," Varro said. "But it looks like I'm the next smallest of our group. I want to scout a good approach."

Setting aside all his gear and weapons, but leaving on his mail shirt, he climbed into the sturdiest tree on the ridge. Though a mail shirt was heavy, it was flexible and made little noise. However, changing in and out of it was not simple. So he fought branches that caught in its links and reached the highest branch that didn't threaten to break under his weight.

He clung to the cool and rough bark of the trunk and stared down. Pisa was at most a half mile away. Trees shaded off down the slope until spilling out into grassy plains. The Iberians milled there like swarms of beetles. Their lines were haphazard and clustered. Varro noted a strange pattern to their arrangement, bringing to mind a porous sea sponge. The pores were of course the gaps left between campfires and tents.

The sun burned down to the west and painted the horizon orange. Long shadows stretched from the Ligurian camps and pointed at the walls of Pisa. To Varro, it appeared like a shadowed hand reaching for the city. Atop the walls, braziers burned and flickered with the shadows of men on guard for an attack. He followed the parapets to towers that fortified the wall corners. It was not a square city, but one that had spread and grown naturally with the terrain. The walls reflected the meandering shape.

He marked the darkest areas of the Ligurian camp in his memory, expecting these to be the easiest passes through the enemy. He could see nothing that appeared like a Ligurian headquarters. Barbarians seldom employed such organization, and the Ligurians appeared to have even less of it. They arrayed no ranks of war machines against Pisa. But he saw they were constructing a covered battering ram. Even in the fading light, men still labored at it, bringing supplies and carrying away debris.

Feeling his grip on the tree tire, he climbed down. Falco helped him land on his feet, and Varro shared all he had observed.

"They've left enough gaps in their camp that we should have no issue reaching the walls. The trouble will be in not becoming victims of the guards there." Varro pointed out the general direction of the best approach. "We can set our camp nearby. It's a suitable spot to intercept messages to and from the Ligurian outpost. They're probably not writing to each other, and the messengers might not speak our language. But it still might aid us."

Falco cleared his throat. "We could just follow the messenger to the Ligurian leaders. They're the ones we want."

"True enough. If we can eliminate their driving force, they might collapse as a unified army. Let's find a place to camp where we can watch this approach and remain hidden. There's only so much light left. We'll rest and then we attempt to get into Pisa."

They cooperated in silence to construct a small camp with a low profile. They heaped concealing branches on their tent and built a staked enclosure to catch anything man-sized that might sneak up on a blind side. A stream passed too far for easy use. But it was their only source of fresh water. So Varro prioritized filling their extra skins and mixing in their wine to preserve it longer. He hoped to only remain in place for a few days before setting out for Consul Minucius.

They slept after their labors, no one taking any watch, as all would need to be alert during the night. Varro was the first to awaken, as usual. Falco snored as if he were in a deep dream as did Curio beside him. He favored his broken arm in his sleeping position. Varro regretted the injury, not only because he hated to see his brother wounded but also because Curio was the best choice to get inside Pisa safely. Now, with a broken arm, he could only play a supporting role in their mission.

When the other two didn't awaken naturally, he shook them until both were groaning and rubbing their eyes. Falco yawned like a tired old hunting dog.

"Is it time to become the unnamed heroes of Pisa?"

Varro brandished the parchment, safely contained in a leather tube.

"This message will be in the hands of Pisa's commander tonight."

When Curio awakened, both Varro's and Falco's chuckling fell silent. He groaned as he struggled to rise with a single arm. For a moment, his sleepy eyes blinked softly. Then he shook his youthful head and scratched at the skin under his brace. At last, he noticed the others staring at him.

"We're getting ready to go," Falco said, sounding as if he had just admitted to sleeping with Curio's wife.

"That's right," Varro said. "We're going to need your aid."

He gave a derisive frown and held up his good hand.

"Do you think I'm a child? Fortuna go with you both tonight. I know I can't help with my arm like this. I'll watch the camp. If there is danger, I'll warn you. If I have to abandon this position, I'll carve my sign into a tree to let you know where I went."

Varro sighed with relief, and Falco rubbed the back of his

neck. They both helped him stand and stood in awkward silence for a moment. But they soon snapped back to normal. They set aside most of their gear, needing to preserve their mobility for the work to come. Varro carried Flamininus's message in a small satchel he slung across his shoulder. Otherwise, he carried only shield and weapons. With their preparations completed, they clasped arms.

"I don't expect we will return until tomorrow night," Varro said. "Once inside, we will deliver our message and then wait until darkness again to exit. In the meantime, see what you can learn about the Ligurian camp."

"I'd write some notes," Curio said, scribbling in the air. "But my writing arm is in a sling."

Varro put a hand on each of their shoulders. "And learning from hard experience, if any of us become separated, we will use this place as our rally point."

There was no moon, and clouds covered the stars. Varro and Falco both left their helmets at camp, not wanting to risk an errant reflection giving them away. Besides, their profile would read more like a Ligurian when they carried their enemy's shields.

"He took it better than I thought," Falco said as they crossed through the last of the woods.

"I think after Iberia, Curio is a little less bold than he used to be." Varro thought back to those dark forests and the brutes who made them their homes. "I know I am."

"Me too," Falco said. "I feel naked without a helmet. This shield really isn't much, either. Only my gladius and pugio are worth anything."

"If we end up fighting, then we've done something wrong. It's all just a disguise to get us up to the walls."

"And then we walk through them?" Falco chuckled. "What's the plan?"

"I've learned better than to make a detailed plan. Whatever we plan will be invalidated the moment we're up to the wall. So we get to the wall first. If we get that far, then no one saw us, Roman or Ligurian. We'll call up to the guards. They ought to be curious about fellow Romans shouting from the foot of their walls."

"Or maybe they'll just drop rocks on us first and figure it all out later. That's why I wanted my helmet, Varro."

"It won't come to that. They'll likely open a gate just enough for us to pass."

Now they had come to the edge of the trees and all their levity vanished with the wind that rushed in waves over long grasses. The Ligurian camp ahead gleamed with clusters of campfires and bonfires. The scents that Varro had only tasted earlier now slammed over him like a fist full of rotted meat.

Falco put his hand over his mouth and nose and grimaced.

"We're near their latrines," Varro whispered.

"You couldn't have scouted a better position?"

They crouched low, Ligurian shields on their arms and hands on the pommels of their swords. Their gray cloaks turned them into vague humps that moved through the grass. Varro imagined anyone seeing them might wonder if the stones of the earth had come to life. They kept low to the grass until reaching the rear lines.

The hide tents were quiet and empty. Varro and Falco huddled low, so that grass touched the bottom of their chins. Varro felt the tickle of the blades as he scanned side to side.

"Where are they?" Falco asked in the barest whisper.

Varro shook his head. He did not even hear snoring, which he should have this close to the tents. But they had come this far without detection, and Varro decided to push ahead.

By now, it was a familiar dance to the both of them. Enemy encampments, once penetrated, usually lacked the regularity of a Roman camp. This served to their advantage. Unlike in a Roman camp, in a barbarian one there could be a dozen reasons for someone moving about after dark. None questioned a glimpsed shadow or the sound of a foot scratching on dirt. The lack of coherence and schedule aided pretenders like Varro and Falco.

So they glided from tent to tent, assuring a clear path before moving to the next. The empty spaces Varro had spotted from above were indeed gaps between camps. This represented the tribal nature of the Ligurian army. They clustered together in family and tribal units, leaving dark spaces for them to traverse in peace.

The walls of Pisa seemed enormous now. It was a newer city, at least newer than Sparta, whose walls came to mind when looking at those before him. Varro felt cold water in his stomach and realized that his hands trembled. The walls were suddenly too similar to those he had fallen from in Sparta. Only through the graces of his beloved goddess, Fortuna, had he survived. If he dared to scale city walls again and fell, wouldn't the goddess see it as an affront to her generosity? She would let him die this time.

"Why did you stop?"

Falco piled up behind him. He felt warm hands on the back of his exposed arms. In the darkness, the reflections of light from the wall shimmered in Falco's eyes.

"We're close now. If I fall, retrieve the letter. Do not abandon the mission no matter what happens to me."

"Fine," Falco hissed. "Is now really the time for a rousing talk?"

Varro knew it wasn't and he just delayed facing his fear. He had scaled fortress walls in Numidia. But those bore no resemblance to what he faced now and were not as tall. The fear welled up in him, but he forced his feet ahead.

Then he stopped once more.

It was not fear now that halted him, but a thick line of Ligurian warriors.

Again Falco bumped into him. He stilted his curse, and leaned forward to see the cause of delay. They were both already low in the grass. But when spotting the ranked enemies ahead, they flattened out.

Varro's heart raced as he lifted his eyes over the top of the grass. The Ligurians had assembled at the edge of light cast down from the high walls. Despite their numbers and supposed lack of discipline, the Ligurians made little noise.

Falco's finger extended in the corner of Varro's sight. He turned to follow it and found the ladder teams ready to rush Pisa's wall.

"We picked the wrong time." Falco whispered so close his breath was hot and wet on Varro's ear. "Let's back out before we're caught."

That it was a perfect night to infiltrate the Ligurian camp also meant it was a perfect night for the Ligurians to encroach on Pisa's walls. Now that Varro was on his belly before the assembled barbarians, he realized the truth of it. Without another word, he scrabbled backward on his stomach through the grass and Falco joined him. They would try again the following day. Now was too dangerous.

Then the barbarians shouted, their throaty war cries exploding in unison. They thrust their spears skyward and stamped the ground, spreading vibrations through Varro's chest as they rushed forward.

Out of the surrounding darkness, scores of disorganized Ligurian tribesmen rushed to join the first wave. Blasting horns punctuated the wild calls shattering the night's still. Varro felt as if the entire world had erupted into chaos.

Both he and Falco stood up to flee the way they had come.

And faced a wall of onrushing Ligurian warriors.

"Fuck!" Falco shouted. "Where did they come from?"

"Join them," Varro said, turning and raising his Ligurian shield. "Because we're not getting through them."

11

In his youth, Varro would imagine the battles his great-grandfather and father described to him. In his mind's eye, the Carthaginians and their allies appeared like barely human monsters. Their elephants were gargantuan abominations that terrorized the battlefield. His father, when in the right mood, described slaughters horrifying to Varro's impressionable mind. He fed his imagination visions of blood and bodies and parts of bodies littering vast landscapes. It was a vivid and frightening—and unfortunately realistic—depiction of battle.

His imaginings, however, were also filled with heroic Roman citizen-soldiers who fought for their farms and their city. They strode between monstrous enemies and destroyed them. They and their centuries moved at will among the battlefield, or so it seemed from how his elders described these battles. Every Roman was free to engage whatever threat he deemed most pressing to win the field.

Now, on this night before the walls of Pisa, Varro's young imaginings were completely demolished.

Swarms of sweating and screaming Ligurians pressed to either side of him. They were all drunk, for the scent of wine lay heavy over the mass of them. Their faces were red and eyes focused ahead with the intensity of crazed men. Varro had no freedom of movement. Unlike the battles he had imagined in his youth, he could do nothing but flow along with the crowd of drunk madmen carrying ladders to Pisa's vast walls. He wouldn't be a heroic citizen soldier flying about the battlefield to visit death upon his enemies. He was a cork bobbing in the turbulence of a barbarian sea.

Falco fared little better. But he stood taller than those around him. Varro could at least track him in the dim illumination. Even as the waves of attackers carried them into the light of Pisa's walls, the swell of Ligurians appeared as little more than heads of shaggy hair.

"Don't lose me," Falco shouted.

"I'm trying!" Varro had no choice other than to go where the enemy shoved him. But he worked across the current toward Falco.

Pisa was now alert to the danger. Torches burst into light atop the walls and guards rushed to their posts. Varro could see the flashes of pale javelins streaking down on the first ranks to touch their ladders to Pisa's walls. The Ligurians sheltered beneath their long shields as their companions set their ladders.

"We're going up there?" Falco shouted over the heads of the men surrounding him. But Varro could tell from his confused look that he could no longer see him in the crowd's darkness.

Varro bounced and fumbled along with the surging men. As they neared the rear of the lines, more and more of them raised their shields to defend themselves from projectiles. He did the same, realizing that for the moment he would lose touch with Falco. If they both worked toward the middle, he hoped to find him.

The idea of setting ladders to scale city walls was an ancient one. Varro had seen it done before and realized it had some benefits despite the obvious risks. Eventually, one ladder would succeed where a dozen others failed, and the attackers would have a foothold. If enough ladders succeeded with enough speed, the defender would be overwhelmed and unable to shift defenses in time. It was also harder to stop a dozen broken points in the line than a single large one.

He resisted each step forward, eliciting angry shoves from those behind him. But they flowed around him and his effort to stem the advance was pointless. They had no apparent leader to goad them on. Every man was bound by a warrior's honor to scale the walls. If circumstances had been different, Varro might have admired that trait. Now he cursed it.

The mobs divided into groups that lined up behind a ladder. Some ladders had already been pushed away, the defenders using long poles to shove the ladders off the wall. But for each of these, climbers weighted down other ladders. Once filled, they would become impossible to dislodge without tremendous effort.

Javelins continued to streak down. Varro kept up his shield, fighting the flow relentlessly shoving him toward the walls.

The thin shafts now ranged behind the ladder teams and found better targets. Varro's shield thudded as a javelin shattered across it. Ahead of him, men pulled their heads down behind their shields as if in a hard rain. The javelins sprinkled among them, some quivering into the ground and others finding flesh. He watched as a Ligurian sank to his knees, pulling at a javelin that had pierced through the top of his shoulder and exited from his back.

The flickering braziers above cast an otherworldly light over the scene. Romans had dropped blazing pots off the walls, both to drive back assailants and illuminate the ladders. These crashed and exploded in brilliant streaks of orange flame before fading into low burning puddles of oil. But it was enough light to mark the enemy for the wall defenders.

Falco leaped up between the shields of the throng surrounding him. He seemed like a man drowning in a lake, coming up for air, hoping to grab a floating branch. Varro called to him, but he was too far ahead. The shouts of rage and agony, along with the crash of javelins and stones striking the attackers, drowned out anything else.

With a curse, he gave up on ever getting free of this mad gang of Ligurians. Sometimes one of them would speak to him as if excited about the prospect of dying on the ladder. But they would either pass by or fall back into the churning mass.

Someone led the Ligurians, as Varro glimpsed a knot of men standing back and shouting encouragement to his warriors lining up for the chance at the walls.

A thunderous explosion rocked Varro from behind, sending him flying into the man before him. The entire mass collectively heaved away from the blast. Varro's shield stuck on something and held him upright long enough to regain his footing. The push forward had stopped.

In the amber half-light, he saw a massive stone had crushed two men to bloody paste, then rolled through the throng to shatter others in its path. The gash it left in the Ligurian mass swiftly filled in with more men.

Varro looked up and saw the vaguest hint of something gray arcing high into the air and realized another stone followed the first. It landed a dozen degrees away from the first cast. The Ligurians had shifted to avoid another shot, but suffered another crashing amid them.

Even at a distance, the impact still rippled over Varro's face, bringing the foul odors of blood and sour wine. Bodies flew into the air while others vanished under the path of the stone as it bounced into the dark. Men screamed and crashed into each other. The disorganization and panic broke up the rear ranks, which would make the ladder defenders' jobs less strenuous, at least for a brief time.

His admiration was short-lived, however, as the push ahead renewed. Varro soon found himself queued for a ladder.

Scanning the walls, he saw two ladders had established a hold. Other ladders full of men slowly rocked back, sometimes falling back to the wall and other times tipping backward to vanish into the mob below. Their screams faded into the cacophony of battle.

His own ladder seemed secured as the Ligurians lined up its entire length. However, the Roman defenders were making easy work of the attackers. As he waited, bodies plummeted down the wall to bounce and shatter on an ever-growing corpse pile beneath the ladders. They were so close that when they landed, their blood flecked Varro's legs and their abruptly ended screams tore at his ears. He looked away, rather than dwell on what might happen to him if he fell.

Varro drew his gladius and readied his shield.

He hadn't considered getting into Pisa this way. But he couldn't step out of line. To do so, the Romans could easily pick him out. He might even appear like a leader trying to direct his men, and therefore become a priority target. Though he couldn't see the parapet at this angle, he knew centurions were up there shouting orders and directing the defenses. He could imagine the order, one that he might give as well. "That one in the open. Kill the bastard and there'll be one less nuisance to deal with."

Not that he could step out of line had he wanted to. He didn't know if all forty thousand Ligurians had selected this point to attack, but looking behind it seemed so. Darkness enveloped the Ligurians' rear. Their pale shapes milled through the black night, wary of the onager shot that threatened them, but still pressing the attack. If the Ligurians took him for their own, he would appear as a coward and likely be attacked for it. He had bested multiple opponents at once before, but never forty thousand to one. Turning back, he accepted the gods were sending him up this ladder.

Falco emerged again, standing in line like Varro. His face was desperate, and blood smeared his cheek. But when he saw Varro he broke into a smile and waved.

The incongruity of it all made Varro laugh. The two of them lined up as if patiently awaiting their turn for a blessing at a temple. Falco patted his head, indicating he missed his helmet.

Again, Varro chuckled and shrugged. They were actually fighting, and as he said, this meant they were doing it wrong. So the gods did listen to him, and took glee in twisting his words against him.

The terror of battle can do strange things, even to a veteran's mind. Varro had seen it in his recruit days. They could suddenly rage, cry, or laugh, always in inappropriate situations. So it was with Falco who still laughed as if enjoying the best day of his life, and not as if the enemy were forcing him up a ladder to battle his fellow citizens.

Someone shoved him with a curse, and he shuffled into the gap before the ladder. No corpse had fallen from the wall this time. Perhaps it went over the other side, or so he hoped. If the Ligurians were gaining a foothold, Pisa might be breached.

He set his foot on the bottom rung of the ladder. The struggles above shuddered all down its length to vibrate against the soles of Varro's caligae. The line above him advanced. He shifted his shield to his back and held his gladius in hand. It was unlike the Ligurian swords and so stood out from the column of other swords also held aside. The man behind him commented on it, and Varro mumbled a reply that was lost in the thunderous clashing all around.

Now he began to climb. One rung at a time, he clung to the jumping and shuddering ladder. The pale streak of a man went screaming to his death below. Varro looked down. The man had landed hard atop his fellows. He hadn't died but screamed and clawed at his leg, which was bent at an angle through his thigh. His death was assured to be slow and painful, unless a javelin or stone hit him from above. But the defenders wouldn't be merciful, even if he might be an easy target. They would let his agonized screams demoralize his fellows.

But nothing stopped Varro's ladder from advancing. The Ligurians had gained the parapet. He struggled to look around the man before him by hanging off to the side of the ladder. He glimpsed Roman helmets and they seemed to backing away from the ladder, showing the Ligurians had gained the parapet here.

The man behind him yanked him into place with a curse. Varro nodded as he lined up properly. Across the distance, Falco's ladder was also advancing, and he was nearer to the top than Varro.

He realized what he needed to do now. The overwhelming confusion of the moment had stunned him into blind obedience. But he was on a different mission from the Ligurians and still a loyal son of the Republic.

Raising his sword, he tightened the grip on it. The bronze blade shined with the brazier light above. Then he twisted on the ladder and swept down and behind.

The Ligurian beneath him looked up the moment the blade slashed across his eyes. He howled in pain and grabbed for his face, and then fell backwards off the ladder. His foot struck the man beneath him, knocking his helmet aside and halting him.

Now Varro turned upward again. The line had stalled and the ladders swayed as the combatants at the top struggled. He stood so that his face was level with the next higher man's backside. So men looked aside as they waited to climb. This made it easy for Varro.

He slipped his blade into the Ligurian's ribs as easily as sheathing it. Blood bubbled up from the deep puncture and flowed back over the blade. But Varro withdrew the sword, then hauled the man off the ladder to send him screaming to his death.

None of the men above him noticed or expected treachery beneath them. So Varro climbed higher and repeated the murder of unsuspecting Ligurians, peeling each one away as he died and sending them to the ground.

Below him, the Ligurians closed the gap that had—to them—inexplicably opened. Varro climbed up to where the Ligurian at the top of the ladder yelled at his companion to make room for him on the parapet.

With only a glance to spare, he looked across to see Falco reaching the parapet.

Varro slipped his gladius into the kidney of the man above him. He arched his back in horror, and Varro grabbed the center of his tunic to throw him from the wall.

He reached the top knowing he counted his opportunity in heartbeats. The Ligurians beneath him, at least the man directly beneath him, had witnessed Varro's treachery. He might not understand the words, but he understood the threat of them. He would soon be treated to the same killing stroke he had effortlessly delivered a half-dozen times on his climb to the top.

To the right, a Roman soldier who reminded Varro of Curio in his recruit days struggled against a brawny Ligurian. To the left, another Ligurian wrestled back a concerted Roman effort to push through him. It was shield to shield there, and Varro judged it better to attack than to linger.

Before the enemy below him caught up, Varro scrabbled into the opening between the two Ligurians. His sword barely had room to work. When he cocked his arm, his elbow struck the man behind him. The Ligurian shouted encouragement to him. Varro smiled.

He drove his gladius into yet another exposed back. The enemy staggered around, eyes wide in a bloody face. Varro did not indulge him, but threw him from the wall to fall into the city below.

"To the ladder," he shouted at the red-faced defenders who now peered over their shields. "More are coming."

Without waiting to see the result of his order, he turned to the other Ligurian forcing open the parapet landing. He had driven the young Roman back using his massive shield. Only the weight and size of the Roman scutum had kept the soldier from being battered flat. Varro couldn't tell if the soldier had support behind him, but expected Falco to have reached the landing from that side by now. Support would arrive soon.

He stabbed the Ligurian through his side, feeling the blade bend against bone before ripping it out again. The enemy's knees buckled, and Varro shoved him off the wall into the blackness at the foot of Pisa's walls.

The recruit remained huddled behind his shield.

"You're fine," Varro shouted. "We've won back control of the ladder."

The young soldier popped up from behind his scutum. His face was milk white and eyes as wide as a terrified horse. He might not even be a proper soldier, Varro realized, but just a boy pressed into defending his city.

With no time to waste, he turned back to the ladder. The Ligurian that had been behind him now reached the top. The defenders Varro had relieved plugged the gap. Two of them hauled the Ligurian over the side while others shoved the ladder away.

The parapet was wide enough for two men, and made of heavy wood. Still, it shuddered and bounced and revealed gaps in the boards. The struggle by the ladder was in the hands of the defenders now. He couldn't work inside to aid them. So he turned back to the young soldier.

Halfway around, he struck what at first felt like a wall. He rebounded back and found himself unable to see anything but the peeling green paint of a scutum slamming at him.

His own shield remained on his back. As the second punch came, he had nothing to do but back away from it.

"I'm a Roman!"

But the young soldier punched again, stepping up for what Varro knew would be a stab from his gladius. If the boy was only a recruit, he was well drilled on the use of his shield.

Varro flinched back and avoided the strike, but now came up against the Roman ladder defenders. He had no more space to retreat.

The chaos of battle ruled the parapet. Men screamed and swore, blades clanged, and shields thumped. The smell of blood and smoke hung over everything.

"I'm not your enemy! I'm Roman!"

Varro's words did not reach anyone, or if they had, then they made no impact. He had come up the ladder and carried a Ligurian shield. So what if he spoke Latin? It was not unusual. To the defenders of Pisa, it would be a safer thing to kill him than listen to what might be a Ligurian trick. After all, except for his mail shirt and perhaps his hair, he looked exactly like one.

Varro realized he had to fight his own side.

The young soldier struck again, likely emboldened by believing he had killed the enemy that Varro actually had. He drove forward. Varro still had his shield on his back.

He was forced to parry the strike, precisely aimed for his gut, as all soldiers were instructed to do. Knowing that the young soldier hadn't the experience to improvise, Varro easily predicted the attack. He swept it aside to make time to fetch his Ligurian shield from his back.

As he did, he kicked the scutum shield, driving away the soldier so he could make space for himself. Yet the determined youth dived back at him.

They scuffled back and forth as Varro pleaded with his attacker.

"Listen! I have a message for Marcus Cincius!"

"I have a message for you barbarians!" The young soldier now found his voice. "Die!"

The charge and strike was drill-perfect and easily avoided. But Varro lacked the footing to take advantage. The entire battle unfolding around him had come down to this one young man. He lost track of everything else. It pained him to have to bring down this fine soldier. But he had no other choice. He prayed the lad would survive.

He met the renewed attack with his shield out and gladius low to catch the youth in his leg. Their shields clashed in a dull thud, and Varro felt the successful drag of his blade slicing muscle. He felt the youth's sword turn on the inside of his shield, bouncing to run its blade along the edge of his ribs.

The mail shirt was perfect defense from just this sort of blow.

But the leather strap of the satchel containing the message for Marcus Cincius was not so protected.

The young soldier's gladius sliced the leather strap, and the satchel fell away.

"No!"

The soldier collapsed as Varro reached for the satchel that slid away from him.

It hit the parapet boards and it appeared it might slip through the gaps and become stuck. But then it flipped over the edge and vanished into the darkness below.

Varro cursed, but the young soldier grabbed his ankle. He seemed determined to trip him. But Varro pulled out, and in his rage kicked the youth in the face. The hobnails of the caligae did horrific damage, breaking bone and tearing skin. The act caused instant regret, and Varro stretched out a hand as if to take back the terrible act.

The soldier's grip released his ankle and he pulled out.

Behind him, he heard orders shouted.

When he turned, the Romans had pushed away the ladder.

Varro's message lay somewhere in the darkness below.

And an entire parapet of grim-faced Roman defenders raised their shields and set their swords for him.

Varro looked down on the bloody soldier at his feet, then to the Ligurian shield on his arm, then back to the Romans drawing closer.

It seemed the Ligurians were in retreat as suddenly as they had attacked. With a glance, Varro saw great gray waves of attackers flowing back into the darkness below.

Varro put down his sword and shield, then raised both hands.

"I'm Centurion Marcus Varro. I have an urgent message from Senator Flamininus to Marcus Cincius."

Then the Romans rushed him.

12

As Varro sat in his cage, he considered whether it had been wise to surrender his sword and shield. His face still throbbed with the battering he had experienced at the hands of his fellow soldiers. They sat around a fire in their makeshift camp close to the walls. Some returned to their tents to sleep, some continued to stare at the walls as if expecting a renewed attack. Unfortunately, others never returned to their tents.

Their eyes gleamed with the orange light as they cast dark glances at him, his captor giving him the worst of all the scowls.

His tongue probed all his teeth, finding them intact. Old age would eventually remove them, but he hoped to keep them until then. The drubbing he had received while trying to surrender made him fear losing some of them.

While Pisa had repelled the Ligurian attack with ease, Varro still sensed the tension in the posture of the soldiers and people. They constantly looked at the walls, expecting to see more barbarians daring the parapets. He heard distant sobs, shouts of anger, and barking dogs. Citizens stood in the doorways of their homes, too tired to stand but too anxious to sleep.

They had called him a traitor. None of the blows Varro had endured hurt more than that. They left him no room to explain. He had come over the wall with the enemy. He attacked and wounded one of their number. There was no message in his possession, and they would not search the ground below for a satchel containing one.

So now he sat in a cage, grateful they separated him from the other Ligurian captives. Those went elsewhere, probably first to the interrogators and then likely to a larger cage than Varro's. They might keep them for prisoner swaps or ransom. But if the siege lasted and food grew scarce, they would simply be killed and hung from the walls.

If only he could contact the commander, they would know relief was coming soon.

Falco had mounted the wall as well. So was he in a different cage, Varro wondered? No one would believe his excuses, either. Varro hoped that eventually someone in authority would learn of two alleged traitors both with the same stories had arrived with the Ligurians. Then they might be pulled out of their imprisonment and have their gear returned.

But Varro had to survive long enough for that to happen, if it would happen at all.

His burly captor finished speaking with his companions, then walked over to Varro. He held something in his meaty hands and shifted it behind his back when he arrived at the cage. He just stared through the bars at him.

Two deep lines carved out the limits of his mouth, where a square jaw extended farther than it should. His eyebrows were bushy dashes over small eyes. His teeth glinted in his snarl.

"Why did you betray Rome? What did the Ligurians pay you?"

Varro sighed and looked aside as if he had something more

pressing to attend. But his captor was insistent, and he beat the cage with his heavy fist.

"I'll wring it out of you if you won't speak."

"I am Centurion Marcus Varro, recently of the Tenth Hastati in the Iberian campaign. Before that I served in Macedonia, also as centurion of the Tenth. I've twice received the Grass Crown and have more citations for bravery than you have wits. I did not betray Rome. As always, I serve it. And you are delaying an important message to your commander by keeping me caged."

"You carried a Ligurian shield, came over the wall with them. You tried to kill Clodius. Ruined his face, poor lad."

"I am sorry about Clodius." Varro meant it, but realized his captor would not hear the sincerity in his voice. "He was a good soldier and was just too panicked to listen to me. I merely tried to bring him down long enough to get past him."

"By kicking out his teeth and breaking his nose?" The burly captor wrapped one hand around a cage bar, still keeping the other hidden. "You were going to stomp his head in if we didn't get to you first."

Varro lowered his head. He had let rage into his heart, and now paid the price for it. Even in battle, he had to keep his rage in check, perhaps even more so. Rage and wild emotion have no place in a battle. It is already dangerous enough without rash action, such as the kind that had only strengthened his appearance as a traitor.

"What is your name?" Varro asked. "I've given you mine."

Again, the burly man slammed the cage with his fist.

"I'll ask the questions, traitor. Now, are you going to tell me what the Ligurians paid you?"

"They paid me nothing," Varro said, sighing. "Why are you holding me aside? If I am just a traitor to you, then shouldn't I be with the other Ligurians?"

"You're right where you should be." The lines etched on the

burly man's faced drank in more shadow as his smile widened. "Be glad it's me asking you the questions and not the interrogators."

"Another curious point," Varro said. "If I'm the traitor you say I am, then you are denying your city desperately needed intelligence. In fact, you might provide an advantage to the Ligurians by leaving me here. So, who is the real traitor?"

While pleased with his sharp wit, Varro shrank to the back of his cage as the burly man grew larger as he pressed against the bars. His voice was low and threatening.

"Careful of what you say, traitor. You'll be handed over to the interrogators soon enough. But you might be in no shape to talk to them after I'm done with you. Now, I want to know how much they paid you, and where did you hide it?"

Varro's lips pressed together as he suddenly realized this man was seeking profit even as his city suffered in the grip of a vast, inescapable enemy.

"If I tell you, then you'll send me to the interrogators?"

"And if you don't," the burly man said with a satisfied smile, "me and my boys will have our own interrogation. One you might not survive."

Varro pursed his lips in thought. These urban centuries must have a different standard for the men in their ranks. He could never imagine something like this from a regular trooper in the legions. But then they were recruited from the same pool. If ever he found such a man under his command, he would show them no mercy.

The burly man rapped the iron bars. "Am I putting you to sleep, Centurion Varro?"

"No, I was just considering my options here. It seems no matter what I do, you'll likely kill me. If I tell you where my hidden treasure is, you'll kill me so that I don't report to your superiors. If I don't tell you, you'll kill me because I'm a loose end. If I convince you of my mission, you will also kill me to escape your own punishment. So, I'm a dead man in a cage."

His captor smirked, still keeping his hand behind his back and one hand wrapped around a cage bar.

"You're smart. That's why they made you a centurion. But you weren't happy, were you? They don't pay us enough. They force us to serve, year in and year out. It costs us our livelihoods and our families. But no one cares. So you see a chance to get your hands on Ligurian gold. How much? Where did you hide it? Tell me, and you don't have to die in pain."

"You'll have to keep me alive until the siege is over," Varro said, now drawing up to his full height. His head pressed against the bars above him. "Or else I could lie about the location and you'd never find it with me dead."

This seemed to have been a wrinkle in the burly fool's plans. Even in the flickering shadows of the campfire lights around them, his confidence slipped and his eyes widened. But then he regained himself and continued to smile.

"This city is a mess. Plenty of places to hide you until we're free. So, where is your hidden gold?"

Varro had guessed what the burly fool held behind his back. It was why Varro remained his captive rather than be turned over to headquarters like other prisoners. Besides the strangeness of finding a Roman among the enemy, they found something stranger still when relieving him of his weapons.

Now Varro pulled closer to the bars and leaned in conspiratorially, keeping his voice low and coy.

"It's genuine gold, you know. Not a coating."

The burly captor's small eyes widened, but he tried to feign confusion.

"The pugio you have at your back," Varro said. "The golden owl head inlaid on the pommel. It's why you took me prisoner. It could just be a mere design. But you know it's not just that, and you want to ask me about what it means."

The small eyes went flat.

"True. I saw the same design on a pugio carried by a rich visitor here before. But his was silver. Yours is gold."

"So, do you really want my Ligurian gold, or are you looking for something more?"

"I want both," he said.

His voice had dropped into a whisper to match Varro's. Their exchange was becoming hypnotic, with soft voices and slow movements. Indeed, Varro felt almost as if he were seducing the man.

"I lead a brotherhood of sorts. Soldiers who refuse to let the rich drive us into poverty. You've seen for yourself that our members are wealthy. Forget what the Ligurians paid me. If you want the gold that much, I will tell you where I hid it. Belonging to the brotherhood, however, is worth ten times as much. Now, you've been smart enough to figure that out. If you kill me, there goes your chance at so much more."

His captor's small eyes flitted from side to side. He struggled to appear confident and in charge. But Varro knew a rapacious greed was eating through his heart and his will.

"No, I can't trust you," he said at last. "I wouldn't let you into my society if you beat me and threw me into a cage."

"Then you're a bigger fool than I thought," Varro said, now stepping back from the bars. "Everything that happened until now has been an accident. I can forgive it all, given the confusion. But you've demonstrated you are observant, smart, and of a like mind when it comes to how the Senate runs things. Our brotherhood only takes in the sharpest of the sharp, and we profit where others lose. You've been losing all along. Now here I am, and I am impressed. Set me free. Help me complete my mission here, and you'll prosper even as all of Pisa suffers."

Varro's captor now backed away from the cage and was staring at the pugio in his thick hands. He was on the hook, and Varro only had to sink it into his flesh.

"That's not all. You won't have to remain in Pisa. You'll slip out with me. We're on to better things after this."

"Did you really have a message for the commander?"

"Of course not!" Varro waved his hands. "But I have a contact to meet at headquarters. Our brotherhood does not wait on Rome when our business is in jeopardy. Now, I've told you so much already. Give me your name, and soon you'll have a pugio just like that one. Silver at the beginning. But as you rank up, you might earn the gold one as I do."

"You came over the wall with the Ligurians."

"I did. How else was I to get in here? I offered them a deal. I was happy to take their offer of gold for intelligence on the inside. I received half up front, and half later when I reported back. I was supposed to get into Pisa and act like I was part of the guards here. But you stopped me. I have to congratulate you. No one has done that before."

"Arruns Fronto, optio of the Fourth Wall Guards."

Varro smiled. "Welcome to your new future, Optio Fronto. See me to the headquarters, under guard if you will. Let no one suspect us. You'll meet my partner there, and we'll finish our business."

The clicking of the cage lock brought forward the optio's partners. They seemed confused, but Fronto was not only their leader, but also the biggest among them. So when he brushed them off, they obeyed.

"You, come with me." Fronto stabbed his thick finger at one of his men. "We're taking him to headquarters."

"But, sir—"

Fronto's glare ended any debate. The soldier stood aside as the cage door squealed open. Varro saw both men were prepared for him to flee or attack. It would be a shame to die by his own pugio, he thought. Besides, he was not foolish enough to attack with so many others around him. So he exited the cage with hands up and eyes downcast. Both men flanked him, each with a hand gripping his arms and the other hand resting on their weapons.

They passed through the camp with the optio's men watching them go. The hour was late, but Pisa remained awake. Onlookers lined the streets. Most of them searched the city walls, but others gave Varro scornful looks as they passed. He would have to wait for a better opportunity to make his escape. It felt strange to think of everyone as enemies, but for the moment that's what they were.

While Pisa's citizens searched for returning Ligurians, Varro looked for places to execute an escape. They tramped down dark streets, which should have made a break simple. But every time he felt Fronto's grip loosen, a group of citizens would emerge. He thought little of Fronto and his corrupt friends, but he could not risk hurting the citizens he had come to help. So he followed on with both men wordlessly dragging him ahead.

Varro was running out of time before they would figure out his ruse. He cleared his throat as they traveled uphill toward the garrison at Pisa's center and pulled gently at Fronto's grip.

"This is just for you," he said, then tilted his head toward the other guard.

The burly optio frowned but then realized what Varro meant. They were about to reach the garrison headquarters. Varro could see men on guard before the stairs leading up to heavy red doors.

"All right, I got him from here," Fronto said. "You go back and wait with the others."

"Sir, why?"

Varro felt the subordinate's hand tighten rather than release him.

"Because that's my order to you. Look, he's not armed and our boys are right in front of us. No need to worry about him escaping. Now do as you're told."

The soldier looked at Varro, then gave a slow nod to his officer. "If you say so, sir."

He stepped back, but he didn't immediately move off. Fronto had to pull Varro out of his subordinate's grip. Only then did the guard return the way he had come.

Fronto regarded Varro with grim determination. "All right, it's just us two. Don't think about running or doing anything stupid. I trust you, but only so much."

Varro watched the guard vanish down the street into the darkness. When he was certain he had gone, he gave a thin smile.

"My contacts are only a short distance from here. Let me do the talking and everything will be fine."

They approached the garrison fortress as if Varro was still a prisoner. In fact, the guards on duty didn't spare them a second glance. Varro led them around the side toward the darkness. His heart raced, not knowing the exact layout and what he might find ahead. But the moment had come upon him, and Optio Fronto had to be dealt with.

He saw a well ahead emerge from the darkness. He briefly closed his eyes giving thanks to Fortuna for this blessing, then turned to Fronto.

"He's just up here," he said in a whisper. "That's the well I'm supposed to meet him by."

Fronto said nothing, only giving a curt nod. In one hand, he held Varro's pugio; his left hand flexed as if expecting a fight. He might be gullible, but he was wary. Varro knew he would have to be fast and brutal. Otherwise, he would truly become an enemy of Rome.

They approached the well. Varro made a low whistle as if signaling his contact. He held one hand out to slow Fronto's approach. Both men instinctively crouched low. Varro eyed the pugio, its carefully honed edge catching the faint light shed from the garrison above.

"I don't see anyone." Fronto stood straight and his voice grew louder. "What does he look like?"

Varro whirled on him, striking for his weapon arm. Fronto had bested him once, but that was with the aid of his companions. Now, one-on-one, Varro proved himself as the better fighter.

He captured the optio's arm, then wrenched it over to neutralize the weapon in hand. He yanked forward, sending Fronto flying into the side of the well. His head thudded against the stone, and he gave a deep groan. Varro kept his hold on his arm and drove his knee into Fronto's face.

The optio let out a growl, and to his credit, the blow to his head did not slow him. Varro lifted as the burly man shoved himself upright. He opened his mouth to curse, but Varro slapped his palm over it. Then he hooked his foot behind Fronto's and tipped him backward over the edge of the well.

The pugio glittered between them. For an instant, it seemed Fronto would drive the blade into Varro's flesh. The two men groaned in their effort to defeat the other. But it was Varro's desperation that defeated Fronto's strength.

With his body pressed to his enemy, Varro levered back Fronto's head so his neck lay exposed. Then he twisted the pugio around so that it plunged into the exposed flesh. The optio screamed at last. But it was a short gurgle of blood, and Varro could feel his body going slack beneath him.

"If you hadn't been so greedy, you might have lived another day."

Blood flowed between his fingers, and Fronto sank back against the well.

Varro reached for the pugio, his hand slicked with blood. At the same moment, Fronto lashed his arms out. It was the spasm of a dying man. His legs kicked and his life escaped him as one long wet groan. But in that instant, he slapped Varro's hand.

The pugio spun in the air as if toying with him.

Then it plunged down into the well. The blade scraped and clanked, and eventually splashed into the darkness.

Varro gave a brief shout but pressed his lips shut. He was still within sight of the garrison. As Fronto struggled in his dying moments, Varro lifted him by his legs and dropped him into the well.

He stepped back, breathless and covered in blood. He had escaped captivity by his own side. But now he no longer looked like a Roman centurion. He, in fact, looked like an escaped captive.

Fronto's death weighed on him, even if he had left Varro with little other choice. He hoped one day he could forgive himself for all the evil he had done in the name of a greater service. But tonight he simply felt like a murderer.

That he was covered in blood would surprise no one. Pisa had just endured a surprise assault. That the blood was fresh would generate too many questions. He could think of nothing else to do. He stripped his tunic off and dropped it into the well. So much lay at the bottom of that dark shaft. He couldn't think of it now. Standing in his underwear, he felt the chill of the night wrap around his exposed body. He had no place to go other than where he had meant to go from the beginning.

Now his approach to the garrison drew attention. The soldiers on guard immediately frowned at his approach. Before he could even speak, one extended his arm and pointed away.

"Keep on walking. We're not taking in the injured here. Go to the square. That's where you'll find aid."

Varro did his best to straighten his shoulders and summon his centurion voice.

"My name is Marcus Varro, centurion of the Tenth Hastati. I'm here on behalf of Senator Flamininus with an urgent message for your commander. Please take me to him immediately."

The guards doubled over in laughter. But another voice called out from behind and cut it short.

Varro turned and found Fronto's subordinate breathless and red-faced. He raised a soggy tunic in his left hand and pointed with the other.

"Get him," he shouted through his wheezing. "He killed Optio Fronto."

13

Varro stared in horror at his accuser. As he pointed, he held up in his left hand the bloody tunic that Varro had just dropped into the well. The watery blood pattered on the stone as he approached, continuing to jab his finger at Varro.

"He killed my officer! His body's in the well!"

An icy terror coiled in Varro's stomach. The guards that had just so recently told him to move on now drew their swords. Varro heard the hiss of the blades as he fled the closing trap.

He didn't know the layout of Pisa. It was all darkness and confusion, alleyways that went nowhere, buildings that had no purpose. All he knew was that Pisa sat on the mouth of a great river. And that river was Rome's sole reason for wanting to control this city. He fled into the dark, thankful for a starless and moonless night to welcome him into the favorite shelter of criminals. For what had he become other than a criminal? Once more, violence had provided only a short-term answer to his problems.

Though he was tired, fear propelled him. He heard the guards' feet stamping on the stone stairs of the garrison fortress. He didn't look back, couldn't look back. It was a headlong plunge into the unknown. The guards shouted for him to stop, and he knew by running he incriminated himself. Of course, they would pull Fronto's body from the well. He was a known officer, and Varro was a half-naked killer. He had to run.

His sole advantage was in complete lightness of foot. Combined with his terror, he sailed ahead of his pursuers. Though they hailed other citizens, none of them responded. They were too tired, too frightened to do anything.

Varro cut hard to his left and bounded in between two buildings that looked as if they were holding each other up. He heard his pursuers close behind. Their hobnails clacked on the stone, and now in the dirt between buildings, they dragged on the earth. They continued to shout for him to stop, but it only drove Varro to run faster.

Bouncing against the walls as he fled, he ran towards the light, a faint and gray rectangle at the end of an alley that seemed more like a tunnel. He skidded out into the street, saw the two guards flickering in the dark behind him, then bolted to the right.

He exited into a wide street where citizens still watched the walls of their city. That Varro was nearly naked made no difference. He seemed to have exited into a poorer part of the city where such conditions were normal. He wished for bigger crowds, but there were enough people here that if he slowed down he might blend in. Against his instincts, he dropped to a jog as he pushed into a throng of dark and sweaty men discussing what the Ligurians might plan next. They frowned at his interruption, but accepted him. In fact, Varro joined them in their speculations.

His pursuers emerged from the alley, and Varro watched them warily. The small group he had joined asked what he thought the Ligurians might do next. He mumbled an incoherent answer, watching as his pursuers picked the right direction. The frustration at his enemy's success lent his words an edge, which his newfound friends interpreted as righteous anger. They patted his shoulder and promised Rome would crush the barbarians surrounding them.

The guards were more persistent than Varro expected. Rather than shrug and turn back, they too slowed their pace and studied the citizens gathered in the street at this unusual hour. In fact, the presence of garrison guards dispersed many of the citizens who lingered.

Varro used this as his excuse to leave his fake friends. He wished for a cloak or even an oversized tunic to hide himself under. Instead, his bare skin glowed in the scant light falling out of a nearby home. Even as he tried to walk away, he heard a renewed shout for him to stop.

He broke into a run.

From behind, civilians cursed as his pursuers shoved through them. Varro didn't know where he was going, but trusted he would find a place to ditch his pursuers. Apparently, Fronto must have been well loved by the guards at the garrison for these two to remain in pursuit.

He raced through streets, some empty, all dark, and all echoing with the thudding footsteps of his pursuers. It seemed there was no place he could escape. The city was finally calming, and now fewer people were on the street. The stitch in his side pulled him off balance. He was on the verge of surrender when he looked down a narrow street. A cart heaped with trash sat at the bottom of a hill.

He fled that way, looking behind to be certain his pursuers had not yet rounded the corner. In three steps, he bounded up and into the trash. It was mostly old rags, rotting hay, and other odorous waste. But it covered him enough that the guards would not spot him easily in the darkness.

They paused halfway down the hill realizing they lost him. Varro heard them mumbling between each other. Again, it took all his effort to contain his urge to flee. It was harder now to stay silent, as he still panted from his exertions. Fortunately, his pursuers were equally tired.

He heard them debate which way he had gone. Varro hadn't realized they were less certain of his location than they seemed. After a while, he heard the clack of hobnails as his pursuers turned back. That they walked and didn't run told Varro they had surrendered. He allowed himself a small smile for having evaded capture.

He huddled in the trash, something squishing beneath his knees. Maybe it was the remains of a spoiled fish. He didn't want to think about how far he had fallen in so few hours. As exhausted as he was, he felt able to lie here all night. It might have been a good idea, but for the oppressive stench. So, confident of his safety, he emerged from the trash. The rags sloughed off his body and bits of garbage clung to him. But he stepped out of the cart and into freedom.

For all the chaos of the last few moments, the street was quiet and dark. He made his way down its final stretch, careful to slide along the walls and out of sight from potential pursuers. In the distance, he still heard shouts, barking dogs, and the faint cries of the wounded. It was strange to think that all these people were now his enemies, or at least would regard him as an enemy.

He examined his hands and torso, all smeared with filth and blood. The trash had been an expedient hiding place. But now he regretted the stench it coated him in, fearing it would give him away to anyone nearby.

It was a strange thought that he was now on the run in Pisa. His message was lost. His gear was lost. Indeed, his honor was lost. It was time to find all these things again.

He wondered about Falco. Hadn't he climbed the walls with him? He doubted Falco had perished on those walls. He was too good a fighter to be defeated in such a paltry battle. But then, where had he gone? Perhaps he was mixed in with the prisoners.

Varro wouldn't find him hiding in this dark street. Yet Pisa was too large and too wide of an area to search. Not to mention, it wasn't his objective.

He still had not forgotten what he had come here to do. Somewhere along the edge of the southern wall was his message. It was still likely wrapped in its leather satchel, sitting beneath a pile of corpses. He would have to find it, dig it out, and bring it to the garrison headquarters.

Then hope that he could reach the commander and convince him of his authenticity.

He slapped away the dirt and the garbage clinging to him and realized that he had to find something to wear. Even in the disarray of a siege, he couldn't wander about the city half-naked and expect to be ignored. Certainly he could find a home with unattended laundry ripe for theft. He regretted stealing from the poor, but he would serve them better by completing his mission.

At last, reaching the end of the street, he peered out carefully, certain that no one was following.

But the moment he emerged into the faint light of a distant fire, a heavy figure collided with him. It rammed into him, knocking him flat. Varo sprawled out, winded and beaten. But his reflexes did not fail. He knew instinctively that a punch or a sword would follow on the strike. He flipped to his left, and a foot stamped down where his head would have been. The hobnails scraped on the stone, blowing puffs of air across Varro's face.

"Thought you'd get away." The voice was rough and weary. "Well, I knew you'd have to come out eventually."

The figure reached down and snatched at Varro. His heavy palms slid across his body, finding no purchase from the sweat and the slime covering his skin. It was Varro's opportunity to worm away and regain his feet.

There was no one on the street. In the distance, shadows flickered through what light remained. Calling for help would avail him nothing. Whoever came would be on the side of the guard. The guard himself was not tall, maybe only to Varro's chin, but he was determined.

And he held a sword in hand.

"Surrender," he said with curt finality. "I've got you. The chase is over."

"He wasn't as innocent as you think." Varro held up both hands as if to surrender. But he looked beyond his would-be captor and saw a long stretch of road leading into darkness. "I was defending myself."

"Of course you were." The guard leveled his sword and emerged from the darkness. Shadow obscured him, but Varro read the determination in the lines of his face. "Now just keep your hands up. You gave me quite a chase. I don't want to go through that again."

"You won't have to," Varro said.

He feinted left and then sprinted right. He had lulled the guard into believing he had given up. Now he tried to bring his sword around in time to catch Varro, but he bounded past.

The chase was on again, and the guard howled in frustration. "I'm going to cut your balls off!"

Varro had no intention of losing any part of his anatomy. The moment of rest was all he needed to regain his breath. Even after a summer of inactivity, Varro was still in better shape than most active-duty soldiers.

He bounded down the street, looking desperately for a new avenue of escape. Behind him, hobnails clacked on the stone pavement.

Then he heard a screech and scrape and the guard cursed as his body thudded to the ground. Varro stopped short. He turned and found his pursuer laid out on his back in the middle of the street.

Running back to the guard, he dropped atop his body. The fall had momentarily dazed him. Were it not for his helmet, he might have broken his skull against the pavement. Varro snatched the helmet away, then slammed it against the guard's head. It snapped to the side and the guard went limp beneath him.

"Sorry about that. Your tenacity was not rewarded, but I admire it still."

He grabbed the guard by his ankles and dragged him to the side of the street. Though it was dark and no one was around, he could not risk being seen. His heart thudded against his ribs as he worked with desperate speed. The guard's tunic was a poor fit, but better than nudity. The helmet was likewise too tight. So, he let the chin strap dangle. The guard was already groaning by the time Varro had relieved him of his sword, his pugio, and the rest of his harness.

"Again, sorry about this. But better to steal from you than a poor civilian."

He wished for something to bind the guard's hands, but he had wasted enough time. He was already groggy and groaning about revenge. But Varro now looked like a soldier, and the soldier looked like a criminal.

The only things he left behind on the soldier were his sandals. He preferred his own and intended to get them back. But he had also seen how running with hobnails on stone could lead to disaster. Until he could clear his name, he had to remain unseen. Hobnails were good for many things, but stealth was not one of them.

He jogged away from the moaning guardsman, now sure of his escape. He found another dark alley to gather his thoughts.

Fronto had confiscated his gear and stored it in his own tent. Now that he had acquired temporary weapons and an ill-fitting tunic, it was less important to recover his gear. That could come once he had cleared things up with the commander. Finding his message from Senator Flamininus was his primary objective. Then he should seek Falco. His support would help in dealing with Pisa's commander.

He let himself sink to the ground, his back against a rough stucco wall. The message became less relevant with every day that passed. Soon Consul Minucius would arrive to relieve Pisa. Delivering that message with only days between its arrival and the consul's made little sense.

Tonight's disaster could not have been foreseen. He regretted wasting time on Paullus. It all felt far away now, but soon his mission would either complete or fail. Then he would face the question of Paullus's disappearance.

Rather than dare anymore this night, he allowed himself to sleep. The moment he knew he had been safe, the urge to close his eyes had become overwhelming. Now he couldn't fight it. He would search for the message with the dawn.

He awakened the next morning to a voice vibrating through the wall behind him. A man was shouting for something and banging on what sounded like a table. Varro leaped up and grabbed for his stolen gladius.

Pisa had come to life again. At the end of his alley, he saw people crossing back and forth across the bright square of light. He had slept past dawn. All of his joints ached, but especially the backs of his legs and calves. He stretched and rubbed them, then straightened his back and headed toward the opposite end of the alley where there was less activity.

He stepped with confidence into the street. He dressed as a garrison guard, and so needed to act like one. The citizens here went about their business like any other day. Varro had never been inside a major city under active siege. He had imagined those living under such conditions would walk with their backs stooped and their eyes forever searching for danger. Indeed, he saw some who came close to that description. But most acted as if forty thousand Ligurian barbarians did not surround them.

Varro was unsure of the wall he had come over. He only knew it was not near the river. That was to the north of the city, fortunately, where most of the population conducted their daily business. So, he moved against traffic, confidently meeting the eye of anyone he passed.

The madness of the night before had left few scars on the city itself. Some buildings had been burned, probably more from accidents caused by panic than the attack itself. There was a terrible odor that hung in the air. It was the usual foul stench of crowded cities, but worsened by the smell of decay. Varro knew that despite appearances, chaos might erupt at any moment. The Ligurians might be disorganized and inexperienced in siege warfare, but it would only take one breach in the hard shell of Pisa's defenses to plunge the city into bitter suffering.

Arriving at the southern walls, Varro looked up at the ruined parapets and then at the corpses below them. He had no doubts that his message was somewhere in the mess of bodies, charred wood, and lost weapons. He had arrived unchallenged but now saw soldiers and citizens alike picking through the refuse. Rotting corpses would bring disease, and friends and enemies alike had to be burned for the sake of the city. It was mostly citizens at work, young boys pressed into service by the urban centuries. The soldiers stood about resting on their spears and shields and helping only where needed.

Varro had two approaches to this problem. He could try to sneak up the side of the wall and then investigate the debris for signs of his satchel. Otherwise, he could act as a guard. He might even join a team, though his poorly fitting tunic might draw attention. Worse still, they might ask him for details of his rank and his unit. Varro was uncertain how the urban centuries organized themselves. He knew that at least the rank of optio existed, but there might be fewer centurions than normal legions.

He settled on a third option. As he stood back from the line of workers and soldiers, he noted the most likely place of his defeat last night. It had been all confusion and darkness, but he could remember certain outlines of buildings that now stood prominently in the morning light. So, rather than try to sneak up on the spot or integrate himself with an existing unit, he just simply began his search.

And it worked.

The satchel sat atop two slain Ligurians. He did not want to look carefully at their ruined bodies. But it was obvious why no one had approached these corpses yet. They were thick with flies, as flies were everywhere along this part of the wall. But their innards still glistened inside the cavities of their shattered bodies. Their blood and bones now dried on the pavement beneath them. Certainly, all along the wall, more bodies like this lay in wait for someone to scrape them up.

Varro picked his way among broken stones, shattered wood, bent weapons, and dented helmets. He lifted the satchel away by the long strap that had been cut from his body. He held it up and aside. Blood still crusted on it and flies swirled angrily, as if they had nothing else to feast upon.

He reeled it in, nose wrinkled in disgust, then opened the flap to find the parchment rolled up safely within. He had found his message.

He turned to retreat from the carnage, but encountered a line of guards behind him. One was immediately recognizable.

"I knew he'd come back to the wall." The guard who had accompanied Varro to the garrison and later found his officer dead in the well stood with hands on his hips. "He wants to go out the way he came in. But that's not going to happen. He will not see the outside ever again."

14

Varro was tired of running. He clasped the satchel containing Flamininus's message to his side. His other hand reached for the stolen gladius at his hip. He drew it and leveled it at the four men arrayed against him.

"I have proof of my claims," he said, holding up the satchel. "Not that the four of you are concerned with anything like the truth. You want me dead to cover your crimes."

Their leader, who had identified Varro the prior night, drew his sword in response.

"Claim whatever you like. Fronto's body was pulled out of the well last night, and I know you killed him. Now, we're taking his revenge."

Had it been only the four men against him, Varro might have considered a fighting retreat. But he lacked even a shield. Worse still, nearby soldiers now appeared interested in the brewing conflict. These soldiers, who had been glad to idle while civilians labored at clearing the mess of bodies, turned to watch the growing conflict.

It occurred to Varro that these men did not have to be his

enemies. If he acted with confidence and proclaimed himself with conviction, he might persuade them. It was an unlikely possibility, but fighting was a losing situation.

In his hesitation, his accusers fanned out around him, leaving him no path to escape. So, he instead looked at the other soldiers watching from the distance and begged for their help.

"I'm on an important mission," he said. "I carry a message from Rome to the commander Marcus Cincius."

He held his satchel aloft to emphasize his point. It drew the attention of other soldiers, but served as a call to battle for his accusers.

"Enough of your lies!" The new leader of Fronto's cronies, sword already drawn, charged.

Contrary to his instincts, Varro backed up and kept his sword forward only in defense. He looked toward the other soldiers and shouted out to them.

"Help me! I must get through for the sake of all."

He had no time to say more before he had to run. It galled him to flee yet again. But rather than flee he ran toward the other soldiers. They seemed startled and unsure of whose side to take. Varro held his satchel forward like a battle standard. Behind him, the corrupt soldiers did not relent.

"Stop him! He's wanted for murder!"

Now soldiers and civilians alike stopped working. The soldiers drew their weapons or lowered their spears. Civilians fled, realizing they were about to be ensnared in a fight that did not concern them. Varro ran to the wary soldiers, sword lowered but still in hand, with his satchel held overhead for all to see.

"This message must get through. It is vital for all of you."

Fronto's cronies now trapped Varro between themselves and his would-be saviors. Their counterparts on the other side brandished their weapons, and the cronies were wise enough to draw short of clashing with them.

To Varro's relief, an officer emerged from the tangle of soldiers in front.

"What's this, then? Drawn weapons? Who the fuck are we fighting? Everyone stand back and lower the damn weapons."

He was a stout man with a recently broken nose and bulging eyes that glared out from beneath his dented helmet. Varro immediately felt a kinship with this man. But whether he felt the same toward him remained to be seen.

Varro's accuser answered without delay.

"Sir, we caught this one murdering a fellow soldier. I saw it myself. He stabbed my optio in the back and threw him into the well by headquarters. The body is there, sir."

The officer's face folded up in disgust, and he scowled at Varro.

"Is that so? What have you got to say for yourself?"

Holding forward his satchel, he met the officer's eyes.

"I am Centurion Marcus Varro, recently of the Tenth Hastati Iberia. I am here on a special assignment from Senator Flamininus. He sends a message to your commander Marcus Cincius. You may inspect the bag, but you must not break the seal on the message. That is for your commander only."

Varro's chest tightened when he allowed the satchel to pass into the officer's hands. Other soldiers leaned in to see if Varro had spoken the truth.

"We caught him coming over the walls with the barbarians, sir." The leader of the four cronies stepped closer. "And whatever else he says, he murdered my optio. That's a fact, sir."

Varro stared at the officer before him as he fished out the rolled-up papyrus. The senator's official seal caught the morning light, shadow blackening the lines. He bent his lips, then let it drop back into the satchel. The surrounding men likewise nodded as if they were convinced. Varro extended his hand.

"I will have that message returned. And you will see me to your commander. I will explain everything to him." Varro now looked over his shoulder toward the four cronies who stood at his back.

"These four have a good reason to want me dead. After all, they took me captive and sought to extort me. Therefore, they have placed all of Pisa at risk for their own benefit."

Varro extended his palm, his expression flat and firm. The officer seemed to consider both sides of the situation.

"This is over my head," he said. He put the satchel behind his back. "Let's take everyone to headquarters. Someone there ought to figure this one out."

"You'll have no problem with me," Varro said. "But you will return that message. It is my duty and obligation to deliver it to the commander myself. I will not allow that message to leave my sight."

The officer's eyes narrowed and he stepped closer to Varro, tilting back his chin.

"I know who you claim to be. And who you claim to serve. But that means nothing here. I'm in command until a superior officer tells me I'm not. And I don't see anyone else around. So, you'll come with me as will your friends and we'll all have a little talk down at headquarters."

Varro had no choice. He bristled at the command but knew the officer was merely doing his duty. He had also saved Varro from a fight he would not have won. So he inclined his head.

"I'll do as you say. But I ask a single favor. Do not break the seal on the message. It is for your commander only."

The fiery challenge in the officer's eyes abated, and he seemed about to speak.

Then Varro heard the scrape of a foot on the stone behind him.

Years of training and instinct took over. He stepped aside and spun about, raising his sword.

The lead crony had driven his own blade at the center of

Varro's back. It was a reckless and desperate stab. But now Varro was no longer the target. His attacker had intended to end his life in a single thrust. And so his force carried through.

The blade sank deep into the officer's gut. He wore only a simple bronze chest piece. He left his shield aside to supervise the work being done under the walls. It cost him his life.

He slid forward grabbing the hand that had stabbed him, blood gurgling from his lips, his eyes bulging to the point of bursting. "You fucking bastard! You won't..."

Seizing on the confusion, Varro shouted, "Murderer! He killed the centurion."

The officer crashed to his knees and slid off the sword that had impaled him. The cronies, now realizing they were surrounded and outnumbered, were forced to fight.

Varro understood his opportunity. The leader of the cronies had wanted to silence him, even if he had rightly accused him of murder. It was the miscalculation of a fool.

And Varro's chance.

He rammed his sword into the neck of the cronies' leader. The blade sawed to the bone, nearly taking his head off. He collapsed upon the centurion, his lifeblood mingling with his victim's.

The regular soldiers outnumbered the cronies two to one, leading to a brutally short clash. In the space of a dozen exchanges, three more bodies collapsed to the ground. Only one made any sound, a low pitiful moaning verging on a sob.

The stunning violence left the remaining soldiers breathless and confused. One man shoved aside the body atop his officer, then flipped him over and held his face in both hands like a lover. It seemed to Varro as if he were silently begging the officer to return to life. But he had gone on to whatever fate awaited him beyond death.

Varro crouched down next to him and placed a hand on his shoulder.

"I'm certain he was an excellent officer. He did not deserve to die this way."

Varro felt others step behind him, and their blue shadows crept over the corpse of their officer like a death shroud.

"I must get through to your commander." Varro spoke in soft and comforting tones, unfortunately accustomed to speaking like this to the grieving. "The message I deliver will vindicate his death."

Varro stood again. He had used that soft moment to slide his satchel out from beneath the dead centurion. His helmet lacked any feathers or decoration to mark his rank. But to Varro's mind, he could be nothing less. He had all the qualities of a good leader. He regretted the pointless death.

The soldiers were quick to regain their wits. Death was everywhere, and the only thing shocking about this one was it happened at the hands of their own side. Soon, another assumed command and ordered all the bodies to be carried to the square where they would be burned. Cremating the unfortunate and nameless centurion with his killers was an insult, but also expedient given the state of siege.

Three men led him back across Pisa. He was uncertain if these were escorts or guards. None of the men had any mood to speak, and Varro realized it was better this way. Carrying his blood-soaked satchel, he made the long trip back across Pisa to the headquarters he had fled the night before.

In the daylight, he saw how perilously close the well was from the front steps of the garrison. He could never have dispatched Fronto as he did last night even under the barest illumination. Two guards remained at attention on the steps, though clearly not the one Varro had knocked out. He prayed he had not made his report yet. With luck, he was still somewhere in Pisa recovering.

Varro's three guards spoke briefly to the men on the steps, and they waved him through.

"You're going to the centurion of the watch," said one of his escorts. "He'll decide what to do with you from there. We'll have to give our reports."

"I understand," Varro said. "Just remember who killed your officer. When I make my report, I'll be clear about what happened. Hopefully, you'll never have to deal with scum like them again."

Whether he made an impression on his guards, Varro didn't know. They simply led him into the stone building and placed him in the custody of other soldiers.

Varro was immediately relieved of his weapons and the blood-soaked satchel. He knew better than to protest now. The commander was in this building, and he was soon to complete this mission.

He sat on a plain wooden bench with one man to guard him. What ensued was a long period of administration. A secretary had come with a wax slate to capture Varro's information and his purpose. It took him several trips back and forth between whomever he reported to and Varro. Each time, he had a new set of questions regarding the various deaths since Varro's arrival. He tried to remain patient and understanding, realizing anything less would be of no benefit to his mission. But he still had an urge to scream in the face of all these administrators. Did anyone realize a Ligurian horde waited outside, or that they might attack again? He appreciated composure in adversity. But not administration over urgency.

At last, a new man came to greet him. He wore a clean cream-colored tunic, and from his straight back and muscular legs Varro knew he was a soldier. He relieved the guard and took Varro up a flight of stairs. They didn't speak. Instead, the creak of wood underfoot was the only sound.

They emerged into a large war room. There were maps of hide and parchment spread out on a heavy desk. A pugio tacked down one corner of a map. Behind the heavy desk, a balding man, squat with a square body, leaned on the desk with both hands spread wide to support him. His beige tunic showed sweat stains at the collar. The muscles of his face pulled taut, drawing his features to the center so it seemed his cheeks were wider than reality.

Varro's escort stepped forward and put both hands behind his back then stood to attention.

"This is the one, sir. We've collected his statements." He then produced Varro's bloody satchel and held it forward. "And here is the message he claims to be delivering."

Commander Marcus Cincius did not look up from his map. Instead, he waved a hand toward the corner of his cluttered desk. "Put it there, and you are dismissed. Thank you."

The escort gave Varro a thin smile as he left the war room. He waited in silence, listening to the escort's footsteps echoing down the stairs behind him.

The commander focused on the map spread out before him. Varro leaned forward to study it as well. It was a scratchy and faded layout of Pisa. He could tell by the wide river outlined in thick ink lines. It ran through the city like a dagger. Piles of colored stones seemed to represent the Ligurian forces, as these were piled up and encircled the scratchy ink walls. Less encouragingly, piles of naturally colored stone spread out all around the map walls. Only small clusters held points like towers and gates in any concentration.

Commander Cincius jumped a palm full of stones in his hand as he considered the map. He held one flat piece between a thin finger and thumb, and this hovered from one small cluster to another. With a long sigh, he let the pile of stones clatter to the desk beside him. He still didn't look up, but rested heavily on the table.

"If only soldiers were as common as stones. We can hold out, but for how much longer? It won't be long now before the Ligurians find a way over the wall. They came close last night. I suppose I should be thankful they're not smarter in the art of siege warfare. But thankfulness is in short supply."

He looked up and stepped back from the table. He ran his thin hands along his bald head and let out another long sigh. His eyes narrowed on Varro.

"Centurion Marcus Varro, sir. I come with an urgent message from Senator Flamininus."

Strangely, the commander merely nodded. Instead, his tired and baggy eyes searched Varro. Whatever he saw, it seemed to cause him discomfort. His brows drew tighter, and he folded his arms. A faded tattoo showed under the sleeve of his tunic. Varro couldn't tell what it was.

"The message is right here, sir." Varro lifted the bloody satchel and held it forward. The commander's eyes drifted to it, but then slid back to Varro's.

"It seems you've been involved in this series of incidents last night. You are a centurion? Then you ought to know what should follow."

Varro swallowed hard. He replaced the satchel on the desk and stood to attention. He knew what ought to follow and knew better than to say another word. Commander Cincius returned his hard stare until a tiny smile formed. It seemed a gesture he was no longer familiar with but had once known.

"Be at ease, Centurion. I'm sure there is a good story behind all of this. I've heard so much about it." The commander nodded toward the satchel on his desk. "Fresh blood. I hope it's Ligurian."

"Of course, sir." Varro once more proffered the satchel.

This time, the commander accepted it. He held it out by the strap like a dead fish. He then used his own dagger to lift away the satchel flap. Flamininus's message slipped out, and the seal remained unbroken. Varro breathed a sigh of relief. That message had been through as much as he had. Other than some blood stains, it appeared the message had survived. Now, Varro hoped he would as well.

The commander broke the seal, and his eyes swiftly absorbed the contents of the papyrus. Then he threw it aside. Varro watched it curl up and roll to the edge of the table, where a stone stopped it from falling to the floor.

"The message at last. I assume you suffered a great deal to get inside these walls and then to reach me here. The blood on this satchel tells a good bit of that story."

"It was an ordeal, sir." Varro looked at the abandoned papyrus. "I trust you understand relief is on the way. Given the delays we experienced in getting here, I expect the consul's army is not far behind us."

The commander gave a perfunctory nod. "Yes, yes. I have understood that for a while now. What I need is not messengers crawling through the Ligurian camp and then over my walls to deliver the same message over and over. What I need is the legion to show up and drive off these barbarians."

Varro tilted his head. "Sir, I don't understand. You have only just received my message."

"Your message." The commander folded his arms behind his back and stepped around the desk. When he reached Varro's side, he placed a hand on his shoulder. He gave it a gentle, sympathetic squeeze. "But your message is not the first to arrive. A few days ago, while the Ligurians were still figuring out their plans, another messenger from Senator Flamininus arrived with the same message. I'm sorry, Centurion. You suffered much for no better purpose than to repeat a promise that I'm now eager to see fulfilled. And I know you can't do anything about it. So, I will send you back to the consul with the same message I gave to the last man. It is simple. A message you can carry in your head and be assured you'll deliver it with complete accuracy. Hurry. That's my reply to the consul."

"Sir, I don't understand. We were not near Pisa at that time, and there was no one else to deliver this message. I'm certain of that."

But there was someone else, Varro realized. In that moment of understanding, he saw the commander's smile widen.

"He suggested another might follow him here, but that this messenger would likely be delayed. I assume he was speaking of you. The one who preceded you is quite a prestigious man, not the sort I'd expect to be delivering messages."

"Yes," Varro said. He tried to conceal his bitterness, but even he could hear it in his own voice. "Marcellus Paullus comes from a renowned family. I only wonder how he got here before we did."

The commander shrugged, then reached out for the papyrus. "No matter. I am glad the Senate has finally decided to send help. And it is good that I have it in writing and by a senator's own hand at that. I don't trust many politicians, but I trust Flamininus's word. I only hope Consul Minucius can get his legion on the march. Bring my message to him with the same dedication you delivered this message to me. You will do all of Pisa a great service."

"Of course, sir. I will make it my duty."

But Varro wondered what else Paullus had done without them, and what it might mean for their future.

15

Varro slipped out the southern gate under the cover of darkness. The wall guards wiped sweat from their brows as they closed the doors behind him. He faced the glowing dots of campfire light, then heard the bolt thud into place behind him. The heavy doors of the gate rattled against his back. At last, he was out of Pisa and again facing the Ligurians on their own terrain.

He rested with his back against the doors long enough to get his bearings. As it was when he first approached the city, the Ligurian camp spread out in clusters of warriors and tribes. He had only to stick to the dark spaces between the campfires, and he could trace his way back to the foothills.

It was a strange feeling, but he was glad to be free of Pisa. His own side had mistreated him, which would have been understandable had he not been taken hostage to small-minded greed. He had tried to appear as a barbarian, after all. But once over the walls, he had not expected to become a fugitive. He was grateful to Commander Cincius for reviewing his testimony and attributing everything to the confusion of battle. It also helped that the only living witness to Varro's actions was the lone garrison guard that had chased him through the city. Varro had hit him on the head hard enough that he had scrambled memories of their encounter. Fronto's corpse was an inconvenient question that ultimately did not matter. From what Varro could determine, he was not as well loved as he originally thought.

The commander had fed him and offered him a place to rest. Then he gave him an escort out of the city. In the meantime, he had gone seeking his own gear. But he couldn't locate where he had been held. In the end, he was wearing another man's tunic and carrying another man's weapons. They felt alien to him. They would serve well enough, but the sword grip did not fit in his palm as he was accustomed to. The pugio at his hip was even stranger. It was sharp and well cared for, except for a small nick in its edge that Varro would never have tolerated in his own equipment.

He had, once again, lost his pugio. Before setting out to find Falco and Curio, he swore to find a better way to indicate his membership in Servus Capax. Marking it on a weapon was just not practical. It might serve for senators and others who would never get their hands dirty in the field. But for his purposes, it was a liability. This would be the first thing he would change if he had the authority.

Now he ducked low and swept across the knee-high grass into darkness. He sped between the blank spaces in the camp. He paused and crouched low whenever he heard a voice or spotted movement. On both sides, he could hear the Ligurians laughing and snoring their night away. He moved unseen through the deep lines until he emerged into the trees at the far side.

He was back where he started.

With only starlight tonight, he could hardly pick a path through the sparse trees. Yet he was eager to return to the rally point and discover what had happened to Falco. He also wondered how Curio had passed his days waiting for their return. There was a new phase to their mission, though perhaps not the original one.

They had to get ahead of Paullus.

Whatever that snake planned, Varro was certain it would be to his advantage alone. Sabotaging the Ligurian camp or capturing a leader for intelligence would mean nothing if Paullus was away scheming against them. He did not know why he would do so. He just knew subterfuge was in that patrician's blood.

After a few hesitant turns, and doubling back at least twice, Varro found their well-concealed camp. He paused and crouched low behind a rock. He didn't want to be mistaken for an enemy and have his friends run him through. Neither could he be sure that there weren't enemies now occupying their camp. He had no idea what happened during his absence.

Impatience eventually defeated caution, and he tentatively stood from behind the rock. He whispered, "Curio? Falco?"

Something that he had mistaken for a bush turned to face him. He recognized Curio's bright face, even though it was daubed with mud. Varro now stood up and raised both hands.

Falco crawled out from beneath their hidden tent. "And the hero of Pisa returns!"

The joy of their reunion did not survive the news that Paullus had been there before them.

"That bastard," Falco said, driving his fist into his open palm. "How did he get in there before us?"

"According to the commander," Varro said. "he approached the walls during daylight. The Ligurians hadn't yet made any serious attempts at taking the city until just the other day. They'd been content to terrorize the countryside instead. The city defenders let him in and escorted him right to Commander Cincius."

"Why does he have all the luck?" Curio adjusted his sling. "Instead, I got a busted shoulder and we've been living like animals for no reason."

Falco growled. "Well, I'm going to bleed all the luck out of that little bastard when I get ahold of him. This is a team. He's acting like it's a solo mission. Varro and I risked our lives to get that message through. If he had a better way to do it, fine. But he didn't need to leave us out of it."

Varro narrowed his eyes at Falco and tilted his head back.

"Speaking of luck, how did you get here?"

"Well, I got to the top just like you did." Falco rubbed the back of his neck and looked aside. "It was madness up there. I couldn't convince our boys I was on their side. I tried to defend myself. But the Ligurians kept encouraging me to fight. I was the biggest man on that ladder, and I think they were depending on me to widen the gap. So, when you fell and the Ligurians sounded a retreat I knew I had to get out of there. I was about halfway down the ladder when our boys tipped it over. It wasn't too much of a fall at that point. The bigger problem was all the barbarians who wanted to talk to me. After that, I'd become something like a hero to them. I just laughed and waved it all off and as soon as no one was looking I ran as fast as I could. And here I am."

Varro shook his head. "So, you just left me to my fate?"

Falco continued to look aside, though a small smile came to his lips.

"It wouldn't make much sense for both of us to die up on that wall. Besides, I figured you'd sort it out with our boys. You're better with words than I am."

"Well, words failed me this time."

He gestured they should all sit in the pitlike area of their hidden camp. Varro sat upon a flat rock and stretched out his legs. The other two leaned forward to hear him tell the story of his capture and ordeals within the walls of Pisa. When done, both Curio and Falco were shaking their heads in disgust.

"Well, you can take my shield." Curio dragged it up from the ground and slid it towards Varro. "With my arm like it is I won't have a need for it."

Varro looked at the shield for a long moment. It was the oblong shape of the Ligurian shield that got him into this trouble. However, he had to be practical. He collected the shield off the ground and set it beside himself. He then asked what they had been doing during his time in Pisa.

Curio explained how he monitored the Ligurian camp. He guessed at several likely locations for their leader. However, he could not get close enough to verify anything.

"They were building a covered battering ram." Curio pointed to the north. "It looks too big for the job. If they're going to hit the gates squarely, then they're going to have trouble getting it up the road and lining it up properly."

Varro gazed at the northern stars. "Well, with luck, by the time they figure out how to attack Pisa the tribune will be here with his legions."

"Well, what do we do now?" Falco asked. "Our mission was to collect intelligence. Curio has done about what any of us can do. We can't find their leader, though I guess we could try harder. But I'm worried about Paullus. What is that bastard about?"

Varro groaned and rubbed his legs. He didn't have an answer to Falco's question.

"Whatever he is planning, he has been planning for a long while. Remember, he carried what I thought looked like a palace on the back of his horse. Who knows what he was carrying in there and what purpose he intended for it? We've seen that his servant knew where to go."

"I don't know about that," Falco said. "He ended up a Ligurian prisoner."

"An accident," Varro said. "His master probably abandoned him the moment there was any threat. Paullus has something in mind. But I cannot figure out what it is. He must have known he would be on this mission with us. Otherwise, how could he have prepared all of this in advance?"

The three of them fell into thoughtful silence. Cricket song filled the air as Varro wrestled with this question. In the end, he surrendered with a shrug.

"We should make one last pass at the Ligurian camp. Whatever we can determine about their strength and disposition will help Consul Minucius. After that, we go to meet him as fast as we can. Commander Cincius urged me to deliver his message. Given that the Ligurians have already attempted the walls and are building a battering ram, we have little time."

"It seemed like Pisa's defenders have things in hand to me." Falco rubbed his jaw. "I almost got my head taken off. They might be garrison soldiers, but they fought like legionaries."

"I don't doubt their fighting spirit," Varro said. "I saw the commander's battle map. The moment the Ligurians get a foothold, the city is going to be overrun. He doesn't have the men to face forty thousand barbarians. That is work for the legions."

They continued to discuss various possibilities for Paullus's actions. Ultimately, they could think of nothing better than Paullus wanting to be the hero. To Varro's mind, that was a weak theory. There appeared to be too many other factors at play for it to just be glory-seeking. Certainly, Paullus considered himself superior to them and bridled under Varro's leadership. But there were other ways to achieve supremacy than abandoning them.

Setting aside the matter of their wayward companion, they let Curio lead them in one more sweep of the Ligurian camp. Even with his arm in a sling, he was as agile and stealthy as always. As they wove among the trees back down to the Ligurian lines, Varro lost sight of him more than once. When they arrived, they sheltered among the trees and bushes at the edge of the camp. Under Curio's direction, they crawled north. Along the way, he showed where leaders might be. From the size of the tents and the guards posted outside these, it seemed likely that someone important rested inside. Varro noted these locations, keeping a mental tally of the number of leaders they counted. Whether that would be useful or not remained to be seen.

The battering ram was larger than even Curio described. The main beam was composed of three thick logs all lashed together. A protective housing for the ram operators was halfway constructed. But Varro could see right away it would be too big and unwieldy to make it up to the gates while under attack from the defenders. However, if they landed the ram squarely, Pisa's gates would likely fold up in a single blow.

Falco and Curio covered him while he scratched notes onto his vellum map. In the darkness, he could only make brief notations. He would expand on these later. While he focused on this, he didn't see the Ligurian horsemen leaving the camp. Falco pointed after the three horses that left the camp. Behind them, a small group of Ligurians watched them go. Even in the sketchy light, Varro was certain a leader, perhaps even a chief, was among that group.

All three of them huddled together, watching the small cluster of Ligurians at the edge of the camp. Curio whispered, "We could try to nab the strong one. He looks important."

Varro studied the large barbarian that stood out from the small group at the edge of the camp. He wore a black fur cloak and a circlet flashed around his head. While he seemed important and was far enough away from the main camp to be vulnerable, Varro did not think it a good idea.

"They can bring up reinforcements before we could escape." Instead, he looked toward the horses trotting south along the outside edge of the camp. "But if we can catch up with the riders, we should be able to overtake them. There must be something important afoot. Otherwise, why would one of their leaders come to dispatch a simple message?"

Falco nodded. "I'm sure you can run circles around a galloping horse. But speaking for myself, my legs aren't up to the task."

"Remember what I said about horses? When we need them, the enemy will supply them." Varro sat up straighter and scanned the camp. "Curio, in your wanderings did you locate any horse pickets?"

Without a word, he led them off to the north. Falco complained they were headed the wrong way. But Curio simply waved him forward while crouching low to the knee-high grass. Soon, they arrived at a large tree whose roots grew around a heavy boulder that looked like it clutched it to its trunk. They piled up behind this, and Curio pointed to the flickering campfires beyond.

Varro delighted at the line of horses picketed at the edge of camp. Spiked barriers protected against intruders. The Ligurians evidently planned to keep their horses ready to deploy against a cavalry threat on the flank. They could easily lift the barriers away, and free the horses for mass action. However, they only needed to slip three off the line, something the barrier wouldn't hinder.

In any culture, horses were the luxury of the rich. Therefore, the horses would be always guarded. While Varro could see no one on duty, he knew they were present. He and Falco would approach from either side of the picket line, and Curio would remain ready to lead horses away. With his arm in a sling, he could do little else.

They both drew their pugiones as they crept up on either side of the long picket. It was a rope anchored between two trees, and that is where Varro spotted the first guard. He leaned against it, his spear not even in hand. He seemed to stare up at the sky as if asking a question of his gods. Varro would soon send him to a direct meeting.

He used the horses for cover. Some sidestepped or snorted at his passage, but these horses were used to men moving around them. When he reached the end, he was positioned just behind the tree. He could hear the Ligurian breathing as he pressed to the other side of the tree.

In one deft move, Varro slipped along the rough bark and then flipped atop the unsuspecting sentry. He drove his pugio into his stomach while his left hand clamped over his mouth. The guard flattened against the tree trunk, stunned. In the darkness, Varro saw his eyes flash white and then felt him weaken and droop. He guided him to the grass with the pugio still in his guts.

Varro hovered over him, assuring himself no one had seen him. Only then did he slowly withdraw the blade, then continue to slide around the tree trunk to face the horses again. He wicked fresh blood from the blade, knowing that the scent of it might frighten the horses. They might be trained for battle or may just have been pressed into the service by their owners. Varro did not want to take any chances.

Across the way, Falco had the same success. His tall, muscular shape showed against the stars of the northern sky. Already, Curio led two horses away from the picket.

All of them were soon riding north and on the trail of the Ligurian messengers. Varro knew they would not dare bring their horses to a gallop in the darkness. Neither would he, but he only wanted to trail the riders until they were far enough from the main camp that any sounds of combat would not bring reinforcements.

Even though they moved beneath branches and around bushes in dark woods, Varro's experience in Numidia served him well tonight. He had once led a band of stealthy raiders. They were known as the mountain ghosts. They would stalk Carthaginian caravans on horseback, and strike from the cover of a hill crest or a small stand of palm trees. It had been an exhilarating life, if only for a brief time.

Tonight, he planned the same for these three unsuspecting barbarians.

The riders were evidently attempting to conceal their passage. They moved at a steady pace but shied from their own lines. Varro understood that their mission was secret; otherwise, they would have been dispatched during the day where they could gallop. Therefore, he had to be cautious in trailing them. Though he couldn't see it himself, he was sure the riders checked their rear area for anyone following.

He led their column, with Falco behind and Curio bringing up the rear. Curio's injury limited his effectiveness. But he could still help contain the riders. Varro only needed one alive.

He was waiting for a clearing or other opening where he could overtake the riders. Yet that moment lay hidden in the darkness ahead. They all leaned against the necks of their horses, trying to conceal themselves as they followed.

They would soon come within striking distance. The three riders carried swords and small shields, but seemed otherwise unarmored. They were not large men, probably selected for their size and ability to maneuver at high speed. Their direction now cut to the east.

Suddenly, one of the Ligurians called out and all three horses broke into a run.

"They've seen us." Varro urged his horse ahead and drew his gladius. "Let's bring them down!"

16

The hoofbeats of six horses echoed through the thin woods. Varro led the others in maneuvering between trees and over fallen logs. While the horse was not his own, it seemed to sense the next command. If Varro was not mistaken, the chase excited his horse. Maybe one horse in the lead was a friend. He was grateful for an obedient and swift mount.

The three Ligurians ahead of him were equal to his riding ability. They slipped between trees and leaped across ditches and over logs. Though the night was dark, and starlight dusted a blue haze over their path, the riders glided ahead as if on an empty road.

"Faster!" Varro urged his mount to keep pace. It responded with a snort and pulled ahead of the others.

The rearmost Ligurian turned his horse and then grabbed something out of the darkness. He heaved it into Varro's way.

A thin, dead trunk collapsed across the gap between two other trees. Varro's path led directly into the trunk and threatened to knock him from his mount. The Ligurian shouted a curse and then galloped after his companions.

Varro yanked back on the reins, barely able to turn his horse from crashing into the fallen tree. It screamed in protest as its hooves drove up clods of earth. But it turned in time to avoid a collision. The dead tree was within reach of Varro's hand. He cursed and waved his sword at Falco.

"Go around! Keep after them. I'm right behind you."

Falco thundered past, deftly guiding his mount around the trap. Curio broke to the other side, his horse bounding in long strides. Again, cursing his luck, Varro turned his horse to skirt the tree in his path.

Now he was in the rear and struggling to catch up with the other two. It was rough ground that neither side had any hope of navigating without an accident. Yet all of them were better riders than most. While he was not as refined and drilled as a legion cavalryman, he had learned dexterity and finesse from his Numidian teachers. He could excel in terrain where a traditionally instructed rider would struggle.

The lead Ligurian slipped out of Varro's sight, vanishing into the silvery darkness ahead. He could just see Curio on the right and Falco on the left. Between them, the last of the Ligurian riders shrank between the trees. They were escaping.

As he was about to mouth a prayer to Fortuna, the goddess answered his unvoiced request. The Ligurians' middle horse screamed and then pitched forward. While he could not see the rider's fate, Varro heard his anguished cry followed by a heavy thud and snap. The following rider's horse collided with the fallen one. Though they were enemies, it still pained Varro to see the tangle of horses and bodies roll through the trees and brush before flipping to a stop.

Falco had already drawn his sword and drove his mount at one of the riders attempting to stand. Curio continued past the crash. He could not help with the combat. But he could continue to follow the escaping rider.

The recovered Ligurian staggered under Falco's vicious blow.

He had only time to raise his shield before Falco knocked him flat again. Varro saw no sign of the other rider who had created the accident other than his horse wrestling to free itself from the tangle.

Varro arrived at the twisting mass of horseflesh and shattered shields. Pulling in front of their path, he looked for the other rider. The unfortunate Ligurian lay beneath his kicking horse and was completely still.

"Take him alive!" Varro shouted. It seemed one rider might escape and the other might be dead. If Falco killed this one, then their chase was for nothing.

Falco lowered his sword. Instead, as the rider stood once more, he kicked the barbarian flat. Varro trotted around to join Falco, and now the two of them stood over a bruised and bleeding barbarian. He was young, perhaps only a teen.

He had lost his weapons in the crash, but he reached for a dagger at his belt. Falco leaped off his horse and thumped to the ground next to the barbarian.

"Not today, young man." He brought his shield down on the Ligurian's shoulder, causing his hand to flex and drop the dagger as well as knocking him to the ground. He cried out in shock as he fell for the third time. "You'd have been better off playing dead. Not that you would have fooled me."

Varro likewise dismounted and stroked the neck of his lathered horse. The animal snorted and leaned into his touch. Perhaps he had made a new friend this night.

"Hold him."

Varro turned to the horse struggling atop the heap. The beast's front legs had been broken. There was no way to help it. The other horse beneath and the unfortunate rider both appeared dead. Varro searched for the cause of their crash but found nothing. It had only been a matter of time before one of them ran out of luck.

He whispered a prayer of thanks to Fortuna that it was the Ligurians who fell first.

Upon extracting the rider from beneath his dead horse, Varro confirmed he had died. His face was blue, and a thin line of blood trickled from both nostrils and his mouth. The most severe of his wounds were all on the inside. He had seen this before, both in and out of battle. A man might appear unwounded, even laughing with his companions, then drop dead.

"Do you understand me, boy?" Falco held the teen barbarian by his sword arm. His other arm was dirty and bleeding. It seemed he had jumped clear of the crash. Instead, Falco's battering had delivered the worst of his injuries. The Ligurian struggled and did not answer as Falco repeated his question.

"I don't think he understands you," Varro said. "Bind him and we will search this mess for anything that looks hopeful."

Before doing anything else, Varro put his sword to the suffering horse's neck and ended it. His stolen horse had already wandered away, but seemed willing to remain nearby. Falco's horse likewise stayed near, but away from the blood and suffering. They were both excellent horses, given that they did not flee from the scent of blood and the screaming of the injured horse. Clearly, they had been trained for battle.

While Varro sorted through the bloody wreckage of both horse and rider, he heard the thud of hooves approaching. He looked up to see Curio, his horse's head lowered and panting.

"Sorry, the Ligurian got away. He jumped a ditch, and this one balked."

"No matter," Varro said. "Falco nabbed one."

"A lively one, too."

He held down the young Ligurian with his knee and bound his hands with the reins of his own horse. Like all barbarians, he was fierce and proud, and willing to fight to the death. Falco at last drew his pugio, reversed it in his grip, then slammed it into the back of the boy's head. He flattened with the force of the blow and went still.

"Don't kill him," Varro said. "We may need him alive if we find nothing in this mess."

"All barbarians have rocks in their heads. He'll be fine."

Curio dismounted and helped gather the horses. Varro emptied the contents of pouches and packs, the meager and crude tools spilling out into the thin scrub. He sorted through these until he found a leather tube. He held it up as if displaying a snared hare.

Falco flipped his captive onto his back while glancing at Varro's prize.

"The barbarians don't write?"

"No, they don't." Varro pulled open the tube, which was sealed with a thin strip of twine. "But it would seem they can learn how."

He teased out a scraped and beaten hide of either sheep or rabbit skin. To his shock, crudely formed and smudged Latin letters spread out before him. While the other two returned to their work, Varro ran his fingers along the edge of this crude vellum. Someone had written in charcoal ink and knew enough Latin to convey a basic message.

To Perrius, king of the Boii. From Corado, the king of Liguria. My messengers represent me. You deal with them as you would with me. They know my will and have my trust. Our cooperation brings me great pleasure. Together, Rome cannot stand against us.

At the bottom of the page was a crude mark, like a handprint made in charcoal ink.

Varro read the words three more times, understanding them but unable to fathom their meaning. Was he holding the words of a Ligurian king sent to the leader of the Boii? These two barbarians had never cooperated except during the last war with Carthage, and then only as allies of Hannibal. The Ligurians owned the mountains and coast of the west. The Boii dominated the forests of the east and lands far beyond. As far as Varro understood, these two tribes had no connection to each other.

But he held in his hands proof that these two people sought to join forces against Rome.

"Falco, don't strike the captive again. We're going to need what he knows."

"All right, I was just having a bit of a sport with the boy. After all, I've got a bit of payback to give after that time on the wall."

Varro gathered them around the captured messenger. The boy sat with his arms tied behind his back and his head down. Escape seemed impossible, but Varro knew from experience what a desperate person could achieve.

He read the contents of the vellum, all the while looking down at the boy for signs that he understood. If he did, he kept his head lowered and made no reaction. Either he was well trained, or he did not understand the message he carried. Varro suspected the former.

"Your king writes serviceable Latin." Varro crouched to the boy's level. "He says you represent him to the Boii. But it would seem you don't share a common language other than ours. So, you can continue to pretend you don't understand. It's not important if we know what your message is. Where you're going, there are professional interrogators who will find out."

Falco shoved the back of his head. "You'll start talking when they peel off your skin. They'll start with your toes and end at the top of your head. Imagine looking at all your skin piled in a bucket."

Curio shuddered. "I've seen it myself, and it still gives me nightmares. Why did you have to use that example?"

"Just wanted to see if the lad will piss himself."

To the boy's credit, he only flinched when Falco mentioned removing his skin. This proved to Varro that the barbarian understood Latin. He stood up and stretched.

"The interrogators will figure it out. We don't have far to go to reach them. I'm sure professionals will do a better job of getting you to speak."

Now the barbarian looked up. He was young and only had a sprinkling of stubble on his chin. But his eyes burned with defiance equal to the greatest of warriors.

"I am not afraid."

The tremble in his youthful and accented voice betrayed his words.

"You may have learned our language but did not learn the meaning of interrogation. Spare yourself some agony and talk now. We can't keep you from your fate, but the more we know in advance the less you'll have to suffer later. It's your choice."

Falco wrestled the captive off the ground and shoved him toward the horses.

"I'll give you a hand up, but don't think to escape. Try it and I'll give you a taste of the interrogator's techniques."

Falco mounted his stolen horse and Varro helped the bound captive onto the mount. He and Curio then gathered their horses.

"I didn't know these barbarians had kings," Curio said.

"They don't, at least they have not before. But someone has gathered these Ligurians together. So that must be Corado. The Boii are supposed to be dirty barbarians hardly better than animals. More amazing than the Ligurians writing in Latin is the Boii being able to read it."

"I wonder why?" Curio scratched his head, then shrugged. "I suppose if they don't have their own writing, they would have to steal ours. They must be desperate to communicate with each other to go through all that trouble."

Varro agreed. They set out and put their captive in the center. Varro would lead the column, using his map to navigate the way to Arretium.

With a potential alliance between two barbarian tribes, they had to make haste and warn the consul. One of the Ligurians would deliver the message, even if he lacked his king's official document. Varro thought this was an amazing advancement for both peoples. He had never seen any barbarian tribe use writing as a means of communication. In fact, he wondered if anyone would believe his captured message was genuine. Evidently, both sides had profited from their interactions with Rome. Whether or not they wanted it, civilization was slowly penetrating the thick walls of their warrior-based culture.

Their captive seemed resigned to his fate. He sat backward on Falco's horse with his hands tied at his back. He did not try to escape, though Varro knew he must plan something. Such a young man would be prone to reckless action. Certainly, Varro would have tried to escape were he in this situation. They kept a close eye on him, and any time they rested their horses one of them would keep him at the end of his gladius.

They had now passed half the night and had to make camp. Their prior owners had already fed the horses and they only needed water from a nearby brook. They tied the boy to a tree and made their watch schedules before retiring for the night.

And that's when their captive escaped.

17

Varro held the middle watch. It was the hardest of all three, for it divided his sleep in half. With so much at stake, it was easy to remain awake. But being aware was another matter. He had not noticed their prisoner had loosened his bindings. He didn't realize the boy was on the run until he heard the cracking of tree branches moving away from camp.

He jumped to his feet and gave chase in the darkness. The boy was frantic and did little to conceal his path. Varro leaped through snapped branches and over trampled vegetation as he chased the barbarian.

The boy's thin and pale form grew out of the dark ahead. The night offered only starlight for illumination and made for treacherous footing. Both men risked breaking an ankle or worse in the chase.

With the boy in his sight, he took only four bounds across the shadowed ground to tackle him. The barbarian cried out in shock and frustration. Both rolled through the brush and spilled into a shallow ravine. Varro came out on top and had his pugio in hand and then at the throat of the boy.

"I knew you'd try it. I just didn't think you'd worm out of those bindings so easily."

"It's because you let the idiot tie the knots."

Varro snorted at the comment. Falco had bound him and had taken care to test them before being satisfied.

"Well, you certainly woke me up. I think I was dozing. Now, up you go and back to camp. You're going to speak to the interrogators tomorrow. So make your peace tonight with whatever gods you pray to."

They struggled in the ravine, with Varro's pugio finally settling the barbarian's spirited defiance. He pressed it to the small of the boy's back until the point dug into the skin.

The boy lay face down in the dirt at the bottom of the ravine. Varro pressed atop him with his pugio set to the boy's spine. After regaining his breath, Varro was about to haul the boy to his feet.

Then he heard the crack of a breaking twig.

His captive heard it as well and inhaled to cry out for help. Varro slammed his head into the dirt while pushing his dagger so that it drew blood. The boy squirmed against the pain but bit back on his shout.

While keeping the boy pinned, Varro grabbed dead branches and tossed them across his body to obscure himself in the dark.

He put his mouth next to the boy's ear. "If you make any sound, it will be your last."

"A mercy, then?"

Not appreciating the humor, Varro pushed his pugio deeper into the boy's skin. He tried to pull away from it, yet only squirmed in the dirt.

The crunch of branches and dried leaves drew near. A thin and wavering orange light swept down the side of the ravine. It was torchlight, and therefore not powerful enough to illuminate the bottom. Varro pushed down on his captive to keep him quiet.

Looking over his shoulder, he could not see to the top of the ravine. But he heard and felt someone standing there. Whoever it was let their torch pass back and forth as if searching. The edge of the orange torchlight rolled past Varro's body. He dared to twist so that he could see the figure atop the ravine.

Fearing a Ligurian, it surprised him to find a Roman soldier holding aloft a torch in one hand and a drawn gladius in the other. The orange light reflected off his featherless helmet.

Instinct kept Varro's mouth closed. He did not move, but stared hard at the searching figure. In any other situation, he would be glad to see a fellow Roman. But tonight, in this dark forest still half a day away from Arretium, he wondered why a soldier would search the night. It provoked caution in him.

Now he heard a voice beyond the soldier. It was too muffled and distant for Varro to understand. But the Roman holding the torch replied in a clear voice.

"I see nothing here, sir."

Another muffled answer.

"I heard it too, sir. It was probably just animals fighting."

Varro and his captive both remained as still as stones. Each for their own reasons, they did not want this Roman soldier to find them.

At last, the soldier moved off, retracting the thin amber light of his torch. Varro remained in hiding long after silence reclaimed the woods. Once satisfied the soldier was gone, he eased off his captive's back. Then, with as much silence as he could maintain, he escorted his prisoner back to camp.

The boy cooperated, understanding that he had lost his sole chance at escape. Varro put the boy up against the tree and then got his rope in place. But before tightening it, he punched him hard in the gut. The boy doubled over and expelled all his held breath.

"I know that trick," Varro said as he tightened the bindings. "Falco knows it too. I'm surprised he didn't catch you doing it the first time. No matter, you're not slipping out of these bonds again."

"You were afraid of that soldier." The barbarian lifted his head, having recovered from the shock of the punch. He gave a mocking smile. "You can't trust your own people, can you?"

"Of course not. Experience has taught me to trust no one. Especially not a barbarian who thinks he's clever because he learned to speak my language."

They exchanged hard stares. Varro tightened the rope until his captive grimaced, then sat on the cold earth in front of the boy.

"A Ligurian boy who can speak and read Latin might be useful to me in the days to come. It seems a shame to turn you over to the interrogators. You won't survive their attentions. And before you tell me that death doesn't scare you, I'm telling you that death is what you will look forward to. There are worse things than dying. Tomorrow you will find out what those are."

Whether it was from the threats or just that he had wearied, the boy shed a tear. It was a thin line that ran down an unblemished cheek to vanish into the thin hairs of his jaw. Varro was untouched. In his younger days, he might have felt sympathy for the suffering of this poor boy. Today, however, he was an enemy. For enemies, he drew no distinction in age or gender, having learned by bitter experience that such distinctions led to bad ends.

"You obviously come from a prestigious family. Otherwise, you would not have learned my language. And because of this, your king honored you with delivering his message. You, a boy so young, were given the authority of a king. It must grieve you to have failed in this mission."

The boy sniffed back his tears and raised his chin. "As long as one of us delivers the message, there is no failure. It is you who failed. You killed one and caught me. But the other will get through."

"Yet tears stain your cheeks. You know when you meet your

ancestors in the next life, you'll have to admit your failures. But that is not the cause of your tears. It is truly fear of death. It is just the two of us here. I've been at this far longer than you have. I still fear death. There's no shame in it. You're going to miss your family and friends. Your dog and the fields you played in as a child. Maybe right now you're thinking of a girl you liked. But she'll never know, because by this time tomorrow, you will be ribbons of flesh in a bucket."

The visceral description proved too much. The boy began to openly weep, with tears freely rolling down his cheeks.

"You are lying to me. I can't talk if they cut me up like that."

Varro offered a sympathetic smile. "You weren't listening earlier. They'll start from your toes. The best interrogators will keep you alive until every inch of your skin has been flayed. Being so young, I expect you might be strong enough to survive most of the experience. But if your gods love you, they will kill you by the time the interrogators peel up to your knees. I've seen stronger men than you die from the agony before then."

The comparison jabbed at the boy's pride. He raised his chin again and stopped sniffling.

"I am strong. I am not afraid of your interrogators." But his trembling lip and searching eyes said something else. Varro let silence be his answer, and soon the boy's demeanor changed.

"What do you want from me? You have the message. It's all that I know."

Varro glanced behind as if searching for that message. He pressed the boy to learn more about Corado's plans, but his denials seemed genuine.

"Even if I believe you, the interrogators must still confirm what you've said. Are you certain you know nothing else?"

The boy's eyes pleaded for mercy even though he attempted to sound hard. "I know nothing else. You killed Corado's messenger. I just went to support him, and the one you let through was our guide. I spoke Latin, and so they selected me for this task. But it's not because I come from a prestigious family. My father is a trader. We trade with Rome and others. I learned this language from the day I could speak my own. My father promised it would serve me well."

Varro knew the truth when he heard it. The boy was utterly defeated and had little value beyond confirming the letter they had captured. Even if he was an enemy, it seemed a heartless thing to send him into the hands of the interrogators. He stood, then searched his pack by thin starlight and produced a strip of cloth to gag the boy.

He accepted his fate as Varro tied it off.

"When the time comes, you must confirm that letter to my commander."

His shift had ended, and Falco's would start. He lay snoring in the tent, and Varro tugged at his feet.

"Get up, we've got trouble."

Despite appearing to be dead asleep, Varro's words set him bolt upright. His eyes were lost in shadow, but his heavy brows shot up.

"My sword." His hand reached out for the blade sheathed beside him.

Varro stepped on it. "Hold on, not here. I found visitors in the woods."

As Falco readied himself, Varro explained what had happened. Despite the strangeness of Roman soldiers in hiding, Falco instead focused on their prisoner.

"I had the little bastard tied up good. I can't believe he escaped." Now dressed in his mail shirt and sword harness, he prodded the boy tied to the tree. "Well, looks like he's not escaping again."

Both left Curio to sleep, then followed the path that Varro had taken to pursue their captive. When they came to the ravine, both dropped into a low crouch. Falco looked expectantly at Varro, who then led them along the ravine until reaching where he had spotted the Roman. From there, they crept between trees and bushes in the direction Varro had seen the soldier leave.

They soon found a lone Roman tent that was concealed with branches and brush just as they had done for their own. One man sat on a log and sheltered in a heavy brown cloak. He wore a Roman helmet, and a pilum rested against his shoulder. He seemed to be asleep.

"You're not the only one to fall asleep on duty," Falco whispered.

"What are they doing out here?" Varro saw only a camp large enough for three men. "There are too few for it to be a forward patrol."

With the guard asleep, there was no way to learn more about the camp. While they might be forward scouts, something about them felt strange to Varro. The lack of feathers in the soldier's helmet reminded him of how he and the others operated. Forward scouts might not bother with battle dress, but care more for stealth and evasion. Neither would they carry pila, which would have limited use in their mission.

Varro gestured they should get closer to the camp. He crept through the predawn murk and circled around the rear of the tent. Both he and Falco listened, eventually rewarded with snoring. Still not satisfied, Varro arced wide of the camp until he was far back enough to take it all in from a different angle.

Here was the difference. On this side of the tent, a slave slept on the rough earth outside the flap. He wore a plain gray tunic that blended with his surroundings. In the scant light, Varro could still see that he was fleshier and healthier than most legion slaves. His tunic, though plain, was likewise in better repair. The slave was better suited to serving a tribune or consul than one for common infantrymen.

He leaned back and looked at Falco, who had spotted the slave as well. Both stared at each other in the darkness. Falco's eyes glittered. Without another word, the retreated the way they had come. They arrived in camp, finding their captive slumped against his bonds. At first, Varro thought he was dead, then realized he had merely fallen asleep.

"What do you make of it?" Falco settled on the grass and made space for Varro to join him.

"That slave wasn't from the legions, but the soldiers were. I don't know what they're doing out here, but I suspect it's not in the legion's interest."

Falco grumbled deep in his chest. "Paullus? You think there's a connection?"

"Maybe, but I can't think of why they are so far from the legions. I don't know if we'll get an answer tonight."

With nothing more to discuss, Varro retired to the tent and let Falco complete his watch.

They were up at dawn, and first tended to their horses. They found grass for them to graze on and watered them at a nearby brook. Again, their captive struggled when they tried to mount him on a horse. Falco hit him about the head twice before he complied. "You barbarians never learn when you're defeated."

Varro followed his map to Arretium. Not that it was an explicitly designated path, but he could estimate the correct direction by it. Besides, locating thousands of Roman soldiers in a predetermined location was easy.

The camp emerged from the trees about midafternoon. Varro heard the familiar sounds of camp life carrying across the hazy distance. It was a massive camp, square and strong, with proper ditches and stakes, and alert sentries at all four entrances. Blocks of ordered hide tents shook gently in the breeze. His own horse seemed excited, as its more sensitive nose must have recognized the mass of cavalry horses ahead. Varro stroked its neck. "Time to find you some new friends. You'll like Roman horses. They are more civilized."

They rested before meeting the consul. Varro understood it would take time for his request to reach headquarters, and so wanted to be ready for what might be hours of questioning. As they dismounted, Falco turned their prisoner toward the camp and pointed.

"Look at that. Sure, you have a lot of hairy beards in your mob, but that's a proper army over there. Your people will be driven out of Pisa and will go hide in their mountains like they always do. But this time, it's going to be different. You're going to be crushed."

Their prisoner stared defiantly, but not long. He turned his back without a word, and Falco chirped with laughter.

"It's going to be good to be on the line again."

"I doubt we'll be on the line," Curio said. "We've got horses now."

Varro agreed. "But I don't think the cavalry will take us. Remember how Senator Flaminius warned us?"

They resumed their approach to the camp, coming within sight of the guards after another half hour of travel. Varro could smell the familiar camp life odors. Once he considered them foul and full of terrible memories. As the years passed, however, the scents elicited feelings of familiarity and safety. The same for the sounds of men drilling and their officers shouting, or the thunder of cavalrymen practicing their formations.

Coming out of the woods was like coming home, even if it was to a temporary camp that would take them to war.

The guards raised their shields and approached with caution. They did not look like enemies, but neither did they carry any sign of rank other than their mail shirts. They challenged Varro for the password.

"I wouldn't know it," he said. "We have come from Pisa with a message for Consul Minucius. We also have a captive and critical information for him. Fetch your optio if you must, but don't delay."

The soldiers shared worried looks, clearly unsure of what to do. But Varro's suggestion eased their hesitation, and soon an optio had sorted out that they were not crafty Ligurians. Varro could not entirely blame them for the caution. They had not shaved or bathed in days, and Varro considered if he looked half as barbaric as he felt, then it was right to suspect him.

Their actual Ligurian captive tried not to show his fear, but his eyes betrayed him. He looked between the camp and Varro while seated upon Falco's horse. It seemed he might be calculating his odds of fleeing on foot. But that moment had long vanished.

They were obliged to wait just inside the gate. Their horses would be tended, the optio promised. However, messengers had to be dispatched to headquarters and arrangements made. Their prisoner remained with them, though the optio had wanted to take him away.

"He will need to verify some information for the consul," Varro explained. So the boy remained standing, gagged and bound by his arms, while the rest sat on the ground.

As they waited, soldiers went about their routines. Varro enjoyed the pleasant breeze and watching mundane camp life unfold.

Falco inhaled deeply.

"It always feels great to come back to camp after being in the field for so long. We weren't out there more than a few weeks, but it felt like half a year."

"I want to go to the hospital," Curio said. "Maybe they'll let me out of this splint."

Falco laughed. "More likely, they'll take one look at you and send you home to your mother."

The two traded barbs while Varro's gaze shifted across the camp. He was curious about Consul Minucius. He had inherited a difficult problem in both implacable enemies and recalcitrant soldiers. It would take a great man to navigate those conditions. Flamininus did not seem to hold him in regard. But Varro would form his own opinions.

As he rested, half listening to Curio insulting Falco's brows, which he claimed "were big enough to make camp on," his eyes settled on a figure approaching down the main road.

He was a tall and handsome man, walking with purpose and a smile radiating his high mood to everyone around him.

Varro elbowed Falco in the back and let out a long sigh.

"Looks like we've found Paullus."

18

They stared at each other without greeting or expression, standing in the middle of the main avenue of the camp. Paullus dared a slight smile, as if challenging their unspoken question of where he had been. All around them, soldiers went about their business never suspecting the conflict in their midst.

Varro searched his erstwhile subordinate up and down. He seemed clean and hale, nothing like he should have had he been in the field like the rest of them. In fact, he seemed to beam with confidence.

"I had a feeling I'd find you safe and smiling here," Varro said. He hated to speak first, but he had too many questions. "You will explain yourself. We have just come from Pisa. It irritated the commander to receive the same message twice."

A twinkle came to Paullus's eyes. "But I'm sure he admired your tenacity and dedication to the mission. I see you have acquired a captive. What other intelligence have you gathered from him?"

Falco stepped forward and jabbed a finger at his chest.

"You little shit. You might have let us know what you were up to. Instead, we almost died trying to deliver that message. Curio broke his shoulder saving a man he thought was you. Do you want some intelligence? When we get time alone, I'll beat the intelligence into that patrician head of yours."

Paullus bent his lips as if in disappointment. Instead of responding to the threat, he looked at their captive. He brushed past Falco and took the Ligurian boy by his arm.

"From your reaction, I can see you understand us. Why have they taken you prisoner? I expect you must have important information, otherwise there's no purpose in dragging you here. Tell me what it is."

Though he had promised himself to keep his composure, Varro could not help yanking the boy away.

"You'll find out when we brief the consul. In the meantime, explain yourself. And don't be so smug. There will be consequences for your insubordination, I promise. We are a team, and you committed the worst offense possible when you abandoned us to the enemy."

Clearly feigning hurt, Paullus leaned back with his hand on his chest.

"I didn't abandon Curio, unlike you two. I actually came to his aid. And if it wasn't for me, maybe he would still be a captive of the barbarians." He now gave a sneer to the Ligurian boy. "I suppose I'll hear your stories soon enough. Here comes our escort."

They faced back to the main road, and as Paullus said, three men marched down the road toward them. One was clearly a messenger, dressed in a plain cream tunic, and two soldiers escorted him.

They accepted the prisoner from Varro, then pointed toward the center of camp where the largest tent showed Consul Minucius's headquarters. The messenger looked to Paullus.

"Excellent timing, sir. The consul and his tribunes have gathered for their morning brief and await your report."

They followed their escorts in stony silence. Varro ground his teeth in anger. Not only had Paullus abandoned his team, but he also appeared proud of it. He understood that the patrician class enjoyed different rules and different benefits. But in the field, they were all fellow soldiers. There was no room for class distinction in their tiny group. He doubted he could ever make Paullus understand this. Right now, he had no desire to instruct but only to punish. Yet that would have to wait until he received new instructions from the consul.

To further stoke Varro's anger, when they reached headquarters, Paullus stepped to the front of their group. The messenger entered before them, but Paullus blocked the tent flap. In the meantime, the two guards held the Ligurian boy between them as if he were Hercules himself. They gripped him hard enough to turn their knuckles white and make the boy bite his lip against the crushing pain. Varro felt like he should intervene on the boy's behalf, then reminded himself that this was nothing compared to what would come.

The messenger reappeared and gestured that Paullus should enter, which he did. He turned back and nodded Varro forward as if he were in command.

Falco's whisper was hot against his ear as both waited to enter behind Paullus.

"We're back to this game again. That bastard needs to be taken down a peg, or we will never have peace."

While Varro agreed, he could not respond as they entered the command tent.

It took a moment for his eyes to adjust to the dim light. Most of the illumination came from the creamy glow of the sun on the cloth roof. However, red clay lamps illuminated a wide desk where smooth stones pinned down vellum maps at the corners.

Seven tribunes gathered around the desk, each dressed for battle and their faces lined with determination. These were not all the tribunes under his command, but likely the most senior of those serving the consul. Varro's gaze swept down their stern length to settle on the man seated behind the desk.

Consul Minucius was an unimposing man, though he wore his muscled bronze chest plate well. His short hair was curled and so mixed with gray that it seemed like a puff of smoke. Dark circles under his eyes betrayed the weariness of an otherwise energetic posture. He leaned forward as if preparing to spring across the desk at some unseen enemy. Yet for all this, he did not appear as confident as Cato had, or as authoritative as Flaminius, or as noble as Galba. It was harsh to judge a man by his looks alone, but Varro trusted his first instincts. This consul might be the least impressive he had served under.

Standing at his right was a far more imposing man, also dressed for war in a polished bronze chest piece. His hair had thinned back to the top of his head, and his flesh had shrunk to reveal cheekbones as sharp as blades. But he had a shrewd and intelligent look, reminding Varro of a wolf pack leader. This was the legate, the second-in-command and adviser to the consul.

All of them, Paullus included, stood to rigid attention in the presence of their leader and commander. Right now, Minucius was one of the two most powerful people in all of Rome. Even if he did not project the image expected of a consul, his rank demanded utter obedience and respect.

Minucius leaned back on his stool, the wood creaking in the hushed space. He craned his neck as if to stretch, then nodded to Paullus.

"So, the rest of your men have finally arrived, and they bring a captive. I trust this boy has important information."

The consul made a few other comments, but Varro did not hear them. His mind was stuck on how he had addressed Paullus.

He was now being referred to as Paullus's man, and Varro immediately understood the patrician's smugness. He had somehow subverted leadership of their team.

While remaining at attention, Paullus straightened his shoulders before replying.

"Sir, they have only just arrived this morning and I have not had a moment to brief them. I thought it wise to bring them and their captive here immediately. Like you, sir, I trust the captive carries valuable intelligence. Varro, please explain to the consul what you have discovered."

Only after a long moment did Varro realize the consul, tribunes, and Paullus were all awaiting his response. His mind hummed with confusion and rage. But he was a veteran and a respected soldier. He would not lose form in front of his superiors. So, he swallowed the acid on his tongue and straightened his shoulders as he addressed his commander.

"Sir, we intercepted a message dispatched from the Ligurians encamped outside of Pisa. We chased the messengers and rode down two of them. Unfortunately, one escaped us, sir." He paused for an expression of disappointment or reprimand, but nothing came. "The good news is we killed the actual messenger. It was only his scout who escaped, and we captured this one."

Varro stepped aside and indicated the Ligurian boy. Whatever bravado he had possessed had now vanished. With his arms tied behind his back and two soldiers holding him in place, he seemed to sink into the earth. Varro waved him forward, and the guards complied. They shoved him before the consul's desk.

Reaching into his belt, he produced the hide sheet that contained the message from the Ligurian king, Corado. He unrolled it and placed it on the desk, gently sliding it forward to Minucius.

"This is a document written in Latin from the Ligurian leader to the leader of the Boii. The boy here can confirm the contents and that this letter was indeed entrusted to them by their king."

Minucius's expression shifted to a pained smile. He accepted the hide letter, holding it daintily between two fingers as if it might contaminate him. Both eyebrows flipped up as his eyes scanned across the words.

"You say the barbarians wrote this in our language? I would never believe it if I didn't hold this in my hands." Now he leaned forward on the desk and gave a hard look to the Ligurian boy. "Is it true that your king wrote this?"

The captive had turned white and his lips quivered. Still, he mustered enough bravery to answer. "Those are the words of Corado. He is no king, but he leads us."

Minucius handed the hide sheet to his legate, then folded both hands atop the desk. The legate seemed equally astounded to be holding a written communication in Latin between barbarian tribes that had otherwise been considered unlettered. When he finished scanning the document, he handed it to the tribune next to him.

"While this is important news, it is hardly urgent." Minucius inclined his head toward Paullus. "But your team did well to intercept this message. I will send it to Rome in my next report."

Paullus straightened his shoulders and accepted the compliment. Varro, however, balled his fists against his voice rising.

"Sir, we have also collected strength reports and details of the Ligurians' positions around Pisa. Commander Cincius reiterated an urgent plea for aid. I have updated a map for you to review."

He produced his vellum map and tried to place it on the consul's desk. But Paullus snatched it from his fingers first. Varro withdrew his hands as if expecting to have them sliced off. Paullus instead presented the map with both hands to Minucius.

"Here is the additional information I promised, sir. I would be happy to review it with you."

The consul accepted the vellum and scanned over Varro's careful documentation. "I will have my scouts review this and compare it to what we know now. It will be useful in the coming days. I must congratulate you on a job well done, Paullus. I can see how valuable you and your team will be in the upcoming campaign."

Varro put his hand out to keep Falco in place. He heard the soft growl in his chest and understood his anger. But unlike himself, Falco could not be counted on to keep his temper even in the presence of his leaders. No one appeared to have noticed. The tribunes leaned over the Ligurians' message and criticized their crude ability. Minucius and Paullus were absorbed in their own mutual admiration. It seemed only the legate might have detected something was amiss. He gave no expression, but his eyes lingered on Varro.

"Sir, if I may ask a question," Varro spoke loud enough to draw attention back to himself. Minucius gestured him on. "Will you be questioning the prisoner? He might have additional information he was unwilling to share without further encouragement."

Minucius's eyes flashed at this suggestion.

"A fine idea. Of course, I would have given this order myself. You needn't concern yourself with matters beyond your station. Take him to the interrogators and learn what you can."

Varro heard the sting of rebuke, made worse by the chiding look Paullus gave him. But he saluted and accepted his duty.

"I will see it done immediately, sir. Do you have further instructions for us?"

The question hung in the air like a foul odor that could not escape the confines of the crowded tent. Even the tribunes seemed offended. He didn't understand the cause of their upset, but Minucius was quick to dispel his confusion.

"Your orders will come through your leader. Now, the three of you have my thanks, but don't test my patience. You are all experienced soldiers and know better than to break the chain of command. Paullus, remain here, and you three carry out my orders, then await further details. While you are waiting, speak to Tribune Grumio to get a tent assignment."

Varro saluted, then turned to the guards holding the Ligurian prisoner. They released him to Varro's control. It was an awkward and silent exchange, and the boy was as meek as a day-old lamb. He was about to salute, then exit the tent when Curio stepped up to Paullus.

His voice was edged with ice. "Sir, after delivering the prisoner I request leave to visit the hospital. As you can see, my shoulder was injured."

If Curio had intended to shame Paullus for the injury he had endured on his behalf, it seemed to have no effect. Paullus simply frowned. "Of course, but no matter what the doctors say I will need you in the days ahead."

The console nodded gravely in agreement. If anything, Curio's request seemed to reflect badly on them rather than on Paullus. All he had achieved was to ensure that Paullus appeared as their genuine leader. Varro gritted his teeth against his rising anger and reminded himself not to take it out on Curio once outside.

After saluting, the three of them exited the tent with their captive and the two guards following. No one spoke, other than Varro asking for the location of the interrogators.

When the two guards left them to their responsibilities, they walked a short distance from the headquarters tent. Varro put up his hand.

"Do not speak a word. I know what you're thinking, and we will discuss this later. Right now, we must deliver our prisoner to the interrogators. Those are our orders for the time being."

"Yes, sir." Falco's words might well have been a swear, such was his anger.

Varro guided the trembling slave along the main road, then searched behind. No one looked after them.

He led them off the road, then wove between lines of tents where soldiers cleaned their gear, sharpened their swords, or else rested before an officer gave them a new duty. The men only gave them passing looks, wisely remaining out of business that did not concern them. No soldier wanted more trouble than he already had. So, when they reached the limit of the camp, Varro and the rest were alone.

Falco cleared his throat. "Ah, so we're doing the disobedience thing again. Going to let the boy run just to stick it to Paullus? I don't think it's a bad idea. I just think we're probably going to be caught and hand Paullus his excuse to have us flogged."

Varro ignored the jab and instead pulled the boy in front of him.

"What's your name?"

The Ligurian stared in disbelief. Visions of his own flesh piled into a bucket had left him trembling and pale. Now he stood at the edge of the camp where only a ditch and stakes separated him from a grassy field and his freedom. His mouth worked, but no words formed, as if he could not remember his own name. At last, he answered.

"I am Dano, son of Tascus."

"Well, Dano, remember my name, Centurion Marcus Varro. I am setting you free and sparing your life. If you do know more, it can't be much. And if you know much, then I am a fool. But I'm also thinking ahead. Go to the Boii as your king commanded you. Deliver your message as you must. Say what you will of what you've seen here. And know that one day, if the gods put us on the same path again, you owe me a favor equal to your life. And if no such day comes, then when you trade with Rome, trade fairly. That will serve as repayment for the life I granted you today."

Dano blinked and stepped back, rubbing both arms as if

disbelieving he was now freed.

"We are still enemies, at least our people are. But I will not forget the name Centurion Marcus Varro. This I swear before all the gods."

He turned and fled across the ditch and between the stakes and then into the knee-high grass beyond the perimeter of the camp. He ducked low so that he became a vaguely moving shape headed toward the safety of the far trees.

"Good work," Falco said. "The three of us will be in chains by afternoon and flogged by dinner. It will be great entertainment for the boys, at least."

Varro watched the grass shake and bend where Dano passed and soon saw him rise then dash into the protective darkness of the trees.

"No one will remember him." Varro turned and looped his arms around both Falco and Curio. "From what I've seen, I would be astounded if Minucius remembers the letter we just delivered to him. He doesn't seem very concerned about a potential alliance between Rome's enemies."

Falco sucked his teeth. "He seems a bit of a poser to me. I think Flamininus wasn't wrong about him."

"Whatever the case," Varro said, "he is the consul, and he is convinced Paullus is our leader."

Curio pulled back from Varro's arm. "But he's not our leader. Senator Flamininus can prove it."

"But he's not here, is he?" Falco likewise stepped back and folded his arms. "So that was Paullus's whole trick? When we wouldn't listen to him, he just ran off and convinced the consul we were right behind. All the while, he passed himself off as our leader. That's a lot to go through to ease his hurt feelings. He had to pass through enemy territory on his own. He could have got himself killed."

"It might be part of his plan," Varro said. "But I don't think it's all of it. It still doesn't answer why his servant was here after we saw him leave. How did he know where to go?"

Falco shrugged. "Obviously, they arranged things in advance."

"But that would mean Paullus knew more about our mission than we did."

"Well, that shit will all flow downstream at some point." Falco pinched the bridge of his nose and turned his head aside. "And we all know who it will flow over."

Varro turned to Curio and brushed dirt from his sling.

"You ought to get to that doctor. I did what I could, but it's no substitute for real medical aid. You have Commander Paullus's permission. Just don't use it as an excuse to avoid your duty."

Curio laughed and started back toward headquarters where the hospital tent stood, then stopped.

"Don't you have a gold owl's head on your pugio? Why can't you use that to prove that you're in charge?"

Falco groaned. "Weren't you listening? He dropped his pugio into a well back in Pisa. I swear, Varro, I'm going to have that thing welded to your hip one day."

Varro chuckled and patted the plain pugio on his harness.

"These are not my weapons, but taken from some poor bastard who I brained back in the city."

"Well, Paullus doesn't have one, either. You can at least point that out to the consul."

"You know as well as I that Minucius will not change his ideas now. For one, he doesn't care who is in charge if we're doing what he wants. But more importantly, he will not overrule the word of a fellow patrician for the likes of us. We may be better soldiers than Paullus, but we entered Minucius's tent as subordinates and left the same way. The time to change his mind is past."

Falco growled his displeasure. "Well, let's make sure that Paullus has nothing but shit on his face from here on out. We can fuck up every mission until he gets demoted."

As much as the idea resonated with Varro, he knew none of them would serve with any less dedication than they had before. Their work went beyond themselves and benefited all of Rome and its citizens. Besides, they would suffer any punishment long before Paullus ever did.

The three of them fell quiet, but Varro felt a chill. He looked between his two friends and saw that they were having a silent conversation. Their eyes flashed with grim determination. And Varro knew their thoughts.

"We will not kill him. That is murder. I have committed every sin against the gods, but that is one I refuse."

"Well, good for you," Falco said. "You have two good friends here to do the job for you. Just look away. I'll help Paullus fall off his horse, and Curio can accidentally trample him five or six times until we can't tell who he is. It's not like these sorts of things don't happen in battle."

Varro glared at both of them. "How far have we fallen that the first solution to our problems is murder? Curio, he rescued you from the Ligurians. How can you even consider putting a knife in his back? This is madness."

Curio's face turned red, and he lowered his head. But Falco remained defiant.

"You can be sure he'll put a knife through our backs soon enough. I'm fine if you want to wait to see the blade coming. I just hope it doesn't take one of us out first."

"It is for the gods alone to determine his fate." Varro stared until Falco also lowered his head. "We are better men than our enemies. I don't doubt Paullus is up to mischief. But we don't kill a man because we think he might do something we don't like."

The three stood together at the edge of the camp in stony silence. At last, Curio mentioned going to the hospital and broke the awkward moment. They trudged back across the camp without speaking another word.

19

Varro walked along the rows of tents, still dressed in mail and covered with the grime of his recent travails. He had thought of every way to delay meeting Paullus, and a walk around the camp was his best idea. He had lost his command without a single word spoken, and a fire burned in him for it. Paullus knew how to play these political games at a higher level than himself. He had outclassed him twice now, and he suspected a third time was in the offering.

He had left the others after setting up their tent near headquarters. He needed space to think through all that had happened and where everything was headed. It seemed for the moment that their mission was complete, and they would return to normal soldiering. Yet there was something else afoot, and he had to figure it out. He would not let Paullus outsmart him again.

He roamed the camp, and no one questioned his business. While this was convenient, it was a sign of Minucius's troubled leadership. Everywhere Varro went, he found a laxness that had never existed in any other army he had served in. Certainly, there were veterans among the ranks. However, their experience did not translate into discipline. That he should go unchallenged in areas he had no business in was just one sign of this.

It was now afternoon and most of the men were marching or drilling. The empty tents billowed with a soft breeze. Varro followed the familiar scents of horse and a peculiar style of cooking. Those scents brought him back to the dry plains of Numidia and memories of desperate nights riding free across the land.

Of all Rome's allies, the Numidians were the most reliable. He found them encamped at the eastern edge of the camp, close to the regular Roman cavalry. As he drew closer, he could hear them chirping to each other in their strange language. It had been a few years since he spoke it, but just to hear it brought everything back.

He stood back from their camp, taking in their peculiar horses with their graceful and thin bodies. They were at rest now, the horses herded together in a loose picket. The Numidians moved through them, speaking to them like family. It made Varro think of his horse, Thunderbolt. He had left him to his old friend, Baku. It made him wonder if the wily cousin of King Masinissa was here. He would enjoy meeting an old friend but knew Baku wouldn't leave his cousin's side except in the gravest circumstances.

He was about to turn back when one of the Numidians loitering outside his tent noticed him. Perhaps it was because he stared with such interest, but the Numidian smiled and approached. Varro tilted his head at this, as allied troops never interacted with Roman soldiers. Yet this one strode forward with confidence.

He raised his hand in greeting and spoke to Varro in the language of the Numidian tribes.

"I would recognize that scowl anywhere, sir. You have grown older, and you have shaved your beard. But you've not changed your expression."

A moment of shock and anxiety passed as a wave over Varro's mind. He searched his memory for the right words and begged his lips to form them once more. He was out of practice, but just hearing the language again restored it to him. At least enough of it for him to raise his own hand in greeting and reply.

"I am embarrassed. You remember me, but I do not recognize you."

The Numidian was typical of the tribesmen who coaxed a living from unforgiving plains and jagged mountains. He was short and wiry with deep brown skin and piercing, intelligent eyes. He wore only a cream-colored tunic and head cover, but did not carry a weapon. The heat of a desert wind seemed to surround him even in this milder environment.

"There is no blame, sir. You have dozens of us to remember, but we only need to remember one Commander Varro. Besides, sir, I only served in the Mountain Ghosts at the end. You were called away so suddenly, and the Ghosts were no more after you and the others left. I was told I would learn much from serving with the Romans, and it was true. Even in the short time under your leadership, I learned discipline. I have taught this to my friends here. But they still act like we are in Numidia, and as if we are a tribe and not a unit. But now that I see Commander Varro is here, maybe things will be different."

"I appreciate your praise. What is your name?"

The Numidian was young, and as much as Varro wanted to convince himself otherwise, utterly unfamiliar. But he saluted as he had instructed his Mountain Ghosts.

"I am called Amul, sir. I am a leader of men, thanks to your training."

They clasped arms and fell into friendly conversation. Varro learned that his old mentor, Baku, still served the king as a special advisor. Amul confirmed the Carthaginians remained wary of their borders even after the disbanding of the Mountain Ghosts.

"It seems, sir, that your memory still haunts them. Their caravans travel with twice the guards they used to employ."

In the end, Amul had to return to his men and Varro to the problems he had been avoiding. They parted with the promise to speak again before the campaign ended. Amul believed he and his men would return to Numidia upon liberating Pisa. But Varro warned there may be problems ahead that would require the unmatched skill of the Numidian cavalry. He was thinking of the Boii but gave away nothing specific.

When he returned to his tent, he found Paullus addressing Falco and Curio. They both sat in a posture of indifference outside the tent. Paullus stood with both hands on his hips as if chastising them. The image brought heat to Varro's face. Their earlier talk of murder felt more plausible than ever. But he put aside the thought and straightened his shoulders as he joined the others.

"And where have you been?" Paullus looked at him from the side, not bothering to turn his head. "Curio has come and gone from the hospital. And you have been away that whole time."

"Drop the act. We all know what you did, and who is truly in charge here."

"Well, you might be in charge if we were still on a mission." Paullus now turned and tilted his head to the side in challenge. "But now we are absorbed back into the regular legion. The message to Pisa has been delivered, intelligence gathered, and the report made to Consul Minucius. That was all Senator Flamininus had entrusted us to do. After that, we were to take instruction from the consul."

The heat on Varro's cheeks increased, and again his hands balled into fists.

"Play whatever game you wish. Within Servus Capax, you are subordinate to me and to the others. You're a junior member. Thus far, I can't say I recommend you for further duty."

Paullus gave a thin smile. "I see you no longer fear for your estate. Maybe you think because we are so far from Rome that I cannot possibly alert Flaccus to your violence against his nephews. But you would do well to remember that I am not so stupid. In fact, I can harness my connections even in the field."

"That threat can only carry so far," Varro said. "It makes little difference what Flaccus thinks if you've got us all killed. All except yourself, that is. I'm certain you're hoping we find death in battle. Then, you can have your own little command, and be the hero that you only pretend to be."

The sneer on Paullus's face morphed into a snarl.

"I was just informing the others of their new assignments. You and I will not be serving together. The three of you will assist the allied cavalry. It is well that the enemy provided you horses. Otherwise, I'm not sure what we would have done with you."

Varro looked to both Curio and Falco, who had been watching with tense silence. Their faces were grim, and he could read the murderous intent in them. For a moment, he thought of joining them in their dark plans. But he took a measured breath before speaking again.

"And I suppose you'll be with the regular cavalry. It's just as well. I'm sure the consul has arranged for a suitably glorious position."

He wanted to question Paullus about his servant. But he had not yet unraveled that mystery, and it occurred to him that Paullus would not know what had happened. To his mind, his servant was still a captive of the Ligurians. Varro needed time to figure out what Paullus intended. So, it was best they stayed apart. It would allow him to work with the others and pin down their suspicions.

Paullus seemed to believe Varro's introspection signaled acquiescence. So he tilted his head back and renewed his smirk.

"The three of you will report to Tribune Grumio. I'm certain he will assign you positions equivalent to your ranks in the infantry. No doubt your time frolicking about the desert will serve you well in leading our allies to victory."

Falco groaned and rose to his feet.

"No doubt all the years of sitting on your ass will get you killed in the field. I can only hope you fall off your horse and break your neck. You're soft. That's why you hate us. We're a powerful team. You can force your way into it but can never join. You don't fit anywhere, not in your family, not in the Senate, and not in the legion. You're just a wet streak of shit. One day, someone's going to wipe you up."

Though Paullus was not a small man, he appeared like one before Falco's gathered might. His usual bluster withered, and he struggled to hold a death glare. But he was not up to the moment and turned aside with his sneer intact.

"There is one last order from Consul Minucius. We discussed it at length and agreed that these Servus Capax pugiones are a liability. Others who know what to look for can easily identify us. Therefore, I must surrender them to Consul Minucius today. So, hand them over."

He extended his hand as if expecting Varro and the others to lay their pugiones across his palm.

"No, these are important symbols of what we represent." Varro clapped his hand over the pugio at his hip, even though it wasn't his. "If the consul wants mine, then he can summon me directly and have it pried out of my hands."

Curio now stood to join ranks against Paullus, and both he and Falco agreed. All three of them folded their arms as if challenging anyone to take their weapons.

"You understand that request is entirely possible? It is not my command, but the lawful command of the consul. I know that Senator Flamininus might disagree, but he's not a consul anymore. And after some deliberation with Minucius, we have reached this conclusion. So, I will ask one final time. Then you will leave me no choice but to take more direct steps to carry out orders."

Varro's hand trembled as he drew the pugio. He held it in a

fighting grip, its nicked blade pointing at Paullus's heart. It took all his effort to remember that murder was an atrocity. But he spun it around, then replaced it in the sheath before handing it over.

"Please be less dramatic than him," Paullus said. "I will add my pugio right now. The order stands for all of us and not just you three."

"Oh, it is for you." At least this part of the plan was clear to Varro. "If you can eliminate any sign of rank, then you'll be able to justify the lie about your own."

Paullus ignored the comment and gathered their weapons. He tucked them under his arm and then pulled out Varro's. He ran his thumb along the pommel, giving him a quizzical look.

"Where's the marking? Are you trying to deceive me?"

"I lost mine in Pisa. If you want it, you have to climb to the bottom of a well and fetch it yourself."

Paullus stared at the dagger, his thumb rubbing in a gentle circle. At last, he shrugged and placed it back under his arm, though Varro detected a hint of irritation in his expression.

"I won't ask how it ended up there. Just so long as you are not playing a game. Consul Minucius would not appreciate it."

Varro simply held Paullus's stare. Using the consul's name would not intimidate him.

"Enjoy your moment. When we get back to Rome, you'll find yourself in a different situation. I don't care whose name you threaten me with."

Rather than respond, Paullus narrowed his eyes and looked at all three of them before turning away. They watched him cross the open field and head directly to the consul's tent.

Falco let out a long sigh. "Looks like we'll have to requisition new ones. He could've at least been kind enough to bring replacements."

"I know he rescued me," Curio said. "But I still hate him."

Varro watched him cross the distance until he vanished out of sight behind some tents.

"He is close to the consul, it seems. Normally, I'd say it's the patrician class taking care of their own. But Paullus has gone beyond even that. The little bastard seems to have made himself second-in-command. I wonder what the legate thinks?"

Falco returned to sit inside their tent, scratching the back of his head.

"It doesn't matter what any of them think. It's what I think that you should be worried about. Since all of us just got a demotion, we should reconsider our earlier decision about Paullus. He just needs to fall from his horse. It's a simple accident. Not unexpected for someone who hasn't been active since the last campaign in Greece."

"You know how I feel about that. And I don't think we were demoted. He just wants to elevate himself by bringing us down."

Curio said nothing, but he sat beside Falco. The two of them shared a knowing look. Varro hoped they were not serious but admitted even he enjoyed the idea of Paullus no longer troubling them. Violence was always a seductively simple answer. But he had learned better and could never live with the guilt.

By the evening, they had gone to meet Tribune Grumio as directed. The tribune seemed surprised at their assignment. He grumbled about the lack of clear communication. Varro took this as yet another sign of Minucius's lacking command. But the tribune was grateful for three capable men who could speak the language of the allies.

"I wouldn't think in all of Rome I could find more than two people who could speak to the Numidians. But here I have three in my command. I want one of you for my command group, and the other two will lead the allies in battle. But Centurion Curio, your arm is a liability."

"It's nothing, sir." Curio raised his arm in the sling. "The doctor just wants me to keep it braced as long as possible. I can ride, sir."

"The Numidians will see it as a weakness." Grumio shook his head. "The gods know they are hard enough to contain with a firm hand. No, I shall have you in the command group. It might be a waste of ability, but you will serve as a runner."

The tribune then selected Varro as his second-in-command, given his experience. While they would still camp with the regular infantry, the tribune expected them to begin their new duties with the dawn. He would introduce them to the men, and then they would prepare to march out. Tribune Grumio expected them to arrive at Pisa within two days.

They spent the rest of the day preparing for their new positions. As Falco suggested, they secured new pugiones. Varro was pleased that his replacement blade had been well tended and had no nicks.

The next morning, Varro reunited with Amul. They both shared a laugh at how soon this had happened.

"Sir, all the men are eager to meet you, as well as Falco and Curio. Most have never heard of you, but I have changed that. I hope you don't mind, sir. The name of the Mountain Ghosts should not be forgotten. And now, we can make new legends."

Varro patted the Numidian's shoulder.

"I'm not sure how many legends are left in me. But let's give the Ligurians a fight they won't forget and drive them back into their holes."

They had little time to meet the Numidians before the orders came to form a marching column. In their brief interactions, they tested Varro's language skills and knowledge of their culture. Many were astounded to learn he had dined at King Masinissa's table and could describe details to prove it. They seemed satisfied that Amul had told them the truth and accepted Varro and the others as kin.

Tribune Grumio had a good grasp of the Numidian cavalry. While he was no expert rider, he only needed to direct his men in battle. The allied cavalry would sit on the wings and await the consul's decision to attack. Varro expected little action. In fact, he expected the Ligurians to flee once challenged. They lacked a strong cohesive goal other than pillaging the countryside. Their leader, Corado, was unknown beyond his circle of followers. He had merely rallied enough angry barbarians to himself to cause trouble.

But he was also wise enough to seek an alliance against Rome. This hinted at intelligence and cunning obscured behind a confused siege. If he really forged an alliance, Varro wondered what the barbarians might achieve.

They marched along what were now familiar paths to Varro. He had spent hours poring over his map and perfecting it. He felt strangely cut off being placed in the allied cavalry. Perhaps it was because he had operated independently for too long. He wanted to participate in the strategy. He wanted to explain the details of what he had seen and documented around Pisa. But somehow Paullus was now attempting to do that very thing. He could only imagine what sort of lies he would have to tell, and what damage that might do to the overall battle plan.

No matter what he felt about the Ligurians and their lack of discipline, they still outnumbered the legion. With poor planning and hubris polluting Roman strategy, the Ligurians might win the day.

Varro set this worry aside since Paullus had assumed the responsibility. Minucius's wrath would fall on him first, even if he tried to deflect it elsewhere.

By evening, they camped within half a day's march from Pisa. It had been an arduous trek over unforgiving terrain, more difficult for the horses and the baggage train than the infantry. He missed being able to easily step over obstacles in his path, rather than constantly leaning forward to ensure his horse did not blindly follow the one before him into danger. But this Ligurian horse was a sensible sort. Varro liked him and was considering a name for him that evening.

He groomed the animal alongside the Numidians doing the same. Falco and Curio supervised the preparation of evening meals. So, he had a moment alone to think of his next steps.

Or so he believed.

He heard his name whispered, seeming to come from everywhere. It was an eerie feeling until he realized whoever called him hid on the other side of his horse. He wondered why the animal did not respond to a stranger so close to him.

But when he stepped around the horse, he saw a familiar face.

"Dano, what are you doing here?"

The young Ligurian searched side to side, then gave him a thin smile.

"I think I discovered something you will want to know. Something equal to the value of my life."

20

"What are you doing here?" Varro also looked around, finding the Numidians engrossed with grooming their horses. They loved them above all else and cared for them better than their own family. Grooming one was an almost sacred activity, and so they paid no attention to Varro's visitor.

"Obviously I came back." Dano had a youthful and innocent look, obscured behind the beginning of a beard.

To avoid being overheard, Varro led him away from the horses to the dark space at the edge of camp. Already being on the margins of the camp, it was easy for both of them to slip away for a private conversation. They now huddled together so that a tent blocked them from most angles.

Varro prompted him for his reason to return.

"I had to pay you back. You gave me freedom against the orders of your leader. You treated me better than I would've treated you as my prisoner."

"You've been free for a day. What could happen in that time?"

Dano gave a sly smile.

"I knew I wouldn't be able to reach the Boii on my own. So I planned to return to my people. They would blame me for my defeat. But if I told them something about your camp, they might forgive me. Still, I would carry the shame forever. Then I remembered those soldiers in the forest."

Varro thought back to the strange feeling he had about the soldiers camped in the woods.

"So you went to spy on them? You did this because you wanted to repay me?"

"My father taught me to owe nothing to anyone. I cannot rest knowing my life is yours, even if I would never see you again. The gods know my debts. Besides, it was easy to spy on them. That's where things got interesting and I realized I could pay you back. There were three Romans and three of my people working together. The Romans also had a foreign slave. Only one of my people could speak Latin, and so he led the group."

Varro summoned a memory of the Roman on watch that night. He knew they weren't regular soldiers. The presence of the slave made him think of Paullus.

"I didn't see any need to sneak around," Dano said. "I approached them and told them what happened to me. They doubted me, but I have the rope burns to prove my story. So, they let me join."

Varro struggled to keep his hands at his side, but he wanted to shake the boy and dump out everything he had learned.

"Can you describe what they looked like? Did you learn any of their names?"

Dano's proud smile faded, and his cheeks reddened.

"I didn't learn any of their names. I wasn't with them for long, otherwise, how could I be here so soon? They saw me as just a boy, and so no one addressed me. In fact, my people wanted me to tend their horses while they spoke to the Romans. I ignored them. And I was smart enough not to let anyone know I understood Latin."

The triumphant smile returned to his face, and Varro patted him on the shoulder. It was the encouragement he needed to continue his story.

"They are planning to kill Consul Minucius."

Varro stared at him in disbelief. His mouth fell open, and he looked around as if simply voicing the statement might actually kill Minucius. Dano shrank back as if he feared the same. He lowered his voice as he continued.

"The Romans are going to lead my people around the back of your lines. They're taking about fifty men to create confusion. Then one of the Romans will get close to the consul."

Dano paused here, and rather than speak aloud, he mimicked the thrust of a dagger into someone's back.

"This is grave news," Varro said. He stared across the camp, unable to see past the Numidians' horses. He wondered where Paullus was and how he was connected to this conspiracy. "They did not mention Paullus, the man who met us when we brought you here?"

"No one used any names. They all knew what they were talking about. If I started asking for names, they'd suspect something."

It was a shrewd decision, and Varro appreciated it. He gave a careful look at the Ligurian in front of him. There was more to the boy than it seemed at first glance.

"That was wise of you. Do you know how they intend to reach the consul?"

"Only that the Romans will get close to him as long as my people do their job of threatening his position. In the confusion, they will put their knives into him. They didn't say exactly how they would kill him, but it must be their plan."

"I agree." Varro rubbed his chin, considering the likely candidates for assassins. There were too many to consider. "Did you learn why they want to kill Minucius?"

"So they can win the battle," Dano said as if explaining the obvious to a child.

"No, I mean did the Romans express any hatred for Minucius or for Rome? Right now, there are many people unhappy with being pressed back into the legion. I just wonder if that's at the bottom of this."

Dano shrugged. "Honestly, they talked like merchants rather than killers. You know the type, just doing business. I got a good look at the Roman who spoke to my people."

"So, if I were to capture this man you could identify him?"

Dano's shoulders straightened, and he tapped his head.

"I've got an excellent memory. But you'd have to protect me if I'm going in front of your people again. It took a lot to come back here, just so you know."

Varro smiled and again patted him on the shoulder.

"I do know. I thank you for it. You've repaid your debt to me. But you've done a service to your enemies. How does that make you feel?"

The question appeared to catch him off guard, and he raised a startled hand to his neck. "I just wanted to be free of my debt. When I walk away today, I don't owe anyone anything. If I helped an enemy, well, I wouldn't be the first. I see a lot of things helping my father with his trade."

"There's nothing more to tell me? How did you get away?"

"I'm just a boy, remember? Even though Corado had chosen me to accompany his messengers, it didn't make me important. I just have a skill he needed. So, when it was time to head back to our camp I faded to the rear. When no one was looking, I ran. I knew they wouldn't search for me. They have got to get back with a report. Besides, they never learned my name. I mattered nothing to them."

He lingered a moment, then looked towards the trees beyond

the camp. Varro looked around as well. The Numidians were leading their horses away.

"You realize that you have absolute freedom. That means you don't need to return to your lines. In fact, your people believe you're dead. A dead man has a lot of freedom. Now that we are speaking as equals, I ask that you stay nearby. I could use your help once more, especially when we capture the men who intend to kill the consul. Of course, I would compensate you with more than just thanks. A man with your skill could make a fine living just trading on information."

Dano's brow furrowed.

"I just want to get back to my father and become a trader like he is. He makes a fine living trading goods."

"Still, if you can remain nearby, then I would be in your debt."

"What would I eat, and where would I live? I don't want to get caught again. If I do, your army is so big you might not even know."

Varro had been so impressed with Dano that he forgot he was dealing with an inexperienced boy. He had garnered enough from their relationship already, but he was sincere in his offer. The boy had potential, and he hated to see it wasted.

"Stay near the Numidian cavalry. That's where you'll find me, as well as Falco and Curio. If you change your mind about a simple life as a trader, come to me. You've shown you know how to find me. There's nothing wrong with a little adventure before you begin your quiet life."

They clasped arms, and then Dano ducked down and swept back into the grass. It was twilight, and long shadows stretched across the field. Varro watched the boy slither through it like a snake until he once more vanished into the distant trees.

He rushed to complete grooming his horse, then avoided returning to the tribune. Instead, he gathered Falco and Curio and led them away from their tent line. Both understood he had important news, and no one spoke until they were out of earshot of others. He gathered them close and whispered all that Dano had told him.

By the time he finished, all of them stood with arms folded and heads down. Falco rubbed his jaw.

"You think Paullus is connected to this? I don't disagree, but I also don't see the connection. Just because they had a slave and they happened to be where we last knew Paullus to be doesn't make him part of this plot. Of course, if you say so, then I'm happy to take him out."

Varro waved off Falco's threatening comment.

"The problem with all of this is that we only have Dano's word. While unlikely, it is possible he could be telling us a story. It would be very crafty of him, but maybe he wants to lead us into a trap."

Curio snapped his fingers. "That's true. Maybe Paullus knows we let Dano go and paid him to tell us the story. Then we would do things that will get us in trouble."

Falco chuckled. "We do things to get in trouble, anyway."

Varro thought about the possibility. It seemed far-fetched, but he had learned it was impossible to be too careful.

"No, Dano is telling us the truth." Varro looked between the two of them and finally unfolded his arms. "If Paullus wanted to get us, and he knew we let Dano go, then we be flogged by now. Besides, that's too elaborate a plan. He has a dozen easier ways he could make trouble. If Dano is not telling the truth, then he would've been instructed by someone to lead us astray. There just hasn't been enough time for that to happen. It is all as Dano said it is."

The three of them nodded, and Varro slowly looked around the camp. The sun painted a rose-colored stripe on the western horizon. They had little time before they would be missed.

"We don't have enough proof to bring this to Consul Minucius," Varro said. "We will have to handle this ourselves. Trusting anyone else only risks alerting our enemies. We don't know how deep this plot runs."

Falco grumbled and locked both hands behind his head.

"But why murder the consul? I get he might not be loved by everyone in the Senate. And maybe some angry veterans want to show what they think about serving again. But he's not the reason these veterans have been called back. Killing him won't get them sent home. If anything, it would make it harder."

Varro nodded. "We won't find out why they're targeting Minucius until we capture one of the conspirators. No matter what happens, we will have to take at least one alive. And then all those threats we leveled at Dano will come down on his head instead."

With the day running out, they had to attend to their duties before being missed. Varro at last returned to Tribune Grumio, who did not appear to notice his absence. It was a loose command group and reflected the overall lack of discipline in Minucius's army. While Varro lamented this, it did allow him freedom of movement. If he satisfied his tribune's orders, he could conduct his own business without fear of interference.

At dawn, the consul gathered his forces and gave a rousing speech, exhorting everyone to save Pisa and preserve the Roman way of life in the north. Whatever might be said of his discipline, his oratory skills were sharp. As Varro listened alongside the allied cavalry, he noted that even the more resistant men were swept up in the speech. Whether this would translate to victory on the battlefield remained to be seen.

They marched in a typical column, but without a main road to follow progress was slow. All the while, Varro's mind turned to Paullus and the conspiracy. As Falco had pointed out, he had no proof of his involvement. But Varro knew it was true, nonetheless. Once he had uncovered the conspirators, he was certain the interrogators would learn the truth. But who were these conspirators?

In Varro's estimation, at least one had to be in the consul's command group. He would be the closest when the Ligurians launched their distracting attack. The killer might not even directly assault him, instead choosing to push him in front of a Ligurian warrior. Then it would be considered nothing but a blameless accident of fate. Who would challenge the gods if they selected this day for Minucius's death? It was a smooth plan, much like Falco's plan to eliminate Paullus. That shifty patrician had to be involved but would never be the one holding the dagger over the consul's body.

Unfortunately, being with the Numidian cavalry meant Varro could not observe the consul and those around him. Certainly, the legate would stand to gain the most from Minucius's assassination. It made him the prime suspect, but the murder would not make him a permanent consul. Therefore, there had to be another motivation that Varro could not understand from his limited point of view.

In the end, he gave up trying to guess. He guided his horse and followed the column northwest. It didn't matter why someone wanted to kill the consul. It only mattered that he survived this treachery. That became Varro's new mission, whether assigned by Flamininus or the gods themselves.

He recognized much of the terrain that the army was passing for the first time. He hoped his map informed the consul's strategy. But as they neared Pisa, it became increasingly obvious that his notes had made little difference. Minucius appeared to choose a direct route toward the Ligurian encirclement. None of the points for an ambush or screening terrain seem to be in his consideration.

Curio, who rode in the command group with him and still wore his sling, gave him a knowing look. Since they were on the march, both were restricted to silence. But Varro could read Curio's thoughts perfectly. With Paullus interpreting the map for Minucius, he probably didn't understand what it was intended to show. Once again, Paullus's desire to be in charge regardless of his qualifications now led an entire army into a dangerous situation.

When at last they came to the wide plain where the Ligurian force spread out before them, Varro abandoned any hope of a surprise breakthrough.

Orders came to assemble the battle ranks, with cavalry on both wings. The consul ordered the Numidian cavalry to the left and the Roman to the right. It put Paullus as far away as he could go from Varro. In any other circumstance, he would've welcomed it. But now it prevented him from witnessing anything incriminating.

"Here's your chance, Centurion Varro," Tribune Grumio said. "Or rather a chance for Centurion Falco, since he'll be in the thick of fighting. I'm curious to see what your time among the Numidians has taught all of you."

"He will be limited in what he can do, sir. He is only a single decurion and will depend upon your wise strategies."

Tribune Grumio chuckled and surveyed the plains ahead of them. The smile faded.

"There are quite a few of them, but I suppose we were warned. I can only hope that they don't bring their full weight to bear on us. Our swords will be forever dulled from hacking apart so many bodies."

The tribune's airy boastfulness lifted the spirits of his men nearby. A good leader knows never to show fear before his subordinates. Varro appreciated it, but he realized from Grumio's comment about their numbers that he had a healthy fear of a numerically superior force. This, too, was wise.

The Numidian cavalry was organized the same as the Romans. The Numidians had adopted this formation rather than try to preserve their traditional, looser structures. Since they were commanded by Roman officers, it made for an easier transition.

They numbered about eight hundred strong and were divided into three groups. In the Roman cavalry, these were called turmae.

Each of these three groups had a decurion who led ten cavalrymen. In a Roman unit, all the decurions reported to a prefect who then reported to the tribune. However, the Numidian organization dispensed with this role. The tribune himself gave orders directly to his decurions. Being outside the formal structure of the Roman legion, he had more leeway than he otherwise would. Varro only had a role if Grumio fell in battle. Otherwise, he was going to be more of an adjutant than anything else.

The Ligurians appeared to have been prepared for the Roman legion. Varro remembered the outpost that monitored this area to warn the main force in advance. If he could advise Minucius, he would've suggested sending a task force to eliminate that outpost. Now, the Ligurians had plenty of time to bring the bulk of their warriors forward. They could not risk sending everyone to face Minucius. Otherwise, the forces within Pisa might sally out and challenge them from the rear. But they had sent enough to be a match.

Sitting atop his horse, Varro had a clear view of the advancing Ligurians. They managed a semblance of formation, but it seemed more like they intended to skirmish rather than battle. Therefore, he expected Minucius to counter with his velites. Instead, he dispatched the hastati from the second legion.

No one in the command group spoke a word. But Varro inferred from the sudden silence and stiff postures they were all surprised as he was.

The hastati marched forward with their shields up and in their customary staggered positioning. Across the field, he could hear the centurions shouting their orders. Opposite them, the Ligurians cursed and goaded the Romans into attacking.

Engaging skirmishers with heavy infantry and no other support was simply throwing away the lives of his soldiers. They would never bring fast-moving skirmishers to battle and therefore achieve nothing. On the other hand, the velites were equipped to match their counterparts and retire when they had spent their javelins. Varro's lips tightened against the string of curses he felt building up there.

In the command group with Varro, Curio cleared his throat. He twisted on his horse to see his diminutive friend gesture toward the rear of their lines.

He knew he wanted to go watch for a Ligurian ambush. But he had no opportunity to break away. Varro imperceptibly shook his head. Instead, Curio walked his horse back a few steps as if to be prepared for immediate action. While they couldn't be certain when the ambush would happen, Varro judged it wouldn't be now.

Down on the field, he watched the hastati bravely march forward. Only a handful of men lay on the grass in their wake. The Ligurians employed slingers to great effect, knocking out men from the edges of their maniples. The centurions shouted for a charge when they got close enough. Pila were raised across the front centuries, and Varro experienced a moment of tenseness as if he were about to give the orders to cast.

He heard the shouted commands and watched as the light pila streaked across the gap. Some found their marks, but most speared only the ground. The Ligurians melted away, having anticipated this tactic. Unlike their warriors, the skirmishers had no obligation to move into contact.

Eventually, Varro had to look aside while the hastati chased an enemy that would only turn long enough to cast a stone from their slings before running back toward their lines. At last, the tribune in command halted pursuit and withdrew the hastati from the field. They picked up their brothers who had either been injured or killed as they crossed back to the main line.

On the other side of the field, scarcely a dozen Ligurian wounded remained behind. A few cried out, impaled on the pila.

As expected, the exchange had been uneven and a grievous waste of lives.

Beside Varro, Tribune Grumio drew a deep breath and stroked the neck of his horse. His voice was low, but in the stunned silence, it carried all the weight of a stone hammer.

"This doesn't look good."

21

Sitting atop his horse, Varro considered a name for it. Falco sat on his horse next to him, making the same consideration. Along with Curio, the three of them were part of a long line of cavalry protecting the infantry who were creating the ditch and stakes for their camp. They watched the northwest for signs of Ligurian activity. Nothing had come from the barbarians. So, they had used this opportunity to gather amid their Numidian companions.

"It's not like you're going to keep him," Falco said. "Besides, he knows his own name. And it isn't a Latin one. There is no point in thinking so much about it."

"I suppose you're right. But I'd rather think about that than think about everything else we have to consider."

Curio adjusted his sling. "Just call him Thunderbolt. You know that's what you want to do."

"He was a glorious horse. I hope he is happy with his new master."

The three of them debated horse names a while longer, then fell silent. It was the distracting chatter of men who didn't want to remember the defeat they had suffered. While the loss of some hastati was of little consequence in the overall scheme, it indicated problems at the top. The veterans among the soldiers would realize this, and their lack of confidence would spread to the recruits. It was a dangerous thing to have an already reluctant army become disillusioned with their leadership before the battle even started.

Falco scratched the back of his head, digging his fingers deep under his helmet.

"Do you think maybe they want him dead because he's incompetent? Maybe we're working for the wrong side?"

Varro hissed in a low voice. "By the gods, don't talk like that. The Senate elected him to that position, and the Senate represents the public."

Falco sneered and shook his head. "The deeper we get into the shit, the stranger your ideas become. He's probably consul because he paid someone for the honor. He needs the job to make his career. I'm just saying that maybe someone who knows better doesn't want him to pursue that career. How do we know what's good or bad for Rome? We are just three simple infantrymen who sometimes get to ride horses."

Curio laughed at the comparison, but Varro found no humor in it.

It was a bitter day, he decided. Falco was more than likely right in his assessment. How could he laugh at something like that?

Besides committing the hastati to failure, Minucius had also made the perplexing decision to pull back and establish his camp. Varro was grateful to be with the Numidians. If they complained, they did so in their own dialect and accent that defied Varro's linguistic capabilities.

Once the camp was properly fortified, the tribune recalled the calvary from guard duty. The rest of the night passed following standard procedures and no threats came from the Ligurians.

However, with the Roman positions now well known, they would likely prepare for the inevitable battle. Again, they could not abandon their siege or else risk a counterattack from Pisa. Yet Minucius had conceded surprise with his hesitant probing of the Ligurian defense.

The next day, Minucius arrayed his battle lines before the prepared Ligurian defense. Varro sat on his horse on the left wing with the Numidian cavalry. As second-in-command, he rode at Tribune Grumio's right side. The signifier and tubicen flanked both of them, and at the rear were his messengers, which included Curio. He had removed his sling. Varro had asked him about this earlier, and he said a sling made him a target for the enemy.

He asked Curio to remain alert for the ambush that must be coming. Varro assumed since they had all night to prepare that the Ligurians would approach in the middle of the battle and attempt to eliminate Minucius. Varro had to get to him before that happened.

He had considered telling Tribune Grumio, but it would take more effort and time to convince him than it would be worth. He might even alert the consul and therefore tip off the conspirators. Varro was certain one had to be at the consul's side. The best plan he could come up with was to wait for the attack to begin, then dispatch Curio to watch for the ambush then alert the consul.

Any action for the allied cavalry would come later in the battle. An ambush would come at the midpoint while all attention was directed forward. So he expected to peel away to aid the consul when needed. The only thing he wouldn't be able to do was guard him throughout the entire battle. Assuming his bodyguards were still loyal, the consul could rely on them.

From atop his horse, he heard tribunes and centurions shouting orders across the long ranks of soldiers. He considered his plans. The consul, his command group, and his bodyguard were set far to the rear. Not so far that a mounted man couldn't reach it in good time. But it still presented a risk. He had simply dismissed the possibility of convincing Minucius that his life was in danger. Maybe he was aware of enemies seeking his death and would've welcomed Varro's news. It was too late now.

The battle had started.

Horns blared, and centurions shouted. The velites ran ahead of the hastati, their wolf pelts flowing and their javelins poised to cast. On the opposite side of the field, the Ligurians answered with their own skirmishers. Beyond them flowed a dark river of barbarians eager for Roman blood. Forty thousand strong, they seemed capable of washing away anything in their path. Minucius had only brought half as many swords to battle. But like Varro, he likely counted each sword equal to three of the barbarians. The Roman soldiers possessed better tools for killing in vast numbers. As grim as it seemed, Varro was confident the Ligurians were about to face defeat.

Once the velites had cast all their javelins, they retreated toward the advancing hastati.

"So it begins," Tribune Grumio said. "I expect we will not be called upon until the principes have engaged."

Varro nodded but felt that Grumio had not considered the more likely scenario of countering a Ligurian cavalry charge. He simply sucked his lip and made no answer, knowing that the cavalry still regarded him as an infantryman. The tribune would likely dismiss his ideas.

The clash of the hastati against the barbarian horde vibrated in Varro's ears even at this distance. Their struggle flooded him with memories of his own battles. He did not wish to be on the line again. It was a place of blood and death, where even courageous men begged the gods for mercy. The ground would become soaked with blood, and soon severed fingers and hands would mix with fallen bodies to create treacherous footing. He did not want to experience that again. Yet strangely, he missed it.

Sitting on a horse and waiting for a single moment to strike lacked the intensity of fighting for your life against a wall of enemies. This differed from his experiences in Numidia. There, he ran free and engaged enemies one-on-one. Now he would ride in formation if he were called upon to ride at all.

He watched the hastati in combat. One century would move up and relieve the other of its maniple. A fresh soldier always faced the enemy, but those Ligurians in the front remained in battle until they fell. Rome had the superior system, one rooted in logic and an understanding of human limitations. Barbarian cultures seemed to reject the thought that a man could tire in combat. This thinking cost them their best warriors. If they couldn't win the initial clash, they would likely lose the battle.

Varro kept glancing behind at Curio. Each time, he gently shook his head. Tribune Minucius sat on his horse, hands shading his eyes as he surveyed the battle in progress. No sign of an ambush yet.

Varro heard the familiar notes played to signal the hastati's withdrawal. The principes would now advance into their place. These were the men in the prime of life, the heart of the Roman fighting force. The hastati had done their job softening the Ligurian line. It would now fall to the principes to drive the enemy from the field and back to their mountain homes.

Beyond all of this, the dark silhouettes of Pisa's defenders bristled along the walls. They were little more than purple smudges to Varro's eyes, but he imagined their excited chatter at being relieved. Despite his experiences in the city, he looked forward to its liberation and witnessing its inhabitants' celebrations.

But the battle was not yet won.

He saw the cloud of dust on the Ligurian right flank and heard the soft pounding of distant hooves. Their cavalry was sweeping forward intending to break the principes on the flank.

Tribune Grumio saw this as well and sat up straighter on his horse.

"Stand ready to charge on my order."

Eight hundred Numidian horsemen responded with throaty war cries to their officer's commands. Even in all the noise, Falco's voice was clear. Varro saw his friend rode at the spear tip of their formation. Varro had tried to convince him to remain at the rear so that he could disengage and help with the consul if needed. But it seemed he was too eager to find battle again and made sure that he would lead the charge.

At the rear, and closest to the tribune, was Amul. The Numidian watched the tribune for orders but also gave a nod to Varro. He was eager to show what he had learned under Varro's command. It would be good to see what his training had done for the Numidian. And as the Ligurians drew nearer, the time for that training was at hand.

The barbarians pounded ahead in a barely cohesive formation. Their strongest warriors led and the rest jostled with each other to move toward the front. Again, it was a stark contrast to Roman order and discipline. Varro knew which method would prevail.

When the Ligurians had crossed halfway to their destination, he gave the order to charge. The tubicen blared out the notes on his horn, and the Numidian cavalry bounded into action.

Hearing their high-pitched battle cries brought Varro back in time. Once more, he was riding free across rocky plains to threaten a Carthaginian caravan. There was no hot wind in his face or dust in his mouth, but he could feel both as he urged his mount ahead. He let out the same high-pitched cry and joined his Numidian brothers in their charge against the Ligurians.

From here, the tribune did not need to give further direction. The Numidians understood the objective and how to best achieve it. At the front, Falco raised his sword and hefted his small shield.

Daring to glance behind, Varro saw Curio had joined the charge as well. He wished he had remained behind, but understood that he could not do otherwise. He would simply ride along with the other messengers and defend himself as best as he could with his injured arm.

The Ligurians swerved to engage the Roman countercharge. The Numidian cavalry formed a wedge that drove into the heart of the enemy cavalry like a sword. Falco vanished into the darkness of the barbarians, and the rest of the cavalry followed.

The horses plunged ahead and scattered their enemies. Varro held his own sword wide and kept his small round cavalry shield up.

The first barbarian charged at him, aiming a spear at his head. While dramatic, the attack was impractical. The head was too small of a target, and Varro easily ducked under the spear. He guided his horse with his knees and let his longer gladius cut into the Ligurian's side. The barbarian screamed and tumbled from his horse, then vanished into the chaos.

Horses snorted, and hooves stamped the earth. Men swooped past each other, slicing off arms, piercing torsos, or battering them from their mounts. The unfortunate men on the ground died under the hooves of friend and foe alike. Anyone regaining his footing was trampled down. It was pure madness and carnage.

And Varro rode through it all, his shield taking the worst of his enemies' blows and his sword dealing wicked cuts. It seemed he would ride through them, through Pisa, and into the vast mountains of the north before he would stop. He was once more a Mountain Ghost, dealing in death and misery from horseback.

"Centurion Varro! Return to formation!"

The order shocked him back to his senses. He was riding beside Amul, who was covered in blood and smiling. All around them Ligurian cavalry turned their horses and fled the field.

"To me, Varro!"

Tribune Grumio glared at him, having halted his charge behind the main thrust. The rest of his command group, Curio included, rallied around him. Amul butted his shield against Varro's and nodded to him before riding off to marshal those under his command.

Once more at the tribune's side, Varro realized he was dripping in blood. The salty taste seeped into his mouth and along with sweat, it stung his eyes.

"A fine display of horsemanship and combat," Grumio said. "But you need to stay in formation with the rest of the command group and not range ahead. You could have been cut off and taken down. I expect better of you."

Now Varro felt the heat on his face, and he lowered his head in acceptance of the criticism. He had been rash and let the moment carry him away.

The tribune had them regroup and reform, ready for a fresh charge if called upon.

But it did not seem the consul would order a second charge. The Ligurian line had collapsed, and the barbarians dispersed in a chaotic mess. Even so far away, Varro heard cheering from the walls of Pisa. Only the victorious shouting from the Roman lines drowned it out.

Varro looked back to Consul Minucius. He sat on his horse with his arms raised to signal victory. No ambush or assassination had occurred. The Ligurian plotters seemed as disorganized as their own army.

The Romans moved forward to occupy the field. The Ligurians were now in full retreat, and Minucius could claim to have liberated Pisa.

Though a great victory, the Romans still had to count the cost. Varro led his horse into position and soon passed the mangled bodies of his countrymen. They lay atop each other in piles that abutted their enemies. It was as if both sides reached out to each other even in death. Varro's horse snorted at the scent of blood but did not shy away. The animal took courage from the herd of cavalry guarding the left flank.

The Numidian formation remained loose, but Tribune Grumio continued to shout commands. At the front, Falco waved to Varro. The barbarians were flowing away toward the mountains like a black tide. The defenders on the walls raised their spears and shields in victory. Once the Roman line reached the gates by the river, Pisa would truly know freedom once more.

It was a long afternoon, with velites carrying the bodies of the fallen to the aid stations in the rear, while the rest of the army established a secure perimeter. The consul began immediate operations to establish a fortified camp outside the walls. Some of the Numidians questioned this. Varro explained that while they had liberated Pisa, they did not want to seem as if Rome occupied it. The garrison commander there had full authority over the city. If the legions marched through the streets, citizens might question his legitimacy. Besides, the Ligurians had retreated, but they might return.

By the end of the day, the camp had been established and messengers sent back and forth between Pisa and Consul Minucius. Once more, Falco and Curio gathered with Varro at the edge of the camp.

"They didn't make a move," Falco said. "It seemed like the perfect time, seeing how they had an entire day to set up their ambush."

"Then it means the battle is not over," Varro said.

Curio had replaced the sling on his arm and adjusted it as he spoke.

"But they ran off. Without a battle to hide their deeds, they would have to kill Minucius outright. Won't they get caught?"

Varro pinched the bridge of his nose, trying to guess the enemy's next move. He needed to monitor the situation, but could not escape the responsibilities he had. Then he realized how he could achieve this.

"How does your arm feel?" Varro gave a sly smile to Falco, who read his intent and gently nodded in agreement.

"It's better every day," Curio said brightly. He raised his injured arm to show his restored mobility.

But Varro cut him off.

"No, that's not how you feel. In fact, you reinjured it in the battle."

Curio frowned and raised his arm higher.

"Actually, if I had to, I could fight. The doctors want to be careful with it. A horse kicked me, after all."

Falco groaned and rolled his eyes.

"Gods, can't you follow along? We're getting you out of duty so that you can stick close to Minucius."

"Paullus, actually." Varro patted Curio's injured shoulder. "If there is going to be trouble with the consul, it's going to start with him. I know we don't have proof, but I'm certain he is coordinating everything."

Curio gave a slow nod of understanding.

"And that's why he set himself up so far away. If anyone might suspect him, it would be us."

Falco moved his horse around Curio's so that he screened Tribune Grumio's view.

"I knew you'd figure it out. Don't worry about the tribune, Varro will handle him. Besides, he has more messengers than he needs. You just disappear for a while and stick close to Paullus. The moment you see something odd, do what you think is right."

"And notify us as soon as you can," Varro added. "You will face more than just Paullus. Whatever we may think of him, he is no easy foe. Don't do everything alone."

Curio raised his injured arm. "I just said it was feeling better, not that I was feeling like Mars himself."

They soon settled into their routine. Varro had used his time to meet with the Numidians, Amul especially. The Numidian was eager for Varro's appraisal.

"You were a champion among champions." The comment drew a broad smile from Amul, but in truth, Varro had lost his senses during the battle. He scarcely remembered any of it.

As promised, Varro reported Curio's condition to the tribune. While he seemed perplexed, he did not question the report. Instead, he focused on Varro and his actions during the battle.

"I can see you have earned your medals. But do not get carried away in a cavalry formation. We can't have horses running into other horses, as you can imagine the consequences."

Once more Varro's cheeks burned with the shame of having lost control. He was glad Falco was not nearby, otherwise he might hold it against him. After all, he was usually the one calling for cooler heads. He had let out the slowly building pressure and frustration at not understanding his enemy's motivations. But he had done so in the wrong way and resolved to do better.

An uneasy feeling worried him all night, his mind constantly turning over the question of Paullus. Had Dano given him false information? He did not believe it so, but the plan could have changed. Varro would have no way to know if it had. He only knew the consul faced a threat to his life. If he went to Minucius now, the consul would question the delay in his report.

Whatever his doubts, he had made his choice and had to live with it.

His fragmented dreams were confused and blurred, and throughout them, a lonely and desperate voice screamed.

And when he awakened at dawn, the screaming continued.

Only it was no longer a scream in his mind. It came from outside the tent.

The Ligurians attacked once more.

22

In all his years with the legion, Varro had never experienced a direct attack on a fortified marching camp. Of course, he had heard stories from the veterans of the Punic Wars about such attacks. Nothing they had described could prepare him for the feeling of violation and rage he experienced. As he scrambled out of the tent, carrying his small cavalry shield, his mind filled with visions of dead Ligurians.

"Hurry!" Tribune Grumio screamed at his decurions, his face red and eyes bulging. "Get to the line before we're overrun!"

Tightening his harness, Varro joined the tribune and the rest of the command group.

"Sir, how many?"

Grumio's bulging eyes fixed on Varro's.

"The whole hairy bunch of them. They're practically on top of us now. Hurry!"

Varro caught up with Falco in the scramble for the Numidian cavalry to mount up. They jogged toward their horses.

"Don't lead the charge today. Let someone else have the glory. This might be the conspirators' chance."

"I'm not sure there's going to be a charge." Falco did not finish his thought, but simply pointed ahead.

A black wall of Ligurians massed just outside the camp. A ragged line of mixed Roman forces held them back. The disorganization spoke to the suddenness of the Ligurian attack. Falco was right. Every man had to lend his sword to the battle immediately. There was scant time for tactics.

While the spikes surrounding the camp discouraged an enemy charge, they also made it difficult to exit. The infantry could swarm around the spikes, but these would have to be dug up to allow the horses' passage. As a result, both Roman and Numidian cavalry struggled to exit by all the main gates.

"Sir, we can't wait." Varro ran his horse slightly ahead of the command group. "We need to pull up the stakes."

Grumio bit down on his words, looking between the enemy and the backup at the gates. It was a breach of protocol to remove the stakes, especially with an enemy so close. If the Ligurians forced them to retreat to the camp, the gap would become a liability. Minucius would hold the tribune responsible and deliver severe punishment.

Yet the need was too great. Grumio waved Varro ahead, clearly frustrated.

Working through Amul, Varro gathered a dozen of the Numidians, and they pried up the stakes. It was desperate and demanding work, but once they had extracted enough, the cavalry flowed through the opening.

Amul beamed. "We ride to battle again, sir. Once more, a chance to kill our enemies. It is a glorious day."

"Yes, kill the enemies and worry about glory later." Varro then snaked back through the lines of horses headed out of the opening and found his own mount.

They flowed out in a loose formation, heading to the left of the Roman line such as it was. Varro looked for Tribune Minucius among the chaos and found his standard rising over the rear ranks. By now, Curio would have reached Paullus. He had to trust him to keep the consul safe from treachery. The battle ahead would demand all his attention.

The emboldened Ligurians shouted curses and taunts as they pressed the Roman defenses. Spears and sling stones arced overhead, scattering among the Romans and reaping a bloody harvest. Until the consul and his tribunes could assert command, every centurion was acting on his own initiative. But the centuries had become intermingled. Varro could not see any cohesive formation, just a long and thick line of brawling soldiers. To fight to their best ability, centuries needed to coordinate within their own maniple. But now unfamiliar centuries fought on either side. The infantry knew its job but didn't know its neighbor.

All of this passed as a blur, and Varro charged alongside his tribune toward the enemy. They had placed the camp where the Ligurians had abandoned their incomplete battering ram. Despite the supreme visibility this location afforded, the Ligurians had come upon them unseen until the last moment. As such, their cavalry was already charging the left flank.

The Numidian flank.

Grumio appeared as incensed as Varro was. His eyes were bright with fury, and he held his sword high.

"Kill them! Send them screaming to their gods!"

Varro felt his horse shiver as if exulting at the open plain beneath them. Eight hundred Numidian horses thundered alongside him. The wind scoured his face as he rode for the mass of raging barbarian horsemen.

The two sides joined like interlocking fingers. Varro watched the leading cavalrymen vanish into the swarm. The Numidians appeared weak beside the hulking Ligurians. They carried only a small shield and javelins. They did not wear any armor or carry any other weapons. It would appear the enemy outmatched them.

But Varro knew better.

As the Numidians rode through their enemies, their javelins found their marks. Their lithe horses kept them out of reach and propelled them forward to the next enemy. They left bleeding and broken enemies in their wake, unhorsed or else slumped over the necks of their beasts.

At last, Varro and the command group crashed into battle.

Unlike the Numidians, they fought like traditional Roman cavalry. Varro's weapons dictated a different style. His gladius was not effective on horseback unless he drove his horse aside the enemy. This was impossible to do at a gallop. But Varro adopted a more dangerous stance, leaning out of the saddle to use his sword. Rather than target the rider, he sought the horse. He had to be careful not to lose his grip or sink the blade into the horse. His only other backup weapon was his pugio, an even worse weapon to use on horseback.

They were about to exit the other side of the Ligurian charge. This time Varro was certain to stay near Grumio. He turned to be sure he had not ridden ahead in his excitement. The tribune was splashed with enemy blood, and his face was taut with rage. He raced behind Varro with his signifier on his right side. He held their standard aloft in one hand, fought with the other, and guided his horse with his knees. As expected, the signifier was the best soldier in the tribune's command.

So when a Ligurian rode past and skewered him with his spear, Varro nearly fell out of his own saddle. In a blink, the signifier was gone and his horse galloped on without him.

"The standard!" Grumio shouted and turned his horse hard.

Varro did the same. A fresh knot of Ligurians bore down on him. He raised his shield to protect his left and struck out to his right. The blade of a spear tip scored his shoulder, his mail deflecting any injury. His shield likewise protected his left, but shoved him toward his sword-side enemy.

It took all his skill to remain in the saddle as his enemy swooped past, slicing for his head. He had only a moment to look at the hate-filled, wild eyes of his foe and then ducked. The crack of the blade over his head faded into the background as his horse carried him onward.

"The standard!" Varro echoed the tribune's words. The standard had to be retrieved no matter the cost.

Having passed through a clot of enemies, he now turned his horse into the dust from the charge billowing in his wake.

Grumio had guided his horse back to the fallen signifer. The proud standard of the Numidian allied cavalry lay in the grass beside its dead bearer. The rest of the command group likewise turned their horses back. But for this instant, Grumio was alone.

The enemy that had swiped at Varro now converged on him. Where Varro had been lucky, the tribune was not.

The spear that had only touched Varro's shoulder now rammed directly through the tribune's back. The force of the blow shattered the spear shaft, and Grumio toppled from his mount. Another Ligurian hacked at him as he thundered past, but the blow only struck the tribune's horse on the saddle, which was now empty.

The Ligurians understood their achievement, and as they rode away called out to their brothers. If they captured a Roman standard, they would become both famous among their own and humiliate the Numidians.

Varro understood his duty.

"Retrieve the standard!"

The command group circled around their fallen officer. The Ligurians turned their horses to face the determined resistance. But the prize was too valuable to resist, and they spurred their horses forward.

The command group met the charge, while Varro had already

placed his horse before Grumio's body. He had fallen atop the standard, and his blood leaked onto its shaft.

Glancing up to see the others engaged with the Ligurians, Varro slipped off his horse. He shook his head and snorted in protest. He was fine to ride through danger, but had other thoughts about standing idle amid a swarm of charging horses.

"Easy, guard me a moment, then we will be away."

Varro experienced the singular terror of being on the ground amid fighting cavalry. All around him, brown and black blurs raced past. Weapons flashed and battle cries echoed as combatants swooped in and then away. The ground shook beneath his feet as hooves thundered all around.

"This must be what a bug sees before it's crushed," he muttered.

He flipped Grumio onto his back. The broken spear shaft held him up from the ground. His eyes were wide in shock, but still rimmed with indignant fury. Whatever they looked upon now was nothing of this world.

Leaving the standard on the ground for a moment, he hefted the tribune's body. His horse seemed to understand his intent and shied away. Varro had to chase him a few steps before placing Grumio's body over the horse's rump. All the while, the sounds of battle behind him rang in his ears.

He fetched the standard out of the grass, feeling Grumio's fresh blood on his palm. He raised it up and shouted a war cry.

A dark shadow fell across him, and he reached for his gladius, which he had thrust into the ground. Instead, it was the tubicen who extended his hand to accept the standard.

"Allow me the honor, sir. You are in command now."

So it was. The simple statement left him without words. Both sides had charged through each other, then reformed for a second pass.

He saw Falco approaching with his unit of ten riders. His face was full of stern shadow cast by the morning sun. He saluted Varro, immediately recognizing the change in command.

"It seems our enemies have not tasted defeat yet." Varro carefully remounted his horse, who again protested the extra burden he now carried. He handed the standard to his new signifier. "Keep this safe and hold it high."

He had not formally practiced cavalry tactics, but he understood the basics from his time in Numidia. Besides, his Numidian cavalry knew what to do next. His orders were superfluous.

"The consul still stands," Falco said as he passed Varro to find his position in the formation.

Their charge had carried Varro far from the main battle, but he could easily see Consul Minucius regaining control of his lines. Before him, the Ligurians hurled themselves in a mad wave at the stubborn Romans. They saw their advantage slipping away and appeared to be making a final attempt to break through the line.

With the tribune's body slung over the back of his horse, Varro could not ride at the same speed as the others. But it was his duty to ensure such a brave and fine officer as Tribune Grumio received proper honors and a burial. He could not leave him on the field to become a trophy head for some barbarian. It was hard enough to leave the signifier behind.

The second charge went as well as the first. The Romans sliced through the disorganized Ligurian riders, and the Numidians proved their worth. When Varro emerged on the other side at the rear of the charge, he found the enemy continuing to ride for the north. The cavalry on the left flank had been defeated.

He formed up his Numidians for further orders. They were flush with victory, and Amul chanted the name of the mountain ghosts. Those nearby took up the chant, but Varro waved him down. The battle was not won, and to celebrate was premature.

Falco remained in the rear ranks, but still beyond speaking distance. Varro watched him searching over his shoulder, checking for signs of danger in the rear. But Varro did not expect the Ligurian ambush here. At least not with their marching camp protecting the rear area. It would be quite a feat to sneak even a dozen Ligurians through that camp and to the consul's position.

By now, the consul had arranged his lines, but at a substantial cost. It was no simple thing to move a century into or out of battle when everything was so disorganized. To do this across all his lines was even harder. The soldiers paid the price and were now sprawled out on the ground either dead or dying.

However, the Ligurians had spent their advantage and gained nothing. The Roman attack already bowed their lines back and would soon break through. Varro already noted men breaking from the rear ranks like specks of dirt washing away in a current.

He watched for his signal to attack, but nothing came. They had performed their duty and repelled a cavalry attack on the flank. While Minucius would probably not credit them for what they had done, Varro knew the Numidians had spared the Roman line a devastating flank charge. If he remained in command, he would be certain to recognize them for this.

The fighting continued, and Varro found it difficult to stand and observe his brothers struggling against a stubborn enemy. Every thud of a shield on shield shook him to his core. He could feel the itch in his palm for the grip of his gladius.

As always happens in battle, the enemy broke without warning. In one moment, a soldier is fighting for his life, and the next there is nothing but space before him.

The Ligurians turned and ran for the mountains where they had sheltered after their defeat the day before. The Romans cried after them, deriding their cowardice. Even Varro's Numidians raised their javelins and cursed them in their own language.

Whether it was from anger at being surprised or realizing a tactical opportunity, Consul Minucius signaled pursuit.

The order immediately tempered the cheering, and centurions

all along the line shouted for order and silence in the ranks. This was not to be a disorganized run, but a disciplined march to where the enemies believed themselves safe.

Though he did not agree, Varro had no choice but to obey. Until ordered otherwise, he was acting as tribune of the Numidian cavalry. He left Grumio's body in the care of the velites that collected casualties. The two young men who accepted the corpse seemed astonished to be holding someone of such a high rank. But rank did not offer any protection in battle. In fact, it was a liability on the field. Grumio had been brave to charge alongside his Numidians. They would accord him honor for his death and remember his bravery.

The allied cavalry rode wide on the left flank as an escort to the main line. The Ligurians fled before them, gaining ground faster than the Romans could match. Already the first barbarians to have fled were climbing into the foothills.

As far as pursuits went, this was tedious. The Ligurians had successfully made their escape while the Romans plodded after them. Varro knew that the average soldier had enough stamina and strength to close that gap and still fight. So he didn't understand why Minucius pursued them with so much caution. To his mind, the consul was ceding their advantage.

When they arrived at the foothills, Minucius called a halt to the pursuit. He had sent all the Ligurians back to their mountain homes and seemed content to walk them off the fields surrounding Pisa.

The army then settled into a holding pattern. Their camp was not far, and they still parked the baggage train there. Varro expected they would return and make plans to fortify Pisa.

But by the end of the day, his expectations had been proved incorrect. They brought the baggage train up to meet the legion.

By late afternoon, they were marching into the mountains to put an end to the Ligurians once and for all.

23

Varro stood to attention with the other tribunes assembled in Consul Minucius's command tent. The consul sat at his desk with his head lowered and pinching the bridge of his nose. No one spoke and all eyes were likewise downcast. Only Varro dared to search the other faces from under his brows. The silence was cut by the sounds of camp life beyond the tent. Nearby, a centurion shouted at his subordinate.

"Are you so stupid that you don't know how to stand straight? Dear gods, why have you cursed me with such worthless men?"

The muffled shouting reflected Varro's sentiments exactly. From the barely discernible stirring among some of the tribunes, he guessed others felt the same way.

Paullus, despite not being a tribune, somehow had managed to attend the consul's brief. Doubtless, he had used his self-appointed leadership of Servus Capax to gain access. He was one who did not flinch at the centurion's cursing. Perhaps he did not see their situation as clearly as some others did.

At last, Minucius raised his head and searched around the room until he fixed on one man. His voice was low and gravelly.

"You are certain we are completely cut off in either direction?"

The question was directed at the unfortunate tribune standing directly across from him. He had overseen the scouting detail to confirm the Ligurian encirclement. He stiffened at the question and looked straight through everyone as he answered.

"Sir, my scouts have confirmed it. Also, it is plainly obvious that we cannot escape from this pass. You can see the barbarians behind their barriers, sir. They guard the way forward and the way back. The mountains on either side cannot be scaled."

Silence reasserted itself, and the nearby centurion continued to curse his men.

"How stupid can you be? Frankly, I am amazed the walnut between your ears produces anything like thought."

Varro sympathized with the centurion. He wished he could hurl the same curses on Minucius and his uninspired tribunes.

"Then we're going to need a plan," the consul said. "I'll need to know exactly what we're facing and every detail of this pass."

Varro swallowed hard against the risk of speaking out. The consul's haste had led them into a trap, and now he offered platitudes as a solution. He was disappointed no one else in the tent had the nerve to call him on it. Of course, he realized he was no better. Still, they were duly appointed to their ranks while he was merely acting tribune. At the least, the legate should have spoken. Yet he too remained silent.

It had been a trying two days of pursuit. After their initial success in routing the Ligurian attack, Minucius followed them into the mountains. His mission had been to relieve the siege at Pisa, but being a consul was free to expand the scope of operations. On the first night they made camp in the mountains he called a general meeting. In his address he swore to end the Ligurian threat forever. At the time, the men rallied behind this idea. However, Varro thought it was ill advised. The consul seemed oblivious to the number of enemies he had just faced. On the open field, the Romans would always prevail. But to travel into the mountains risked exactly what had just happened this morning.

The Ligurians trapped them in a pass.

The consul's call for action ignited a spirited debate among his tribunes. Varro listened to variations of full-frontal assaults. It seemed as if each tribune wanted his command to be the centerpiece of the battle. Whether it made strategic sense seemed secondary to the amount of glory it might accord the tribune. Minucius nodded throughout, looking like a man who could not choose his meal from among seven of the same courses.

All the while, Varro remained silent and studied Paullus. Over the last two days, he had assigned Curio to spy on him. He had learned nothing new, but then Curio had not yet made his report. He did not appear like a man intent on murdering Minucius, but rather like one eager to please him. He jumped on every suggestion that caught the consul's attention and derided any that he disliked. Varro considered this must be his plan to get close. He was certain Paullus had to be involved in the plot as well as others in this tent. Yet he could not discern who those would be.

The debates about which tribune should attempt to smash through the blockade eventually reached an impasse as hard as those the Ligurians had built. No one could get through.

Consul Minucius leaned heavily on his desk in a posture of defeat. It was a bad look for the most powerful man in Rome. No wonder Senator Flamininus held him in low regard.

When the news of their entrapment had reached Varro this morning, he had already been planning how his cavalry could aid in a breakthrough. He had come to this brief expecting to share the plan but found Paullus here. His presence was like cold water on a campfire. Varro was reluctant to share his thoughts with him present. He wasn't sure how Paullus could benefit, but believed he would find a way to twist it to his advantage. He had proved more than once how slippery he could be.

However, the need for a fresh idea outweighed his concerns. Neither the consul nor his tribunes had any imagination. It seemed to Varro that the reluctance of this muster of the legion went beyond just the common soldier and extended to its leadership.

Varro stood forward, then cleared his throat.

"Sir, I believe I have an idea how to defeat the Ligurians. The Numidian cavalry will create a breakthrough for the infantry to exploit."

He had to repeat the statement twice before Minucius noticed him among all the other arguments. He frowned at Varro as if he were speaking from a distant hill. Then he held up his hand for silence and the others ceded the floor to him. Paullus regarded him with hooded eyes, but Varro ignored him and concentrated on the consul.

"Sir, it is well known that our men often joke about the Numidians and their poor appearance. I should know, because have I been one of their number."

"I thought you were great lover of their people?" Consul Minucius appeared to speak genuinely, but the comment drew snickers from the dark corners of the tent. Varro ignored these.

"That is true, sir. I have vast respect for their abilities as horsemen and warriors. We all know their history. Without them, many of our battles would have been far more desperate. They are horsemen without compare, and I have seen many in my time."

One of the tribunes who had snickered now spoke up. "In your time? How old are you? Aren't you an acting tribune? I'm not sure how expansive your experience is."

This emboldened another tribune to speak. "We don't need a

history lesson. We need a practical plan. Do you have one or are you going to just praise your men?"

At last, Minucius raised both hands to each tribune before returning to Varro. "Go on, but please get to your point."

"Of course, sir. I only mention their appearance and abilities because it is important to my plan. A few days ago, we taught the Ligurians a harsh lesson in the effectiveness of the Numidian cavalry. But it was only for their horsemen, and the majority of their warriors have no opinion yet. Sir, the barbarian mind holds appearance in the highest regard. When the Ligurians see a disorganized mess of dark-skinned, thin, unarmored men riding lanky horses, they will not take them seriously. I will instruct the Numidians to act as if they are fearful and incompetent. Give the enemy what they expect to see, and that's all they will see."

Minucius rubbed his chin in thought then pursed his lips.

"You believe you can approach the barricades and then launch a surprise attack because they will scorn the Numidians? Rather, I think they would leap into battle against a weak enemy."

Paullus at last spoke, agreeing with Minucius. "I know you believe the Numidians are great warriors, but we cannot underestimate the Ligurians as well. Your idea won't work."

"My idea is not finished. I said nothing of a direct attack on the Ligurians." Varro inclined his head to the consul. "Sir, the Ligurians would certainly strike at weakness. But they will not have time. We all know the speed and agility of the Numidian cavalrymen. As the Ligurians sneer at the disorganized horsemen approaching them, they will not expect a sudden, organized charge."

He paused, if only to add drama to his next statement.

"The Numidians will not attack the defenders, but instead will ride through them in dispersed formation. According to what we know, the Ligurians make their homes just beyond this pass. My horsemen will thread their barriers and strike at their unprotected homes. Their wives and children, their livestock and farms, all of it will be put to the torch. Now, they can either guard the pass or defend their homes. I have no doubt which they will choose. The Ligurians have not been committed to this cause from the beginning. They will not remain here while we slaughter their kin and destroy their homes."

Minucius's eyes widened with glee, and he balled his fist to thump the table.

"Of course they would not. They have come only to pillage, not to risk all they possess and love. When they turn, we will have our breakthrough. We will no longer be hemmed into this pass."

The consul's enthusiasm for the idea won over his sycophantic officers, and even those of a more independent mind seem to agree as well. Paullus glared at Varro for an imperceptible moment before breaking into a smile.

"It is a good use of allied resources, sir. Better that they should take the risk. And of course, they will be led by our brave acting tribune."

Paullus might have thought he had trapped Varro into risking his life, but he would have it no other way.

"Of course, sir. I will not allow anyone else to assume the risks of this operation."

Minucius agreed and then called for a planning session on how to exploit the opening the Numidians would create. Varro found himself outside of this conversation. He simply stood at attention while others laid out their plans before the consul. Notably, Paullus involved himself in this as well.

It astonished Varro that he should be so close to Minucius. Even if it was a ruse, it seemed overdone. His eyes slipped to the legate, who stood with arms folded while listening carefully. He seemed as if he judged everyone in the crowded tent. His role was to act as an advisor to the consul. Thus far, Varro had observed nothing from him. Paullus seemed to have that role. Maybe Minucius was overawed by having a relative of the great Scipio Africanus in his command and sought him for advice over his own legate.

In the end, the consul dismissed Varro to prepare the Numidians for action. Paullus did not move from the consul's side. He gave a thin smile to Varro as he left.

Outside the tent, Varro saw the angered centurion and his line of five soldiers. They had apparently failed inspection. The entire time Varro and the rest had debated in the tent, the centurion had been bawling out his charges. It brought a smile to his face. At least some things were constant in this army.

He crossed the rocky ground of the mountain pass to where the Numidian cavalry picketed their horses and made their camp. Stark, gray stone walls rose on both sides as if to emphasize their plight. They also served as a backdrop to the yellowed hide tents that bobbed with a gentle breeze.

He met Falco just outside his command tent. They caught up on all that had happened in the tent. Falco was already aware of the plan, and glad that the consul had embraced it.

"We're never going to punch through that blockade, not with them dropping rocks on us from both ends. Your idea was a good one. And speaking of good ideas, Curio's back. He is in the tent, grabbing a nap while you were with the consul."

The two of them piled into the tent and slid aside Curio. Falco watched the tent flap for anyone approaching. Varro slapped Curio's leg.

"Time to make your report, soldier. Wake up!"

Curio rolled over and groaned. "You couldn't have taken longer? I haven't really slept in two days."

Falco peered out of the tent and then drew the flap tight. "Don't be so dramatic. I've caught you sleeping when you said you were awake. Just like Varro on watch."

They allowed Curio a moment to wipe the sleep from his eyes.

He no longer wore his sling, though a dark bruise showed under the sleeve of his chain shirt. Varro and Falco both leaned in to hear what Curio had learned.

"He's been a busy man," he said through a yawn. "In fact, I watched him sneak away the first night."

Falco slapped his knee. "You were right, Varro. I knew this slippery bastard was up to something. Go on, tell us what he did."

"He was skilled in sneaking through the camp, which surprised me. He was watching but never found me."

Varro scratched his chin. "I doubt he was looking for you specifically. Remember, he doesn't know that we are aware of anything."

"Well, he was plenty cautious." Curio mimicked keeping his head down and looking over his shoulder. "You would think he was carrying Minucius's body to bury it in the woods. But he was carrying something, a bundle close to his chest."

Varro tried to imagine the scene: Paullus crouched low as he slipped between the ordered rows of tents, and Curio following close behind. It made him smile to think he had no idea Curio trailed him.

"He was headed right for the Ligurian barricade. I was getting nervous because we were so close. But he just held up both hands and walked the final distance."

Curio raised his hands and imitated surrender.

Falco hissed low. "Talk about a snake. Now he's dealing with our enemy."

"It gets better," Curio said, lowering his hands. "It wasn't barbarians that came to meet him. They were three of our own. They were hiding with the Ligurians, probably waiting for him to show up. Before they greeted each other, Paullus showed them something he wore about his neck. It looked like a medallion, but I was too far to see details."

Varro could see it in his mind and spoke it aloud for the others.

"Those were the soldiers we located in the woods. The three conspirators that Dano said he could identify."

"Funny you should mention him." Curio sat up straighter. "I spotted him poking around the edges of our camp last night. I don't know what he's up to, but he's nearby."

"Probably gone back to his old ways and scouting for the enemy," Falco said. "He was helpful while he was our prisoner. But he will forget us fast enough."

While Varro did not hold the same doubts, he was less interested in Dano. Instead, he urged Curio to finish his account of Paullus's treachery.

"They had a brief discussion," Curio said. "I couldn't get close enough to hear it. But I was close enough to see what Paullus did. That bundle he held to his chest had three pugiones in it. He gave one to each of them. They examined the pommels, then looked toward our camp like they were thinking about how to get in."

"Those were ours!" Falco again slapped his knee and grabbed Curio by his bad shoulder, causing him to wince. "They were looking for the Servus Capax marks."

Varro sat back, his head swimming with a myriad of ideas. He turned inward, no longer seeing the room or hearing his friends.

Everything came together with sudden clarity. All the mundane details made sense now.

When at last his mind returned to the tent, he found both his friends staring at him.

"You've got that look," Falco said. "You figured something out, haven't you?"

"We've been working according to Paullus's plan from the beginning, from when he wanted to join us. He needed us as an excuse for his covert plotting. Remember when he met us outside of Rome? His servant had come with a horse laden with gear. He knew we would dismiss it as a quirk of a pampered patrician brat.

He was following my old saying. Show them what they expect and that is what they will see."

Falco folded his arms and frowned. "What do you think was in there?"

"It was gear for three men, including provisions and camping equipment. Those three he is dealing with are not legionaries. They are hired killers. They needed disguises to pass themselves off as real soldiers."

Now Curio folded his arms. "But you said they referred to each other as soldiers. One of them called his officer sir."

"It could be that they have a hierarchy of their own, or once they have assumed a role, they remain in it until the job is done."

"So Paullus outfitted the killers to look like legionaries." Falco paused to peek out the tent flap once more. A flash of morning light slashed into the dim tent, then vanished. "But did he really think he could carry so much to Pisa and not be caught?"

Varro shook his head. "He was certain I would order him to send back his slave and extra gear. I did exactly what he wanted. He had previously instructed his slave to take a different ship and meet him at a specific location, one probably designated by his co-conspirators."

Curio and Falco looked at each other, and Curio asked their question.

"What do you mean by co-conspirators? The three men he met the other night?"

"Whatever is happening, Paullus is just one piece of it. I'm certain something larger is happening that we don't yet understand. But we are beginning to develop a picture of it. Someone higher than Paullus wants to eliminate Minucius. Paullus is just a tool, though a willing one. He has no place in the world other than to sit at home as a rich man's son. It does not satisfy him. So someone has tapped his discontent, and probably offered him a hidden path to the power he seeks."

Falco rubbed his brows then folded his hands behind his head.

"Why can't we stay out of this shit? Just once. Are you sure about all this?"

"I wish I had room for doubt. But there's more to tell, all the things we missed along the way are now clear.

"Paullus was in a rush because he needed to meet up with his servant. Whoever has organized this whole plot set out a tight timeline. He couldn't be delayed. That's why he insisted on the merchant captain sailing that day."

"But he left when the Ligurians ambushed us," Curio said. "Then he came back to save me, and then went on to warn Pisa. How does that all fit into this plan?"

"I know why he saved you. As I expected, it was not from the goodness of his heart. You had something he needed before he could continue with his mission."

"What could he have needed from us?" Falco spread his hands wide in question.

"We all saw it but didn't recognize it," Varro said. "When that sailor threw Paullus's pack into the surf, Curio fetched it for him. Some items spilled out when you pulled it out of the water. But you retrieved them while Paullus was raging at the sailors."

"That's right!" Curio leaned forward and touched the base of his neck. "He had something wrapped in a cloth. He was so mad that I didn't want to bother with him. I threw the cloth back in the water but kept what it held. It was an iron medallion. It had a worn-down image on it. It looked like a snake. Anyway, I stuck it in my pack and figured I would give it to him later. It didn't look like anything valuable or important. I thought it was a charm."

Varro shook his head. "But it was important. He sorted all his gear immediately and discovered the medallion was gone. Right after that, he became reserved and easier to deal with. Actually, he was distracted by the loss of that medallion. At some point, he realized you had it."

"But why not ask him for it?" Falco asked.

"Because he is nervous. Curio might've just handed it over without another word. But in his own mind, he feared us asking questions. He was also planning to escape, and maybe make it seem as if he had become a casualty. I cannot say how he planned to leave us, but the Ligurian ambush was his best opportunity. When we separated and left Curio with the Ligurians he had a chance to retrieve his medallion. His co-conspirators would not recognize him without it."

Curio rubbed his injured shoulder. "So he freed me and lifted that medallion. I don't have to look. I know I don't have it anymore."

"You saw him present it to the others. You don't have it."

"Why not just kill Curio?" Falco gave a sheepish look to his small friend. "Of course, I'm glad he didn't. But it seems the practical thing to do. And why warn Pisa, for that matter?"

"The three of us have a part in his plan, if that's not obvious by now. Had he killed Curio, we would've known it. First, he wasn't certain where you and I were while he was dealing with Curio. We might have caught him. Second, we would've known from Curio's wounds that a Roman killed him. He did not want to arouse our suspicions. Instead, he acted as if he sought only glory for himself. He completed the mission to Pisa to strengthen that illusion as well as gain credibility with Minucius. Again, he showed us what we expected to see and we accepted it."

Falco growled at the thought. "I can't believe him. He got to the consul first and set himself up as our leader. Of course, a nephew of the great Scipio would be the leader of an elite squad like us and not the other way around."

"That was exactly his plan. It allowed him to separate us while keeping himself close to his target. He also expected we would be glad for the distance between us. Again, he knew us too well. Now you must realize why he collected our pugiones and handed them over to the killers."

Curio was breathless as he spoke. "He's going to frame us for the murder."

Falco snorted at the idea. "How would that work? Consul Minucius has seen all three of us. We don't look anything like them."

Now Varro cocked his head and gave Curio a patient smile. "What did the three men who Paullus met with look like? I don't need to know their eye color. But was one tall and one short? Was one about my height?"

Curio's face paled, and everyone had the answer.

"The consul has only met you two once, and he hardly knows my name. It's unimportant since he'll be dead. You're both unknowns to all except the Numidians, and I am only marginally better known. Paullus was eager to get me out of the command tent today. He never used my name when he addressed me. He doesn't want anyone to have a clear memory of me. Because later, when they find our daggers in Minucius's back, he wants to be able to point to us. Of course, everyone knows his name and trusts it. I'm certain other conspirators will also hang the blame on us. The Numidians are not citizens, and their testimony will not matter. We will be found guilty, and we all know how the legion works. Justice will not be delayed."

They sat in gloomy, reflective silence. Varro saw his friends' expressions melt to dejection. He let them consider all he had guessed and hoped they would find a hole in his theory. But he knew they would not. When the silence grew uncomfortable, Varro brightened his voice and sat up straighter.

"I don't recognize these two sad faces before me. It's as if Minucius is dead and we are awaiting execution. Both of you should be glad instead. Paullus has no idea we figured him out. And this gives us the advantage of absolute and devastating surprise."

Falco's cheeks reddened—a rare thing for him.

"Maybe what you say is true. But we're all expected to carry out that brilliant plan you shared with the consul. Of course, that is exactly the moment these traitors will strike."

"I can fight for the consul." Curio tried to raise his bad arm but stopped halfway before he grimaced in pain.

"All of us will fight." Varro narrowed his eyes at the tent flap and imagined his next steps. "I agree with you, Falco. We must act now. Bring Amul here. It's time for the mountain ghosts to ride again."

24

"You have to admit, he is more handsome than you are."

Falco stroked his jaw as he admired Amul dressed in Varro's mail and helmet.

"Sir, it is the greatest honor to ride your horse into battle," Amul said. "But what will anyone think when they hear me speak? I do not have the same voice."

Varro put his hand over his mouth and tried not to laugh. Curio did, but Falco had the patience to explain.

"No one in the Roman line will be listening. They will be waiting for you to pull off your trick. Besides, you're a bit darker than Varro. Worry more for how you look than how you sound."

Amul studied his loosely fitting chain shirt but seemed unconvinced.

"I will address the men," Varro said. "Then you will take over. No one will question me, and they all know you are a great leader. You focus on the mission, just like we did back in Numidia. Fool those barbarians into thinking you aren't a threat, then fly through them and kill their families, burn their homes, and make them regret ever challenging us. Don't let them bring you to battle, and circle back to this pass. I guarantee by the time you return, the Ligurians will be gone."

Amul straightened his shoulders. "I will see it done, sir. No one will know you are not with us. I will bring honor to all our names."

Varro clapped him on the shoulder and assured him of his confidence. Amul left to gather the Numidians. Their plans had been shared with the Numidian decurions and all that remained was to reinforce their role.

Minucius arranged his forces as if preparing for the full-frontal assault his tribunes had demanded. They stretched out in long lines that filled the pass. The Roman cavalry bunched at the opposite end, but would have no part in the battle for lack of space for their horses.

This was not so much a ruse as it was preparation to exploit Ligurian panic. Once they understood where the Numidians were headed, they would turn their backs on the Romans. The barbarians at the other end of the pass would be slower to react, not realizing what had happened. Minucius would begin his attack and ensure a Roman breakthrough.

The address was brief, as Varro did not want too many Roman eyes drifting between him and Amul and wondering at their differences. When finished, he handed the reins of his horse to Amul. The proud Numidian saluted, mounted up, and then ordered his eight hundred horsemen forward.

As they feigned disarray, Varro found it easier to work his way to the far end where he met Curio and Falco already prepared in hiding.

They dressed like normal soldiers, with no chain shirts or bronze greaves. While Falco and Varro had instructed the Numidians, Curio had found them infantry gear. Each one now carried a red scutum and wore a bronze helmet with three black feathers. On their harnesses were a gladius and pugio. Their only other protection were bronze chest plates. Varro's shield and weapons were stacked to the side.

"I feel naked in this." Falco stroked his chest.

"It's what we wore for years," Curio said. "We'll be fine."

"We need to look exactly like the infantry." Varro retrieved his gear. As he strapped on his chest plate, he watched the Numidians amble forward as if they didn't know how to ride. Across the gap in the rocky, uneven ground, the Ligurians peered across their wood barricades. He saw one point and turn his head in laughter.

"It won't be long now. Once Minucius gives the order to advance, I expect the Ligurians in the rear to spring their ambush."

They watched as the Numidians made a show of their incompetence. More of the Ligurians came to watch the spectacle. They lined the barricades and laughed easily among themselves. Amul shouted at his men as if frustrated. But Varro could hear snippets.

"Don't look too confident. Spread out. We are almost there."

Varro smiled. "Good thing no one else understands him."

The Numidians had reached sling distance, and Varro saw the barbarians preparing their shots. He resisted an urge to order their shields up. Of course, Amul kept a wary eye on his enemies. The Numidians began to form up as if preparing a tentative charge.

Beside him, Varro saw both Falco and Curio leaning forward. They balled their fists, feeling the same anticipation.

The suddenness of the charge surprised even Varro. Amul's shouts vanished into the thunder of eight hundred Numidian horses riding for the gaps between the barriers. They raised their javelins and shouted their war cries. Dust flew up around them, blurring them into dark smudges.

With their unparalleled skill and surprise on their side, they steered their horses through the Ligurian gauntlet. As far as Varro could see, not a single Numidian fell from the saddle. Their lanky horses might've lacked the impressiveness of Roman cavalry, but they were lithe and fast. They left their enemies spinning in confusion and desperation.

Across the gap, the Roman line stood in disciplined silence. It seemed at last this legion had found its pride. Perhaps it was from the desperation of their entrapment. Their ranks were still and ordered, and only an occasional breeze set their helmet feathers waving. Behind them, Minucius and his command group watched from horseback. Varro noted that he had wisely placed lookouts to his rear in acknowledgment of the threat there.

The Numidians continued to pour through the gaps. Ligurians scrambled to shore up their defense, but it was too late. The speed of the horses denied them. Varro and the others crouched low and kept their shields to the ground. They could not approach Minucius until the Roman line advanced or else risk being spotted.

The last of the Numidians galloped out of the pass. The Ligurians seemed uncertain about which way to turn. Varro could only guess what transpired behind those barriers, but he noted fewer men guarding them.

At last, Minucius ordered his hastati ahead, signaling his intention to capture the pass.

"Time to move." Varro picked up his shield and then kept low as he walked along the edge of the pass. Falco and Curio followed behind.

Yet in that same instant, the mass of Ligurians in the rear raised their swords and shouted defiant battle cries. They swarmed across their barriers and charged for the rear lines.

The sight of so many barbarians suddenly charging sent horns blaring all down the Roman line. The triarii reversed themselves on Minucius's command. Apparently, they were prepared with their own ruse. It was well played but stymied Varro's efforts to reach the consul.

"Shit, we're cut off." Falco stood up as did the others.

"We'll go between the lines," Varro said. "Let no one stop us."

He broke into a run, and the others followed on either side. The triarii raised their shields and set their spears to receive the Ligurian charge. The consul had wisely relocated between his advancing lines and the defensive line. The triarii clustered around him, and he seemed impervious behind a wall of chain shirts and heavy shields.

But Varro knew he was never more vulnerable.

As they sprinted between the lines, men turned their heads. Optiones on both sides glared at them, but likely assumed them to be messengers. That three men would be running about the lines without orders was unthinkable.

The Ligurian charge now smashed into the triarii defense. The clapping of shield on shield and sword on sword rang in Varro's ears. Ahead of him, Consul Minucius and his command group struggled to monitor both fronts.

Varro did not see any threat but knew this had to be the conspirators' chosen moment. After this day, they had no means to make Minucius's death appear as an accident of fate. The battle would end today.

To his left, the principes advanced behind the hastati. To his right the grizzled veterans of the triarii forced back the barbarians seeking their flanks.

He neared the consul's position now but still did not see anything amiss. The conspirators had changed their plans. At this point, he had no choice but to reveal what he knew.

Before he could reach the consul, one of his infantry bodyguards barred Varro's path. The centurion towered over Varro, his heavy face drawn taut.

"Hold on. What are you three doing here?"

The burly centurion's voice was a match for his intimidating size. He carried a drawn gladius and looked eager to sink it into flesh. His scowl searched between Varro and the others.

"Stand aside," Varro said. "I have a message for the consul."

"Three messengers?" The words were heavy with skepticism.

Falco was the centurion's match in size, and he squared off with him.

"Glad you can count but get out of the way. This is urgent."

The centurion gritted his teeth, displaying yellow incisors like a wolf.

"You give me the message, and I deliver it to the consul. That's how this works."

Varro knew better, but before he could protest, everything changed.

Behind the consul, who monitored the triarii lines, a squad of Roman cavalry charged. However, the space remaining in the pass left no room for horses. The triarii line stretched nearly to the stone walls on either end. The disruption from the horses attempting to thread the narrow gap granted the Ligurians an opening.

Consul Minucius screamed in rage and pointed at the chaos.

"What in Jupiter's name are they doing? Close that gap!"

The flow of horses from the rear drove combined with the pressure from the Ligurians to the front caused the Roman line to break. Barbarians flowed into the opening, screaming victory.

Varro groaned at the reversal in fortune. Even with the cavalry obscured by the ranks of triarii, he knew Paullus led the ill-timed charge.

Everyone in the command group turned toward the jumbled mess on the flank. Only the centurion blocking Varro's path did not.

He was Falco's height. Varro glanced down to his hip.

A stylized owl's head on the pommel of a pugio winked at him.

Varro charged into the centurion, smashing his shoulder against his shield and pulling it away.

"He's one of them!"

The stunned centurion staggered backward, and Varro slid past him. As he did, he expertly lifted the pugio out of its sheath. The grip bit into his palm, as if rejoicing at finding its true owner again.

Someone else shouted Varro's exact thoughts.

"Protect the consul!"

The Ligurian envelopment pushed toward the command group. Even if they were unaware of the plot against Minucius, every barbarian coveted the glory of killing a Roman consul. Whoever could achieve such a thing would live forever in barbarian history.

As Varro slipped by, Falco grappled with the equally sized centurion. He could see nothing else as he ran for Minucius. His bodyguards, both on foot and horseback, now turned to face the charging barbarians.

His eyes desperately scanned for a pugio in one of their hands or for anyone attempting to reposition close to Minucius. But they were all focused on the impeding clash, their battle cries thin amid the din of battle to either side.

The barbarians threaded the narrow gap between triarii and principes. That they would be destroyed had to be obvious to even them. But their lust for eternal glory drove them forward.

By now, the principes had reversed and were rushing back to defend the consul and shore up the triarii. It had to be the most bizarre battle Varro had ever experienced.

The consul did not know which way to turn, being besieged at all sides. To his credit, he drew his cavalry sword and prepared to join his men in a fight to the death.

That's when Varro saw the conspirator.

Barbarians swarmed the consul's position, and in that chaos another of the conspirators revealed himself. Minucius had turned his horse to face the bulk of attackers on his left. This presented his back to Varro and the bodyguards surrounding him on that side. They now shifted to protect the flanks and keep the Ligurians from enveloping them.

Just as the Ligurians attacked, a conspirator hidden amid the infantry bodyguards drew his pugio. He then grabbed Minucius by the hem of his tunic and yanked back. The consul's strike against his enemy fumbled and he nearly toppled from his horse. Shocked at an unexpected attack from his rear, Minucius turned and cursed.

At the same moment, the conspirator thrust his blade at Minucius's side.

Varro pounced on him, tackling him to the ground.

The conspirator was armored in a chain shirt and bronze greaves. He was strong and smelled of garlic. He cursed Varro as he pushed against him, working his pugio out from under himself.

Horses stomped all around them, while their riders slammed against each other. A hoof thumped beside Varro's shoulder as he wrestled with the conspirator. He felt the prick of a bronze blade against his gut as his enemy shifted beneath him.

"Who are you?" Varro managed the question through gritted teeth. "Surrender now!"

He couldn't get a look at the man's face as they rolled amid the horses. Above him, he heard Minucius call out for help.

"To me! The line is broken!"

The conspirator locked his legs into Varro's, then shifted to bring himself around. They were face to face now, and each one gripped the other's pugio. All the while horses danced around them, their hooves threatening to crush anything on the ground.

He didn't recognize the face that met his. The conspirator had no distinguishing marks other than pock scars on his cheeks. His face was flushed red and he groaned with the effort of pushing his blade towards Varro's neck.

"Did Paullus give you the order? Is he your leader?"

In answer, the conspirator butted his head into Varro's. He fell back, a blinding explosion of white pain filling his vision.

He recovered quickly enough, but his conspirator was faster. He sprang to his feet, and then looked for a path to escape.

Behind him, Falco shouted, either in pain or in victory Varro could not tell. Curio wrestled with the third man to his left, strangely assisted by a Ligurian.

Minucius still sat upon his horse and fought against the barbarians jostling to reach him.

"You're trapped." Varro recovered from the dizzying blow and then staggered up to his feet. The conspirator had nowhere to run. He gave Varro a hollow smile, then leaped once more for the consul's back.

In a single bound, Varro covered the distance. The consul turned his horse at the precise moment, clearly guided by the gods themselves. The conspirator instead drove his pugio into the consul's horse, which reared and screamed at the stab to his flank.

And Varro drove his into the conspirator's back.

Blood poured from his mouth, and he arched backward against Varro. He was laughing, his blood-flecked face drawn into tight lines.

Varro dragged the conspirator away from the battle. Minucius struggled to bring his horse under control, but he pointed to Curio.

"There is another! Aid him!"

His commands were nearly lost in the cacophony of battle. All of Minucius's other bodyguards were absorbed into the fight swirling all around. Both triarii and principes now engaged the defiant Ligurians. He had only Varro to depend on.

He dropped the wheezing body, leaving the pugio implanted in his back. Drawing his gladius, he rushed to Curio's defense. The Ligurian that had fought alongside him now lay dead and Curio fought alone. This conspirator was likewise dressed in a chain shirt and heavy bronze greaves.

Despite his claims otherwise, Curio could not fight. Instead, he sheltered behind his scutum while his injured sword arm hung uselessly at his side. However, he had interposed himself between Minucius and the conspirator, using his scutum at an angle to keep his attacker at bay and away from the consul.

The conspirator had clearly given up on his mission and now sought to vanish into the swirling combat. It was only through Curio's efforts that he could not escape.

Varro slammed into the man, driving him to the ground and pinning him beneath his weight.

He bucked up against Varro but could not break free. Over the maddening noise of battle, he heard Curio shout.

"Move your head!"

Shifting his head aside, he felt the bronze edge of Curio's scutum graze his shoulder as he slammed it down on the conspirator's helmet. It pinged against the metal and rebounded.

But Varro felt the body underneath him go slack.

He rolled off the conspirator, then staggered to his feet. Curio stood smiling, his injured arm dangling at his side and his scutum resting against him.

"I had him all the way. But thanks for speeding it up."

Varro looked down on the fallen conspirator.

"I hope you didn't kill him. Where's Falco?"

They both searched the scramble of fighting men. All around, the Ligurians scattered for cover. The Romans gave chase, revealing the dead and dying rolling on the ground. For an instant, Varro feared he would see Falco among them.

Then he rose to his knees out of the mass of bodies around him on the ground. Had they not been friends since childhood, Varro might not have recognized him. His face was covered in blood so thick his eyes appeared like polished white stones in red wine.

"Thanks for leaving me to do all the fighting. The big one fell over like a dead tree. All show, that one. Not a real challenge."

At last, the Romans shouted in victory as the Ligurians scattered in every direction.

They had freed themselves and claimed the pass.

Before Varro and the others could add their own cheers, Consul Minucius and the remnants of his bodyguards and command group encircled them.

Minucius's eyes gleamed with rage as he pointed his sword at Varro.

"I will have answers for this. Surrender your weapons. The three of you are under arrest."

25

Consul Minucius thrummed his fingers on his desk as he considered Varro, Falco, and Curio standing in front of him. His legate also stood behind him with arms folded, and four other tribunes likewise stood in postures of grim determination at the back of the command tent.

Varro had explained all that he could, leaving out his suspicion that Paullus was somehow behind the conspiracy. Now, it was up to Minucius to accept the truth.

Inside the tent, the air was thick with tension. But beyond its gloomy confines, Varro heard celebrations of victory and salvation. The Numidians had returned just before the consul summoned them from their makeshift prison to headquarters. Amul had tried to reach them while they were under guard and nearly came to blows with the soldiers who held him back.

"You misunderstand," he shouted in his broken Latin. "They are heroes. They are brave men, braver than you!"

Varro had shaken his head and silently warned him to leave. There was no need to embroil him in this fiasco. It was bad enough that the three of them were being held as if they were conspirators. His only solace was knowing the surviving conspirator had been sent to the interrogators.

Now they had explained themselves to the consul and he seemed unsure how to determine the truth.

Minucius studied the three pugiones set out before him. Two were still stained with blood. He picked one up and examined the pommel closely.

"I suppose that based upon what I have seen myself you three acted in my defense. Your service to Rome has been exemplary, and today it was no less so. However, you were wrong to keep the conspiracy away from me. You risked my life."

He glared at Varro as if expecting an answer.

"Sir, I made the most expedient decision that I could in the time that I had. Falco and Curio simply followed orders."

Minucius gave a slow nod. "Your orders, Centurion Varro? I thought Marcellus Paullus led your organization. He'll be here shortly, by the way. He'll have to answer for the confusion with the cavalry."

One of the tribunes at the rear rubbed the side of his nose. He had command of the Roman cavalry and had earlier deflected the botched charge to misinterpreted orders. Of course, Paullus's status accorded him protection that would've otherwise resulted in flogging for anyone else. Nevertheless, it sounded as if he would be held to account of some kind.

"Paullus was too far away from us. We had no easy means to communicate with him given the speed of battle. We acted on our own accord."

Minucius narrowed his eyes as if suspecting Varro somehow lied to him.

Now his legate finally weighed in.

"I believe these three men. Had they acted as you expected, then your enemies would have been forewarned. Without a doubt, one of your servants or slaves kept the conspirators informed. We will soon know which one after the interrogators are done. But these three men were wise enough to draw them out. And they were alert to any danger to you. As you saw today, they acted in time to foil the plot against you."

"I suppose I must agree with you," Minucius said as he lowered his head. "But I do not like Centurion Varro replacing his command without speaking to anyone else. I understand his reasons, but there should be repercussions."

Varro straightened his back and looked through everyone to the darkness at the rear of the tent. However, Falco spoke up.

"Sir, Amul is a good leader. You saw what he was able to do following Centurion Varro's instructions. It allowed us the chance to save your life."

Normally, speaking out of turn would've earned Falco a withering rebuke. But Minucius now appeared more philosophical. He leaned back and bent his lips in consideration.

"I will shortly learn what the interrogators have discovered. I appreciate your wisdom in leaving one alive. I would know who wants to see me dead and why. The three of you honestly know nothing of the reason?"

Varro shook his head. "Sir, all that I know I have already said. We stumbled upon these men plotting with the Ligurians outside of camp. Curio shadowed them and determined their intentions. They never once revealed any reason for their actions."

A messenger interrupted the proceedings and announced Paullus's arrival.

Varro did not turn to look but remained at attention. Yet he could feel Paullus slithering into the room like a snake. As he announced himself, Varro felt a chill of revulsion and anger. He took heart that once the interrogators had finished with the conspirator, Paullus would find himself in chains. They might have to handle him carefully, but even the nephew of Scipio

Africanus cannot be exonerated for orchestrating the murder of the serving consul.

The messenger who arrived with him stepped before Minucius's desk and saluted.

"Sir, the prisoner is dead. The interrogators found him unconscious. He has been at the hospital all this time, but the doctors were unable to save him."

The tremble in the messenger's voice underscored the gravity of the news.

Minucius's jaw clenched and the muscles on his cheeks twitched. When he had marshaled himself, he spoke in clipped words.

"The interrogators never questioned him?"

The messenger confirmed what they all knew. The conspirator had somehow taken his own life before anyone could torture him. The unspoken question was why had he been left alone.

After dismissing the messenger, Minucius sat in stony silence while his legate and tribunes studied their feet. Answers they had been anticipating were now impossible to get.

Paullus stepped forward into the silence, then saluted. After announcing himself, he paused as if considering his next words.

"Sir, as you've seen my men are quite capable. They were able to uncover the conspiracy on their own. This is a mere setback in the investigation, and not cause to abandon hope. With your permission, sir, we could continue investigating. It is one of our many skills."

Varro grabbed Falco's wrist, not to restrain him but to keep himself from punching Paullus. He dared to glance at him. He wore a plain white tunic and appeared to carry no weapons or any other gear. However, Varro noted a pin-sized drop of blood by the collar of his tunic.

He had killed the conspirator. Varro would never learn how he did it, short of conducting his own interrogation of Paullus. No doubt his rank and wealth afforded him a means to reach the conspirator and silence him.

While Varro rocked from this sudden inspiration, Minucius considered the offer.

"I'll put that aside a moment. I need to understand why you initiated that charge. You had been given no such order, and you persisted in it against common sense. It almost seemed as if you wanted the Ligurians to break through."

Before Paullus could answer, the legate cleared his throat.

"You can understand why, Quintus. I needn't remind you of how confused orders can become, particularly in desperate situations like today. Paullus is eager to demonstrate his ability. I'm sure he misunderstood something. You know how fast those horses can charge. Before he realized the mistake, he was already among the Ligurians. It was a terrible and unfortunate accident. I do believe a reprimand is in order here. But I think Paullus is sufficiently embarrassed, and he'll have to live with the shame. That's a suitable punishment, don't you think?"

Paullus straightened to attention. "It is as the legate says, sir. I accept whatever punishment you hand down. I deserve it all."

Minucius seemed to retreat, holding up a hand and leaning away as if wishing he could escape the responsibility of judging such an esteemed man.

"I will have to submit an official reprimand. There is no way around it. But I suppose you have learned a valuable lesson, and you'll have to explain yourself to the wounded and the friends of those who died for your misjudgment. That's a stiff enough punishment for any man."

And so Varro learned who was the conspirator in Minucius's command.

He tried to keep his expression flat as he looked to the legate. He had been the one to give the conspirators access to the consul and had probably arranged for Paullus to eliminate the final one.

An icy fear tingled along his spine, knowing that he stood between two men capable of any evil.

No matter how Varro felt, Minucius seemed to have experienced great relief. He clasped both hands behind his head as if winded from a long run.

"Now, back to the matter of the conspirators. I can't understand why I was targeted. I have those who disagree with me, and I know I am not in recent favor with many of the men in my command. But this just smacks of something bigger."

Varro remained at attention, as did the others. He wanted to grab Paullus and throw him across the consul's desk, then scream, "Here is your traitor." But he knew better. He was not out of danger yet. Paullus and whoever he worked with, including the legate, would try to make his death appear accidental as well. Falco and Curio shared the same danger.

Yet he reminded himself that Paullus only knew what Varro had just explained, and that left out all his suspicions that included the wily patrician. As far as he knew, his hand in all of this was still hidden. It was an advantage Varro had to preserve for as long as possible.

The legate cleared his throat and leaned close to Minucius's ear. The consul nodded at the whispers, occasionally looking to Paullus and then Varro. Yet he mostly he stared at the three daggers laid out on his desk.

When the legate stood back once more, Minucius steepled his fingers over his desk and nodded to Paullus.

"Whatever is going on, it reaches beyond the confines of this camp. I'm certain this all has its roots in Rome. Therefore, I'm dispatching you and your team to do the work you do best. Find out what is the bottom of this skullduggery. The others in this tent will aid me in investigating the camp for other conspirators. The four of you do not have the rank required to do what must be done. Do you understand your orders?"

Varro understood clearly the legate was sending them off under Paullus's watchful eye. Doubtless, there would be some discussion as to how best to dispose of three troublesome soldiers on the return journey.

While Paullus confirmed his understanding, Varro pressed his lips tight against a sly smile. The moment they were beyond the camp, he had his own ambush prepared.

Minucius at last dismissed them, waving them off as if shooing away the entire matter of his attempted assassination.

"Paullus, I would still speak to you about who you should work within Rome. The rest of you go with my thanks. I'll be certain to send you the good wine tonight. I wish I could do more, but given our current circumstances I have not only to only handle the conspiracy, but also secure Pisa. There's much to do yet."

Varro saluted as did the others, and all three of them exited the tent.

"The good wine," Falco said flatly. "We saved his life three times over, and we're going to get a skin of wine for it?"

"We didn't do it for the reward," Varro said. "We did it for them."

He extended his hand across the camp. Thousands of soldiers and allies now celebrated their freedom. Just this morning they had been expecting death. Even the normally dour centurions did little to contain the celebration.

Falco tilted his head and groaned. "If you say so. He could send some women along with the wine."

Curio laughed. "And who would he send? The barbarian women? I bet they have longer beards than their men."

"Let's not waste time here," Varro said. "We get to discuss a few things, away from our fearless leader."

Mention of Paullus drew them all to silence. Varro knew he could not avoid Amul and the Numidians for long. So they went to greet them first. Besides, he had to retrieve his gear.

"They came running just like you said, sir," Amul said as he returned Varro's bronze helmet. "We burned many homes and left many children without their mothers. The barbarians will learn a hard lesson from this."

It pained Varro to think of destroyed families, but this was hardly new to him. It was the terrible price people paid for war. None of it would've happened had their men not taken up arms against Rome.

It took longer to work through the excited Numidians, who were proud to add their names to the long list of Numidian achievements in service to Rome. He could not deny them their moment, particularly when many credited him for it. They went among the tents and congratulated as many as they could. At last, he had to call Amul aside for a private word.

"We have been reassigned to duty elsewhere," Varro said. "If I have any say, I will recommend you for leadership. The consul is short on tribunes now. He might appoint someone, but I think you will do the actual leadership. I know you would do well."

For his traditions, Amul belittled himself and tried to deny the honor, but in the end, he acquiesced. "If you believe in me, sir, then that is all I need to know."

At last, Varro and the rest retreated to their tent and prepared for the march back to Rome.

"Paullus doesn't understand the danger he is in." Varro spoke in a low voice as he rolled up his blanket, then stuffed it into his pack. Falco and Curio leaned in close to hear. "He is probably thinking of how to dispose of us between here and Rome."

Falco gave an evil smile. "But he doesn't realize it's a time to dispose of him."

Varro shook his head. "This is not a matter of vengeance. He'll need to be taken alive for questioning. He's the only one who knows what is really happening. We can't silence him."

"Remember what I said? You don't have to be the one to do it."

Falco sat back and folded his arms, giving a sly smile to Curio. "Just look away and let the two of us handle Paullus. When you look back, all your worries will be gone."

Again, Varro reiterated his stance. But even Curio twisted uncomfortably.

"I know he didn't do it because he liked me, but he saved my life. It feels wrong to stab him in the back."

Falco puffed out his cheeks, then let go a long sigh.

"You know what feels worse? Him stabbing you in the back. Because don't you know it's coming? Maybe not on the march, but certainly later. He will wave his little medallion at somebody. Then one day you'll be asleep in your nice bed, but you'll never wake up again. He won't leave loose ends. That's what we are to him."

Varro put his finger to his mouth for silence.

"Make sure you have enough rope to hold him. We'll let Senator Flamininus handle the situation. We're not going to kill him. He's too important alive, not to mention we are better than him."

It took longer for Paullus to seek them out than Varro had expected. In fact, they waited for him at the edge of the Numidian camp. He was beginning to fear Paullus had slipped away, somehow guessing the threat against him. But by late afternoon he came leading his horse. All his gear was stowed in bulging packs strapped atop it.

"You can use my horse if you want to ease your burdens," he said with a wide smile. "I knew you wouldn't be able to keep those stolen horses. The cavalry always needs replacements."

Varro declined the offer and then saluted. "You will lead the way, sir."

A moment of astonishment flashed across Paullus's face, but the smug smile reasserted itself.

"Well, I would defer to you and your map."

"You'll remember, sir, that I presented it to the consul, and you reviewed it with him. It seems that my notes made no impression on the consul's plan. I wonder why that is?"

Paullus dismissed the question with a curt shrug.

"Surely one of you three is more capable than me at finding the road back to Rome. We have no time to waste and must set out at once. I have requested provisions for five days. I pray that will be enough to last the distance."

The four of them set out from camp, leaving by the southern gate. The guards there gave them confused glances but asked no questions. No one had come on the consul's behalf, nor had the promised good wine arrived.

While he had saved the man's life, Varro had a low opinion of Consul Minucius.

Curio led their column but did not range far ahead. Varro sensed tenseness in his two friends and hoped Paullus did not recognize it as well. He seemed carefree, almost joyful, as he led his horse in the middle position. Falco brought up the rear and had promised Varro in private he would not stick Paullus in the back.

They emerged from the pass and made good time across the plain before Pisa. The river was once more open to traffic, and boats were like black leaves floating on its surface. The setting sun turned the walls of the city deep amber. As their column passed through the detritus left by the Ligurians, Varro could not believe so many enemies had once encamped here.

Paullus broke the pensive silence. "I want to make it to the safety of the trees before complete darkness."

"Wouldn't we be safer camping in the open?" Varro played his expected role but hoped to gain the trees as well. He didn't want anyone to witness Paullus's capture.

"Is that your advice, Varro? I don't pretend to have your experience. If you think it is better, then that's what we'll do."

Falco called out from the back of the line.

"Jupiter's balls! If you're going to fucking lead, then make the decision. You knew how to run off into the forest by yourself. Now you're not an expert anymore?"

Nothing could diminish Paullus's good mood. His laughter was light and chiming.

"Very well, let's head for the trees. If we're being followed by anyone from camp, it will give us better cover."

They crossed the fields and Curio led them to the hidden location they had made prior to delivering the message to Pisa. They tied off Paullus's horse and began an imitation of setting up camp.

In the gloom, both Falco's and Curio's eyes seemed to glow with expectation. As Paullus sorted through his pack on the ground, Varro gave a shallow nod to both.

Their swords hissed from their sheaths and caught the dim rays of the last light of the day.

Paullus stood up at the sound and drew his brows together when he discovered three swords arrayed against him.

"What are you doing?"

"We are arresting you," Varro said. "We know what you've done. Curio saw you meet the conspirators hiding among the Ligurians. We also know you wanted to frame us. It's over now. Keep your hands up and step away from your horse."

Paullus raised both hands and backed up as directed. His face slackened and his brows drew together in worry.

"I do know what you're talking about. You're making a mistake. Remember who I am and who I know. You don't want the kind of trouble I can bring you."

Varro ignored him. "Falco, hold him steady. Curio, tie him up."

Paullus remained still, but his shock evaporated, and the smug smile returned.

"Very well. I submit to your authority. But I look forward to justice."

26

Varro kept his sword ready and lowered at Paullus's stomach. Falco gathered his arms behind him, while Curio measured out a length of cord. All the while, Paullus held Varro's gaze with a thin smile.

"Are you sure you know what you're doing? What sort of proof do you imagine you have against me? Curio's word against mine, and that's it. That's all you have to pin your hopes on?"

Though he knew better than to engage in this debate, Varro couldn't help it.

"You will give us the information we need. You must have that medallion on you, the one you returned to get from Curio."

A cloud passed before Paullus's face, but it did not linger. As Curio began to wind the cord around his wrists, he tilted his head back and laughed.

"You're so naïve. Do you think I'll be handed over to the interrogators based solely on your witness? I look forward to your expression when nothing comes of this. Even if everyone believed you, nothing would happen."

Of course, nothing would come of this. Varro realized it now.

Paullus had not done anything wrong, other than perhaps steal their pugiones. Still, he believed in justice and believed in Senator Flamininus.

"You know what I think," Paullus said. "You've ensured your own destruction. You're always so quick to act on what you believe is right that you don't consider what is practical. This entire affair wasn't even your business."

Varro straightened up. "So, you admit it? You've had this plan since before you joined us."

Curio pulled the bindings tight, and Falco guided him away from his horse to the middle of their small camp.

"Now what do we do with him? Tie him to a tree?"

Paullus maintained his smug silence but his smirk trembled.

When Varro didn't respond, Falco gave Paullus a shove toward the tree.

"He's right, you know. He won't go to the interrogators. Let's do our own interrogation right now. We'll get a confession and he'll sign it."

Rather than quail at the threat, Paullus regained his footing and sneered.

"You've been living with this man for years, but you don't seem to know him. I trust my life to Varro. He is too moral to torture me. It would make him cry long before I admitted anything."

Varro balled his fist, then pounded it into Paullus's face. He snapped back, tripped on the uneven ground, bounced off a stone, then rolled onto his side. He lay there in silence while Varro shook out his hand.

"I'm a changed man. You've done a good job convincing me I need more evidence. Falco, we should build a fire and heat up our blades. He was so eager to steal them from us, maybe we will burn them into his flesh. That way he can carry them forever."

"Now there's the best idea I've heard all night. I'll gather the firewood myself."

"Stand me up!" Paullus struggled to right himself, but with both arms tied he needed help. "Do you want to know everything? I don't mind telling you without the torture. Because whatever I say won't matter."

The three of them shared cautious looks, but Varro gestured for Falco to assist Paullus to his feet. A bruise formed on his cheek below his eye, but he still smiled.

"It's a simple thing to understand. Minucius is in the way of what my family wants. He has also earned a fair share of enemies of his own. So, the enemy of my enemy is a friend. Even three fools like you can understand that. An open assassination would create chaos in the Senate. But as consul, he risks his life in service to his great city. It would be a miserable fate to die in battle. But it's not unexpected or unexplainable. He almost did it for us, getting us trapped in that pass until the Numidians broke us out. For that, I am grateful to you Varro. But gratitude only goes so far. You ruined intricate plans and made new enemies without even realizing it. One of these days, all three of you are going to disappear. It's as simple as that. No matter what you do to me today, you're as good as dead."

"Do you want to break his teeth or let me?" Falco cocked his fist. Varro waved him down.

"Save the threats. You've no idea how many times we've been at the edge of death. Your words don't frighten anyone, especially with your arms tied. But you should be afraid of us. You are a snake that coils at the bottom of a deep hole. We're going to drag you into the light, and that will destroy you."

Paullus's sneer at last faltered. Varro expected him to beg or attempt a deal. Yet he remained silent and bowed his head.

He mumbled something that only Falco seemed to understand. He stretched his head forward to hear better.

Paullus head-butted him. Bone thumped against bone and

Falco staggered backward. His heel caught on a rock and he sprawled out on the ground.

Curio, who had become bored and sat on a log, now leaped to his feet and reached for his sword.

Stunned at the violence, and hamstrung by the need to keep Paullus alive, Varro's gladius remained still.

But Paullus wasn't finished.

He kicked Curio in the gut, knocking him down beside Falco. He called out to the darkness.

"Kill them!"

Then he bolted to the side, seeking the high bushes surrounding the campsite.

The shout galvanized Varro, and he leaped after Paullus. At last, he raised his gladius as he crashed through the bushes.

Paullus staggered ahead of him, maintaining his footing despite his hands being bound. However, he could not balance on the uneven ground without the aid of his arms. He slipped with a curse and rolled down a shallow slope.

Varro's sight turned red. He forgot all thoughts of preserving Paullus for what he knew and desired only revenge.

Yet as he bounded ahead, he heard the thunder of hoofbeats vibrating through the ground. Behind him, Falco and Curio both cried out in shock and rage.

Torn between capturing Paullus and returning to aid his friends, he did the practical thing.

He allowed Paullus to escape.

His caligae scraped against stone and earth as he twisted in midstride. He sped back toward the camp and saw the dark shapes of horses leaping over fallen logs and low brush. He counted three crashing into the campsite.

Both Curio and Falco had regained their feet when Varro joined them. But they were surrounded by two men on horseback and a third who had no room to join the fray. Both dueled with their attackers. Varro had no chance to see the details other than they dressed in brown and green and carried small shields and cavalry swords. Their horses were black, and their eyes flashed white as they stomped the ground. Curio and Falco kept them at bay but would not be able to sustain it much longer.

Varro attempted to reach them, but the third horsemen had circled around the outside of the camp. He now drove his horse into Varro's way, a wall of black muscle knocking him aside.

He collapsed to the ground, and his gladius flew from his hand and then slid down the slope. The mounted attacker reared his horse, its hooves flailing out to smash Varro's skull.

He rolled aside, stopped by the thick roots of a heavy bush. But he avoided the two hooves that slammed down where his head had been.

With a grunt, he rose to his feet, only to duck away from a swiping blade. Once more, he fell over the bush that had stopped his roll. He flipped and landed on his face by his gladius.

His hand snatched the blade immediately, but he remained on his stomach. His opponent cursed and drove his horse forward through the thick brush. It was the delay Varro needed. He got to his feet and readied his sword.

When the horse burst through the underbrush, Varro saw its exposed chest, a broad target for his gladius. The horse's momentum carried it forward, even as the rider hauled back on the reins.

The blade punched out.

A heavy weight thumped between Varro's shoulder blades, sending his strike wide and flattening him to the ground. Before he could flip, a foot stopped down on his sword hand and a second blow struck against the back of his helmet. He flattened out as the rock used to strike him thumped into the earth beside his head.

The horse continued past, but someone fell on top of him. The weight of two knees drove into the small of his back and expelled all the air in his lungs.

As many times as Fortuna had saved him, she looked away at this moment.

Paullus's breath was hot on his cheek as he wrenched Varro's arms behind his back.

"You didn't think I would come out here alone?"

He thrust Varro's face into the bitter dirt, then slapped his cut bindings next to it.

Someone tied off Varro's arms while Paullus slid off his back. Whoever fastened the knot left it loose. Perhaps Fortuna had not looked away after all.

Paullus dusted himself off as the man behind Varro drew him to his feet. He heard the horse that he had hoped to kill now circle around to join Paullus.

The two men looked at each other and exchanged nods. From the rider's appearance, he seemed like a Ligurian. He could not see who held him from behind but guessed it was another barbarian.

Back at the camp, Falco and Curio had likewise succumbed. Varro was grateful that these Ligurians did not appear to understand Latin. Otherwise, they might've carried out Paullus's orders. Instead, they had taken all of them as captives.

The riders had dismounted, and their horses wandered to the edge of camp in search of forage.

Paullus retrieved Varro's gladius and now swung it idly at his side as they walked back to the camp.

"Servus Capax is a failure. What good are you if you can't do what is necessary? You couldn't even be counted on to remove Minucius. Your strict morality limits you to the point of uselessness. So, it falls to me to do the practical thing. And you know what that means."

Paullus joined the two other Ligurians and ordered Varro to

stand beside Falco and Curio. Blood ran down Falco's head, and Curio's injured arm hung uselessly. Both were cut and bruised, and their eyes sagged in defeat. Two Ligurians flanked them, both seeming too big for the horses they had ridden.

When Varro took his position beside Falco, he now faced the man who had captured him.

Dano said nothing, but his eyes seemed to plead for silence.

It took all Varro's willpower to keep the smile from his face. The rope around his wrists was already coming free.

The last of the barbarians directed Dano to stand behind Paullus, the two forming what seemed like an honor guard on either side.

Paullus folded his arms and looked between all of them, gently shaking his head.

"I don't take any pleasure in this. I know you think I do, but I am not so heartless. It means nothing to you, but the memory of this day will probably haunt me for the rest of my life. However, I must be practical."

Varro tilted his head back, and while he spoke, gently pushed against Falco's shoulder.

"If it bothers you so much, then don't watch. Are these the Ligurians you worked with to plot against Minucius? Let them do it for you. You haven't the guts to be practical."

Falco pushed back against Varro's shoulder, signaling his friend was ready for action.

Paullus's face darkened at the insult.

"Then again, as a courtesy to a fellow citizen, I should cut your necks. You shouldn't die at the hands of these barbarians. They've served their purpose, though they should've killed you straightaway. I will have to reduce their pay for it."

Varro's hands were now free, and he looked to Dano who stood behind Paullus. The young Ligurian gave a barely perceptible smile.

The trap was ready.

"Didn't I warn you," Varro said, "that your life would go smoother if you treated others with respect? I think you're about to learn a valuable lesson."

Dano shouted something in his language, and the barbarian next to Curio pulled him away from danger.

Varro spun on the barbarian flanking him. He slipped his heel between the Ligurian's feet, then shoved him over. He howled in fury and surprise as Varro followed him to the ground. His Servus Capax pugio was already in hand, and then driving into the ribs of the hapless Ligurian. He arched his back, barely able to slap the thick hand onto Varro's face before collapsing into death.

He rebounded to his feet and spun towards Paullus. The sun now fled behind the horizon leaving only a thin light to paint the scene before him in shades of gray.

Curio struggled against the Ligurian leading him away from camp. Across from him, Dano had disarmed Paullus. But the other Ligurian opposite Paullus had recovered from his surprise and now stepped forward with his sword raised.

Varro bolted the short distance, pugio in hand, and tackled the Ligurian. Both crashed against a tree, the force of the blow knocking the wind from the barbarian. Varro had the advantage of a shorter weapon. Once more the white-edged blade slipped into the Ligurian's side, piercing his kidney. He dropped his sword with a groan, and Varro stepped back to let him crumble into the brush.

A different scene greeted Varro when he turned back.

Falco had crossed the gap but kneeled in the dirt with both hands over his face. Dano lay flattened on his back as if enjoying the rising stars in the purple sky above.

Meanwhile, Paullus mounted one of the Ligurian horses. He kicked it forward, guiding it between the trees and into the green darkness of the forest.

Varro rushed to Falco's side, but his friend was already getting to his feet. He shoved him away.

"It's just a scratch. His pugio caught my brow. Don't let him escape!"

When he pointed after Paullus, he revealed his face full of blood.

Dano was likewise recovering from whatever blow had flattened him.

The final Ligurian joined Dano and helped him to his feet.

"Take a horse!" Dano thrust his finger toward the nearest black horse.

It was down to Varro now. Paullus was an expert cavalryman, able to navigate terrain that would foil the average rider. But Varro believed in his own horsemanship.

Without time to grab a suitable weapon, he tightened his grip on the pugio and made for the horse.

Then it was as if a hand had batted all the sound from the forest while it held its breath. In the next moment, the forest exhaled hundreds of birds screaming into the air. Their flight was so hectic that leaves and twigs showered on the camp.

At the same moment, the horses screamed and bolted. The violence had not disturbed them, yet some unseen force sent them fleeing in terror.

Varro could not wait to understand the cause, and so set off running after Paullus. He left a wide trail as his horse crashed through the woods.

He ran with a single-minded purpose. Paullus would answer all his questions. He would not go to the interrogators. Instead, Varro would cut the skin from his face until that sneer was nothing but bloody ribbons. He would learn everything.

Then a sound like a mountain avalanche rocked him.

He could not keep his footing and found himself thrown

between trees and boulders. New rocks jutted up like fangs of the earth. Trees swayed and collapsed in jumbled piles.

Yet he persisted, trying his best to hurl himself after Paullus. He could glimpse him now. He had lost his horse and fled amid the chaos of the rocking and churning forest. Trunks waved and branches showered down all around them.

Varro tried to scream, but his voice was lost in the impossibly loud grating of stone on stone. Cracks formed beneath his feet, as if he were running across a frozen lake rather than rocky earth.

A thick branch landed across his back and drove him to his knees. Hard stone gashed his skin, and the weight of the branch forced him to the trembling dirt.

Yet this ended the rocking and grinding.

All he heard was trees collapsing and branches falling in the aftermath of the earthquake.

He sloughed off the branch, his pugio still in hand, and resumed the chase.

Only now he did not know where he faced or where Paullus had gone. He was disoriented, and his charge stuttered to a halt.

Searching all around, he heard Falco and thought he saw him flickering between trees that now leaned together in a tenuous balance. He didn't see Paullus.

Varro waited patiently, certain that he had used the confusion to hide. But he was no expert and lacked the patience for stealth.

It only took a moment for him to break away.

Not more than a dozen yards away, Paullus staggered to his feet. Branches and dirt fell from him as he loped away. His left leg dragged as if wounded.

"You're hurt!" Varro shouted as he followed. "You can't escape."

Paullus allowed one terrified glance over his shoulder but pressed ahead.

Leaping fallen trees and weaving between freshly exposed rocks, Varro caught up.

He grabbed Paullus by his shoulder as he limped ahead. Varro jabbed his pugio into the small of his back, arresting any attempt to escape.

"The gods have foiled your last trick." Varro noticed that Paullus had lost his weapons in the earthquake. "They even disarmed you for me."

He spun Paullus around and set his pugio to his throat.

"You didn't expect traitors in your little group, did you?"

"I admit, that was a surprise." His arrogant smirk had returned, though it twisted with the pain in his left leg. "But don't credit yourself too much. Remember what I told you. If you think killing me will do you any good, you're mistaken. I once threatened you with Flaccus and his cronies, but he will be the least of your worries."

Varro pressed the blade harder against Paullus's neck.

"Who are you working for? You have a medallion. Curio saw you reveal it to the killers you hired. You're going to explain that to me."

Despite his flesh bending at the tip of Varro's pugio, Paullus held his smirk.

"You don't have the skills of an interrogator. You won't know if what I tell you is true or not. You'll probably kill me by accident. I know that you are smart enough not to try. So, I'm not afraid. Nor am I afraid that your two idiotic friends will do it for you. Because, Varro, you are as predictable as the sun and moon. All good men are. And that is why you are useless in your role."

Varro stared at him. He had never felt such hatred tremble up his arm and into the tendons of his hand. It was as if his pugio begged to drink the blood beneath the skin pressed to its edge.

"You will go to the interrogators. I am taking you back. There are too many questions to answer. Even if you lean on your uncle's reputation, Minucius is not without his own allies. You seem to have forgotten he is aware of your treachery."

As confident as he appeared, Paullus's shoulders relaxed as his posture slackened. He held up both hands in a gesture of surrender, just as Falco reached them. He was breathless and leaned on both knees.

"Good. You caught him. Now finish him. Push that dagger home."

"He is our prisoner. He needs to answer for his crimes, and we need to learn what he is up to."

Falco shook his head. "Again with this? When you step on a snake, you don't apologize to it. You crush its head before it can bite you. Look, I'll do it for you."

Varro held Paullus's triumphant gaze. The pugio remained in place even though he had both hands in the air. Varro bit his lip. It was a simple thing to draw a line through his neck.

"I am in command, and I say he is our prisoner. You will not question me in this again."

Falco let out a long, tired breath.

And then the world shook again.

27

A force like the ground punching his feet sent Varro flying. The pugio in his hand nicked Paullus's chin as he flew away. It was a superficial cut, and suddenly Paullus was free once more.

More trees collapsed as the ground raged. Varro slammed into Falco, and both narrowly avoided a crashing tree that landed between them and Paullus.

Even in the deafening roar of the earthquake and the shattering forest he could hear Paullus cackling as he fled.

Falco pushed Varro away as more branches and limbs collapsed all around them. It seemed as if the forest was hemming them in and aiding Paullus's escape. Again, a limb bounced off Varro's shoulder and spun him around.

The violent rocking continued as he braced himself against the sturdiest tree he could find.

Paullus loped forward and it seemed as if he might actually escape despite his injuries. Falco struggled with branches that formed a fence around them.

As if to emphasize the drama of the moment, Paullus turned and raised his fist.

"You see who the gods favor! When we meet again, it will be your death!"

Falco roared in frustration as he wrestled with the limbs that fell into their path. But Varro remained clinging to the strong tree.

Paullus turned to continue his flight.

And then vanished.

Moments after his disappearance, the rocking and churning of the earth ceased.

Varro remained holding the tree and Falco stopped wrestling with the branches that caged them. Both watched for Paullus to reemerge from the wreckage. But when nothing stirred, Varro stepped away from the protection of the thick tree trunk.

"You know, if you look behind it's completely open."

Falco turned and stared in amazement, then put his hand to the back of his neck.

"If my face wasn't covered in blood, you'd see a lot of red there."

They both stepped out from the debris fencing them off from Paullus. They then picked a path across the broken earth, stepping over heavy cracks and twisted limbs.

They found Paullus lying in a deep crevice that had opened in the earth. He lay on his stomach as if napping. But Varro saw the blood leaking from beneath his head.

Falco whistled. "The gods couldn't have been clearer in their decision."

Varro stared at the body at the bottom of the crevice.

"The gods did not decide for us, but for our enemies. He was the last one who knew about the plot to kill Minucius. He could've exposed everything, and I know that gutless snake would have the moment the interrogators got him."

Falco glanced over the edge. "Whoever he worked for has been making sacrifices at the temple. He's never speaking again."

Varro let his shoulders relax and then sighed. "We can't leave his body here. We don't want to be suspected of killing him. We need to show that he died in a fall and not with a dagger in his back."

"That won't prove anything. We could've thrown him off a cliff or bashed his head."

"We cannot abandon his body. I know he was scum, but he was a Roman citizen as well. Let's give him a proper burial if we're not taking him back. Do you want his restless ghost haunting you forever?"

"Well, that's the best argument you could've made. I'll help you down."

When Varro reached the bottom, he discovered that Paullus still had a pulse in his neck. When he informed Falco, he groaned and raised his fist to the sky as if cursing the gods. Together they lifted him out of the crevice and carried him back to camp.

Curio, Dano, and the Ligurian who had aided them all waited among the wreckage of what had been their secret camp. After two earthquakes, the tree cover had all toppled, and the rocks that had screened the camp had either broken or sunk into the earth.

"You got him!" Curio stood, and a fresh sling held his arm in place. "I said you would succeed."

Dano crouched over the Ligurian who had kept Curio from danger. He glanced up and flashed a smile before returning to the fallen man. A branch had pierced through his side like a spear, and Dano held his hand as his lifeblood leaked into the dirt.

They set Paullus down and Varro did his best to bandage the wounds with the scraps of cloth available to him.

"I'm not cutting my tunic for him," Falco said as he stood over Varro.

He sat back and adjusted the bandages on Paullus's head. Curio had also helped care for the fallen traitor.

"Even if he didn't mean well by it, he saved me once. So I helped with the bandages. That settles things, right?"

Falco puffed at the statement. "Sure. I give you permission to hate him again."

Leaving Paullus aside, Varro went to kneel by Dano and his injured companion. The Ligurian's flesh had become an ashen color and sweat gleamed on his brow. Varro saw that the branch had pierced his liver, and nothing could save him.

"I wish I could thank him."

Dano shrugged. "Of the three he was the better, but I promised him you would pay good silver. He was a mercenary, after all."

Varro raised his brows and chuckled. "It doesn't matter why he fought for me, only that he did. The better question is why are you here?"

Dano set the Ligurian's hands over his chest, then gave Varro a sly smile.

"Because now you owe me, Centurion Marcus Varro. I like that better than owing you."

"Yes, I owe you now. Is that why you stayed close, or is there another reason? Curio saw you around the Numidian camp. You've been following us all along."

Dano blushed. "Like you said, there's nothing wrong with a little adventure before joining my father again. It was a simple enough thing to get back with these three. And that one you call Paullus needed someone who could speak both languages."

"How long have you been working with Paullus?"

"Not long. I only joined a day before we set out. He gave orders to ride ahead to the forest outside of Pisa. We were to shadow you from the trees. After that, he wanted us to stay near and await his command to attack. He would pay well for each one of you killed."

"But they took us prisoner instead."

Dano folded his arms and gave a satisfied smile.

"I told them we could get more money for the three of you alive. I convinced them to ransom you back to the Roman legion. In the meantime, I convinced this one he would earn even more silver if he worked with me." He patted the chest of the Ligurian before him. "You must understand our people. After honor, there is nothing greater than silver and spoils. That's what all of this was about. The tribes want the wealth of Rome. They can talk about Rome being the great enemy of our people. But it's all about men wanting glory and riches."

Varro looked at the Ligurian lying between them. He had expired, his shallow breathing at last stopped.

"As you said, I do owe you. Is it silver you want? If so, you'll have to travel with me to Rome before I can pay."

Dano appeared to consider the offer, but then shook his head.

"I still have a message to deliver to the Boii." His smile widened. "I don't know much about those barbarians. I understand they live in tents and travel around like animals. I can't see what we have in common other than wanting to take from Rome. As you said, it might be useful to have someone on the inside to help you. That could be me."

Narrowing his eyes, Varro pretended to harbor doubts.

"Well, I would have to discuss this with my companions. And I'm not sure what sort of price you want for the service."

"We can talk about that. You'll make me rich later. Right now, this is more exciting than lugging wares for my father or stealing chickens from a Roman farmer."

Varro rubbed his chin as if in deep thought, then turned to Falco and Curio who still sat beside Paullus. "What do you think? Can we find a use for a skinny Ligurian boy?"

Falco sniffed. "It didn't go so well last time we added a new member."

"I don't like having another small man on the team." Curio

scratched under the sling supporting his arm. "I'm supposed to be the sneaky one."

Before Varro could say anything, Dano stood and put up both hands.

"I don't want to join as a member. I don't know what the three of you really do. Just this one time, while it's still more fun than dangerous."

Varro stood as well and set his hand on Dano's shoulder.

"Then we'll consider you provisional. We will work out your fee later. For now, you should prepare for a trip to Boii territory. Get set up there and we will meet soon. First, we must take Paullus back to his family and make our report. But I expect to be sent into the field immediately."

With their arrangements made and Paullus clinging to life, they found a place to bury the Ligurian. They then made camp for the night. On the following morning, they thanked Dano once more and promised to bring him a reward for his bravery when they next met.

Then they set out for Rome and all the troubles that awaited them there.

28

Sitting in a private room on the second floor of a sumptuous tavern, Varro watched Senator Flamininus examining the iron medallion held between his fingers. A personal bodyguard stood at the door and looked down the hall to where voices murmured gently below.

Varro sipped from a porcelain cup. The wine was the best he had tasted in months. As the senator studied the medallion, Falco splashed more wine into his cup and then Curio's.

"I've never seen this before." Flamininus's soulful eyes flickered with light from the oil lamps hanging from the ceiling. "The snake imagery suggests a few possibilities to me. But I will have to investigate. All the traitors carried these?"

"Yes, sir," Varro said. "This identified Paullus to his accomplices. I don't believe they had met prior to the attempt on Minucius's life. That would mean someone else orchestrated the entire affair."

The medallion clapped against the wooden table as Flamininus set it down. All four of them stared at it like a specimen pinned to a board. The senator's tongue probed his cheek as he thought.

"That is more than likely the situation. Thank you for bringing this to me."

Varro had expected a stronger reaction. The news of an attempt on a serving consul's life should have alarmed him. Instead, Flamininus had listened without expression, asked a few questions, and then let it go with a promise to look into things.

Sitting in this private room, rewarded with fine wine and praise, he still felt as if he were being mollified. Was Senator Flamininus aware of the plot before he sent them to Pisa? Did he intend for them to be framed? It was an absurd thought, particularly after he had worked so hard to exonerate them from Cato's charges of desertion, among other things.

Indeed, there was more going on than he understood.

They had been back in Rome for two weeks before Senator Flamininus arranged for this meeting. In the meantime, they had the unfortunate responsibility of caring for Paullus while his family arranged to take over his ongoing care. Of course, Rome's finest doctors lined up to treat the man. Each one promised to revive him, but in the end, it seemed the gods had decreed eternal sleep as Paullus's punishment.

Throughout their journey back to Rome, Falco had insisted the gods had only slowed Paullus long enough for them to finish what they had started. "What will happen when he wakes up? We won't even be around to defend ourselves. Better to silence him now. Just pinch his nose shut. He's hardly breathing as it is."

But Varro knew that even if Paullus awakened from a long sleep after being struck in the head he would not be the same man. He might remember nothing, or be unable to speak, or worse. Varro did not fear Paullus anymore and saw no reason to stain himself with the crime of murder.

Instead, he feared those who had instructed Paullus from the shadows.

"Thank you all for what you have done." Flamininus recovered from his gloomy thoughtfulness and then raised a cup. "You have once more exceeded my expectations. The people of Rome owe you more than they know."

They all raised their cups beside Flamininus, then drank deeply of the sweet wine.

"Sir, Paullus threatened to turn Senator Flaccus against us." Varro shifted his cup aside as if to make space for the topic at hand. "It was how he had strong-armed me into sponsoring his membership in Servus Capax. I was wrong to let that influence my decision."

Flamininus gave a weak smile. "The gods have corrected it for you. And there is no shame. You now have more to lose than ever before. It is natural that your enemies would turn it against you. I have been watching your estates, though from a distance. From what I see, all is well. I suggest that you three return for a short rest and check on your affairs firsthand. This letter from the Ligurians to the Boii is more concerning than any other news. If they join forces, we will have trouble. So the Senate will act fast. I will need your help once more."

Varro straightened up, then glanced at both Falco and Curio. It was the moment to inform the senator of their decision. Flamininus sensed the tension between them, and his brows furrowed. However, he had the wisdom to remain silent and looked to Varro for an explanation.

"Of course, you can count on us, sir. But this business with Paullus has got us thinking."

With Varro leading, the three of them slipped their Servus Capax pugiones onto the table. They were to carry no weapons in the presence of a senator, but they had hidden theirs beneath their tunics. Flamininus's eyes dropped to the weapons set before him but did not stir otherwise.

"Take these back, sir. We will not carry them anymore."

Flamininus's left eye twitched, as it often did when he grew agitated.

"These mark your membership in Servus Capax. Varro, yours is gold to show your rank. You have no choice but to carry these."

"There are other ways to indicate rank that are not so easily copied or lost." Varro pushed back the tunic hanging over his right forearm. "The three of us will get the symbol tattooed here. Rank can be indicated with one or more stars over the owl's head."

Flamininus's expression soured. "I think the pugiones are a better choice."

Varro pushed the three daggers across the table.

"With respect, sir, you have no choice. We are returning them to you and not asking for your permission to do so. Carrying these as a sign of Servus Capax has been a burden and a danger to all of us. I have lost my pugio more times than I can count. Paullus was able to change and strip rank by simply taking these weapons from us. You are not the one who must bear these everywhere he goes. We do, and it's easier to always carry the sign on our arms."

Flamininus's face shaded red and his lips grew thin, but his voice remained even.

"This is a tradition established by your great-grandfather, Varro."

"Then it is one that ends with his great-grandson. We have earned the right to make this change, sir."

While Senator Flamininus might only have kept his silence a moment, Varro felt it expanded into hours. When he spoke, he lost some of the warmth in his voice.

"It has been interesting to see the changes in you three since we first met. I will take your suggestion forward. There is some merit to it. Your allegiance will be indelibly marked on your flesh.

It will be harder to divest your identity if your life depended on it. Are you willing to accept that risk?"

He looked between Falco and Curio before answering.

"In all the years I've carried the pugio I've never had to show it to anyone and neither have I had many others recognize it. I think it is a manageable risk, sir."

Flamininus gave a curt nod. "Do not get those tattoos until I tell you. In the meantime, hold onto these. If I take up your suggestion, then you can return them or hold onto them as a memento."

"Thank you, sir." Varro then lifted his cup once more and offered a toast to all their future success. The senator seemed to have regained some of his spirit after the drink.

"Actions against the Boii will begin soon. The Senate is considering all of the North in a state of rebellion. So, arrange your affairs and await my summons. The three of you are indispensable now. I will remind Consul Minucius of the rewards he owes you since he appears to have forgotten. As for my reward to you, it's not more money. But you do need guards to watch your estates when you're away. I will arrange for this, of course subject to your review. They will be former legionaries, which I'm certain you will appreciate better than muscle hired off the streets of Rome. They need work and you need their services. Sadly, I have too many veterans petitioning me for help making a living. So this is a perfect match."

Varro and the others agreed and offered their appreciation for the help.

Their conversation drifted to lighter topics, though their daggers remained on the table. At last, Flamininus ended their meeting but left coins enough for another round of wine. He urged them to enjoy their night, but that they should be ready when he calls them again.

Once they were alone, they collected their weapons and stuffed them back beneath their tunics.

"You did a good job," Falco said.

"I agree," Curio said. He then imitated how Flamininus's lips thinned at the challenge to his authority. Falco slapped the table and laughed.

"You look just like him. How do you do that?"

They drank the fine wine and discussed returning to their homes. None of them felt as if they were going home. Falco perhaps said it best for all of them.

"The three of us were made men in the field of battle. A villa and farm are where we go to die, not to live. I hope Flamininus calls us soon."

They clinked their wine cups together and toasted the sentiment.

Varro let the sweet taste linger, then set his cup down.

"But it is nice to have a safe place close to friends where we can rest once in a while."

Falco and Curio agreed, and they toasted once more to friendship.

HISTORICAL NOTES

In 193 BC, the Roman Senate faced trouble on numerous fronts. In the north, both the Ligurians and the Boii gathered for trouble. Rome completed a census, and taxes were collected from a war-weary citizenry. The gods also seemed displeased, rocking the land with earthquakes. In fact, these were so frequent and the ceremonies intended to appease the gods were so involved that citizens protested. The Senate eventually forbade the reporting of an earthquake on any day the appeasement rites had already been enacted.

Disaster struck when the Ligurians put aside their internecine struggles and swept out of the Apennines to rampage across the north. They sacked the port of Luna where Cato had staged his Iberian campaign several years prior. They devastated the countryside and eventually surrounded Pisa with 40,000 warriors.

The Ligurians lacked cohesion and made a few tepid attempts to capture Pisa. They knew next to nothing about siege warfare and so settled for razing the countryside until someone figured out how to get over the walls. The Roman prefect at Pisa, Marcus Cincius, sent a messenger to Rome and begged for relief.

The consul charged with the north for this year was Quintus Minucius Thermus. His response was to assemble two urban legions and march to Pisa's relief within ten days. However, he met with stiff resistance from a recalcitrant public. Hundreds of those summoned protested to the Tribune of the People, Tribunus Plebis in Latin. Rome echoed with shouts of "I call upon the tribunes!" and the muster ground to a stop as the Senate reviewed the requests.

Being citizen-soldiers, the men of Rome felt they had justifiably fought enough. Ever since the Second Punic War, Rome had been involved in one military adventure after another. Each new muster of the legion called upon the same men to fight and now called upon their sons as well. What had once been viewed as a sacred privilege was beginning to feel like a death sentence. Rome brimmed with disabled soldiers unable to find work. The able-bodied who did return discovered their farms in debt or sold off. Few men returned to better lives after serving Rome in the legion.

In the end, Minucius got his troops. The Senate granted no dispensations for service and declared the North to be in a state of rebellion. All citizens, Latins, and allies who were summoned therefore had to answer the call. The citizen-solider was on the march once more.

Minucius did not trust his hesitant soldiers and this might have led him to the tentative and probing approach he took to handling the Ligurians. Given the Ligurians were only concerned with loot and personal glory, they were easy to drive off once directly confronted. Minucius pursued them, imagining he would end the Ligurian threat for all time. This was pure folly, considering the Ligurians had proved notoriously difficult to dig out of their mountain redoubts in prior attempts. In fact, this was only the opening act in a protracted war to bring the Ligurians under control.

Nevertheless, Minucius pursued them but found his camp

attacked one morning. Repelling the Ligurians was a near thing, and for a time it seemed he might have lost the day. However, his reluctant soldiers prevailed and he followed the Ligurians into the mountains.

They then blockaded him in a pass, and once more it seemed his soldiers were doomed. Fortunately for him, he had eight hundred Numidian allied cavalry with him. These allies volunteered to lead a breakout effort.

They appeared unassuming and weak, being small and unarmored. Their horses looked ungainly compared to the Roman cavalry. They played up this appearance and were able to approach the Ligurian outposts unopposed. Yet once within range, they cast off their act and bolted through the barricades and out of the pass. They attacked the Ligurians in their own territory, setting fire to their homes and killing their families. The Ligurians were forced to retreat and Minucius's army was saved.

There was never any plot to kill Minucius, at least none known to history. Like any powerful man of his time, he would have had allies and enemies in equal measure. Paullus is a returning character from a previous story and remains a fictional member of a historical family.

Now Varro, Falco, and Curio are finding a new voice for themselves. They are no longer inexperienced boys but hardened veterans. They know what is best for their mission and how to carry out their orders independently. As always, they are in over their heads. But as long as they stay true to their brotherhood, they can brave any danger and face any threat.

Or so they believe.

NEWSLETTER

If you would like to know when my next book is released, please sign up for my new release newsletter. You can do this at my website:
http://jerryautieri.wordpress.com/

If you have enjoyed this book and would like to show your support for my writing, consider leaving a review where you purchased this book or on Goodreads, LibraryThing, and other reader sites. I need help from readers like you to get the word out about my books. If you have a moment, please share your thoughts with other readers. I appreciate it!

ALSO BY JERRY AUTIERI

Ulfrik Ormsson's Saga

Historical adventure stories set in 9th Century Europe and brimming with heroic combat. Witness the birth of a unified Norway, travel to the remote Faeroe Islands, then follow the Vikings on a siege of Paris and beyond. Walk in the footsteps of the Vikings and witness history through the eyes of Ulfrik Ormsson.

Fate's Needle

Islands in the Fog

Banners of the Northmen

Shield of Lies

The Storm God's Gift

Return of the Ravens

Sword Brothers

Descendants Saga

The grandchildren of Ulfrik Ormsson continue tales of Norse battle and glory. They may have come from greatness, but they must make their own way in the brutal world of the 10th Century.

Descendants of the Wolf

Odin's Ravens

Revenge of the Wolves

Blood Price

Viking Bones

Valor of the Norsemen

Norse Vengeance

Bear and Raven

Red Oath

Fate's End

<u>Grimwold and Lethos Trilogy</u>

A sword and sorcery fantasy trilogy with a decidedly Norse flavor.

Deadman's Tide

Children of Urdis

Age of Blood

Copyright © 2023 by Jerry Autieri

All rights reserved.

No part of this book may be reproduced in any form or by any electronic or mechanical means, including information storage and retrieval systems, without written permission from the author, except for the use of brief quotations in a book review.

Printed in Great Britain
by Amazon